J.P. Jordan's debut novel is a fascinating tale tying together the current abuses of the church with the insurance world. The characters and story kept me engaged with many unexpected twists right to the end. *Men of God* takes a rightful place alongside of other best-selling mystery fiction novels.

- Walter Kilgust, Esq.

Men of God is an incredibly fast read! An intriguing mystery told from an expert's point of view. From a law enforcement perspective, the book was well-researched and true-to-life. Can't wait for Jordan's next novel.

- Detective Bill Larson (Retired)

Intriguing! Captivating! The local setting kept me involved as if I were part of the story. *Men of God* contains a number of twists and turns. Just when you think you have it figured out, the author takes you in another direction. Once you start reading, you will find this book very hard to put down.

- Kevin L. Fronek, CPA

A good mystery should keep you guessing until the end, and Jim Jordan's debut book did not disappoint. *Men of God* had a unique storyline with interesting characters. I'm looking forward to his next books!

- Dawn Campion

Jim Jordan's new book, *Men Of God*, is an investigative thrill ride with a unique perspective. The story is told from within an insurance company's internal audit department, which brings a new and illuminating take to our ideas about what investigations are.

Nick Hayden, the protagonist character, goes from war-torn Afghanistan to driving a desk at a Midwestern insurance company, a job he reluctantly takes. When he stumbles across what may well be a serial killing—of clergymen—Hayden draws on all his experience and intuition in pursuit of the truth.

As a debut mystery, Jordan's *Men Of God* is a well-told story that clearly shows us how well he constructs a thriller. The story has just the right combination of pace and intrigue and topical themes to engross and hold the reader's eye.

As a local bookseller, I'm always interested in characters and stories that tie into our community. *Men Of God* does not disappoint. I can't wait to read the next Nick Hayden story.

- John Maggitti, PhD
Novel Bay Booksellers
Sturgeon Bay, Wisconsin

MEN OF GOD

J. P. JORDAN

ten16press.com - Waukesha, WI

For information, please contact:

TEN16 Press
ten16press.com
Waukesha, WI

Cover design by Kaeley Dunteman

To Nancy, my wife and partner of more than forty years!

Thanks for your support, ideas, and encouragement in helping me to achieve a life goal in publishing a fiction novel.

To many more bottles of wine in developing subsequent projects.

With love.

Jim

PROLOGUE

The old man cursed under his breath as he began to lug the heavy garbage can across the courtyard to the industrial dumpster. His brain raced as he thought through the series of events that had brought him to this God-forsaken place. *This work is beneath me. Damn those that sent me here. I have no business being here . . . I have my work, my place in the world . . . No one like me should have to perform manual labor like this.*

The controversy had taken a toll on him. Over the course of the previous months, he had aged considerably, as evidenced by the patchy white stubble on his face along with the long strands of stringy grey hair sticking out from under his woolen hat. The oversized brown rubber boots and the mismatched clothing he had selected for warmth added to his grizzled appearance and reflected his grim demeanor and churlish attitude. *I've been abandoned. Damn the journalists and their smear campaign.*

Contemplating the darkness and the chill of the March morning air cutting through him, he heard the growing rumble of the Chicago & Northwestern freight train in the distance. It served as his daily wake-up call, wanted or not. Just another irritation for him at his new residence. Although the tracks ran through the heart of the metropolitan area, more than a mile away from his dormitory, he could not believe the noise generated by the train at that hour of the day. Like clockwork, the train's roar hit its apex every day at four in the morning, making him wonder how anyone could live in such a place. *Another bleak day in cursed Wisconsin. Damn the lawyers.*

Large white flakes swirled about him in the wind making for an eerie glow in the ancient mercury vapor lamps lighting his way. As the snow began to accumulate, it only served to make his work even harder. The typical sound of rolling thunder from the large wheels of the container reverberating off the courtyard walls was now muffled. Instead, it was replaced by the crunch of snow under the container and the old man's grunts as he dragged it in fits and starts through the growing mess on a path he was creating. Fortunately, he was able to keep his curses to himself. But with each heavy pull, he resolved to have a serious conversation with his new superiors about other, more appropriate, work for him at a much more civilized time of day that better suited his schedule.

As the old man's brain churned deep in thought, he was unaware that someone was watching him from across the street. A figure, clad in black, had taken up a position on the roof of a vacant four-story building, kitty-corner to the courtyard. For this observer, it had become a familiar spot, once the diligent research of several weeks resulted in locating the old man. Following the old man's fall from grace, his whereabouts had been largely unknown. At least, that was the case until an obscure billing statement, a mere attachment to a report, landed in the right inbox. Once it became clear where the old man had been sent, several weeks of surveillance established his patterns of behavior. Having the luxury of time, the observer chose the day of reckoning. Garbage day fell on Tuesday, becoming the day, 4:00 a.m. the time. The courtyard of the rehab facility served as the place.

The night vision telescopic sight attached to a 7.62 X 51 mm M40 rifle, the preferred weapon of Marine snipers, framed the old man. The muzzle of the rifle rested on the wall of the structure, where the figure had pushed away the accumulating snow. Several .308 Winchester full metal jacket bullets would provide more than ample stopping power.

There was no other activity in the vacant buildings adjacent to the area at this time of day, nor any functioning video cameras that might lead to discovery. The growing roar of the approaching C&N train provided the perfect cover. There would be no need for a suppressor to quiet the shot from 200 yards. It was just the two of them.

The old man completed hauling the fourth of his five containers and was beginning to sweat at the effort. He began to anticipate his return to the building, a warm cup of coffee, and a hot shower following his final trip across the courtyard. As he was about to begin his final circuit, he paused briefly to take a deep breath, incredulous at the decibel level of the passing train, the rumble now reaching its crescendo.

Standing alone in the dark courtyard, he began to sense something was amiss. There was no real reason for that feeling. He had been at this routine for several weeks, but the sensation sent a chill up his spine, despite the sweat. Then, looking down, he saw a strange red dot appear on the front of his jacket. Transfixed for a moment, the curious glint of light caught the zipper of his coat, reflecting into his eyes. Before he could make sense of the glow, he felt the heavy thud of being punched in the chest, accompanied by the poof of feathers exploding from his down jacket.

As the old man's brain scrambled to put things together, he pulled down on the zipper of his coat, shocked to find a plume of red emanating from his abdomen. *Oh my God . . . have I been shot?*

From the perch on the vacant building, the black-clad figure calmly ejected the shell casing, which dropped into the snow. Then, with sharp precision, a second bullet was chambered and fired. The next round found its mark alongside the initial entry point, killing the old man where he stood, knocking him over the trash can.

The results were observed through the scope. How appropriate was it that the old man died lying in a pile of garbage? Waiting calmly for any sense of alert in the area and then finding none, the lone individual retreated from the rooftop perch into the snowy morning as the sound of the departing train faded into the distance.

CHAPTER 1

"Chuck Nowitzke," he shouted angrily into his cell phone after being awakened from a sound sleep. He bolted upright in his bed. "Jesus Christ, what time is it and who the hell is calling me?" Not recognizing where he was for a moment, he slowly began assessing his surroundings. *I'm in a hotel room.*

After a brief pause, the response came. "Chuck, it's not Jesus. This is Marcus Clark . . . your new boss. It's five thirty in the morning. I know this is your first day on the job, or it will be after eight o'clock, your official start time. But we need you and your expertise at a crime scene now."

Nowitzke, still trying to process what was going on after coming out of a REM cycle, had the fleeting thought this could just be a bad dream. Then, gathering himself, he responded. "What type of crime, sir?"

Clark followed up succinctly. "A shooting and probable homicide. Since you're new to the area, would you like a squad car to pick you up, wherever you are?"

"Yes, that would be great. For the time being, I'm staying at the Radisson downtown on College Avenue. And sir, I'm sorry for my outburst."

"No problem, Nowitzke. First impressions don't really matter to me all that much," Clark said with a touch of what Nowitzke was pretty sure was sarcasm. "Be ready to go in fifteen minutes."

Jumping into the shower, he hastily washed his hair and skipped his shave. Then, still dripping wet, Nowitzke tried to air-dry himself before pulling on a pair of khaki pants, a crushed shirt, and a wrinkled blue sports coat from the suitcase that had been sitting in the corner of the room overnight. His assumption that he would have time to iron his clothes before reporting to his first day of work turned out to have been a bad one. Sitting on the corner of the bed for a moment, he considered how he had arrived in Appleton. A veteran detective in his mid-forties, he was starting over . . . again. Another new department. Another job. Another new ex-wife. Life was looking up. A fresh start was what he needed. However, after years of investigating murders in Milwaukee, this was not the way he had envisioned his first day in Appleton, roughly a hundred miles north of Wisconsin's most violent city. Refocusing on the matter at hand, he found his loafers on opposite sides of the room before grabbing his winter coat and heading toward the elevator. Looking at his reflection in a mirror of the lift, Nowitzke saw a paunchy man with a shock of brown hair, a thick mustache, and scruffy beard staring back. The detective held the gaze longer than he had time for, shook his head, and sighed. After sliding his forty-caliber Glock into his belt holster, he grabbed his black backpack and was ready for work. Stepping into the expansive lobby, he found a Starbucks kiosk that had just opened for the day. He purchased a large coffee with cream and a muffin before hitting the avenue just as a squad car pulled up in near blizzard conditions. *Shit. Loafers were the wrong choice.*

The middle-aged, slightly overweight officer, who was wearing a leather jacket over his uniform, lowered the passenger side window. "You Nowitzke? I'm your ride."

Opening the front passenger door, Nowitzke responded, "No shit. I didn't think you were an Uber driver trying to make a few bucks on the side with your cruiser. Of course, I'm Chuck Nowitzke." He wondered who else might be stepping into a police cruiser for a voluntary ride this early in the day.

"Damn, you caught me," said the officer with a grin before introducing himself as they pulled away from the curb. "Bill Gaines."

"Do you have any information about the murder?" Nowitzke asked

Gaines, noting the near absence of all traffic given the weather conditions and the time of day.

"Not much," Gaines replied. "Supposedly, the victim is an elderly man who was found by a coworker. The actual call came in just under thirty minutes ago, but I don't know much more than that. Another officer was immediately dispatched to the location to preserve the crime scene. Don't know much about the address either, aside from it being in a run-down part of town. By the way, we don't get too many murders in Appleton, so this is a big deal for the city and the department."

"How long a ride to the scene?" asked Nowitzke, taking a small sip of coffee that was steaming through the hole in the lid.

"We should be there in five minutes."

Nowitzke began to relax, contemplating his plan when he was prompted to look over his shoulder. He was startled by a tongue licking his face through the metal grate separating the front and back seats. "Holy shit! I assume that's your big dog in the back seat?" Nowitzke exclaimed, turning to the 100-pound German Shepherd sitting quietly in the rear of the cruiser.

Gaines chuckled. "Meet Harvey, Detective Nowitzke. He's at your service, if you need him."

"Aside from eating, what exactly does Harvey do for a living?"

"Harvey does a little of everything, including drug and bomb sniffing, but he can also perform article searches," responded Gaines.

"What's an article search?" asked Nowitzke, pushing some of his muffin through the screen to Harvey.

"Harvey is trained to find items that don't necessarily belong in a certain setting. Basically, he can locate things with a human scent on them . . . and please stop feeding him. He's going to puke all over the car."

Disregarding the admonishment, Nowitzke shoved the rest of his muffin through the slot, making a friend for life in Harvey. The three officers, two- and four-legged, continued in silence for the balance of the short trip through the snowstorm to the crime scene.

CHAPTER 2

Nowitzke was beginning to grasp that he had not planned well for the weather. That realization was confirmed when he stepped from the squad car into the wet ankle-deep snow feeling the Slurpee-like mix squish into his loafers. "Fucking beautiful," he mumbled to himself as the cold mush sent a shiver through his body. He owned boots. They were just in a box in a storage unit on the south side of Milwaukee. He'd hoped that there would be no snow this spring. Just another bad choice, but only a misdemeanor amongst other personal felonies in the grand scheme. Leaving Gaines and Harvey, Nowitzke trudged through the snow to find another squad car with its light bar flashing on the street adjacent to what appeared to be a gated courtyard.

Although still a rookie, Officer Anissa Taylor had followed the book, staking out an expansive area using every foot of yellow police tape she had at her disposal. Even before the light of dawn and in the blowing snow, Nowitzke couldn't help but notice Taylor's striking good looks. Given only her silhouette, the detective thought to himself it had been some time since he had seen another patrol officer fill out the uniform the way Taylor did. While she didn't have much latitude with her dress, Nowitzke also noted her blonde hair tucked in a tight bun that accommodated her hat. But, even in the near darkness, Nowitzke could not get past Taylor's dark piercing eyes.

Biting his tongue to keep from making any stupid remarks, Nowitzke introduced himself as the detective assigned to the case. It became clear Taylor combined twenty-something looks with an equal measure of youthful enthusiasm, even at the early hour. "Sir, I'm Officer Taylor," she chirped, extending her hand with an eager greeting. Nowitzke couldn't determine if the source for her excitement was connected to her personality or the fact a dead body was lying less than a hundred yards away. He'd need to get to know her better to learn that.

"Good morning. What do we have?" asked Nowitzke, taking a sip of his coffee.

Taylor essentially repeated what Gaines had already offered, adding only that the body was lying in the center of the courtyard, in a pile of garbage, surrounded by a moat of blood-soaked snow. Pointing to the victim, she surmised he had been hauling garbage to the dumpster when he was apparently shot. However, since her orders had been only to establish the perimeter and to hold off for Nowitzke's arrival, Taylor could offer little more, except that his first name was Ed.

As they talked and walked toward the entrance leading to the courtyard, neither Taylor nor Nowitzke noticed a small, slightly built elderly man emerge from the structure adjoining the courtyard opposite their location. Approaching Nowitzke and Taylor, he yelled across the area to them. "Officers, I was the one who found Ed's body and called the police."

Nowitzke yelled for the man to stop in place, but he continued moving towards them.

"I called the police this morning," the man continued. "I found the body and have already been out to offer Ed last rites when it became apparent he had passed."

"Last rites? You're a priest?" questioned Nowitzke.

"Yes, I'm Father Michael Coughlin. I worked with Ed. One of Ed's duties was to take our garbage to the dumpster early every Tuesday. He was required to make sure everything was in the dumpster before the truck comes. When he didn't return to the dormitory for morning prayers or breakfast, I went out looking for him and found him there," gesturing to Ed, whose body was now covered by the accumulating snow. Coughlin was meticulous in his description of the facts, but Nowitzke thought he seemed remarkably calm, especially for someone not used to discovering dead bodies on a regular basis. "There are two sets of prints in the snow. Mine and Ed's path to and from the dumpster. Sorry if I did anything that hurts your investigation, but I thought he had just fallen and needed help. I certainly wasn't expecting to find him dead."

"Father Coughlin, I understand you might be upset with the death of your friend, but what you did seems reasonable given the circumstances. Prior to coming into the courtyard, did you hear or see anything suspicious that might be connected to Ed's death?"

"No," replied Coughlin.

"Was there anyone who had it in for Ed?"

Coughlin was silent, shaking his head "no," but hesitated for just a second, seeming uncertain. That second gave Nowitzke a momentary pause.

"Thanks. You can go back inside and get warm, Father. Officer Taylor will join you in a moment to take your initial statement."

Taylor suddenly became wide-eyed, pulling Nowitzke to the side and quietly whispering out of Coughlin's earshot as he slowly returned to the building, "Sir, I'm not a detective . . . I wasn't supposed to do anything more than preserve the scene."

Nowitzke whispered his response. "Taylor, you're a sworn police officer, right? They covered statement taking at the academy, did they not? The department gave you a gun, didn't they?"

Nodding to each of Nowitzke's questions, Taylor seemed hesitant, her erstwhile exuberance now seemingly tempered. "It's just . . . it's the first time I've ever been involved in a murder investigation."

"Welcome to the club," countered Nowitzke. "You're my only resource for the time being. Remember your training. We're looking for evidence, a motive, suspects, all the usual things associated with any crime. Oh, and find out who Ed was and why anyone would want to kill him. I got a strange vibe from Father Coughlin a moment ago. Also, while you're back in the warmth of the building out of the elements, remember that I'll be freezing my ass off out here working to gather any physical evidence in near whiteout conditions. I need you to get in the game. By the way, do you have a camera in your squad?"

"Yes." Taylor moved as quickly as she could on the slippery mix to retrieve it from her vehicle.

After handing the camera to Nowitzke, he looked Taylor directly in the eyes. "Oh, and after you've got Coughlin's story, contact the medical examiner to get his ass down here along with some back-up help. Then, see me with what you've found." After turning toward the body, Nowitzke paused, looking back at Taylor. "By the way, based on how well you've done so far to assist in preserving the scene, I know you'll do a great job." Nowitzke shoved his coffee cup into the snow to steady it and paused to survey the entire site surrounding the corpse. Then, using Taylor's camera, Nowitzke recorded the scene, taking video of the courtyard and the general vicinity to document what he found, narrating as he proceeded.

"The victim's tracks are clear, showing movement between the building and the dumpster, with drag marks from the bins. There is an additional set of footprints, confirmed by Father Michael Coughlin, made when he saw the body and attempted to assist."

He then changed the camera's setting, proceeding to methodically take a series of still photos of the same area. Circling it from ten feet, Nowitzke then began to focus on the body. He paused briefly to take the last swig of his now-cold coffee as his mind went into full gear, now turning his attention to the adjacent structures and what he could see of the neighborhood.

First, there was no doubt this was indeed a shooting. Although the medical examiner would officially confirm the cause of death, it didn't take an expert to see the bullet wounds in Ed's chest from where he stood. Nowitzke went back to video recording so he could capture his thoughts.

"It is plain that whoever pulled the trigger did not do so in the courtyard as there are no unaccounted-for footprints in the snow. There is also no physical evidence that there had been any scuffle or confrontation with an unknown assailant, such as a homeless person," Nowitzke recorded.

As he waited for back-up, Nowitzke began to ponder potential locations where the shooter may have been situated. Based on the position of the body, he immediately ruled out any place in or around the large dormitory-like building into which Taylor and Coughlin had retreated. Also, Nowitzke saw the courtyard was essentially protected by an old and very thick brick wall, twelve feet high and topped with ornate metal scrollwork. From his vantage point near the body, Nowitzke could see nothing that looked like a shooter's perch elevated to his left or his right. That left the final direction opposite the dorm, which had the same high walls, but also a heavy metal gate off-center to the courtyard square. The gate offered an entrance to the space off the street behind the facility where Taylor's cruiser was now parked. Although the electronic gate was open now, it was only eight feet high. Beyond it, Nowitzke could see only one building that rose above it. Gazing up at that structure, Nowitzke reached into his pocket to retrieve his cell phone. Without taking his eyes off the building, he dialed Appleton PD, identifying himself and asking that Officer Gaines and Harvey return to the scene. Nowitzke ended the call and looked around.

"What is this place?" he asked himself aloud. "Ed, what the hell did you do to get yourself shot?"

Nowitzke heard someone yell in his direction. "Good morning!" came the shout, echoing off the courtyard walls, as a stout man entered through the open gate.

Nowitzke yelled back, "Stop right there, this is a homicide crime scene under investigation."

"Good, then I'm in the right place. I'm the ME, err, the medical examiner," the squat man replied as he continued his march toward Nowitzke's position.

Dr. F. Walter Schmidt had physical dimensions that made him look almost as wide as he was tall. Standing just barely over five and a half feet tall and weighing probably 270 pounds, Schmidt was the kind of man who moved slowly on a good day. Watching him negotiate through the deep snow, Nowitzke thought that the ME resembled a human Weeble, the classic kids' toy that supposedly wobbled but wouldn't fall down. Taking what seemed like an eternity to cross the courtyard, Schmidt finally made it to Nowitzke. On arrival, and gasping for breath, Schmidt promptly doubled over, yet managed to offer his hand, awkwardly reaching up to Nowitzke introducing himself as "Wally." Nowitzke noticed that, despite the winter conditions, Schmidt was sweating profusely as a plume of steam rose off the ME's bald head when he removed his knit cap. Combined with a long, thick, greying beard, his black round-rimmed glasses completed the living caricature of the medical examiner. *Hope this guy doesn't keel over after his walk and we have two deaths here.*

"What do we have?" wheezed Schmidt.

Nowitzke pointed to the body. "I'm no expert, but it looks like a dead guy." Schmidt raised his eyebrows until Nowitzke spoke again. He recapped his conversation with Coughlin, his preliminary findings, and his view of the crime scene. "Someone must have taken a long shot at the victim from outside the yard. But I've been waiting on you to do your magic before investigating where the shots might have come from."

"Well, a late winter storm will slow down response times. Do you have any idea how long the victim has been here?" asked Wally, observing the body now covered by a fresh layer of snow.

"No, Officer Taylor is taking a statement from the individual that found the victim." Looking at his watch and seeing it was now seven thirty in the morning, Nowitzke continued. "Based on what the priest said and the timing of the initial report, I'm guessing the time of death was several hours ago."

"A priest?"

"Yeah, there's a story buried in there somewhere, but I'm not sure what it is yet. I wasn't going to make an old man stand out here in the snow telling me the whole story, but all Father Coughlin would really offer was that the victim's name was Ed. He didn't elaborate on who Ed was or what he was doing here, let alone why anyone would go to the trouble of shooting him. We'll figure out who Ed was soon enough. I was most concerned with preserving the scene, considering the storm."

Looking at Nowitzke, Schmidt asked for some assistance in examining the body. Ed was positioned as though he had simply laid down on the garbage pile. Both men could see where the bullets had torn through the victim's jacket, but little else. Upon opening the coat, however, the ME noted two large holes in Ed's chest surrounded by a large bloody stain on his white t-shirt. Schmidt then asked Nowitzke to help him turn the body over. Providing most of the effort, the detective grabbed Ed and began the delicate maneuver before slipping in the slick pool of blood that had gathered underneath the slushy snow. Nowitzke landed on his butt in the ooze, staining his pants. "Shit!" cursed the detective, his exclamation loud enough to reverberate off the courtyard walls.

Schmidt gave a throaty laugh after watching Nowitzke's ungraceful fall. "Club soda should get the blood out of the khakis, but it won't help much with the pieces of guts and tissue stuck to your pants."

"Thanks for the tip, asshole," Nowitzke shot back, looking askance at the ME as he stood up. Once upright, the detective began to laugh at himself and Schmidt's comment. Schmidt joined in the laughter.

After rotating the corpse, both saw Ed was missing a large portion of his coat and his back where the bullets had exited.

"Well, I'll take a wild stab at the cause of death," said Schmidt. "Looks like the victim took a couple of shots from a high-powered rifle to the abdomen."

"Jesus, Wally, how many years of education did it take to make your determination?" responded Nowitzke.

Unfazed, Schmidt continued. "Both projectiles passed completely through the victim. With all this snow, it might be a challenge to find the remnants of the bullets. Of course, we will do a full autopsy, including toxicology tests, but this looks pretty straightforward."

No shit. As Nowitzke processed Schmidt's comments, he noticed an impromptu committee forming. As Taylor was returning from the dormitory, two additional police cruisers arrived on-site with light bars engaged, sending blue and red colors bouncing off the surrounding walls. Nowitzke watched from a distance as Gaines emerged from one vehicle and appeared to ask the second officer to secure the gate. Gaines then walked around to the right rear door of his vehicle to retrieve his dog.

"I thought finding the slugs might be an issue," explained Nowitzke, looking in the direction of the approaching K-9 unit, "but I'm hoping Harvey can help out."

"Who is Harvey?" asked Schmidt, looking up from his work before seeing the large dog bounding in the snow directly towards them with Gaines in tow.

Nowitzke cornered Taylor, asking how Coughlin's statement went. Taylor responded, "Fine, but I'm still putting things together."

"We can talk about what you've found in a bit," replied Nowitzke. "I have Officer Gaines and his pooch looking for the remnants of the bullets. Also, I think I have an idea where the shots came from," he added, pointing to the building across the street. "Can you do a quick sketch of the courtyard with dimensions to help with documentation?"

Taylor smiled. "Absolutely."

"I assume you have a phone on you?" Taylor nodded in the affirmative. After exchanging phone numbers, Nowitzke continued, "Once I confirm the location of the shooter, I'll need you to do a 3-D version of a diagram. Your drawing will document the angle of the shots from their point of origin to the victim."

Nowitzke then engaged Gaines, providing an overview of what he believed had occurred. "Do you think Harvey can locate the slugs in the snow?"

"That's something he should be able to do," answered Gaines.

"After you've combed the courtyard, give me a call on your cell phone," said Nowitzke after trading numbers with the K-9 officer. "I may want you and Harvey to check out the area where I think the shots came from."

Gaines led Harvey moving north in a disciplined pattern toward the dormitory, while Nowitzke headed in the opposite direction leaving his unofficial team to do their assigned tasks.

Walking through the courtyard gate and acknowledging an officer who was providing crowd control, Nowitzke crossed Franklin Street. The blizzard was subsiding. Amazingly, the sun was fighting to make a late morning appearance. The road was full of slush as it was a side street and not a priority for plowing. With every step, Nowitzke felt the squish of snow into his now-sodden shoes, the cold climbing from his feet directly upward through the core of his body. However, now on the hunt for a killer, adrenaline took over, masking any physical discomfort.

Pausing in front of the vacant building he had targeted as the possible perch of the killer, Nowitzke noted two sets of tracks near the entranceway: one set into the building and another out. Though the tracks were degraded into nothing discernable, Nowitzke retrieved the camera from his pack, documenting the area for whatever it was worth.

Turning away from the door, his eyes scanned the outbound trail as it moved east down the sidewalk. Nowitzke set out to follow the path on the off chance it would lead him to the shooter. *Stranger things have happened.* Based upon what he could see, whoever left the tracks was not a long strider. Yet, it was hard to make any intelligent assumptions about the slushy footprints. The tread of the prints he was following appeared to be a waffle pattern, similar to what tactical boots might leave behind. Finding the best representative sample, the detective put his pen alongside the track for scale and snapped a photo. He judged the size of the footprint to be roughly ten or eleven inches long.

The path took him several blocks from the vacant building, through a dilapidated industrial area into an older residential neighborhood. Ultimately, the sloppy tracks dead-ended abruptly when Nowitzke came to North Richmond Street, a major thoroughfare that had been plowed down to the concrete. Whatever route the shooter followed from there vanished, courtesy of a local municipal snowplow driver. He crossed North Richmond on the slim chance that the footprints would reappear, but the locals were already digging out from the storm with snowblowers. *Damn.*

The detective made his way back to the building and studied what he believed was the main entrance to the former manufacturing structure. He doubted there would be much light inside and fished out a flashlight from his backpack. His second assumption was that the building had likely become a shelter for the local homeless. The heavy metal entrance door, with a windowpane of embedded chicken wire, no longer sat squarely in its frame. Somehow, the lower half of the door had been bent to allow access to the building, albeit to slightly built people. Although he was not as thin as he had been early in his career, Nowitzke began to squeeze through the door when he heard his coat catch and rip on the rusted frame. "Son of a bitch. First the shoes, then the pants . . . what next?" Nowitzke continued through the entrance, unconsciously touching his Glock to confirm it was still there given his suspicions he might not be the only person inside. As he looked around, those thoughts were confirmed by the piles of food wrappers, ratty sleeping bags, and old newspapers accompanied by the strong smell of urine. The structure had been "home" to people on a regular basis, but there was no evidence anyone else was currently in the building. As his eyes adjusted to the available light, he could not see any discernable footprints in the dust on the floor.

Sunlight was beginning to stream into the building through several large windows, illuminating his way. Nowitzke put the flashlight away and looked up into the cavernous structure, which he guessed was previously an industrial facility of some sort. After finding a stairwell, he began to trudge upward on the metal steps looking for access to the roof where he believed he would find the shooter's perch. Taking his time to look for any visible evidence along the way, Nowitzke's journey dead-ended at the top floor where he felt a cold breeze. There, he saw another heavy metal door cracked open, allowing blowing snow to accumulate on the floor.

Nowitzke began to push on the door, although it barely budged because of the snow that had wedged around the opening. Another more concerted effort using his shoulder was just enough to move the door, as it opened with a groan. Poking his head through the opening to take a quick glance, lest someone was still on the roof, Nowitzke found himself alone as expected. He placed his backpack in the vestibule, briefly pausing to observe the area. In fact, someone *had* recently been on the roof. There was a discernable path worn in the snow, even though there were no distinct footprints from which to cast shoe size or treads due to the warmth of the sun. Nowitzke removed the camera from his pack and shot some video of the area and then snapped off a series of still frames to document his finding. Moving onto the roof, he saw the path ended roughly twenty feet away where the shooter had been positioned with the snow having been cleared from the wall of the building. Looking down into the courtyard across the street, Nowitzke fished his phone out of his pocket and called Gaines. "Any luck finding the slugs?"

Gaines responded. "Actually yes. Harvey located both within minutes, but they are pretty mangled."

"Turn south and look up," Nowitzke replied, waving to signal where he was located. "Bring Harvey up here so he can check out the roof. Tell Taylor to turn around too, so she can get a sightline on me and complete the diagram of the shooter's position relative to the body. Also, work with her to establish the chain of evidence on the bullets." Gaines waved back, and then Nowitzke saw Gaines and Taylor go into a brief discussion when she promptly gave a thumbs up to the detective on the roof.

Minutes later, Nowitzke heard Gaines cursing from below as he struggled to open the front door of the structure. After some choice words and the sound of screeching metal, Nowitzke could hear the growing rumble of feet on the metal steps working toward the top floor. Nowitzke met them at the doorway. "This is where the shots came from. I'm not sure how much we'll find up here, but I want to be thorough. Have Harvey give it a sniff."

Gaines directed Harvey onto the slush-covered roof. The dog's nose went into the snow as he again began to search methodically back and forth. Seconds later, Harvey moved to the area where the shooter had been and promptly sat down. Carefully clearing away the snow, Gaines suddenly stopped and called the detective over to the spot. Nowitzke pulled a surgical glove from his pocket and brushed more of the snow away. After he had dug down to the roof surface, Nowitzke found a copper-colored bullet casing lying against the wall. He secured the evidence in a plastic bag pulled from a jacket pocket. "Good dog," declared the detective. Harvey responded like any other 100-pound pet who was being praised. He approached Nowitzke excitedly and began to rub his head against Nowitzke's leg while the detective scratched behind the dog's ears.

"Tomorrow, Harvey, you'll get a dozen muffins on me."

CHAPTER 3

When Nowitzke returned, Wally was wrapping up his work. He and Taylor had already placed the corpse into a body bag. The ME had backed his van into the courtyard to load Ed's remains for the trip to the hospital and the autopsy. With the evidence secured, Nowitzke officially released the scene, informing all the officers they were free to go. Wally turned to Taylor to ask whether Father Coughlin had provided the full name of the victim.

As they began walking towards the ME's vehicle, Taylor pulled out the notes from her conversation with the priest and began flipping through the pages looking for the details. "Ed was a Minneapolis native here for treatment . . . oh, and he was a priest as well . . ." she said, searching for a last name. "Here it is . . . Donovan. Father Edward Donovan."

Both Nowitzke and Wally immediately stopped, exchanging knowing looks. "I believe you have your motive and a potential laundry list of suspects, Detective," offered Wally.

Nowitzke replied, "Yeah, Fast Eddie had a lot of enemies."

Taylor was confused that both men seemed to know of the victim. "Fast Eddie? Who was Father Donovan?"

"Have you been living in a cave?" said Nowitzke, looking quizzically at Taylor. "Fast Eddie has been in and out of the news on a regular basis for at least a year. He's a pedophile priest who was finally caught in the last few months. A total scumbag who had molested boys and girls in the greater Minneapolis area for about thirty years. Last I heard, the diocese had to come up with big bucks to pay some of Ed's victims."

"Disgusting. If that's the case, what's Donovan doing here in Appleton?" asked Taylor.

"The question of the day," responded Nowitzke. "But before we can get to that, let's get in your cruiser and follow Dr. Schmidt to the hospital so we can witness the autopsy. Then, we need to have a more in-depth chat with Father Coughlin. Based upon what we learn from him, we'll probably need to see Chief Clark about an all-expenses paid trip to Minneapolis."

Donovan's post-mortem revealed no real surprises given the two large holes in his chest. As Taylor and Nowitzke were leaving the exam room, Wally indicated he would get back to them with anything out of the ordinary once the toxicology tests were completed in several weeks. Having seen her first autopsy in person, Taylor was a shade of light green by the time both men escorted her to an anteroom. As they said their goodbyes, Wally slipped a ten-dollar bill to Nowitzke, which he immediately put in his coat pocket. Nowitzke guided Taylor to a wooden bench, where she promptly put her head between her knees.

"Slow, steady breaths, Officer Taylor. Autopsies are tough on first-timers, but you'll get used to them," said Nowitzke in a calming voice.

"What was the ten bucks about?" asked Taylor.

"About whether you'd puke or pass out," replied Nowitzke. Pulling the bill from his pocket, he flashed it at her with a smile. "You did great. I knew you wouldn't barf."

"Nice. How was your first autopsy?" asked the rookie officer.

"Incredible. I blew chunks all over the ME's shoes," said Nowitzke with a laugh to which Taylor joined in.

Both Nowitzke and Taylor changed their focus to a more extensive interview with Father Coughlin now that Donovan had been identified. Nowitzke noticed that Taylor's energy levels had returned to where they had been early that morning.

Stepping out of the hospital, neither could believe how the weather had changed by mid-afternoon. After the start of the day with near blizzard conditions, the sun finally appeared in earnest and was quickly melting the morning snow, creating a general mess with large, newly formed puddles of runoff.

Taylor's police cruiser pulled back into the courtyard where the day had begun. The officers noticed a maintenance man hosing down the pavement where Donovan's body had been found.

"Let's have another chat with Father Coughlin, shall we?" said Nowitzke as they entered the building. "Lead on, Taylor, you know the way."

Although the exterior of the building had some character with an old stone facade, it belied the interior of the facility which did not have the same level of charm. The entranceways and staircases were constructed of heavy oak and were likely impressive in their day. But now, they were scratched and dull. The walls were a tired institutional grey-green color. In fact, it was hard to determine if they had been painted that way at some point or were simply discolored from years of neglect. The air in the structure had a musty quality. Heavily scuffed black-and-white checkered floor tiles led their path to an ornate bronze-colored Otis elevator. Nowitzke eyed the lift warily to get a sense of whether it really operated or was there for show. However, having taken the elevator that morning, Taylor confidently slid the door open and climbed in, welcoming Nowitzke into the cage before engaging the controls to move upward toward Coughlin's office on the third floor. As the door closed, the enclosure paused briefly and dropped an inch, eliciting an audible gulp from Nowitzke, before moving in the requested direction.

The elevator opened directly outside the doorway of the small, dingy office occupied by Father Coughlin. The priest sat behind a massive wooden desk that had to be ancient, framed between photos on the wall behind it of Jesus Christ and a cheap reproduction of the Transfiguration. Coughlin rose from an old high-backed leather chair to greet Nowitzke and Taylor as they entered. Although they had met earlier in the day, Nowitzke did not remember the priest as being as small as he was now. He was a tiny man with a shock of white hair who didn't look like a priest in his plain-colored shirt and jeans. Coughlin also wore a gold chain attached to reading glasses along with a large gold-colored crucifix that seemed to strain his wiry neck.

Coughlin steered the officers to two worn leather chairs positioned opposite his seat and politely asked if anyone wanted coffee as he closed the door. Both declined.

Returning to his position, the priest paused briefly to look out the third-floor window as if holding off the interview for a few moments longer. "If you don't like the weather in Wisconsin, just wait ten minutes," mused the priest. Dropping into his chair, Coughlin was met with two stone-faced cops not interested in talking about meteorological conditions.

Nowitzke abruptly launched the conversation. "Father, what exactly is this place, and why was Ed Donovan here?"

Coughlin drew a deep breath. "This facility is called St. Luke's Annex. 'Luke, the beloved physician' per scripture. It is a place of seclusion, contemplation, and healing. The Annex, as it's known, is a private facility that provides treatment for people in need, and we do a fine job in doing so."

"What type of treatment exactly, Father?" Taylor chimed in.

"Many kinds . . . treatment for addiction to drugs, alcohol, depression . . . Our goal is to help our guests recover so they can get back to their lives as productive clergy members." Coughlin's voice had a calming tone about it that would have been appropriate for a public television documentary.

It was Nowitzke's turn. "So, is this facility for religious leaders in general or strictly for priests?"

"Only clergy from our denomination are eligible to use this rehabilitation center," responded Coughlin.

"Who knows about this facility?"

"As I said, this is a *private* treatment center," the priest replied curtly. "We don't advertise, Detective."

Nowitzke then dug into the matter at hand. "Why was Fast Eddie here? I'm assuming it wasn't because of drugs or alcohol issues."

"First of all, Detective, Edward Donovan was a highly respected cleric," said Coughlin, stiffening in his chair. "We did not refer to him by any street name the media hung on him. Ed was here for addiction treatment much like his fifty-plus other brothers currently in residence."

"What type of addiction exactly?" asked Taylor.

Coughlin again paused. "Officer Taylor, I'm not at liberty to discuss the specific nature of Father Donovan's treatment. It is confidential to say the least."

Nowitzke responded quickly and loudly. "Look, Father, we know Donovan was a pedophile with a trail of victims and we are here as part of his murder investigation. I appreciate you can't divulge specifics about his treatment, but can we speak in generalities about what takes place here . . . and not focus on the drunks and depressed?"

Coughlin clearly took umbrage with Nowitzke's tone and choice of words but managed to control his emotions and went back to his soothing style. "Sure. As I said, this treatment center is owned by our church and is charged with the mental health of our patients. If a person charged or convicted with alleged sexual misconduct were to be sent here, they would receive testing and state-of-the-art treatment, including counseling, that would put them on a path to wellness."

"Testing? What type of testing?" asked Nowitzke.

"I'm not sure I want to discuss that in the presence of Officer Taylor," said the priest, looking at the young woman.

"Why?" countered Nowitzke.

"Well," stammered Coughlin, "Because she is a female. What we do here is sometimes . . . highly personal."

"Father, Officer Taylor is a law enforcement professional and, again, we are talking hypotheticals here," replied Nowitzke as the volume of his voice increased.

Shifting uncomfortably in his chair, Coughlin responded. "A guest who is here for a sexual addiction as an alleged pedophile would go through a complete intake protocol. That would begin with an EEG, an electroencephalogram. This is a simple procedure where small, flat discs are attached to the scalp of the patient to detect brain waves. The subject would be shown photographs of children to determine a level of arousal."

Nowitzke and Taylor listened intently to Coughlin's description, but also began to squirm unconsciously in their chairs.

The priest continued. "Following the EEG and, assuming there is a positive indication of potential issues, a second, more invasive test would be used involving a penile plethysmograph. In this process, a ring is placed over the subject's penis to measure changes in circumference based upon a level of arousal when again being shown photos of children."

"A peter meter?" chimed in Nowitzke, causing Taylor to unsuccessfully stifle an embarrassed laugh adding to the awkwardness of the conversation.

Coughlin grimaced but continued. "Interestingly enough, that is how many of our patients refer to this examination tool. Following a diagnosis, the patient would then go through extensive psychotherapy, a classic psychiatric technique to allow the patient to identify and overcome any rationalization about his behavior. Using relapse therapy, a tool commonly used in many types of addiction treatment, the goal is not to change the individual's orientation, which is essentially impossible, but to help the individual anticipate situations and settings that increase the risk of abusing a child. A final option is to provide the subject with drug therapy with medications to suppress male hormones."

"Chemical castration?" retorted Nowitzke. "So, where was Donovan in the course of treatment?"

"Detective, as I said, I am unable to confirm anything about specific patient records. Suffice it to say, Father Ed had only come to The Annex in the past month. Frankly, I don't know how anyone would have known he was a resident here."

"Changing gears . . ." Taylor began, "who did Donovan hang out with, and did he have any friends or enemies here?"

"Officer, The Annex is a place of understanding where we do not assign judgment. Our guests go only by their first names and no patient knows about anyone's personal history, unless perhaps they would choose to share it, which rarely happens. We do not encourage patients to spend time with any type of media, and we ask them to surrender all devices that would tempt them to seek news of the outside world. I can tell you only about twenty-five percent of the residents are being treated for sexual disorders. While all our patients have a reason to be here, there is no pecking order of issues. As for Ed, I was just getting to know him. He was a bit of a loner, keeping to himself. I didn't observe he was developing any friendships, but he didn't appear to have any enemies either. As far as I know, no one here recognized him from the news coverage that his . . . situation created. We struck up a conversation one morning over a chess board. We had a regular daily game, which led to an ongoing dialogue involving any number of topics ranging from theology to football. Even though he was a patient, we had a budding friendship. Frankly, my impression was that Ed was a charming and extremely intelligent man who honored his calling."

"You mean aside from the part about abusing children for much of the past three decades?" added Nowitzke.

Coughlin responded with silence.

"Father, you mentioned your organization is doing great work. Are you able to cure all of your patients?" asked Taylor.

"Officer, treating addiction is a difficult endeavor. Like all the rest of us, our patients are imperfect, and success is difficult to define."

"Well, I understand individuals being treated for drug and alcohol addiction hurt themselves, family, and others. The big difference with sexual disorders is the pain they inflict upon innocent and trusting people, particularly children," countered Nowitzke. "What's the rate of recidivism for your patients under care for sexual addiction?"

"It varies based upon how you measure a re-offense."

"I'm not interested in mincing words," said Nowitzke, whose voice was steadily rising during his questioning. "You have your own experience here at The Annex, and I suspect you've read the research if you are talking about 'success.' What do the psychiatric journals say?"

Coughlin began to stand as if to call an end to the interview.

"What does the research indicate?" repeated Nowitzke, pressing the matter. "What are the chances a pedophile treated the way you describe will commit a similar crime?"

"The recidivism rate ranges from 10 to 50 percent," conceded the priest. "But the research is imprecise."

"So basically, a local TV weatherman has a better chance at forecasting the weather in Wisconsin than your *success rate* here for a person likely to prey upon a child after treatment?"

Even though he had maintained his calm demeanor while Nowitzke pushed his buttons, Coughlin finally cracked. "Officers, I don't like your tone or insinuations. This interview is over."

"Father, if we need additional information, we will be back," said Taylor.

As they all stood, Nowitzke turned to Coughlin. "We'd like to look at Donovan's room."

"Detective, our residents live in a Spartan style. Rooms have only single beds and desks. No TVs, no radio, no cell phones. A Bible is all they need as part of their rehab."

"Father, nonetheless, we'd like to take a quick look, just to tick the box," replied Nowitzke.

With that, Coughlin led them out of his office and down the hallway to a drab room with more stained green walls. Donovan's apartment was just as Coughlin described. Aside from the water-damaged window overlooking the courtyard, there was a bed, a chair, and a Bible sitting squarely on the desk. Nothing more. Nowitzke held the door as Taylor and the priest entered the room.

"You see?" retorted Coughlin.

The search of Donovan's room took all of thirty seconds. Taylor casually walked to the window beside the desk. After glancing out the window, she mindlessly picked up the Bible and flipped through the pages. As she did, a paper that had been tri-folded in a letter style fluttered from the book to Nowitzke's feet. The detective picked up the document, unfolded it, read it, and made a face.

Centered on the plain white sheet of paper were the typed words, *"14. If any one steal the minor son of another, he shall be put to death."*

"What do you make of this?" Nowitzke asked, handing the letter to Coughlin.

After studying the short message, Coughlin had nothing to offer. "I've never seen it before."

"Is this a Bible verse?"

"No. I'm not sure what this means," replied Coughlin, shaking his head.

"I would guess it had something to do with why Donovan was here. Do the inmates—err, residents receive mail, Father?" asked Nowitzke.

"Generally, not. I suppose they can get mail, but most don't simply because their location is highly private and a guarded secret."

"Looks like someone knew where to find him. Without an envelope, we have no way to trace the letter," said Nowitzke. He took a photo of the document, placing the original in an evidence bag and tucking it away in his backpack.

He turned back to the priest. "Father Coughlin, I need some names of people from the diocese that can fill in some of the gaps about Donovan's past."

"I'm not at liberty to give you anything further, Detective. My impression is you don't have the best interests of the diocese in your heart."

"Listen, Father, I could give a shit about your diocese. I can't imagine anyone there would be willing to talk to me about Donovan anyway. My goal is only to solve Fast Eddie's murder."

Coughlin turned down the hall, leaving the officers in his wake.

Nowitzke was about to trail the priest when Taylor grabbed his arm to stop him. "Father, I thought you said Donovan was your friend? Don't you want us to solve his murder? I'd want that for a friend and colleague," said the younger officer. "But, I'm not sure we can do that without someone who can help us."

Coughlin continued walking down the hall.

"Please, Father," implored Taylor. "Just the name of one person who can help us . . . ?"

At the echo of her question, Coughlin stopped and turned. Ignoring Nowitzke, the priest spoke directly to the young woman. "One name only, but I have no clue about where you would find him since he left the priesthood. Dwayne Hammonds." With that, the priest turned from them again and shuffled away, not looking back.

The officers retraced their steps back through the maze of identical halls in silence. As they made their way along, several individuals, presumably patients, greeted them with smiles. Both cops exchanged looks, wondering which were the molesters. Getting into the cruiser, Nowitzke looked at Taylor. "Nice work with Coughlin, Taylor. You earned your paycheck today." The compliment brought a smile to her face.

"Where do we go from here, Detective?"

CHAPTER 4

Their next order of business was to provide Chief Clark with an overview of the findings, as well as to process the evidence gathered. A file was created, and the shell casing found by Harvey was shipped off to Ballistics on the chance the shooter had left a print.

As Nowitzke entered Clark's office, his disheveled appearance with a torn jacket, blood-stained pants, and sodden loafers clearly caught the Chief's attention. Before he could comment, Nowitzke dropped into one of the Chief's office side chairs and launched into a detailed briefing, seconded by Taylor who filled in any gaps. Clark absorbed the recap of the day's events, the evidence, and the Coughlin interview. After twenty minutes, Clark stopped Nowitzke to rephrase what he had heard.

"Essentially, you're saying a high-profile pedophile priest from a major city in another state was a patient at a private, almost secret, Appleton-based facility and was shot twice by a sniper with a high-powered rifle, in my town, on my watch?" Nowitzke and Taylor nodded silently in unison. Then, Nowitzke made the argument that the next steps of the investigation should include a trip to Minneapolis to follow up with local police agencies regarding any open investigations. Logically, it seemed to make sense that the shooter somehow learned of Donovan's temporary residence in Appleton and came to resolve the issue.

Nowitzke completed his report by lauding the work of Taylor and insisting that her continued presence was critical for the ongoing investigation.

"Here's the thing, Chief, the sheer number of potential victims, who are now our potential suspects, makes it necessary for us to go digging into past complaints, interviewing church staff who worked with Donovan, and reviewing the available evidence that had been accumulated by local police agencies over the years. We need to go to the Twin Cities. And we need to find Dwayne Hammonds."

Clark immediately approved Taylor's travel to Minnesota but asked both investigators to provide him with regular ongoing reports of their findings. As the meeting was breaking up, Clark took a parting shot at Nowitzke's appearance. "Please try to dress more professionally for our Minnesota brothers and sisters."

"It's been a long day. I won't go into details about my look, other than to say I did provide you with a souvenir," replied Nowitzke.

Clark looked at him quizzically.

"Several pieces of Fast Eddie that were on my pants are now stuck to your chair."

****

Before the sun rose the following morning, Nowitzke and Taylor met at the Appleton airport for their hastily arranged trip to Minneapolis. Since they were flying standby, waiting on space on one of the regional jets, they were not confirmed until a mid-morning flight. However, they took advantage of the dead time to get a head start of tracking down Dwayne Hammonds. Yet, their effort became a collective adventure in frustration. Taylor's call to the Minneapolis diocese regarding the whereabouts of the former priest got the expected answer with a clipped response. "He no longer is employed here." All other questions about where to find the man were rebuffed before the conversation abruptly ended with the click of the phone. Nowitzke's calls to local law enforcement and several local parishes yielded more of the same. "Yes, he had been a priest, but we have no idea of his whereabouts. Check some of the homeless shelters in the Minneapolis area." It was not clear to Nowitzke or Taylor whether Hammonds was working at a shelter or residing at one. After scanning the web for a listing of local shelters, the officers divided the various facilities to look for leads. Taylor finally scored a hit on her fourth call at Jane's Place on 3rd, where Hammonds both worked and was a part-time resident.

Now, after locating their lead, the officers still had time to kill before their flight. Meandering into a coffee shop, they ordered breakfast, both choosing coffee. However, their food choices diverged from there with Taylor selecting yogurt and fruit while Nowitzke went with eggs, bacon, and hash browns. After the food arrived, Nowitzke looked up at Taylor, who was sitting across from him. The twenty-something officer was physically striking and well dressed in a sharp, black business suit that hugged her frame tightly, a clear contrast to Nowitzke's disheveled look. "Taylor, can I ask you a question?"

"Yes, sir," she replied, sitting up a little straighter in the booth.

"Why did you take this job? I mean, I've pulled your personnel file. You've got a college degree. You seem to have your shit together based on what I can tell. And, don't take this the wrong way, but you're a knockout. I don't get it," concluded the detective, taking a sip of coffee.

"Well, thanks for the compliment, I guess. Being a cop is always something I wanted to do. I'm following in my dad's footsteps. He's a cop in the Upper Peninsula of Michigan. He's my hero for a lot of reasons. I want to make him proud."

The two officers went back to eating when Taylor looked Nowitzke in the eye. "Sir, why are you a cop?" she asked with a little trepidation. "Clark gave me some of your background, and I was impressed. What are you doing in Appleton after working in Milwaukee?"

After a prolonged pause, Nowitzke wiped his mouth with his napkin. "Good question. I guess if I wasn't a cop, I'd probably be one of the guys you'd be trying to catch. I grew up in a tough neighborhood in Milwaukee. We didn't have much, and I was on a bad path. I was destined for prison or the military until an officer who arrested me for doing something stupid took an interest in me and got me straightened out. As for moving from Milwaukee, it was a combination of personal reasons and, well . . . just seeing too much of the worst in people."

An overhead speaker announced that their plane was boarding. Nowitzke picked up the check and they walked to their gate. "By the way, Taylor, I generally answer to Nowitzke, but you can call me Chuck."

The young woman stopped and stuck out her hand as if they were meeting for the first time. "Call me Anissa, sir." Nowitzke shook her hand with a smile.

Upon arriving in Minneapolis, Nowitzke rented a car while Taylor got an electronic fix on the Dwayne Hammonds' shelter. Rolling up to the former warehouse in their rental car, the officers saw a buzz of activity with people of all ages and races moving in and out of the facility. Nowitzke and Taylor approached the receptionist at the main desk and asked to see the executive director. Within minutes, a petite, well-dressed black woman emerged from an office from behind the counter, completing some business on her cell phone. Nowitzke and Taylor waited patiently before the call ended.

"I'm sorry," the woman apologized in a friendly tone. "It's Monday, and all hell is breaking loose. I'm Opal Leonard. How can I help you?"

Both Nowitzke and Taylor flashed their badges and Leonard seemingly took on a stonier look. "We're looking for a gentleman named Dwayne Hammonds. We were told he worked here and was a part-timer," said Nowitzke.

"Why do you want to see him? Is Dwayne in trouble?"

"No," said Taylor. "We believe he might have some information about a man who was recently murdered . . . Edward Donovan."

"Fast Eddie. Fucking pervert," said Leonard, then realized too late she had spoken out loud. "I apologize."

"No apology required," said Nowitzke, chuckling at Leonard's faux pas. "Donovan was a terrible human being. Recently he was shot and killed by a sniper in Wisconsin at a treatment facility owned by the church. We need some background on him from Mr. Hammonds to help find the shooter."

"What, to give him a reward?" asked the director.

"Probably not," chimed in Taylor with a smile. "Is Dwayne here?"

"Yes, he is. Please be gentle with him. Dwayne has become a godsend for us. He is a humble man who handles every task no one else is willing to do. A true servant to humanity. He was a priest who was given a raw deal over this whole Donovan mess. He would not keep silent about what he saw, so the Bishop gave him a choice. Resign or be fired. Dwayne chose to leave the church on his own terms."

Leonard led the officers through a labyrinth of halls before finding the former priest reading the Bible to a young woman who appeared to be in a catatonic state, sitting up in a chair. Hammonds had shoulder-length grey hair and wore a torn flannel shirt and old jeans that were cinched around his waist. He looked up as the small group approached. "Dwayne, these police officers would like to have a word with you about Edward Donovan."

CHAPTER 5

As they waited for coffee at a downtown diner, Nowitzke explained across the table to Hammonds that Donovan had recently been murdered by a sniper at a rehab site run by the church.

"I'm not sure how helpful I can be. What exactly would you like to know?" asked the former priest.

"Our job is to find his killer. We understand that you might have some insights about Donovan's rise to fame and subsequent fall from grace," said Nowitzke. "How did you know Donovan?"

"We came up through the diocese at roughly the same time. For whatever reason, I was assigned a large parish before moving onto the diocese offices to take an administrative role. Edward's career began as a simple parish priest in a poverty-ridden and dangerous part of North Minneapolis. Like him or not now, he had tons of energy back then, breathing new life into his parish with a combination of personal style and a focus on social justice. Interestingly, while he was loved by his parishioners, the leadership at the diocese office considered him to be a pain in the ass."

"How so?" asked Taylor.

"Well, he begged for money from the diocese to start new programs and make improvements to the structure of his church. When he was told no, he went directly to CEOs of Minneapolis-based Fortune 500 companies. He persuaded many to donate funds along with getting time from their employees. Donovan's superiors were not happy to say the least. They saw him as robbing from Peter to pay Paul since several local parishes complained that Donovan was taking money away from them."

"So, he wasn't necessarily making friends?" asked Nowitzke.

"Yes and no. Donovan upset many local priests. But after a rocky start, the diocese warmed to him as they watched him become a budding superstar for his fundraising ability. He rebuilt his church, increased attendance, and attracted the local elite from throughout the metropolitan area to attend his parish. In North Minneapolis, of all places. He developed an amazing contact list with the personal phone number of every important leader in the area. In a short time, the Bishop wanted to leverage Donovan to provide more resources for the entire organization."

"But . . ."

"I would guess you could say Donovan suffered from one of the seven deadly sins. Pride."

"What do you mean?" asked Taylor.

"Donovan became wildly popular and high-profile to the extent that he became known in Minneapolis at large. The local press nicknamed him 'Fast Eddie' due to his paradoxical style, which had him in the fast lane juxtaposed with his sacred vows. I think he took pride in that moniker. Fast Eddie hobnobbed with the Minneapolis privileged. He was seen at every high-profile event. Vikings games. The opera. He somehow wrangled a box at the city's philharmonic orchestra. His celebrity grew as he was named *Minneapolis Quarterly's* 'volunteer of the year,' hailing him as a cultural icon. Donovan reveled in the attention." Hammonds paused. "Can we get something to eat?"

Taylor passed a menu to the thin old man. "Please order what you want."

When the food arrived, Hammonds started eating like he hadn't seen food in a week. Then, after gulping down half a sandwich, he continued. "I have to give the devil his due. Donovan was incredibly successful and worked hard. But . . ."

"But, what?" asked Nowitzke.

"Early on there were rumors about him floating through the diocese offices. At first, I wouldn't believe any of it. I thought it was just jealousy about Donovan's success. Then, I noticed that Fast Eddie seemed to move from parish to parish on a regular basis . . . about every two years or so. He stayed at inner-city locations, improved each one, and then moved again. The Bishop told me that the church was using Donovan's playbook to improve the diocese a parish at a time. Donovan was offered several promotions but he turned down each. Said he wanted to stay in the trenches."

"Maybe he viewed that as his calling?" offered Taylor.

"Perhaps, but the rumors grew and so did my suspicions. As an administrator, I should have had access to his personnel file, but it disappeared. Turned out it was kept under lock and key in the Bishop's office. *That's* when my suspicions became real." Hammonds shoveled another sandwich into his mouth and hastily swallowed. "About five years ago, my phone rang. It was a call from a young lady who said Donovan had molested her special needs child. I took down the information and went to the Bishop. He told me he would handle it directly. About a week later, I called her back to make sure the matter was resolved. She started crying, saying the Bishop told her it was all a misunderstanding. Then, when she pressed for a resolution, the Bishop questioned her parenting skills, her alcohol and drug use, and threatened to call social services. She was cautioned to keep quiet or potentially lose her son."

"What did you do?" asked Nowitzke.

"Frankly, I was enraged. I gave the woman the name of a high-powered personal injury attorney and then started my own investigation of Donovan. I went back some twenty-five years. To cut to the chase, Donovan was molesting young boys and girls the entire time. He took advantage of their social situation, which often involved broken homes. When some parents complained, the leadership of the diocese wrote them off quietly, vowing to handle the matter. However, when I checked back with some of the families, I found that they were all told that law enforcement shouldn't be contacted. Since no one family had a broader picture of what was taking place, each of Donovan's transgressions were viewed as a single one-off misunderstanding. Under implicit threats from the powerful church, each of the victims and their families were 'encouraged' to drop any allegations and move on." Hammonds buried his face in his hands and started to shake. "That son of a bitch hurt kids. Children. He violated their trust. And the Bishop knew about it all. Donovan. The threats to keep parents quiet. Everything. He did nothing."

Nowitzke controlled his anger and glanced at Taylor to see how she was handling Hammonds' story. Taylor sat staring beyond Hammonds, staring at something far beyond the diner walls. Nowitzke turned back to the elderly man. The three remained silent, until Hammonds spoke again.

"The original young lady who called me followed my advice and hired the attorney, Ben Karlsson. From what I knew, he was very successful at returning large verdicts for his clients, including those that had been sexually abused. He was like a lion, not afraid to take on anyone or any organization. His first order of business was to contact the Minneapolis District Attorney asking that criminal charges be filed against Donovan. The DA listened, but suggested they meet with the Bishop, his legal counsel, and Donovan to work out any 'confusion' over the issues. In my position as an employee, I was invited to attend. Like the proverbial fly on the wall, I watched things unfold. I was surprised Karlsson took a subdued approach, especially after all the glad-handing, then stonewalling at the meeting by the Bishop. But I could see Karlsson was cunning. He anticipated this and set a trap. Prior to the meeting, he called the police to come to the site of the meeting after working with the mother to swear out a complaint.

"The Minneapolis Police Department arrested Donovan as he left the offices of the diocese that day. I almost couldn't contain myself when they took Donovan to a police cruiser in handcuffs. Karlsson also tipped off the news media about the big story that would set Minneapolis on its ear. Donovan's perp walk became front-page news captured by all the local papers. He was the lead story on every Minneapolis-based television channel that evening. With the 24-hour news cycle, the story was picked up by every major TV network, including Al Jazeera. With all the publicity, the families who previously complained about Donovan realized they'd been duped by the diocese and threw in their lot with Karlsson to represent them."

Nowitzke and Taylor could not move, paying rapt attention to the former priest's story.

"During the discovery phase prior to civil trial, Karlsson grilled the Bishop in his deposition for the better part of a week. Karlsson was like a surgeon, making small cuts as he questioned him. When he caught the Bishop in a lie, he carved more deeply. Karlsson delved into what his Eminence knew and when he knew it. He also questioned the Bishop about his strategy of moving Donovan from parish to parish without any disclosure to the churchgoers. Since he was under oath, he was cornered. I thought the SOB would lie. But he didn't. He filled in the gory details despite a constant look of panic, looking like he was pleading for help from his big-time defense attorneys. Even his own team of lawyers, each earning hundreds of dollars an hour, could do nothing . . . other than look serious and object to procedural issues from time to time.

"Then, Karlsson announced his plan to depose every victim and to outline the sordid details of each crime for public consumption. Even though the diocesan attorneys believed most of Donovan's victims would never agree to testify, the threat to the diocese became real."

"Where were you in all this, Mr. Hammonds?" asked Nowitzke.

"I had a ring-side seat. But that led to my eventual downfall as well. Even though I was not involved in any of the crimes, I had a crisis of conscience early in the process. I concluded I wanted no part of this church and would accept whatever the consequences were. So, I regularly called Karlsson and fed him all the details he needed to win his case against the diocese. I eventually became his lead witness, deposed in front of the Bishop and the remainder of his leadership team."

"Becoming *persona non grata* in the process?" asked Nowitzke.

Hammonds sighed and nodded. "Let's just say I'm no longer invited to the diocesan Christmas party. Anyway, since a cover-up is even worse than the original crime, the diocese saw the handwriting on the wall and quietly began settlement talks involving its insurance company. Their liability carrier had only had a short-term relationship with the account but had limits of $10 million for each policy term. As the insurer of choice for two years, the carrier coughed up $20 million.

"To me it sounded like a fortune, but I'm no lawyer. Karlsson scoffed at the offer, calling it a 'good start.' Since the church did not have additional sexual molestation coverage, it was in a quandary. The diocese claimed it was broke. But, Karlsson's voice grew louder saying the statutes be damned. He started dropping phrases like 'repressed memory theory,' which really got the attention of the defense attorneys. With the price increasing, the diocese was advised by its lawyers to come up with more money. Following some serious arm-twisting, it was eventually agreed a settlement of $110 million, after the insurer's contribution, would be split twenty-six ways by the victims.

"The church filed for Chapter 11 bankruptcy protection but chose to raise money by selling off several properties. Ironically, most of those parishes sold were the same ones resurrected by Donovan early in his career. In the end, the diocese got its revenge against the families for their snitching."

"Unbelievable," concluded Taylor.

"But there's more," said Hammonds. "Karlsson engineered a settlement document where all terms of the deal, including the names of the victims, were to remain sealed and confidential. As a former member of the diocese, I just violated a portion of that agreement."

"What ever happened about the criminal prosecution of Donovan?" asked Nowitzke.

"The criminal charges against Donovan were problematic. Social media had already tried and convicted Donovan and the church in the court of public opinion. All that was left was for the District Attorney to do his job. With pressure mounting on the DA to prosecute Fast Eddie to the fullest extent of the law, including the suggestion of several medieval-style punishments, the mother who started the entire saga dropped all charges."

"Why? Did the diocese do something to her?" asked Taylor.

"No. She later told me that her son had already received a substantial settlement and they wanted to put the matter behind them. She had no interest in testifying in a criminal court. She took the money and left the state to start a new life with her son. I couldn't blame her."

"So, Donovan got off without any jail time?" questioned Nowitzke.

"Yes. Since none of the other victims had sworn a criminal complaint, the DA had no choice but to drop all charges against Fast Eddie. The reaction of the greater Minneapolis area was outrage. How could Donovan just walk away? To save some face, the DA declared that justice demanded Donovan go to therapy for his addiction. For its part, the diocese declared that Donovan would never be allowed to serve as a priest ever again. For good measure, I was also given my walking papers."

"Assholes," retorted Nowitzke. "Excuse me, Mr. Hammonds. So, Donovan walked away, but you lost your job for doing the right thing?"

"That's a pretty accurate assessment. However, as I said, I knew I couldn't stay there anyway. So now I'm at Jane's Place on 3rd."

Taylor gritted her teeth after hearing the final chapter of Hammond's story. "Did you ever hear anymore from Donovan?"

"Only rumors really. Supposedly, Donovan pulled out his cell phone and contacted some of his former well-placed buddies. His ego was planning a triumphant return to Minneapolis. He just didn't understand he had become a pariah. An untouchable. No one returned his calls. I think he was truly shocked. I haven't heard anything further about Donovan until today."

"Any ideas about who shot him?" asked Nowitzke.

"There are any number of suspects. I suppose I'm on that list as well. But those that Donovan molested were pretty unsophisticated. I don't think they would have been able to locate him, let alone shoot him in the manner you've described."

"Should we be talking to Karlsson? Is he a source of information?" asked Taylor.

The priest shrugged with a weary smile. "Only if you want to hear some of his war stories."

CHAPTER 6

After talking with Hammonds, the rest of the week went downhill quickly. Nowitzke and Taylor came up empty in finding potential suspects from their counterparts at Minneapolis PD. There were simply no complaints sworn against Donovan on record, aside from the most recent one that had brought him down. Even though they had the young mother's name from media reports, they could not locate her as she had left town with her son and the settlement to start fresh. There was no forwarding address or other helpful information. Even though they wanted to talk with her, it was clear from everything Nowitzke and Taylor read that the mother was likely not the shooter.

"Anissa, looks like mama hit her version of the lottery and skipped town," concluded Nowitzke.

While the balance of the other victims seemed to be the most likely pool of suspects in Donovan's death, those names were now sealed just as Hammonds said. When Nowitzke approached a local judge about obtaining the names of the victims as potential suspects in Donovan's murder, it was a short discussion. The judge told Nowitzke he would need a compelling reason beyond the speculation of what she perceived as a fishing expedition challenging the victims' right to privacy. However, the judge finally agreed to review the sealed judgment *in camera*, or in a closed session, to determine whether any of Donavan's victims might have the motive, means, and opportunity to commit his murder. Ultimately, the respected jurist rejected his request, or, as Nowitzke told the story, "she told me to pound sand."

Taylor's background check of Donovan was of little help. Donovan's parents were both deceased and his lone sister was living in California. A quick telephone call to the woman to notify her of her brother's death was met with disgust. She was of no help when asked about her brother. *No, she had not seen him in decades. Never call this number again.*

After speaking with several of the local parish employees at churches where Donovan had worked, it became apparent the priest never had time for them. The staff described Donovan as a loner. While they were shocked he had been murdered, they really didn't miss him.

The DA was not helpful either, given the licking he took in the press. He was more interested in distancing himself from Donovan with an upcoming election.

A look at phone records led Nowitzke and Taylor to several of the local CEOs in the area. Each described Fast Eddie as a bully who liked to wield his perceived power to his benefit. None referred to him as a friend, but also, none struck Nowitzke as potential killers either.

Not surprisingly, Nowitzke and Taylor were also rebuffed by the diocese, referring the officers to their legal counsel.

Everything was a dead end. The net result was that, for all his bluster and notoriety, Donovan had led a sad and lonely life.

After their final follow-up on Friday afternoon, Taylor and Nowitzke walked back to their hotel when they happened upon a local pub billing itself as catering to "scholars and scoundrels." Though, as Taylor observed, the real money they were after belonged to the young well-dressed professionals who worked downtown. It was clear to both officers that the young men and women at the bar were interested in seeing and being seen.

Grabbing a table, Nowitzke ordered a Boddington's on draught matched by Taylor's chardonnay as they dissected the week. What had they missed, if anything? Two orders of fish and chips and several rounds later, they came to no new conclusions. With no suspects, minimal physical evidence, and no real leads, this case had the makings of rapidly becoming as cold as the late Minnesota March evening. In the morning, they would head home.

Miller Investigative Services
CONFIDENTIAL/ FOR YOUR EYES ONLY

SUBJECT: NICHOLAS HAYDEN

DOB:	October 13, 1991
PLACE OF BIRTH:	Sturgeon Bay, Wisconsin
CURRENT RESIDENCE:	Sister Bay, Wisconsin
MARITAL STATUS:	Single
FAMILY:	Father, William "Bill" Hayden (deceased)
	Mother, Caroline Hayden (deceased)
	No siblings
EDUCATION:	B.A. – History, University of Michigan
MILITARY SERVICE:	United States Air Force
CURRENT OCCUPATION:	Unemployed

SPECIAL NOTES: Pararescueman. Highly decorated combat veteran earning multiple citations and honors, including a Purple Heart. Numerous tours of duty in Afghanistan. Recently retired due to injuries sustained in the field. Parents recently killed in an automobile crash. May be suffering from temporary PTSD.

CHAPTER 7

The black BMW 328xi glided up the lengthy tree-lined driveway of Weston Insurance Company, located in Neenah, Wisconsin, a community of 25,000 people perched on Lake Winnebago about an hour south of Green Bay and maybe two directly north from Milwaukee. The warm sun, combined with the smell of freshly cut grass courtesy of a maintenance man on his riding mower, made for a beautiful spring morning. A distant but pleasant sensory memory, particularly after serving at duty stations around the world for the last several years. Passing small groups of what he guessed were employees enjoying a morning walk during their break, Nicholas Hayden took in more of the day, lowering the car's windows while popping the sunroof. The smells and sensations took him back to his youth when he had been his family's lawn guy. Although he had grown tired of that chore back then, he also recalled mowing being far more enjoyable than wearing a snowmobile suit while blowing snow for six months a year. In fact, according to the television meteorologist he heard while getting dressed that morning, it was to become unseasonably warm for May with temperatures pushing into the 80s.

Reaching the end of the half-mile-long drive, he pulled the Beamer up to a group of young women wearing fashionable office clothing, combined with the requisite sneakers, to ask for directions to visitor parking. As he turned down Ozzy's Boneyard blaring on his radio, one of the ladies stepped forward to offer help, but they all became more interested in adding to the conversation upon getting a glimpse of the handsome young man in the sports car. After receiving several mock requests for a ride, he was directed to the space in front of the three-story building's main entrance. The modern structure, constructed of glass and brick, was carved out of the sylvan setting, making a strong first impression to visitors.

After pulling into the first available parking space, Nick sat in his car. He could feel his blood pressure starting to rise. Taking several gulps of the fresh air, he gripped the steering with such force that his knuckles turned white. Beads of sweat formed on his forehead and things went dark for a moment. Then after what felt like an eternity, but was actually less than a minute, he could feel the sensation starting to pass. The beautiful day had returned and he was here, unsure of exactly why. He had made more of an effort in getting dressed and groomed for the day's meeting that he had in weeks. Then he realized he hadn't put on a suit since the funeral.

Admit it, he thought to himself, *you haven't worn shoes since the funeral.* But, after squeezing his size 12 feet into what felt like size 10 dress shoes, he'd packed an overnight bag with a few changes of nice clothes, as directed, since the interview might result in a stay of several days. *Fine with me,* he thought. *There's nothing in that house to go home to, anyway.*

After one final cleansing breath, he got out of the car and entered the lobby that extended the full height of the building, topped by several massive skylights. The interior of the lobby was tastefully decorated with several groupings of plush leather chairs and couches clustered around small coffee tables, giving the area a clubby feel. On the beige tiled floor, several colorful accent rugs added to the look, which was completed by a collection of large plants and indoor trees. Along the primary wall, he noted a series of paintings of solemn old men of varying vintages, presumably a tribute gallery to former leaders of the company. Enclosed in several glass cases along the wall were a collection of industry awards and local trophies, the expected trappings of a company signaling to visitors the organization's accomplishments and value to the community. Large flat-screen televisions hung from several walls announcing important information for employees, rotating between key internal metrics, an RSS feed of news, sports, and local weather, the daily menu at the in-house cafeteria, and a list of visitors that he noticed included his name. In the background, subtle light rock music was piped into the lobby. The net effect of the entire entranceway produced a businesslike yet comfortable setting. It also reminded Weston employees of the importance of success.

Moving through the lobby, he noted the only other person in the great expanse was a young redheaded receptionist. She wore a floral print dress and sat behind a small desk within an enclosure, flanked by two modern art paintings. As he approached, she looked up from some reading, quickly offering a welcoming smile along with a greeting.

"May I help you, sir?"

"Hi, Cassie, that's me," responded Nick, noting the receptionist's name tag and pointing to his name on the electronic readout. "I'm Nick Hayden. I have a ten o'clock meeting with Mr. Swenson." Cassie asked Nick for photo identification, and after making a photocopy of his driver's license, she made a brief call announcing Nick's arrival to an unknown party on the other end of the line.

Cassie directed Nick to the plush chairs he had passed on his way in, indicating that Mr. Swenson's administrative assistant was en route. Nick dropped into a high-backed and extremely comfortable brown leather lounge chair. The type that one could easily fall asleep in, to the sounds of a college football game on television on a Saturday afternoon. However, as he prepared to meet Swenson's assistant, he reminded himself to sit up straight to make a good first impression. As he waited, Nick noticed a recent edition of Weston Insurance's internal house publication, the *Weston Insurance News*, or *WIN* for short, sitting on a coffee table. The cover of the magazine featured several employees who had spearheaded a recent local charity auction standing behind a large prop check for $50,000. Flipping to the first page, Nick noted the president's message along with his accompanying headshot. Although he had met Emil Swenson years earlier, Nick thought the man pictured had aged considerably, even though he still looked quite distinguished.

Skimming the article, Nick noted several bullet points buried in the copy highlighting the organization's prior year financial performance. After a cursory look, it became apparent the company had indeed flourished in achieving its goals and was making a profit in all areas of their business, but one—the religious niche Weston had entered several years before. It was, apparently, the only problem area for the organization, and he began to delve deeper into the article.

Lost in concentration, Nick did not notice the figure patiently standing over him. Suddenly sensing a presence, Nick looked over the top of the magazine and quickly sprang to his feet, embarrassed he had been so engrossed in the publication. Standing before Nick was a handsome woman in her late fifties wearing a smart business suit. She was tall, with deep brown eyes and grey-streaked hair in a shoulder-length cut that gave her credibility, with a youthful flair.

In a friendly tone and with a broad smile, she introduced herself as Anita Lathom. "Mr. Hayden, I'm Mr. Swenson's primary admin. Welcome to Weston Insurance. Can I offer you coffee?"

Hayden asked Anita to call him "Nick" and indicated he had "coffee-ed out" on Starbucks that morning but would take some water if it was available. Anita nodded politely, asking Nick to accompany her to the elevator where she slid her credentials through a card reader to summon the car.

It was a short ride to the third floor. When the doors opened, Nick noticed an abject silence. To the left, he saw an entranceway to what looked like executive offices. However, Anita steered him to his right where he entered what he assumed was the corporate board room. With lightning efficiency, Anita produced the requested bottle of water from behind the wood-paned doors of a Sub-Zero refrigerator built into the wall. "Is there anything else I can get for you, Mr. Hayden . . . Nick?"

"No, ma'am."

"Mr. Swenson will be with you shortly," Anita said in a very formal tone as she left the room, closing the heavy double-wood doors behind her.

With a quiet moment to contemplate his surroundings, Nick noticed a similar level of luxury that had flowed through the lobby. In Nick's mind, it was functional and elegant, but just short of opulent. The boardroom was dominated by a large, highly polished table. To the naked eye, it looked as if it had been literally carved from a single piece of wood. Nick wondered how it was put in place on the third floor, as none of the entrances or the elevator seemed large enough to accommodate the behemoth. Perhaps, he mused, a double-bladed Chinook helicopter had dropped it into its place as the building was being constructed. The table was surrounded by a dozen bright red leather chairs, which stood in contrast to the plush white carpet. Nick congratulated himself for only ordering water, figuring his odds of spilling his beverage on the expensive carpeting would have risen exponentially had he chosen coffee. So far, so good. He exhaled slowly and silently.

At the other end of the room was a ninety-inch television screen along with state-of-the-art electronics. Aside from the various sculptures and paintings in the room, which Nick surmised were exceedingly expensive, the main attraction of the space was the view. Three of the walls in the room were floor-to-ceiling glass, providing an incredible look at the forest surrounding the building.

Nick was lost in the view when a small door opposite the primary entrance to the room opened. Emil Swenson, President and Chief Executive Officer of Weston Insurance, entered the room with a smile and his hand extended. Although Nick guessed Swenson was approaching seventy, he had the energy of a man who was much younger. The CEO had a pale complexion with black hair and natural grey sideburns. Swenson was nattily dressed in an expensive three-piece pinstripe suit with a bright red tie and matching pocket square.

"Nicholas, so glad to see you again after all these years," said Swenson in a booming voice.

"Good to see you again too, sir . . . and please call me Nick."

"Nick, you are no longer in the service. Please dispense with the 'sir' stuff and call me Emil. While we hardly know each other, I considered myself a friend to your mother and father. God rest their souls. I don't know if you remember, but we met once when you were a young teen before Bill's retirement. Then, you were busy with high school. Then, off to college. A Wolverine, no less? Then, the service, posted around the world according to your parents. Based off my conversations with them, I guess I've been a close observer of your whole life. Given the last couple of months, how are you doing, Nick?"

"Thank you, sir . . . Emil. It's been a blur to say the least. I had left the Air Force and my duty station in England and had just started making plans to come home to Wisconsin when I got the news. I'm still processing what took place." *How, in an instant, a teenage driver who was texting could kill my parents.* "The toughest part for me is that, after having been a part of any number of incursions and rescues in the field and never getting what I considered much more than a scratch, that they could be killed by something as stupid as a car accident." Nick paused briefly to gather himself. "I never got to say goodbye to them."

Swenson listened stoically following a few moments of dead air. "Nick, I am so sorry for your loss. If there is anything I can do for you, please let me know. I miss Bill and Caroline, as well. They were so proud of what you had accomplished for yourself personally and then what you did for your country. I don't know how many times we shared an evening together with a glass of wine after dinner, reminiscing about the past and talking of the future. More than once, the talk shifted to you and what you were up to. In many ways, I feel like I actually know you very well."

The two men settled into chairs before Swenson continued the conversation. "Thanks for making the trip here today. I understand your life over the past several months has been tumultuous, both personally and professionally, but I have a proposition for you. I'm not sure if you know this, but I also served my country in the Navy. When I separated from the military, one of the most difficult things I encountered was working my way back into civilian life. Things were very different in society for returning veterans when I served. Finding work from many employers amounted to a Hobson's choice, take it or leave it. Eventually, I met another guy who had been in the service, and we made an instant connection. Whether it was through pity or not, he took a chance on me, offering me work with Weston Insurance Company. I figured I would take the job and look for something better after a couple of months, but that never happened. I landed on my feet as a young sales manager after a short time in the field. Believe me, when I started, I didn't know shit about insurance . . . pardon my French. But I was successful in sales and made an early mark at Weston. While I was never a great technician on the insurance products, I did know people. Many years later, after advancing in management, I hired another squid, your father, for sales. It turned out my instincts were correct. Bill became our best representative before he retired young. Who knew a Seabee could sell? Over time, our success paralleled each other."

Nick nodded along, the story familiar as he had heard it growing up from his father. He wondered if this was the extent of the invitation, nostalgia and looking back. He couldn't think of anything else he could offer this highly successful man. But he was wrong.

"I would suspect you are currently unemployed after your separation from the service. In my years of leading the company, I have maintained a personal philosophy that we need to integrate veterans back into the workforce. In my estimation, veterans need a hand, not a handout," Swenson went on, his voice rising as he spoke. "I've done my best to help many young men and women back into civilian life with meaningful work. I guess this is my long-winded way of saying I'd like you to come to work for our company."

Nick looked at him with a subtle smirk and chose his next words carefully. "Emil, I certainly appreciate the offer. I really do need a job, and please don't take offense, but after jumping out of airplanes and making life-or-death decisions, and even knowing how successful my father was at your company, I can't imagine the thought of selling insurance."

"I appreciate your honesty," Swenson replied. "Nick, I love our sales force. I consider it to be the best in the industry. Every time I speak to our staff, I remind them 'Sales pays the bills here.' I'm not offering you a job as a salesperson. You have a history degree from the University of Michigan and a distinguished military record. Personally, I view you as having great potential in other areas. Respecting your sacrifice, I want to take another chance on a Hayden, even though I believe the deck is stacked in my favor. I think my instincts are still good."

"Emil, I can confess I don't know shit about insurance . . . I speak fluent French, as well. What would you want me to do?"

Swenson popped out of the plush red leather chair, straightened his tie, and took a deep breath, standing as he prepared to answer the question. "Weston has been enormously successful in my time. Under my watch as leader of the company, we have become experts at entering niche business segments taking advantage of available opportunities. It has allowed us to grow exponentially and create profits that support our workforce, their families, our policyholders, and our community. In fact, a critical aspect of our business plan is the continual study of multiple niches with the goal of entering a new market segment every year to help fuel more growth. That strategy transformed Weston from a small Wisconsin-based insurance company into a respected national carrier." Swenson paused briefly. "But it has become apparent we may not be the experts we think we are. Perhaps our success has led to hubris. We have a major problem with the performance of one division that has become very unsettling, calls elements of our strategy into question, and must be addressed immediately. In fact, the board has agreed with management's recommendation to leave the segment, a first for the company. If it's not done right, I'm concerned about the psychological effect on our employees and the message it sends to all of our stakeholders."

Listening intently, Nick chimed in, "Is this the religious segment I read about in your newsletter in the lobby?"

"Yes," said Swenson, looking somewhat surprised that Nick had connected the dots so simply. "Nick, I need a leader to get us out of that segment. We need to do this honestly and ethically and in accordance with all state laws. But also, we need to do a deep dive into the circumstances that led to our failure so we don't repeat our mistakes in the future. Although this is only one portion of our business, we are hemorrhaging red ink. We need to address it quickly. I need someone who can move through the material associated with the policies for the religious institutions and pinpoint where the decisions were made that created the problems we have."

"Emil, I've already told you I know nothing about insurance. You should be able to find someone much more qualified than me to lead the effort."

"I don't need an expert on insurance, I need someone who can learn the basics quickly, then research documents to determine causes. I need someone who can ask tough questions without completely offending the people he's asking. And I need someone who does *not* currently work here so I know that the information is accurate and there are no asses being covered. You would have free reign to do what's needed. In fact, I'd like a full post-mortem on this line, including follow-up after cancellation. Someone ended up with that business after the accounts left us. Was the next company after Weston any smarter or were there other factors that led to the profitability issue?" Swenson paused. "Frankly, I've already settled on you as the person for the job. I won't take no for an answer. I'm sorry for being so direct, but it's my Type-A personality kicking in."

"Emil, aside from knowing absolutely nothing about your business, there are practical issues. For starters, my parents' house is a couple of hours north in Sister Bay, and I don't want to spend that amount of time in the car every day."

Swenson contemplated Nick's objection, lost in thought for a moment before picking up the phone on the desk. "Anita, have the auditors left The Lakehouse? Uh-huh. Okay, have housekeeping clean it within the hour. Oh, and see they stock the refrigerator for Mr. Hayden please. Thanks."

The CEO turned to Nick. "It's all settled. Weston owns a small cottage on the edge of town where we can put you up in for the duration of your contract. You can head home on the weekends, but you'll have a place to stay while you're in town. Also, you will have full authority to handle the review of the religious institution business, including whatever technical staff you'll need. In addition, I will have an administrative assistant assigned to you that can help you navigate internally here at Weston. Nick, see Anita on the way out this afternoon for directions to what we call The Lakehouse. We can discuss specifics of your assignment at dinner. Feel free to wear jeans and I'll swing by to pick you up at seven tonight."

The meeting ended abruptly as Swenson left the boardroom, leaving Nick dumbstruck, his mouth open, trying to figure out what had just happened. *I think I was just hired by an insurance company. Shit.*

After Nick returned his badge to Cassie in the lobby and she had watched the BMW pull away from the property, the receptionist's phone rang. "Hello, sir . . . The man's name was Hayden . . . I don't know why he was here, sir . . . He met with Mr. Swenson. I . . ." Before she could continue, the call ended with a loud click in Cassie's headset.

CHAPTER 8

Anita's directions took Nick west just minutes out of Neenah, to a quiet forested area that bordered a series of lakes. He pulled off a paved road onto a dirt path, flanked by a private property sign simply labelled "Weston," which led him to the cottage. Exiting the car, Nick paused for a moment to hear the strange sound of nothing. His head took a moment to wrap itself around the idea that, aside from winds whistling through the tall pine trees, it could be this quiet so close to the city. Winter deadfall, consisting of branches, pinecones, and dried needles, covered the sparse grass. He stood there savoring the smell of the woods like the only person left in the world.

Walking up the front pathway, constructed of brick pavers, to the main entrance, Nick found the key where Anita said it would be, in a cleverly disguised birdfeeder attached to the porch, where the bottom held birdseed and a secret compartment. Before opening the front door, he immediately questioned the use of the word "cottage" to describe the substantial custom log home. The heavy wood door opened into a great room that seemed to reflect the taste of the decorators at the Weston Insurance complex he had just visited. The house was constructed of heavy timbers with a ceiling peaking at fifteen feet. At one end of the room was a massive stone fireplace that also reached from floor to ceiling, featuring a carved rough-hewn wooden mantel. At the other end of the room was a modern kitchen right out of a designer's magazine, complete with high-end stainless-steel appliances, dark granite countertops, and a large island with four bar-height chairs located under pendant lighting.

No expense had been spared in decorating the place. Even though he had only an overnight bag, he walked to the other side of the room adjacent to the fireplace to find it shared a wall with the master suite on the backside. The bedroom was large with a wall of windows facing the lake. An immense ensuite bathroom with a tiled walk-in shower whose series of nozzles rivaled a state-of-the-art car wash completed the space.

The length of the west wall of the home featured large windows, bathing the room in the afternoon sun and providing a view of what appeared to be private lakeshore. Nick dropped his bag, went back to the fridge, and found a cold Stella Artois. Whoever the unknown staff was, they had done an exceptional job in stocking the kitchen with enough food for the week. As he sipped his beer, he found two more bedrooms and a shared full bath in between them. A large room in the center of the house, outfitted with a large-screen television and a full bar, indicated Weston made guests' comfort a priority. Nick found his way back to the sunroom, which led to an expansive deck overlooking the water. The outdoor space came complete with a built-in gas grill. After opening the two sets of sliding doors to let the fresh air enter the home, he found a plush brown leather chair and sat in the sunroom to enjoy his beer.

Nick reflected upon his exchange with Swenson, wondering about the chain of events. The day started out innocently enough, with a courtesy trip to meet a friend of his parents. But it somehow led to a job offer. While it was clear Swenson was accustomed to getting his way, Nick had serious self-doubts about his ability to complete the requested work with any level of credibility. His history classes had been what seemed a lifetime ago, and although he was sure he could handle research and archival work, skills that would come back with a little effort, he doubted he could pick up the complexities of insurance work quickly. *The last thing I want is to screw things up, my first attempt at my "new" life.* It wasn't until one Stella was gone and a second half drunk that a solution popped into his head. It dawned on him that even though Swenson had offered him the job, there had been no mention of compensation. *Clearly, a way out of this mess. I'll just turn down whatever Swenson offers and tell him I have other opportunities I'm exploring . . . although God only knows what they are.*

Satisfied with his strategy, Nick finished his beer and rose to get another when he noticed something seemed out of order, in a place where order was the order. The Lakehouse had any number of expensive-looking decorative pieces placed throughout the cottage. It had also been immaculately cleaned by the staff as requested by Swenson. However, the cleaning crew either missed a large brass telescope in the corner of the room where glass windows from the walls came together or it was broken on its hinge. The barrel of the telescope was pointing at a forty-five-degree angle down and to the left, rather than toward the sky, looking awry. Hayden put his beer on the coffee table and walked toward the piece. Placing his eye to the lens, he began to play with the focus knob while not changing the angle of the scope. In seconds, what began as a blurry shape was transformed with the turn of a knob into a floating raft complete with a comely young woman sunning herself in the warmth of the day wearing only a white bikini bottom. No sooner had Hayden made the final adjustment bringing the picture into focus, the tanned young woman unexpectedly sat up as if becoming aware of another's presence. The mermaid looked around briefly, but then turned, seemingly glaring directly up through the barrel of the telescope into Nick's eye with a force that made him jump backwards. Then, in one fluid move, he saw the woman grab her top while deftly slipping into the water.

Contemplating the image of the angry woman, he felt he was losing control of his body once more. Growing unsteady, he grabbed a piece of wall as he began to sweat once more. *Jesus, not again.* Nick's breathing became labored and he wondered if he might pass out. He tried to calm himself, repeating out loud, "She's angry, not hostile. There is no danger. There is no danger," trying to convince himself. Then, it was over as quickly it had come.

Moments later, Nick heard the muffled roar of a vehicle turning over, interrupting the peace. Based upon the growing revs, whatever it was seemed to be heading in his general direction. Within seconds, it became apparent he was going to meet his new neighbor as an open-top green Jeep Wrangler came to a skidding halt on the stones of the private drive, sending them in all directions. The momentum of the Jeep seemed to propel the young woman out of the vehicle as she stormed toward his front door wearing a white robe. Nick heard incomprehensible yelling and pounding on the door with the intensity of a police raid working on a major drug seizure. Not at all sure that he wanted to face her, but certain that she would continue until he did, he opened the door to find a tanned, willowy, brown-haired beauty who was cursing in general, but also screaming, "I told you assholes to leave me alone!" However, when she saw Nick standing in the foyer with his beer, she immediately fell silent, seeming confused by the tall unknown man who had greeted her.

After a moment, the woman collected herself. "Where are the perverts that have been spying on me?" she calmly asked.

"I don't know," Nick responded. "I think they moved out."

"Who the hell are you?"

"I guess I'm the new pervert in residence."

Still looking confused by the face she didn't recognize, she replied, "Well, quit looking at me with that damned telescope," and began backing toward the Jeep, seemingly embarrassed by her tantrum.

"Hey, look, I didn't . . . I mean I looked through the telescope just to see what was out there. But I didn't intend to look at, um . . . I'm Nick Hayden. Who are you?"

"None of your fucking business, Nick."

The young woman hit the gas, leaving as quickly as she had arrived, kicking up a shower of stones while also directing a middle finger in Nick's general direction.

"Who said multitasking was a myth?" Nick asked himself rhetorically.

CHAPTER 9

Dinner with the CEO was at a typical Wisconsin supper club that took Nick back to his youth. Cheap-looking knotty pine covered the walls while multiple neon beer signs added color to the place. While he wasn't necessarily paying attention to his destination on the ride, Nick couldn't determine whether the lake he was now looking at off the front deck of the restaurant was the same as the one that sat behind The Lakehouse. *Should have paid more attention during that Wisconsin Geography unit in fourth grade.*

With a view of the setting sun from the deck, a server came out to take their drink order. Swenson took the liberty of ordering deep fried cheese curds. "I'll bet you haven't had these in years, Nick," he commented with a smile.

"Actually, no, sir. But I needed to raise my bad cholesterol," joked Nick, dunking several of the delicious golden nuggets in ranch dressing. As he began to relax, Nick found it hard to imagine that as high-powered a man as Emil Swenson had appeared to be earlier in the day, he could now be enjoying a brandy old-fashioned sweet and fresh walleye. It seemed clear to Nick that while Swenson could play the executive, he also treasured his Wisconsin roots. And, this wasn't an act for Nick's benefit. Emil was obviously a regular at the place, as all the bartenders and wait staff knew his preferences and called him by his first name. He knew their names too. As the evening continued, Nick began to like the old man and his lack of pretentiousness. He could also see bits of his father in Swenson. Over the course of a three-hour dinner, which moved quickly, the two men got on well, talking about all the perfunctory subjects including the unseasonable weather, world events, and the Green Bay Packers. Finally, Emil steered the conversation back to business and the matter at hand. Prepared for the discussion, Nick had rehearsed all the reasons why he could not accept the offer.

"Nick, I hope I didn't come on too strong for you this morning. It's just that I love my company and my job. My goal is to make it a world-class organization, and I make decisions accordingly."

"Emil, no apology is needed. I've dealt with many strong people over the years. I respect your passion for Weston Insurance. I'm just not sure I have the skill set you need for what you want to be accomplished."

"Nonsense. You'll do fine work. After our meeting, it dawned on me we did not discuss the subject of compensation and ground rules." Swenson pulled a white envelope with a Weston logo on it from his jacket pocket and slid it across the dinner table to Nick.

The moment had arrived. Nick was ready to back out of the situation gracefully. However, after opening the letter and breezing through the terms, his eyes opened wide enough to grab Swenson's attention.

"Is the proposed compensation fair?" asked the CEO.

Ruthless bastard. The size of the number was far beyond Nick's expectation, throwing him off stride as he forgot his prepared speech and exit strategy. In fact, it took everything Nick could muster before regrouping to answer with a pitiful, "Yes."

"One last thing. I'd like to meet with you regularly to discuss how you're doing personally and to get updates on your progress. You report only to me, no one else. Is that clear?"

Again, it was all Nick could do to raise a second, "Yes."

With the deal now done, the men finished their drinks to round out the evening. As he dropped Nick off at The Lakehouse, Swenson offered some parting words. "Welcome aboard, Nick. Let's meet in my office at eight thirty tomorrow to get started. I'd like to talk through specifics of where the division stands, as well as getting you settled with office space and introducing you to your administrative assistant. Oh, and by the way . . ." he added, reaching behind his seat to grab a loose-leaf binder several inches thick, ". . . here is a primer on the concepts of insurance to help you prep."

All Nick could utter was a neutral "thanks," still wondering what he had gotten himself into. "Looks like I've got some reading to do, sir." Nick let himself into the foyer as the car pulled out of the driveway. Closing the front door behind him, he caught his reflection in a hallway mirror in the foyer. *You big pussy.*

CHAPTER 10

Friday was casual day at Weston Insurance. Nick realized he had missed the memo upon entering the lobby wearing a blue blazer and pressed slacks and spotting several other employees wearing jeans as the uniform of the day. He made a mental note of his rookie mistake as Cassie, the receptionist, got his attention from behind the glass.

"Nick, here is your employee's badge with lanyard," she said, sliding it through the drawer from her cage. "Mr. Swenson's assistant sent it down to me last night. Welcome to the company."

"Thanks, Cassie. I need to grab some coffee before heading upstairs. Where is the cafeteria?"

Cassie buzzed a door to his left that clicked open on her command. "Come on and I'll show you."

Cassie met Nick at the door. Wearing a light floral sweater and jeans, she led him through a maze of hallways, giving him the mini tour. The walk ended in a large carpeted area with tables and multicolored chairs when Nick spotted the coffee kiosk. Grabbing a large dark roast, Nick asked Cassie where the check-out counter was.

"Mr. Swenson pays for our coffee, tea, and juice in the morning; another good thing about being an employee of Weston."

"Very nice. Thanks for your help, Cassie."

"Nick, if there's ever anything I can do for you, please give me a call."

Walking back to the lobby sipping his coffee, Nick tried to decide whether Cassie's offer was for business or pleasure. *The last thing I need is any complications with a woman who will have to produce an ID to get into a bar for the next ten years.* Sliding his newly minted employee badge into the card reader, the elevator doors opened and took him to the third floor.

Nick found the executive wing based on his visit the previous day and quickly located the entrance to the CEO's office.

Nick knocked and heard a muffled, "Come in." Entering the room, Nick saw Swenson seated behind a large wooden desk wearing a golf shirt with his head down, writing in a leather-bound book. Swenson continued writing as Nick observed the large office, giving himself a visual tour while sipping his coffee. Swenson's office was an extension of the winning theme throughout Weston, with a spectacular view of the grounds through the large windows that extended from the adjacent board room. Even though the space was well-appointed, Swenson had limited his personal touches to only his most prized possessions, including a series of photos of him with professional sports stars and celebrities, along with several pieces of autographed memorabilia.

Across the room, Swenson completed his thoughts before looking up from his book. "Good morning, Nick. Do you journal?" he asked. "I've journaled much of my life. It is a part of my morning ritual to spend thirty minutes writing. It's a stream of consciousness kind of thing and includes things I learn, stuff that bugs me, problems and solutions too, etcetera. I find the process settles me and gets me focused on work by clearing out my brain. Not sure how many leather-bound journals I've completed, but it's more than a few. Let's talk about your assignment."

Swenson went to his phone and called his admin, who had apparently arrived after Nick entered. "Good morning, Anita. Would you please track down Mallory and send her in?"

Swenson sat in a large black leather chair and motioned for Nick to sit on one of the matching couches on either side. Just as he became comfortable, Nick heard the office door open behind him along with a familiar female voice. "Good morning, Emil."

"Good morning, Mallory. I'd like you to meet Nick Hayden."

Nick rose and turned to see the woman who had already recognized his name, his new neighbor from The Lakehouse. Time seemed to stop for a few tense seconds as they each gathered themselves. For Nick, she was hard not to recognize. She was sporting jeans and black top that was a little bit too low-cut for office wear and working hard to support her more than ample cleavage. At their first meeting, Nick had been too distracted by her anger to get a good look at the woman who now offered her hand in a stony greeting to him. "We've met," she said tersely, directing the comment back to Swenson.

Swenson looked puzzled. "You've met? When did that happen?"

Nick decided it was all or nothing. "Yesterday, at The Lakehouse. As I was taking a tour of the home, I noticed a couple of boobs hanging out in the area. While I didn't know who she was at the time, or that she was my neighbor, Mallory chased them away," said Nick, trying to make light of his embarrassment.

Still looking confused, Swenson looked at Nick and followed up in a serious tone. "Were there trespassers at The Lakehouse? Do we have a security issue there?"

"No, sir. Based upon what happened yesterday, I'm guessing I'll never see that pair ever again."

Mallory nodded, a laser stare at Nick. "Oh, I can guarantee it."

Clearly feeling like he had missed something but trying to regain control of his meeting, Swenson returned to his chair, motioning both employees to sit on the adjacent facing couches. "Mallory, I have hired Nick to help Weston Insurance investigate why the company failed to take advantage of opportunities in the religious niche market, and his findings will help us when we ultimately dissolve the division. I have assigned you to be Nick's administrative assistant. You will report directly to him. Your role is to help him get the resources he needs, coordinate meetings and information, and help him navigate our systems."

"Yes, sir."

"Please arrange to place Nick in the office adjacent to mine. Also, move your desk outside of Nick's space."

As he watched Mallory respond to her new role, Nick couldn't help but wonder how an administrative assistant under the age of thirty could afford a lake house neighboring the swanky place that Weston had provided for him. He looked for some sign of closeness between Mallory and Emil, something to reveal a relationship beyond the office, but both seemed all business, and no intimacy in look or word appeared.

Nick shook himself from observer to participant. He had invested his time last night skimming the material Swenson provided. Now, he wanted to earn his pay. "Emil, if you have some time, I'd like to get started with some of your impressions of what happened with the religious institution division. I gave this some thought last night after dinner and want to go through a preliminary series of questions. In fact, I'd like to do the same with some of your senior people and frontline staff who might have some insights about what took place. Any impressions or themes might help provide some direction for the next steps of the investigation."

"Certainly, Nick. I like your strategy."

Nick continued. "Mallory, would you mind taking a few notes of the conversation?" he asked, looking over to see if bygones were bygones. "I'll do so as well, and we can compile our findings later."

Mallory nodded, and even looked curious about what Swenson had to say about the fall of the religious institution business. "Sure," she replied to Nick. Things were still cold, but at least the office brought out a thaw.

"Sir, if you could pinpoint an issue or two, what were your observations of Weston's failure in the religious niche?"

"Well, Nick, I really hate to use the word 'failure.'"

"Emil, based upon everything I've read, it sounds like the word 'failure' is more than appropriate. I'm not trying to pick a fight, but Weston had its nose bloodied to the point of taking unprecedented action by leaving this niche. To me, the company has a long-term opportunity to help coach its employees to believe that taking a risk is worth it, even if the results aren't what you intended. It's a teachable moment for the staff with applicable lessons to other situations. One of the tools we're going to use in looking at this failure is from the military, called an after-action review."

"I guess you're right. Frankly, this division was a colossal failure." Swenson sat back in his chair, staring at the ceiling in thought. After thirty seconds, Swenson looked back at Nick. "Two things come to mind. First, adverse selection."

"Adverse selection?"

Mallory jumped in. "Essentially, it's a concept that means prospective insureds and their agents may have had better quality information about particular risks than our underwriters. Either the buyers didn't disclose critical aspects of their business or known issues, or members of the Weston underwriting team failed to ask the right questions or enough of them to understand the risks. Based upon what we knew or should have known, we could have changed the terms of the insurance contract to make things more equitable between the buyer and Weston, tightened the terms, increased our pricing, or walked away from the account."

"Mal is correct," the executive said. "Essentially, the buyers and their brokers were smarter than we were or may have hidden things we should have figured out. To some extent, the pressure to grow may have skewed our judgment. Perhaps we should have had more experienced staff working on this book."

Nick worked hard to not show the surprise he felt. An administrative assistant interrupting the CEO, giving her own definition, instead of remaining silent? And such a knowledgeable definition. Was she really only an assistant? Maybe there was something between the two of them, but he could not determine it in that moment.

Nick looked back at Swenson. "Sir, you mentioned there were two things. What was the second?"

Swenson shifted uncomfortably in his chair. "I've shared this next thought with some of our senior people after looking through the type and scope of the claims that were made against Weston. Nick, our company may have been at fault to some degree for not understanding the risks we took on, that cost us a fortune in losses, but there was a larger factor in our fate."

"What was that, sir?"

Swenson cleared his throat. "Christian fuckers."

Swenson's response drew a nervous muffled laugh from Nick, who repeated the answer in the form of a question. "Christian fuckers, sir?"

"Yes. I think when we entered the market, we naturally assumed we were dealing with morally upright individuals . . . men of God. Why wouldn't we think that? Sure, the segment had any number of challenges, tough exposures, and a lot of competitors. But other companies seemed to be making money in this market and we thought we had a chance to do so as well. However, my early observation is a small segment of the religious leaders we found our way to do business with were unscrupulous folks interested in stealing money or engaging in reprehensible behaviors that are unimaginable. For many of these people, the more they talked about their good works and how religious they were, the worse they seemed to be. We eventually came to believe that the more someone wore their Christianity on their sleeves, there was a very good chance they had little to no moral character at all. The hypocrisy. The hubris. We could have insured strip clubs and had fewer issues. I know that's a huge generalization, and there are many good folks out there, but our results speak for themselves. The type and number of losses Weston has sustained directly because of these Christian fuckers has put our entire company at risk. Decades of work in all segments of our business could all go up in smoke, because of these corrupt people. You know, as I've thought about this whole debacle, and based on what I know now, I wonder if we will get any justice out of our work here." Swenson looked off in the distance and subtly wrung his hands. "Christian fuckers."

Following Swenson's answer, there was a deafening quiet in the room. Then, looking at both Nick and Mallory, the CEO continued. "Well, you have your charge. Please get to the bottom of this as soon as possible. I'm depending upon you both to give us an exit strategy and provide insights about how we ended up in this position. Our company is at stake."

With that, the meeting promptly ended. Nick and Mallory found themselves outside the CEO's door. Nick looked at Mallory. "Do you have a minute? We need to talk." Moving into an open conference room, Nick closed the door behind Mallory and they each took a seat.

He took a deep breath and started before she could get in a word. "Listen, Mallory. I need to apologize for yesterday. Please believe me that when I was looking through the telescope, it was not my intent to spy on you. In fact, I didn't know who you were or that you were on the raft. I'm innocent. I was only curious about why the telescope was pointed in the direction it was."

Mallory considered Nick. Whether it was his bumbling apology or his good looks, the young woman seemed to soften. "Well, I thought someone else was spying on me. Over the last several weeks, the company had a couple of state auditors staying at The Lakehouse. Between the free beer provided by Emil, the telescope, and these geeks who probably never have seen a set of breasts in person, I guess I became their primary source of entertainment. I just assumed you were another asshole trying to get a look at me sunbathing. I'm up for a clean start if you are."

"Thanks. Frankly, I'm going to need your help to complete Emil's assignment."

"Let me get you situated in some office space. After lunch, we can talk about your plan and what needs to happen next." With the air seemingly cleared, they began leaving the room. Mallory stopped for a moment and looked at Nick. "So, let me ask you . . . how good a look did you get?"

Nick paused, searching for the right words. "Let's just say it looked like the water must have been pretty cold." He and Mallory looked down, both trying not to laugh. "By the way, Mallory, what's your last name for the record?"

"Swenson."

"Seriously. You mean, as in like, Emil Swenson?"

"Yes, as in like the daughter of Emil Swenson."

"Small world," responded Nick. *That answers so many questions. And raises so many more.*

"It is here, Nick."

CHAPTER 11

After a day of setting up space, hooking up computers, printers, and other technological whatnot, and finding himself realizing over and over again that he had a high-paying job at an insurance company, Nick Hayden's drive to his new temporary home was one tinged with surrealism. To many, he knew he seemed to lead a charmed life. Take today for example. He had arrived uncertain of basically everything Emil Swenson had tasked him with doing. He was driving home with an office, an assistant, and an objective of huge importance.

Nick knew he was blessed. Blessed by heredity and environment, he was the type of person both men and women were drawn to for any number of different reasons. He had learned from his father, the uber-salesman, that by listening and getting others to talk about themselves, he could gain trust from others, translating into the innate ability to make people feel comfortable around him. Nick developed that skill early and used it often. He'd used it yesterday to earn Emil's trust, and today to make inroads with Mallory.

"How will I use these supposed great gifts tomorrow?" he said out loud before turning up the radio to some serious Rush for the ride home. His brain continued to churn. *How the hell am I going to pull this off? It's only a matter of time before everyone at Weston realizes I'm a fraud. A well-paid fraud no less. And, people will think I'm a friend of Emil . . . Is that good or bad? Oh, and how long before I have one of my little meltdowns for everyone to see? Jesus, Nick, what have you gotten yourself into?*

He thought about growing up and better times. His father and mother, Bill and Caroline, had always been there for him, even when he had tried to take everything they had worked for and flushed it. It seemed like such a long time ago when he'd grown up in idyllic Wisconsin. Nick was an only child but didn't know quite what that meant until he got to middle school. And he certainly didn't appreciate the family dynamic that he'd grown up with. A throwback to another era. Like a black-and-white TV family. He recalled that when many of his friends were going through their parents' divorces, or abuse, or drinking problems, his mother and father were there for him on the sidelines during whatever sport he was playing at the time. His father was a Navy vet and a highly successful salesman for Weston Insurance who had structured his work life around Nick's schedule. His mother, a stay-at-home mom, was always in his corner.

Summers in Door County meant playing sports, and he'd been an athlete through and through from the time he was old enough to ride his bike from home to a local park. The heat of summer was spent on the baseball diamond with organized and impromptu games, while hockey was life during the winter months. Yet football grew to be Nick's passion as he devoted time on the field and in the weight room to improve constantly. His parents had supported him emotionally and financially, shipping him off to numerous camps so he could develop his skill level, speed, and agility.

Nick was so consumed by thoughts of the past that he had to remind himself to look for the landmarks he'd noted yesterday. As he made the turns to The Lakehouse, he thought about junior year, when he had grown into a Division 1 prospect, with college offers pouring in from across the country seeking the services of the All-State linebacker. As a senior, he had transformed his body, adding significant muscle onto an imposing six-foot three-inch frame and leading his team to the state championship. The foregone conclusion by most of the local experts was that Hayden would move to Madison to become a Badger. However, to the dismay of many, Nick, a burgeoning renegade, accepted a full ride at the University of Michigan, preferring to wear the maize and blue. *I'm sure my choice disappointed them. But I had to get away. Everyone in the area knew about the girl. I wonder where Hannah is these days? Shit. What a fuck-up I was.*

He was back at The Lakehouse, and he needed a beer. After grabbing a cold one from the refrigerator, Nick wandered out to the deck, a place he had already designated in his mind as a great spot to think. Even though he was now looking over this beautiful lake, all he could see was his past.

Going to Ann Arbor was the right choice. Nick's college football career had peaked at second-team All-Big 10 honors. He survived four years of pounding with his only lasting physical souvenir being a curved nose as the result of a violent collision with an All-American running back from Wisconsin. *What a tough son of a bitch*, he thought with a wry smile touching the bend of his nose. During his senior year, Nick was approached by several agents about the potential of playing in the NFL. *No one ever figured me out.* Feeling a different calling, he'd decided to enter military service, eschewing the potential for a big payday that made the pro scouts scratch their collective heads. *Paybacks are a bitch,* he thought.

Nick's desire to serve had not come with a specific branch in mind. However, his search began and ended within fifteen minutes after wandering into an Air Force recruiting office where the busy officer in charge handed Nick a DVD and told him to watch it while he finalized details with another recruit. The slick video opened showing a man suited up in full scuba gear, harnessed to a parachute. Nick watched the monitor as the Airman jumped out of the back of the cargo deck of an enormous fixed-wing plane into a long free fall, pulled his chute, landed in the ocean, and swam to a rendezvous point where he was picked up by a Special Forces gun boat. As the presentation was concluding, the recruiter poked his head in the door and asked what type of job Nick might be interested in. Nick had simply pointed to the paused DVD and said excitedly, "I want to do that."

Looking at the still frame on the screen, the recruiter had responded, "Those are PJs . . . pararescuemen. Maybe the most dangerous job in the entire Air Force. On top of that, they're all basically insane. You've only seen the beginning of the career DVD. I'd like to show you some other options, too."

Nick stopped the recruiter mid-pitch, looking him directly in the eye. "I'm not interested in anything else. Sign me up for that or I'll see what the Navy offers."

Let my penance begin. Two weeks later, Nick arrived at Lackland Air Force Base in steamy San Antonio for eight and a half weeks of basic training during July and August. Given his athletic and educational background, Nick had excelled, providing leadership for many of his colleagues, recent high school graduates who struggled to meet the demands of the Air Force. In turn, he became affectionately and respectfully known as "Pops," given his advanced age in the minds of his classmates. Following basic training, Nick was immediately placed into Class 247, a ten-week indoctrination course designed to sort out the unworthy from the one hundred twenty hopefuls bent on joining the ranks of pararescuemen or combat controllers.

It had become immediately clear to Nick and all the other candidates that "Indoc" would push them to their physical and mental limits. Starting with a heavy mix of running, push-ups, and calisthenics, the new grind inspired eight participants to drop on request from the class before lunch on day one. At their first mandatory feeding, Nick had been randomly seated with another trainee who had begun to doubt himself as well. Nick offered a word of encouragement to the Airman and later helped the trainee in pacing runs that would allow his new friend to achieve the minimum qualifying times. Nick's new comrade, known to him only as Costello, improved and stayed in the program. In the process, as part of what was becoming a crucible experience for both, the two men became inseparable.

Although most contenders had trained in anticipation of the brutal course, "The Pool" separated the men from the boys. On the first venture to The Pool, two buses containing a dwindling number of Class 247 left the dormitory. The fifteen-minute trip took place in total silence as fear and tension grew among the classmates, ending at a modern-looking facility housing what could have easily passed for a typical high school pool, complete with pennants hanging from the rafters. The building was constructed of heavy metal girders complemented with windows and opaque ceiling skylights that added ambient lighting. Upon entering the facility, the wannabes were assaulted with the smell of chlorine in the thick humid air. The calm blue water suddenly seemed less so as the instructors ordered the students into the pool wearing what they had on for a timed swim. The onslaught of The Pool had begun.

Flutter kicks became a new term of art for the group. Each student lay on their backs with their hands under their butts and raised and lowered their legs in succession for hours. Following flutter kicks, the drown-proofing process began. Each Airman had their arms and legs bound together as they bobbed up and down in the pool. The physical and mental challenges of the practice inspired many more to quit. Even Nick was pushed to his limits by the demands of the water. *I'm not fucking going to fail now.* However, Nick's early assistance to Costello was paid back in spades. Prior to joining the Air Force, Costello had been a surfer, perfecting his trade on Florida's Emerald Coast, also known as the Redneck Riviera. With a high comfort level in the water, it was now his turn to offer help to Nick. With the course drop rate accelerating, both Nick and Costello remained steadfast and shined during another particularly challenging segment of training known as "buddy breathing." Grouped into pairs, each team shared a single snorkel. Once dropped into the deep end of the pool, the partners were charged never to lose their buddy, trained to maintain a death grip on each other's arms, while also controlling the snorkel as they bobbed in the water. Losing your buddy or your snorkel was a failure. In their off hours, Nick and Costello practiced this training exercise on their own regularly and were prepared for the increasing levels of harassment by cadre members, culminating in their trainers trying to rip away the snorkel from each pair during the final assessment. Nick and Costello had survived another training evolution together and moved on.

On an evening late in the training cycle, the remnants of Class 247, now forty-five strong, had settled down in their bunks at 2100 hours after another grueling day. Thirty minutes later, a group of instructors stormed into the dorm rousing the Airmen with shouts through bull horns commanding them to assemble immediately outside. Intended to disorient the sleep-deprived Airmen, the evening began with a run back to The Pool for flutter kicks, fast swims, treading water, and more flutter kicks. The twenty-hour marathon, known as Hell Night, had begun. Designed to mimic hostile combat conditions and create a highly stressful environment, it was the final push of Indoc to see who was tough enough to make the cut. Five hundred flutter kicks, while being doused with water from hoses. Then, a timed run, followed by another five hundred flutter kicks while wearing a dive mask full of water. Cold, wet, and exhausted, more than twenty hours later, only three men had remained: Nick, Costello, and a recruit from California. After the marathon session had brought so many to their limits, the primary instructor looked at the remaining bedraggled classmates. "How about a three-mile run before chow, gentlemen?" he growled, pointing to the track.

As Nick and Costello prepared to set off to the course, the Californian had balked. The Airman told the instructor enough was enough, requesting to drop on the spot. Immediately after hearing the request, the instructor called all three men together, telling them the physical demands of Hell Night were officially over. There would be no run. It had been a final mental test to measure their reaction, capacity, and any limits of those in the remaining group. The instructor also announced that Class 247 was now officially down to two participants, looking at only Nick and Costello. California looked at the instructor, dumbfounded.

"What do you mean? I did all the work these guys did. I survived Hell Night, too."

The instructor had looked back at him sternly. "Bullshit, son, you just quit. A PJ never knows when a mission is over or how much will be demanded of him. One of the purposes of Hell Night is to find out who the quitters are. There's no shame in that . . . this course is not for everyone. But PJs never quit. Our creed is 'That Others May Live.' You requested to drop, and you're dismissed."

Turning back to Nick and Costello, the instructor barked out a new set of orders with a wry smile. "Gentlemen, you two look like shit. Get your asses to the team room for a medical terminology course."

With the lack of sleep weighing heavily on both, they each considered the prospect of another ominous assignment looming, "death by PowerPoint." Falling asleep during an Indoc training course of any type, including a classroom session, was grounds for dismissal. Nick and Costello had found desks and prepared for the lecture, doing their best to remain upright, focused, and conscious. Ten long minutes of silence passed as they sat in the room alone. Both started to believe they had been forgotten, when several instructors entered the room followed by a shout. "Attention!"

A sergeant followed the trainers holding two grey t-shirts emblazoned with the words "Pararescue Trainee" and blue ascots, a symbol of their successful accomplishment of Indoc. "Gentlemen . . . you two are all that remains of Class 247. You took everything we had and excelled. Congratulations, you are now *halfway* through your training course to become PJs."

Both Nick and Costello were dismissed. Tired, sore, and hungry, the survivors of Class 247 found their way back to the empty dorm and their beds and slept peacefully, not entirely sure what would happen next.

Nick thought about that night's sleep as the flood of memories he'd been experiencing came to an end. He was back in Wisconsin, back at The Lakehouse, and the sun was setting over the lake.

"What I'd give for a full night's sleep now," he muttered to the lake after draining his beer.

CHAPTER 12

The new week began with heavy rain and thunder as the Wisconsin spring took its typical backslide. Nick had been back to his parents' house to pick up clean clothes and some personal items that would make The Lakehouse seem more like his own space, even temporarily. As he began to plumb the inner workings of Weston Insurance, he discovered that some bad weather would not deter Mallory Swenson from her mission. However, other forces were frustrating her, including the lack of availability of some executives who were out of the office for much of the week. As Nick began to become part of the Weston community, he learned that Mallory had been described from the perspective of her coworkers as being either incredibly organized or, less flatteringly, borderline anal retentive. After the meeting with her father and Nick, she took it upon herself to book his calendar for the entire week. Their charge had been clear: stop the religious institution business from sucking more of Weston's money into a bottomless pit and determine what brought the company to this point. And do it quick since jobs were on the line. Nick found his docket filled with meetings with attorneys, followed by meetings with the executives in charge of the doomed program, followed by yet more meetings with the department heads who ran the support functions for the company. When Nick had arrived back at The Lakehouse on Sunday night, he discovered his new neighbor had left a slew of reports and documents for him to review for the next day.

Mallory had reserved a conference room in the executive area as their primary workspace for the foreseeable future. Impeccably dressed in a tailored black business suit, albeit one arguably cut too low, Nick wondered about the message she was trying to send, if any. Yet, he also noted Mallory had done a superb job of prepping him and publishing the slate of guests, as well as readying the room, complete with coffee and donuts in anticipation of Nick's first meeting of the day with Weston's general counsel, C. Jonathan Woods, Esquire. Nick arrived drenched and dripping from the spring torrent that had come down that morning. It hadn't helped that in preparing for the day, he'd polished off half a bottle of Jack Daniels to cope with the stress of the upcoming week. Toweling off in the adjacent office, Nick studied Woods as he entered the conference room.

A generally reserved person with a very thin build and short brown hair, Woods was the epitome of a conservative insurance attorney. Nick had been warned by Mallory to expect a buttoned-down lawyer who, she surmised, seemingly owned an entire wardrobe of black and grey suits, crisp white shirts, and a rack full of colorful power ties. Today's was purple. In fact, Mallory's report regarding Woods included a detail that he was rumored to have back-up shirts and ties in his office closet on the off chance a stain emergency might occur during the day and ruin his look. Evidently, Woods completed his ensembles with rotating Johnston & Murphy shoes, with his only deviation to this traditional appearance being some flash from a collection of Rolex watches.

Woods had been hired personally by Emil Swenson as a claim attorney out of the University of Wisconsin Law School. With a keen intellect and strong work ethic, combined with his carefully chosen attire, he rose to the top of the legal food chain at Weston in less than ten years. He was a busy man, and he placed a high value on punctuality.

Exactly at nine o'clock, Woods had taken the seat at the head of the large oak table in the conference room, crossed his legs, and began rhythmically drumming his fingers on the thick wood to demonstrate his lack of patience for all to see. Both he and Mallory had contemplated the modern artwork hanging from the wall in silence. After five torturous minutes, a harried and half-drenched Nick entered the office with a Starbucks in one hand and his soaked portfolio losing its loose-leaf papers in the other.

"Sorry I'm late, but the weather really sucks today . . ." he said, without eliciting any response from either of his coworkers. Setting down both the coffee and notes, Nick took off his rain-soaked sports jacket, placing it over the back of one of the available chairs. He extended his hand to Woods while introducing himself. Woods stood, accepted the greeting, and paused briefly with his head cocked slightly, studying Nick quizzically before retaking his seat.

"Do I know you, Mr. Hayden?" asked Woods.

"I don't know how you would, sir. I started here at Weston last Friday, and think I've met all of four or five people at the company."

Woods offered a perfunctory, "Welcome aboard." He re-crossed his legs and assumed a grim look that seemed to fit both the day and the mood of the room.

"Mr. Woods, Weston Insurance has had a great track record of success," began Nick ham-handedly. "But I suspect you are aware the company is losing large amounts of money in the religious institution niche?"

Woods nodded knowingly. "Ah, the Christian issue. I think Emil captured the idea more eloquently than I could though."

Nick continued his introduction. "I'm not sure if you've heard, but Emil has charged Mallory and me with studying what took place and getting Weston out the religious business, as well as doing an after-action report regarding how the company arrived at this point." By her subtle smile, Nick assessed that Mallory was pleased he mentioned her role in this assignment to the general counsel.

"While I'm not a board member, I counsel them, along with Emil. I sat in on the meeting as the board passed the resolution to leave the niche. In fact, I agree with the direction the company is taking. I've also taken the liberty of contacting external counsel to research our legal obligations to our policyholders as well as determining any legal challenges involved with Weston's exit strategy in the twenty-three states where we do business in this line." Woods paused again, scrutinizing the younger man.

"Do you have a timetable for when we'll have that research?" asked Nick.

"I should have a preliminary opinion by the end of the week, at least enough to get started anyway. By the way, leaving this market will be a lengthy process. Every policy in place is a legal contract, and since we issue them for a year, Weston will be on the hook for losses for at least that long once we give notice of cancellation to our policyholders. In fact, the company will be dealing with losses from this market for years to come since notices of claim can extend well beyond the termination of the policy. Nonetheless, the emerging consensus from Legal is we don't see any major issues in pulling out of the various states. We just need to get a handle on the specific requirements and then follow each state's rules and regulations, which of course vary . . ." Again, Woods paused, staring at Nick. "Mr. Hayden, did you play football at Michigan?"

"Why yes, I did. It's been a few years though."

Like a switch had gone off in his head, Woods stepped out of his sober persona, suddenly standing and shaking Nick's hand as if starstruck. "Oh my God, when you came into the room, you looked so familiar, but I couldn't place you. I completed my undergrad and law school at Wisconsin and saw you play at Camp Randall several times. I recall that Michigan crushed us in both of those games, and I specifically remember you dominated on defense."

"Frankly, I don't recall too many specific games. The one thing that does stand out about my Madison experience is the broken nose I got there from your big running back, Montee Ball. We had an incredible collision at the goal line, and I lost that battle . . . and my potential modeling contract," joked Nick.

Mallory, watching the surreal guy talk taking place with Weston's general counsel, rolled her eyes at Nick's remark. While it was missed by Woods, Nick caught Mallory's look, but ignored it.

"Nick, if I may call you that, Legal is excited to be working with you," said Woods, offering his business card. "Here's my direct office number along with my personal cell. Please call if you need anything. Again, we should have an initial report back to you by Friday."

"Thank you. Well, actually, Jonathan . . ."

"Please, call me Jon."

"Jon, as I understand it, you've been at Weston for a while. Is there any advice you can offer regarding our assignment?"

Woods pondered the question briefly. "Thinking about this, I'd dig into some of the claim files to see what took place. It might give you a broader idea about the thought process here."

"I appreciate the guidance. Any particular files that I should start with?"

The attorney shook his head. Then, he added, "If you ever want to get out and have a beer while you're staying in town, let me know. It would be great to talk some football with you. Like, why didn't you go to Wisconsin like everybody assumed you would? I'd also like to hear why you didn't turn pro."

"Good questions, Jon, without simple answers necessarily. But, looking forward to it."

After Woods left the conference room, Mallory rose silently, following him to the door and closing it behind him. Once she was sure Woods was out of earshot, she turned back toward Nick, exclaiming with her voice rising. "What the hell just happened here? I've been at Weston for ten years and wasn't sure if our general counsel even knew my name. You show up late for a meeting after only a day with the company, and he gushes all over you. In five minutes, you got the keys to the legal kingdom here, along with an invite to go partying with our primary lawyer, perhaps the most conservative person here at Weston!"

A big smile formed on Nick's face. "Mallory, are you jealous? Maybe we'll let you be our designated driver when Jon and I hit the local bars."

"Nick, it's not jealousy. I just can't believe the level of cooperation you received from Woods. He's always had a major stick up his ass. Up until today, I thought I had a pretty good feel for the people here, but now I'm not sure what to think."

"Listen. I have always been able to connect with people, in general . . . except for you, maybe. So, don't take this personally. He brought up the football thing, which is in the ancient past for me. That was his hot button. I followed his lead answering his questions and made some small talk that will get us both some serious cooperation. I learned a long time ago to talk to people about their interests, not mine. And look where it got us? Jon's suggestion to look at the claim files makes a lot of sense too. Even if there isn't a particular file to begin with, we've got some direction. Once he gets his various legal opinions to us about withdrawing from the states, we can keep Emil posted on how long the process will be. According to the detailed schedule, when are we going to talk to the program manager of the religious niche?"

Mallory looked at her chart. "He's next on the list." After a short pause, "So, you were a good football player? What else don't I know about you? Who'd you play for again?"

CHAPTER 13

Even in Nick's somewhat-addled state, it didn't take a genius to see that Robbie Mueller wasn't as put together as Woods when he entered the executive conference room. Pale, sweating, and a bit disheveled in a wrinkled grey suit, it looked like he hadn't slept much since Mallory had sent him the meeting invitation the prior Friday afternoon. Nick had read that before taking over the leadership of the religious institution program, Mueller had been a rising star at the company. The fifteen-year veteran was on the fast track as a well-respected field underwriter and manager in several of the company's other highly successful programs. However, he had come back to earth quickly when the religious unit he inherited started to bleed buckets of red ink. Until the previous week, he had acknowledged his team's results were extremely poor. But his reports included his belief that with Weston's track record of success in target markets, the company could work itself out of this hole. Never did it appear that he considered the company might leave the segment. As the board's decision had become a reality, the program director seemed to lose his confidence, and his appearance this day only supported that.

Nick saw that as Mueller sat down, he acknowledged Mallory, and they appeared to be work friends of long standing. But he also had a look on his face that suggested he might now be the primary suspect in the corporate need to assess blame.

As they introduced themselves, Mueller seemed to relax a bit when Nick extended his hand and said, "Call me Nick. Robbie . . . err, can I call you Robbie?"

"Of course," he replied.

"Robbie, do you know what our role is here?" Nick asked, pointing to himself and Mallory.

"Well, my understanding is you both are building an exit strategy for Weston to leave the religious market. At least, that's according to what Mallory told me on Friday after I got the meeting invite."

"Yes, that's part of the assignment," Nick replied. "But more importantly, Weston's board of directors also wants us to determine the issues that led to the poor results from the program, given this seems to be a first for the company. The exit strategy is pretty straightforward. Much of what we can do will come from Legal. But, since you are the program director, I'd like to get your insights about why the company struggled in this niche."

Robbie squirmed in his chair and spent a good thirty seconds trying to carefully choose his words to answer Nick's question. "Nick, may I ask you a question first?"

"Sure."

"My answer will be the same either way, but I want to know whether my comments will be directly attributed to me or be part of a larger finding?"

Nick pondered the political nature of the question for a moment. "Robbie, if the answer is the answer, what difference does it make?" Glancing towards Mallory, he continued. "As I understand it, you have been a valued employee around here for a long time. As the program director, people in the building are going to want to know what you think."

Feeling more confident, Mueller got to his primary question much more quickly than he imagined. "Does that mean my team and I will not get fired?"

Looking at Mallory for any read on a question he should have anticipated, Mallory looked at him levelly, with no message on her face. Nick sat back in his chair, staring at the ceiling for a moment. The room was quiet enough everyone could hear rain hitting the roof as he considered his response. "Let me be honest with you. I have no authority to hire or fire anyone. In fact, I'm not sure who's call that is or if it's even been contemplated. I'm simply here to gather some facts and make a recommendation. In my experience though, I would view a forthright answer as one I could respect. In a prior life, I spent some time in the Air Force and was involved with several after-action reports about missions that didn't necessarily go according to Hoyle. Many of those dealt with deaths, severe injuries, and large material losses. If I felt the Airman involved with the investigation provided me with an honest response, I included a reference to it in my report and recommendations. Conversely, if I felt I was getting a load of bullshit or was being stonewalled, I made that note as well. There are no guarantees here for anyone, including me."

"Fair enough, Nick. I appreciate your honesty. To answer your original question, I believe Weston got killed in the religious market because of several factors. In a nutshell, we forgot our fundamentals in underwriting accounts given pressure from top management to grow revenues and profits at all costs. Essentially, we stopped asking the right questions about risks in favor of taking in money. We didn't do our homework about what could go wrong with these types of accounts. We also gave too much power to brokers." After blurting out his answer, Mueller took a sip of water from a bottle he had brought to the inquisition.

Nick looked at Mueller for a moment as his non-insurance brain attempted to digest the response. "Robbie, my impression is that was a pretty decent summary of what took place. Thanks. Mallory, what do you think?"

Entering into the conversation, Mallory looked at both men from her chair. "Based upon what I know, I think Robbie's dead on target with his assessment. I've heard the water cooler talk over the last several years about growing too fast in a niche we didn't understand. It put us on a collision course with our profit goals. I also agree there has been too much pressure from top management to generate top-line revenue results."

After listening to Mallory's response, Mueller exhaled loudly as if he had been vindicated. Mallory's acknowledgement of his evaluation of the problem confirmed he was not alone in this thinking. Assessing Mallory's comment, Nick hit his question back over the net to both of them. "By top management, are you referring to anyone, in particular?"

Looking at each other briefly, the two said together as if on cue, "Emil Swenson."

Nick laughed to himself. "Well, that should make for an interesting conversation with our CEO. I may be the one heading to the door with that answer since I am *not* a valued long-term employee." Shifting his focus back to Mueller, he asked, "You mentioned the team did not do its homework. Doesn't that responsibility roll up to you as team leader?"

The program director looked at the floor, searching for an appropriate answer to a question he must have anticipated. "I suppose you're right. However, I recognized the growing problems within the niche several months ago and tried to have a conversation about the issues with my manager. I guess I was not convincing enough as she was unwilling to talk. Essentially, she toed the corporate line and charged me with taking ownership of the problems, while hitting our team's targets. No discussions. No leeway. Continue the course. Without changing anything, I'm not sure how I was supposed to get better results. Isn't that the definition of insanity? Doing the same thing, but expecting a different result?"

Mallory didn't answer his question. "Nick, Robbie actually took over the leadership of this program just six months ago. Weston has been in this business for the past five years, and the large losses we're now getting hammered with are the result of decisions made long ago on someone else's watch."

Nick looked at Mallory, begging the question. "Who was the leader of the program prior to Robbie?"

"Tina Matheson, our Vice President of Underwriting," replied Mallory. "This program was her baby to start with. She conceived the idea, built the operation and business plan, chose the brokers, and set things in motion. Also, to be fair, early on, Weston was making a ton of money in the religious niche before we lost our way."

"Robbie, who do you report to now?" asked Nick.

"Tina," came the one-word response.

"When do we get to have a conversation with her?" asked Nick.

"I'm still working on timing. Tina is attending a conference this week along with Frank Raymond, our VP of Claims. We'll need to talk with both to complete this portion of our work."

Nick refocused on Mueller. "Anything else I should know, Robbie?"

Thinking before he spoke, the program manager offered some parting thoughts. "Nick, if I were in your position, I'd spend some quality time looking at the claim files in detail."

"You're the second person today who's told me that."

As Mueller left the room, he looked back. "You do know who Tina Matheson is, don't you?" At Nick's quizzical look, Mueller's gaze went to Mallory. "I thought so. Well, Mallory, you can tell him," and with that, he closed the door behind him.

Nick looked at Mallory, watching her expression. She was answering his question, but not really looking at him.

"So, Mallory, what did Robbie mean when he asked you if you'd told me yet who Tina Matheson is? Is there something I should know about her?"

She finally looked Nick square in the face and took a breath. "After she joined the company, Tina held several assignments, but was clearly being groomed by management for bigger things. However, she rose to her current role as vice president based on her work in the religious niche. My impression is this program is what punched her ticket to the C-suite. She is loved by the board of directors, Emil included. I just wanted you to know this before we talked with her or came to any conclusions."

"That's it?" questioned Nick.

"Oh, and by the way, she is Emil's daughter," replied Mallory.

Nick looked at Mallory, confused for a moment. "I thought *you* were Emil's daughter?"

"Yes, I am."

"Then you're sisters?"

"Half-sisters. It's complicated."

"Yeah, it sure sounds like it. What the fuck, Mallory? Your sister has been running the department that has been 'hemorrhaging' money as Emil put it, and no one thought to tell me this? And now he wants me to close down the division she was running into the ground? Oh, and then give the board a full report on what Tina fucked up?"

Then, in frustration with the day and the larger situation, he grabbed a stack of papers from the conference table and threw them at Mallory. "What a shit show I signed up for," he said to no one in particular.

Mallory's expression went from shock at being targeted by Nick to a slow, slow anger.

"Listen, Nick, I had nothing to do with you coming to Weston for this assignment. This is Emil's shit show as you call it. Take it up with him," she said through clenched teeth. Then Mallory walked out of the room. Nick watched her walk all the way down the corridor, not breaking stride once. She yanked open the stairwell door and left the floor completely. It was only after Mallory had disappeared from his sight that Nick looked down and saw his hands were shaking uncontrollably, and his jaw was so tightly clenched he couldn't move it. *Bursts of anger, followed by physical gestures that appear extreme or inappropriate.* He could hear the therapist's voice in his head.

****

The remainder of the day was as overcast and grey as the mood of the underwriting team. Nick ran the interviews with the rest of Mueller's team on his own. Mallory never returned to the conference room. As far as he knew, she might have left the complex itself. As he worked through the individual meetings, there were no other surprises. To a person, there was a strong consensus with all agreeing with the story told first by Emil Swenson and confirmed by Robbie Mueller. Yes, the company's results were poor. Yes, the company should have done a better job in asking questions. The goals were unrealistic. A couple of unscrupulous brokers profited, while Weston floundered in the market. Many of the claims were horrific. Each was sorry to have been a part of this mess. While none of the team members said it, Nick could tell by reading their faces and body language that each would like an answer to the open question, "What will happen to me now?" Nine mind-numbing hours in, the final interview of day one was completed. Nick packed his bag in silence.

After collecting his things, Nick took the elevator down to the lobby. Despite the physical nature of his prior life, he was surprised and embarrassed at how tired he felt after hours of sitting in a chair. He said good night to Cassie in the lobby and headed out to his car for the drive home.

Once Nick left the building, Cassie discreetly followed him with her eyes back to the car. She picked up her phone and dialed the number she had been given. Waiting briefly, the ringing stopped followed by a "Well?"

"Sir, Hayden met with Woods, Robbie Mueller, and the underwriting team today. Not sure what took place, but Mallory Swenson is setting the agenda." She shifted in her chair with the pitch of her voice rising. "Sir, I really don't feel comfortable providing this type of report." After getting a response, she replied. "Yes, sir, I do like my job. I understand. I'll do my best to keep you posted." Through tears that were forming, she heard a click and the call ended.

CHAPTER 14

After parking his car on the wet pine straw, Nick entered The Lakehouse, dropped his portfolio, grabbed a beer, and changed into a t-shirt and shorts before finding his way to the deck for a new personal best of less than sixty seconds. The sun finally emerged from behind the clouds as he sank into the cushioned chair with a view of the lake. *Wet. The perfect end to the perfect day.* Closing his eyes, he replayed the day in his mind. *Jesus Christ, what a fucking mess.* The process added to his growing headache faster than his Stella Artois could calm it. Pondering where his new job was taking him, the intense quiet of the setting helped him relax. Nick stood up to grab another round when he heard the front doorbell ring.

Nick was greeted by a dour-looking Mallory who had arrived in her Jeep. She had a different look than at the office, wearing jeans, a sweatshirt, and sandals with her hair pulled back into a ponytail. As Nick opened the door, she thrust a large cardboard box at him. "More reading material regarding Frank Raymond and Tina," she said with a flinty tone before turning back towards her Jeep. "Oh, and I've scheduled a meeting with one of our brokers tomorrow. We leave at 8:00 a.m. sharp."

"Wait, Mallory," said Nick. He paused, searching for the right words, but there weren't many. "I'm sorry for unloading on you. It was uncalled for and unprofessional on my part. I'm just trying to understand what's going on here."

Mallory seemed indifferent to another apology but did not move any closer towards her vehicle.

"Can I buy you a drink at least?" said Nick. Mallory hesitated and turned toward Nick, still holding her ground.

"I could give you an overview of the meetings this afternoon," he offered.

Nick could see Mallory thinking over the invitation and the earlier incident before slowly moving toward the door.

"One drink," she replied curtly. "Red wine, if you've got it."

Entering the foyer, Mallory seemed struck by elegance of the home. "So, this is The Lakehouse. I drive by it every day but have never been inside. Supposedly reserved for VIPs."

"And me," said Nick, searching the kitchen drawers for a corkscrew. "Found it. Can you help me find some glasses? I have no clue where they are."

After checking her third cupboard door, Mallory announced, "Got them."

Nick opened the screen door for Mallory as they stepped out on the still-puddled deck. After pulling chair covers from a pair of Adirondacks, they both sat in silence as Nick struggled to open the wine before offering her a generous pour.

Sitting forward in his chair, Nick held out his glass and Mallory reciprocated as they touched glasses. "Listen, I just lost it today," said Nick. "And I don't know why. The Tina thing pissed me off, but I should never have thrown anything at you."

"For the record, it will be the last time that ever happens. I just want to be clear. But, at the same time, I can understand your frustration regarding Tina. Emil should have told you upfront."

Neither said a word, letting Mallory's comment sink in. "Can you tell me about the afternoon session, Nick?"

"Sure. Essentially, it was more of the same and aligned with everything I've heard over the last couple of days. A lot of good people were pressured from the top into making a series of bad decisions resulting in the company losing a lot of money. I'm not sure what the remaining staff can add. This is so simple, even a rookie like me can figure this out," he concluded.

Mallory kicked off her sandals and curled her feet underneath her in one motion. "Listen, I think you bring an interesting perspective to this process. Based on what I've seen, you ask really good questions, don't have a political bone in your body, and could care less about making a career at Weston. This makes you invincible to some extent. It also allows you to leverage your ignorance, no offense, by asking every dumb question in the book. This is something neither I nor anyone else at the company could do without feeling like they could lose their job."

Nick thought about Mallory's observation. While what she had said made sense, he still felt somewhat uncomfortable about his role.

"That being said . . ." Mallory continued, "I've arranged for us to meet one of the brokers tomorrow to give you a different perspective on what has taken place. A road trip to Milwaukee. Then, next Monday, we will meet with Tina Matheson and Frank Raymond. Both come with some warts, like we all do."

"How so?" asked Nick.

"It's all in the files I gave you, but I'll give you a thumbnail overview. Frank is an incredibly negative person. He is generally not well-liked and treats the rank-and-file employees like shit. He's a hypochondriac coming up with a new malady on a regular basis, and really pushes the limits of those who do talk with him. Oh, he's also a gun nut. But for all his flaws, he's actually very good at his job running the technical side of the Claim Department. Most importantly, he's Emil's drinking buddy and best friend at the company. He's burned up some of his political capital in that friendship, though, by being vocal about how bad the results of the religious book have been and that Weston should never have gone into that line of business in the first place. Those comments pissed off Emil, who took them personally. But Frank still works at the company."

"Thanks for the heads-up," said Nick.

"Interestingly, he is also very close to Tina," Mallory continued as she sipped her drink.

Nick looked at Mallory to understand what that meant, cocking his head and making a face, wondering if it implied some sort of intimate relationship between the two.

Watching Nick's reaction, Mallory immediately figured out the body language. "God, no, they aren't sleeping together. Thanks for the visual I didn't need. No, Frank is in his early fifties, and Tina has creeped into her thirties. It's nothing like that. He has just always looked out for her."

"Isn't it a bit ironic then that he has been critical of the program she was instrumental in starting?" questioned Nick. "Particularly since he appears to have been right all along?"

"Probably. When I say Frank has looked out for Tina, I'm talking about since she was a teenager. To some extent, he was a father figure for her when Emil was too busy for her, and me. I think he just writes off the religious program for her as being a learning mistake. Clearly, the opinion of someone who loves her unconditionally."

"So, there's no tension between the two?" asked Nick.

Mallory thought briefly. "I think there's always some level of tension between Frank and Tina. It's just the way their relationship works. Frank's a bit of an oddball and Tina is Tina, driven to rise to the top of the company ladder."

"Tell me more about her. She is your sister . . ." he began, fishing for a response while offering to top off Mallory's glass. "I know you said only one, but . . ." Mallory held her glass toward Nick.

"She has great credentials, graduated at the top of her class from the business school at the University of Minnesota. Her first job was at an insurance brokerage firm in the Twin Cities where she learned the business. Then she joined Weston and has been a rising star since."

"Reading between the lines with Robbie Mueller, he didn't seem to hold her in the highest regard?"

Mallory agreed. "From what I've seen lately, Tina has been distancing herself from the religious program. Even though she started it and made many of the seemingly bad decisions that produced the current results, she has somehow managed to rise above this in the eyes of senior management. To some extent, she has left others like Robbie to clean up in her wake and face the consequences. Despite everything, my impression is she's looking to move up in the company, again. From an insider's perspective, Tina is incredibly smart, but she lacks any level of emotional intelligence. To her credit, though, she does have a bit of a presence about her. You'll see next week."

"I need more details about the sister stuff," said Nick with his voice rising more than he intended.

"I'm not ready to give you anything more tonight," said Mallory, who made a pained look in delivering her flat reply. "But I will brief you before the interview with her. I'm just not up for it tonight. I hope you can accept that. Oh, and for what it's worth, I promise to try to minimize any more surprises. Okay?"

Nick was puzzled. Clearly, based on Mallory's look, there was much more left unsaid. He decided not to push based on her new promise. "Can we get access to the claim files that everyone has recommended we see?" asked Nick.

"Frank is big on protocol. Let's bring this up during our interview with him on Monday. He can't tell you 'no.' By the way, did you tell Robbie you were in the Air Force today?"

"Yes, why?" asked Nick.

"Frank is a veteran. I think Army, but I don't know exactly what he did. But the fact you both served might help you connect with him," she said, taking a sip of wine. "So, were you a pilot?" she asked.

After an awkward silence from background material to a personal question, Nick answered, "I was a PJ."

"What's a PJ?" asked Mallory.

"A topic for another night and another bottle of wine. How would you like your coffee tomorrow morning when I pick you up?"

CHAPTER 15

"So, what exactly are you looking for, Mr. Hargreaves?" asked Maggie Wright.

"To be honest, privacy and solitude," responded her newest client in a deep voice.

"We've got plenty of both on Mackinac Island. While maybe not as much during the high season, I've got listings for several homes off the beaten path that should meet your requirements year-round," the perky realtor answered. "Of course, you'll still have to battle the summer crowds to get your groceries or to go to a bar or restaurant. You know we get a million visitors here annually, all crammed into about five months." Then, she leaned across her desk. "Why Mackinac Island, if I may ask?"

"I've been here once before. I think I'd like the laid-back style of living," replied Hargreaves. "I love the beauty of the island. The big limestone cliffs, the heavy forests, the history, the pace . . ." he said, trailing off. "But mainly for the privacy and solitude," he echoed.

"Okay. Just that it's quite an adjustment for most new people planning to live on the island. Many don't realize that cars are not allowed here, except for a couple of emergency vehicles. The idea of walking, biking, or taking a horse-drawn carriage seems foreign to many. Any quaintness with that idea seems to fade quickly," said Maggie.

"I will say that I definitely noticed the horses when I stepped off the ferry. Well, at least the odor of the manure anyway. That, combined with smell of fresh fudge, is quite the welcome for people stepping off the boat. It probably took thirty minutes before I kind of got used to it," said Hargreaves, chuckling.

Maggie joined in with a knowing giggle. "What kind of property did you have in mind? Condo? Private home? A lot?" asked Maggie with a legal pad in front of her preparing to take notes.

"I was thinking a cottage would do."

"Wow, excellent. I have a couple in inventory." She worked quickly on her laptop to bring up the current listings. "Yes, in fact, I've got several choices for you. Two on the west bluff ranging from $2.9 to $5.9, with one on the east bluff at $1.9," she said earnestly. "Each very nice, with tons of space and amenities, history, and, of course, exceptional water views."

"Wait, $2.9 to $5.9 what?" questioned Hargreaves.

"Million," answered the realtor, unfazed. "You did say cottage, right?"

"I did," countered Hargreaves with a confused look. "I had no idea. Don't you have anything at a little more modest price point?"

"Absolutely. I've got a decent inventory," replied Maggie. "Oh wait, Mr. Hargreaves . . ."

"Please call me Barry."

"Alright, Barry. It just clicked with me. The word 'cottage' here on the island has some specific meaning tied to our history. Back in the 1800s, well-to-do families in the upper Midwest discovered Mackinac Island, and it quickly became their vacation retreat. When they came here on holiday though, they needed acceptable places to live, which included housing for their staff. So, they ended up constructing many of the large classic Victorian homes you saw when you came in on the ferry. I guess they wanted to play down their wealth, so they referred to their homes as 'cottages,'" offered Maggie, peering over her desk at Barry. "Just to complete today's history lesson, several enterprising businessmen later built the Grand Hotel too."

"Well, thanks. By the way, the Grand is amazing. I've got a room there with a view of the straits and the Mackinac Bridge. It must have been a pain to get between both of Michigan's peninsulas back in the day before they built it."

"Probably was. I never had to worry about it because they built the bridge long before I was born," said the young woman. "I take it you want a house. What is your budget?"

"In the $800's?" replied Barry, seemingly wondering if that would be enough.

"Of yes, I have options for you," said Maggie. "Since the season is coming to an end, when are you thinking about making a decision?"

"Now," replied Barry. "Why?"

"It's just that I assumed you might want to wait until next spring."

"Is that a problem?" asked Barry.

"Absolutely not. But, depending upon when you physically move, you might have some challenges into the late fall though. Frankly, the autumn is a beautiful time to be here, but into late October, everything shuts down. The majority of the shops close. Most of the horses are moved off the island. After closing on a home, getting your possessions here might be interesting, especially if things drag into the early winter. But I can tell you without question that if you're looking for privacy and solitude, winter here is your time, with lots of snow, strong winds, ice, and cold. And what's interesting is that in a 'good winter,' there is enough bad weather to form an ice bridge between the island and St. Ignace on the southern tip of the Upper Peninsula. The locals even mark the road with lines of Christmas trees for the snowmobilers to find their way. It might not sound like much right now, but it's the quickest way to civilization, if you're looking for it."

"Then let's start checking out my options now," replied Barry.

"Welcome to the island, Barry," Maggie declared, standing and offering her hand in congratulations at his decision.

Weeks later, Barry wrote a check for a non-cottage that had, despite the price, a million-dollar view on the west shore of the island. Interestingly, most of Barry's five-hundred-some new neighbors had never been faced with making a decision to spend winter on Mackinac. They called the island home largely as a result of familial momentum, where generations of islanders were born, married, raised their kids, and died. Thus, many of the locals viewed this newbie with a mix of curiosity, skepticism, and excitement. Yet despite the size of the small island, few, if any, permanent residents met Hargreaves during his first winter as he worked hard to keep to himself.

The locals at The Mustang Lounge, a year-round watering hole, quickly took up their newest resident as a primary topic of conversation. Often, that involved discussion about whether the stranger was permanent enough to warrant changing the official population sign to add one, had they truly had a sign. As the darkness of January set in, the locals set up a pool guessing the date when the new arrival would leave the island. By March, however, the islanders began to keep one eye on Hargreaves' home to make sure the lights in the house were still operating, lest someone should have to conduct a welfare check and find a body.

Ironically, on April Fool's Day, Barry had his official coming out party by entering The Mustang looking to see if he could collect on the pool. While the owner of the bar would not grant his request, he did offer to buy Barry a sandwich and a beer as his personal welcome to the community. In fact, Barry made an even bigger splash by buying a round for all twenty of the day-drinkers who had ventured out for lunch that noon. The stranger quickly became a semi-regular at The Mustang, drinking with the locals and kibitzing on important topics, such as the preseason chances of the Detroit Tigers, fishing, and politics.

Even though he was a likeable sort, Barry's presence nonetheless led to ongoing speculation and conversation. From a physical standpoint, Barry was about as average as one could be. Average height. Average build. Average looks. He could blend into the woodwork with the best of them. However, he did have one attribute that stood out. Barry had a speaking voice that grabbed attention. An FM radio voice. One so powerful as to add credibility to whatever topic he discussed, especially when delivered by a passionate man who was obviously well-read. Many guessed politician or preacher.

But most politicians and preachers did not buy homes on the island. It was also obvious to the locals he was unemployed, yet seemingly well-heeled financially. The crowd at The Mustang could not have cared less. They were used to white guys with money. While that was more the norm for the summer visitors, the locals further excused Barry since he bought the house an occasional round of drinks.

But why was he alone? No one had any ideas. As a healthy male in his mid-fifties with passable looks and money, an unofficial poll of single local women voted him the most eligible bachelor on the island, even though it was a small field.

Where had he come from? Despite his willingness to have a conversation, this subject had never been broached for some reason. Barry hadn't volunteered an answer, and those who made an attempt were firmly but politely steered in a more ambiguous direction. Those who still were curious tried Google, with no success.

Why was he a year-round resident? A person with means, like Barry, could afford to get away during winter for a warmer climate like other well-to-do property owners who made this their seasonal home. Or, was he trying to escape something from his past?

Even though Barry understood he would never be accepted as a "native," he was accorded a higher social class than being a mere tourist, paying his taxes and supporting local charities, two important qualities for the islanders.

As he completed his first winter, Barry Hargreaves remained an enigma and a curiosity to the locals. But with the coming tourist season, all the speculation about Barry became irrelevant since there was more important work to be done.

****

June 2020

With the warmth of spring, Barry shook off any cabin fever by exploring his new home. His daily ritual included hiking the eight-mile perimeter of the island and discovering its various paths, nooks, and crannies. In the process, he fell in love with Mackinac's extensive history.

It became commonplace for the locals to wave at Barry as he passed by with his trademark brown canvas backpack. His kit typically contained a picnic lunch and a book, critical elements for staking out a piece of land to enjoy the cool breezes off the straits and the warmth of the sun.

Although Barry enjoyed numerous picnic spots, his favorite place to spend time was near the Little Stone Church. Officially the Union Congregational Church, this historical site was constructed of local fieldstone in 1904. Barry spent hours studying the granite cut stones used for the buttresses and the courses surrounding the unique stained-glass windows, including a rare piece dedicated to the conversion of Native Americans. From the church located on a glade just off Cadotte Avenue and down the hill from the Grand Hotel, Barry grew to love the view of the hotel, which from the water looked as if it was floating on the thick woods. Gleaming white and topped by a green roof, the magnificent hotel's main terrace was lined with brilliant yellow awnings and a series of large American flags. Set against the blue skies and puffy white clouds, the area looked like a postcard.

In fact, it was so peaceful there that Barry fell asleep on the grass one late afternoon and, in the process, made another discovery that evening. With Mackinac Island's isolated location away from large metropolitan areas, he woke to a sky filled with stars like he had never seen before. Despite living on the island for months, he'd never invested much time in considering the sky at night, but things changed on that evening. He became so enamored with the constellations that he purchased a stargazer's guide and an amateur telescope to learn more. Soon it became common knowledge that on clear evenings, Barry could be found near the Little Stone Church looking skyward.

CHAPTER 16

On a cloudless night in early June, Barry set up his telescope on the front lawn of the church to study Polaris and the Big Dipper. He did not notice a figure dressed in black located in a copse of trees to the north of him across Cadotte Street some fifty yards away. Over the course of two hours, as Barry studied the sky, the person scrutinized Barry, confirming his identity through a LaRue Tactical STOMP, or Sniper Total Optical Mounting Package, attached to a PredatOBR rifle with a Sound Suppressor M308. The black-clad figure patiently watched tourists walking from Main Street back to the Grand Hotel in the green hues of the night vision scope, waiting for the traffic to thin. As the temperature dropped in the cool evening air, the wind off the straits also picked up significantly. While not an issue for Barry, it would complicate things for anyone trying to shoot a specific target on this summer night.

Feeling the chill from the cold front blowing across the island, Barry began packing up his new equipment. Slinging his telescope over his shoulder, he began to walk north to Cadotte Street. As he stepped onto the road, Barry saw the flash of a red laser beam centered on his chest.

Taking aim in the deteriorating conditions, the eyes behind the scope recognized the window was closing on this opportunity. Given the suppressor and the increasing wind, Barry could not hear the *pfft* of the bullet as it exited the barrel. However, a sudden gust pushed the bullet upward before it could strike his center mass, and it instead crushed his larynx and nicked the carotid artery on the left side of his neck, knocking him backward off his feet. With his voice box destroyed,

Barry could not cry out in pain and watched in silent horror as the arterial spray from his neck gushed like a fire hose some ten feet across the blacktop. Recognizing the injury inflicted was fatal, or would be within thirty seconds, the sniper calmly packed the rifle, approached Barry's body, lingered briefly to conduct necessary business, and then ran, disappearing into the darkness.

Around midnight, following a low-key evening at the Seabiscuit Café on Main Street, honeymooners Mike and Jessica Gilmore turned the corner from Market Street onto Cadotte after another romantic dinner. Huddled together in lock step to keep warm against the wind, their pace back to the Grand Hotel quickened in anticipation of their last night on the island and the opportunity to enjoy each other a final time before departing. However, as they approached their backlit hotel up the hill, they both saw something lying in the road up ahead.

"Honey, do you see that?" Jessica asked hesitantly. As the Gilmores closed the distance, Mike replied, "Did someone hit a deer with their car?" Then he remembered there were no vehicles on the island. Finally, they both realized it was a body. Fearing someone was having a medical issue, their walk turned into a full-blown run with their shouts for help lost in the wind. Mike arrived first and was stunned to see a man with a gaping wound to his throat and his final moment of terror captured in his still-bulging eyes. Jessica followed moments later to the grim site. Then they realized they had just walked through the fallen man's blood that pooled on the street around him.

Even with the high winds, Jessica's shriek cut through the night, clearly heard by the entrance security team at the Grand Hotel some five hundred feet away. By the time security scrambled down the hill, the Gilmores were both recycling their individual orders of Great Lakes Whitefish Filet on the lawn of the Little Stone Church.

The discovery of the body triggered a call by Grand Hotel security to Chief Keith Hutchins.

Hutchins had just fallen asleep before his phone chirped. Grasping the urgency of the moment, his head began to spin as his mind processed the report. He quickly threw on jeans, a sweatshirt, and a Mackinac Island PD windbreaker before kissing his wife Barbara goodnight for the second time that evening. Jumping into his squad, one of the few authorized emergency vehicles on the island, Hutchins alerted two other off-duty officers to meet him at the scene.

"Hutch," as he was generally known, decided to wait to contact the Michigan State Police for any assistance until he had a look at the body and the scene. While Mackinac Island PD was used to handling a death or two every year, most cases involved accidents where a tourist lost their life swimming, kayaking, or in another water sport. A murder had not taken place on the island since 1960 when Frances Lacey, a Dearborn woman, had been found strangled with her own panties before being dumped under some brush.

Approaching the site, Hutch remembered the protocol for investigating a murder, his prior experience having provided him with too many opportunities. His first order of business would be to identify the victim and begin the decision-making process from there.

After twenty-five years of service with Detroit Metro, Hutch made the choice to complete his career in a less taxing law enforcement role and sought a leadership position in a more subdued environment. At age fifty-five, Hutch had a tall and lean frame with a hawkish face. His only physical concern was a growing forehead with his thinning brown hair. Despite his age, he had the vitality of a much younger man. When Mackinac Island came calling with an opening for a police chief, it seemed like the next logical step for Hutchins.

On the face of it, Mackinac Island seemed about as tame as it got. For the most part, Hutch's team worked on petty theft, aside from the periodic alcohol-infused tourist-on-tourist assault during the summer season. And, most of those were between family members. During the off-season, the police used their one emergency vehicle to transport local seniors to church, the medical center, or the open shops downtown.

Hutchins had lived on the island for four years. Considering the size of the population, he knew pretty much everyone in his jurisdiction, albeit some of the local lightweight offenders better than others. Positioning his vehicle so the headlamps pointed in the direction of the scene, Hutch exited his squad car and carefully made his way to the body. Although he hadn't known Barry Hargreaves well, and despite his death face, Hutch recognized him immediately.

Hutch understood Hargreaves to be a new resident, a loner and a bit of an eccentric. Mackinac had more than their share of the latter. Hargreaves had not established a network of friends on the island, but Hutch knew him to be reasonably well-liked. He'd had little time to develop enemies. Considering that most murder victims know their attacker, the first big question was whether the perpetrator was an islander or someone from the rest of the world.

Beginning the search for a motive, nothing stood out. As Hutch's mind raced, a second question emerged with bigger implications: with a murderer on the island, should he post an immediate freeze on travel to and from Mackinac Island, just as the summer season was kicking in? A halt to travel would, in theory, keep the killer on the island, but there were some obvious trade-offs. No doubt the management of the Grand Hotel, local restaurants, and the Chamber of Commerce might have strong opinions. Paradoxically, those interests seeking to keep the island open to a constant flow of tourist dollars would also be promoting a destination with a killer on the loose.

However, the final and most puzzling question would not emerge until Hutch began working through his investigation of the shooting.

With only four full-time officers available, Hutchins was not sure his team was built for the demands of a murder investigation. Hedging his bets, he placed a call to Michigan State Police District 7 Headquarters in Gaylord, placing them on notice about providing possible assistance with the investigation. The State Police, who had investigative and forensic expertise, indicated they would stand by and send officers, if needed.

Thinking ahead, Hutch alerted the departments in both Mackinaw City and St. Ignace, the primary port cities where the three major ferry lines to the island originated from, and asked his counterparts from both cities to come to the island immediately to discuss potential logistics issues. He also requested Chief Connor from St. Ignace bring the Mackinac County Medical Examiner. Finally, Hutch directed his deputy, Mike Penvy, to contact Stephen Russ, the General Manager of the Grand Hotel, and Megan Shields, the president of the Mackinac Island Chamber of Commerce, to attend an impromptu meeting at four o'clock in the morning at the luxury hotel. Penvy was also told to assemble the balance of the law enforcement staff to take part in the briefing.

After putting all the moving parts in place, Hutch called a friend, Chad Acosta. Acosta and his wife, Brooks, were card players and had become friends of the Hutchins shortly after their arrival on the island. Acosta was also the Director of Safety and Security at the Grand Hotel. Knowing the hotel had an exceptional security team, Hutchins told Acosta about the murder investigation and asked if the resort had any portable lighting he could borrow to use at the crime scene. Hutch also requested Acosta to check any closed-circuit video from that evening, assuming the Grand might have cameras pointing in the general direction of the Little Stone Church. At the end of the call, Hutch invited Acosta to his planned meeting.

Hutch pulled out a Nikon SLR from the squad and began snapping photos of the crime scene, the body, and the surrounding area. Although the camera had a flash, it was not providing enough light to help document the site in detail. Recognizing the nature of Hargreaves' wound, Hutch postulated there may have been some blood spray, which might provide a lead. Yet, in the dark and on the blacktop road, any blood was almost impossible to see. As he pondered his options, Hutch heard what sounded like a mechanized caravan moving in his direction.

Leading the way was a bright yellow Cushman industrial cart hauling several portable lights along with a generator. Behind it were two other similar carts: one carried staff wearing typical maintenance coveralls with the second carrying several white-coated gentlemen. Once the maintenance staff had set up a generator and the requested lighting, Hutch realized the other employees were waiters. Just as if they were preparing for a hastily arranged cocktail party, the white coats erected a temporary tent on the lawn near the Little Stone Church. Underneath, they set up several tables topped with red tablecloths. Two large urns of coffee were placed on the tables along with trays of sandwiches and snacks for the investigators. Enough for a small army. Hutch smiled for a moment murmuring to himself, "Damn, that Acosta must have pulled some strings to make this happen."

With the lighting now in place, Hutch retook the photos. As expected, he could clearly see the arterial spray from Hargreaves resembling an abstract expressionist painting on Cadotte's blacktop canvas. Although the Gilmores had walked through the crime scene, Hutch studied the now cordoned-off area closely. He could see the tracks from Gilmores, both of whom were wearing Avia sneakers, but he also saw several prints from a third individual he could not account for. Each sample left a bloody waffle print moving in the direction from across the street heading toward the golf course.

Hutch recognized the type of footprint immediately as being from a tactical boot, like the pair he owned from his SWAT days. Speculating a full print was roughly ten to eleven inches in length, the chief also noted the gait of the person moving through his crime scene. While the stride was fairly long indicating someone had likely been moving faster than a walk on their way to the trees, there were also many prints surrounding the body as if the person had loitered there for a time.

Lost in thought, Hutch did not hear the *clip-clop* of the approaching horses. After learning the chiefs from both port cities and the ME would be arriving on the island, Acosta must have taken the liberty of dispatching a hotel trolley to pick up the guests. Bill Connor, the leader of St. Ignace PD, stepped off the carriage first, followed by his peer from Mackinac City, Kathryn Maki. Bringing up the rear was the county's medical examiner, Eric Wittala. Wittala immediately got to work examining the body.

The preliminary opinion was Hargreaves had been killed by a single bullet fired from a high-powered rifle at reasonably close range. In his examination, Wittala found that after the bullet passed through Hargreaves' voice box, it continued on to sever his spinal cord. Death followed in less than a minute. Wittala quietly told Hutch the wound was so severe that Hargreaves' head was remained attached to the body only by some sinew and muscle. The medical examiner also turned over the only other piece of available evidence to Hutch, Hargreaves' wallet. Even though it was an unlikely motive given the scene, robbery was officially ruled out.

In workmanlike fashion, Wittala completed his on-site examination. Prior to placing Hargreaves' remains in a body bag, Wittala cut the strap on the telescope case that had been on the victim's back. As he and Hutch began to move the body into the bag, both heard an audible *plink* on the pavement. Although the projectile had no problem cutting through flesh and bone, it stopped cold when it hit the titanium case before becoming lodged in Hargreaves' jacket collar, then falling harmlessly onto the road.

"Son of a bitch," both Hutch and Wittala gasped simultaneously, looking incredulously at what was left of the slug. Even though it was mangled, it was clearly a stroke of luck to have this piece of evidence. With a gloved hand, Hutch picked up the slug, placing it carefully in a plastic evidence bag. Wittala finished loading the body into the back of the carriage for the short trip back to St. Ignace to complete the autopsy.

As Wittala was set to leave, Hutch asked him to hold up briefly. "I know the complete autopsy will take some time, but can you get me some fingerprints from Hargreaves by morning?"

"Absolutely," Wittala replied. "Any reason for the rush?"

"Just a hunch. Just a hunch," replied Hutch.

CHAPTER 17

Penvy returned to the tent after searching the area for any other evidence. The deputy located what he believed to be the shooter's position across the street from where the victim lay, underneath the trees based upon the angle of the shot and the pattern of the needles on the ground. Taking a roll of yellow police barricade tape and the Nikon, he walked back to the shooter's blind to snap some additional photos.

As the clock moved closer to his pending early morning meeting, Hutch jumped into his cruiser with two remaining items on his punch list. Hutch contacted Acosta by cell. "Chad, were you able to find any video of the murder?"

"Yeah, Hutch. We got some footage on one camera. It's not centered and pretty grainy . . ." Acosta paused.

"And . . . ?"

"I've seen it a couple of times. It is shocking to say the least."

Hutch's remaining to-do stemmed from his hunch. Pulling the Michigan driver's license from Hargreaves' wallet, the chief contacted Mackinac County dispatch to run a 10-27 identification check. An anonymous young woman answered. After identifying himself, Hutch read both the victim's name and license number into the phone. Unsure of what he would turn up, the thirty-second silence ended with the faceless voice requesting Hutch repeat the name and number. Following another sixty-second delay, Hutch got a response, albeit not what he was looking for.

The officer's voice was clear. "We have no one by that name on file, sir."

"Are you sure?" asked Hutch.

"Yes, according to all available records," said the dispatcher.

As Hutch clicked off the call, he thought through this revelation. "You're shitting me!?" he exclaimed to himself as his final question continued to churn.

At four o'clock in the morning, a bleary-eyed group met in the Terrace Room of the Grand Hotel. More accustomed to hosting weddings and other large parties, the large ballroom had already been preset for a business meeting at a more civilized time later that morning. The cheery room boasted walls covered with vibrant green wallpaper and contrasting salmon-colored ceilings. A large wooden dance floor was centered in the room surrounded by carpeting with waves of other shades of green. Although the room had functional recessed lighting throughout, two large chandeliers set the tone for a room that had hosted many high-profile events. The one design element that seemed out of place was a large copper lion that would have been more at home in the Far East rather than anywhere in the Midwest.

Despite the elegance of the room, it was lost on the group as they gathered around a large makeshift grouping of tables set up on the parquet dance floor. A long table full of breakfast pastries, fruit, and coffee flanked a large flat-screen television. Although all those invited arrived promptly, it was early even for those in law enforcement or the hospitality business.

"Thank you all for coming on very short notice." Hutch took a sip of coffee before jumping into the meat of his agenda. "Ladies and gentlemen, there was a murder on Mackinac Island tonight." The civilians in the room let out an audible gasp.

"The victim was a relatively new arrival to the island," Hutch continued. "He was shot by a high-powered rifle just outside the Little Stone Church, where he had apparently been stargazing. The man took a bullet to the throat and bled out on Cadotte Street."

"Who was the victim?" chimed in Stephen Russ with the obvious question.

"Mr. Russ, people here knew the man as Barry Hargreaves."

Listening to Hutch's carefully worded response, Russ followed up. "I didn't know him. To some extent, your answer seems couched. Is there something more?"

"This is part of a mystery that seems to be growing by the minute. A check through the Michigan DMV has no record of a Barry Hargreaves. The driver's license was a fake. At this point, the medical examiner has promised me fingerprints of the victim by morning so we can try to run down his identity. Without knowing exactly who the victim was, it's difficult to come up with a motive. Frankly, we're scratching our heads. Given the caliber of the slug we recovered and the nature of the shooting, this was a carefully planned attack. There's one more thing I wanted to show you."

Looking at Acosta, the large flat-screen monitor was turned on and a flash drive was inserted into the smart TV. "The security team at the Grand went through all available closed-circuit video in hopes of catching anything out of the ordinary." Looking at Stephen Russ, "I recognize a primary goal is to provide a secure environment for your hotel's guests and that most of your cameras are focused on property. But one camera caught a long-distance view of what happened tonight." Hutch pushed the start button, and a grainy black-and-white image appeared on-screen. "Generally, we would not share this type of video with civilians without having pre-screened it, but in the interest of time, I've made the decision to show it."

The video clip picked up after Hargreaves had packed up his telescope and was making his way across the street. Then he stopped abruptly and fell backwards violently as if he had fallen on icy pavement in the winter. However, those from law enforcement knew exactly what had happened.

"The kill shot," muttered Penvy aloud. The civilians in the room were distracted by the comment when they realized what they had just seen on tape.

"Did we just see Mr. Hargreaves get shot?" asked Stephen.

"I believe so," said Hutch, hitting the pause button. Backing up the video, Hutch hit *Play* again and the group watched Hargreaves die once more. The good news for those eating pastries was that the grainy quality of the clip did not show Hargreaves' blood shooting across the road. Then, the group saw nothing but Hargreaves lying on the ground for roughly sixty seconds. The chief moved to hit the pause button once more.

"Hold it, Hutch," said Acosta. "There's more." As the video continued, an individual carrying a suitcase entered the frame, slowly approaching the fallen man. The person stopped briefly over the body and appeared to reach down to touch Hargreaves' abdomen.

"Oh my God. A good Samaritan checking Mr. Hargreaves for a heartbeat!" exclaimed Megan Shields.

As the footage continued, though, the unknown figure extended an arm before bringing it down violently on one of the legs of the victim. Even with no sound, the image triggered a synchronized head snap from everyone in the room. The video continued. The person stood over the body calmly before rearing back, delivering a second blow to the other leg before turning and running out of the frame. Seconds later, the Gilmores came into view. Thankfully, Acosta turned off the feed before showing either of the honeymooners throwing up.

"Who were the people at the end of the clip?" asked Stephen.

"Guests of the Grand celebrating their honeymoon," offered Hutch. "One of our deputies interviewed them both. As you can imagine, Mr. and Mrs. Gilmore were pretty shaken up by the experience. The bottom line is that neither saw the shooting and only happened upon Hargreaves after the fact. They are not suspects."

Stephen winced at the thought of his hotel being at all connected with the murder, making a note to check on the couple and to send a gift to their room later that morning.

"Was the first person we saw approaching Mr. Hargreaves the murderer?" Megan's question seemed to open the floodgates to more questions from the group.

"What do you know about Hargreaves?"

"Why was he shot? Was he involved in some illegal activity?"

"If Hargreaves is not Hargreaves, who was he?"

"Do you have any suspects?"

"This whole situation could be a public relations disaster. What are we supposed to do with a murderer on the loose? What do we tell our guests?"

Feeling like he was losing control of his meeting, Hutch stepped to the center of the semicircle and hushed the group. "Look, you all have very legitimate questions. In fact, I have the same and more. However, it's been only a few hours since this shooting, and we're working this case hard. I'm not looking to you to solve this crime . . . that's my job."

"So, what do you want from us?" asked Stephen.

Hutch drew a breath. "First of all, this type of meeting is atypical and it's highly unusual for anyone from law enforcement to brief local civilians about an active investigation. Although I can't rule out that this is a local-on-local murder, I also have to consider the possibility that the killer is from off the island and now intent on leaving. The purpose of this meeting was to tell you about what has taken place, because it does have ramifications on the tourist trade. You represent stakeholders on Mackinac Island, and I need your input because I understand how the island's economy works. I believe you understand the gravity of the situation. First, we have a killer on the loose during the beginning of your high season, which to me seems problematic as a member of the chamber. With that understanding, the question for each of you is the effect on the island if we shut down the ferry system immediately, as part of an effort to keep the killer here."

For as vocal as the hospitality representatives had been, Hutch's question sucked all the air out of the room. Coming into high season, turning off the tap of tourist dollars for any length of time would be economic suicide, now and potentially into the future.

After sixty seconds of silence, Stephen regrouped first. "Hutch, I understand your dilemma and believe you understand the potential implications, otherwise Megan and I would not be here. A couple of things come to mind. Since you don't know who the killer is, what would you be looking for while you determine when to start the ferry system again? Also, while the ferries probably transport ninety percent of the visitors here and back to the mainland, there are any number of private boats and yachts currently docked in the harbor that can get someone off the island, not to mention our airport. If the killer was smart enough to pull off Hargreaves' murder with a high-powered rifle, might they not have planned to leave short of using the ferry system?"

Jumping onto that theme, Megan chimed in. "Again, based on the premise you don't know who the killer is, how long would the ferry system be closed? Would a day or two even make a difference? It would seem anyone with half a brain could simply wait out any shutdown of the ferry system, if they wanted to get back to the mainland."

Continuing his thought process, Stephen added a couple more issues. "Hutch, we and every other hotel here have guests scheduled to leave tomorrow with others arriving. We also have people to feed. Without a flow of goods and services, the problem gets bigger by the day."

After both Stephen and Megan were seemingly spent, it was Hutch's turn to re-engage. "Thank you for your questions and comments. I also see shutting down the ferry system as problematic and, as you both have pointed out, not totally effective given the options for the killer to leave by other means. That, and the fact that our staff is too small to cover all routes off the island. From my perspective, our best option is to work with our law enforcement counterparts in St. Ignace, Mackinaw City, and the state police in monitoring the flow of people off the island. That might involve delaying the first several ferry departures this morning while law enforcement builds a plan for some additional screening or baggage searches. However, as we finalize our plan, we will do so understanding the implications to your business. I appreciate you both coming to this meeting at such an early hour. As the investigation progresses, we'll keep you informed."

Aside from Acosta, the civilians left the room as the chief's cell phone rang. Hutch moved to a corner of the large room to get some privacy.

"Hutch, it's Eric. I've started the autopsy on Hargreaves and found something unusual on his body. It looks like a letter, but when I unfolded it, there was a single sentence on the page."

"Alright," said Hutch, listening intently. "Go ahead."

"*197. If he break another man's bone, his bone shall be broken.* It's just weird," said Wittala.

"You said you found this on the body?"

"Yes, in an inside jacket pocket."

"Take a photo of the letter with your phone and send it to me please," said Hutch.

"Hutch, after reading the letter, I was curious," offered Eric. "In addition to his fatal wounds, Hargreaves also had two broken legs. Postmortem."

CHAPTER 18

Hutch's brain shifted into overdrive. He continued his conversation with the ME, but also got Chad's attention, pointing to the flatscreen. "Eric, after you left the crime scene with the body, we found out Barry Hargreaves was an alias. According to the state of Michigan, there is no such person. Can you expedite the prints to me ASAP? We need to figure out who this guy was."

"Will do," said Eric, but Hutch never heard it as he had already hung up.

Hutch got the attention of the officers who had drifted to the breakfast pastries. "We've had a development. Chad, please run your video one more time."

All watched the progression of the murder of Hargreaves up until the point when the unidentified person with the suitcase hovered over the body momentarily.

"Is there any way to enhance the picture?" asked Chief Maki.

"No," responded Chad.

"Watch the next couple of frames closely," said Hutch.

The law enforcement team and security staff paid close attention as the potential suspect reached down to Hargreaves. "When I first saw this sequence, I agreed with Megan that the person with the suitcase was a Good Samaritan checking the victim for a heartbeat. Having seen the rest of the clip, we know this person was no do-gooder," said Hutch. "Rather than checking for a heartbeat, I believe this individual actually placed something on the body. Eric just sent me a photo of a document he retrieved from Hargreaves' jacket. The letter contains one sentence. *'197. If he break another man's bone, his bone shall be broken.'"* The chief passed his phone around the room for his colleagues to see the note.

"Man, it is hard to see anything conclusive from this video, but if this person put this letter in Hargreaves' pocket, he must be the perp," concluded St. Ignace's Chief of Police, Connor.

"Also, the contents of the letter fit with what we saw on the tape. The suspect must have broken Hargreaves' legs after he was dead," added Chief Kathryn Maki.

Hutch nodded. "He did. Eric confirmed it just now."

"So, someone came to the island, shot Hargreaves, or whoever he is, and then after he was dead, broke his legs," summed up Chad. "How bizarre is that?"

"Pretty messed up. But what's the story with the suitcase?" asked Deputy Penvy.

"Mike, guns come in all shapes and sizes," offered Hutch. "Maybe the perp used a suitcase gun?"

"A what?" asked Kathryn.

"A high-powered rifle with components that can be assembled or broken down in a matter of minutes," offered Hutch. "The entire gun literally fits in a suitcase. I've read about them, but never seen one before."

"Any ideas about how the suspect broke Hargreaves' legs?" asked Connor.

"Yeah, with one of these," replied Hutch, extending the collapsible baton he carried. "A required piece of hardware for anyone in law enforcement."

"Without a description, we're searching for a killer in dark clothing, wearing tactical boots and carrying a suitcase containing a rifle?" asked Mike.

"At this point we are," said Hutch. He looked at his watch. It was just after 5:00 a.m. "Damn, we're almost out of time. I'm issuing an order to delay the first ferry transports of the day until ten o'clock to buy us some more time. I'll let Megan and Stephen know so they can react.

Chad, with such as unusual situation, can we use some of your folks to supplement law enforcement here on the island as well as in St. Ignace and Mackinaw City?"

"You got it, Hutch," replied Chad.

The collective group went to work to finalize details of their plan.

With less than five hours to put their tactics in place before the killer potentially slipped away, the group agreed they would largely rely on video surveillance at docks on the island and in both port cities to identify potential suspects. However, reinforcements were called in with the State Police sending twenty troopers to assist, along with several employees from the Grand's security team. Chiefs Maki and Connor arranged for all departing visitors to be greeted at their respective ports by a contingent of local officers who would perform random bag searches on any suspicious persons. However, every member of the group recognized that without a description of the suspect, the potential of apprehending the killer was miniscule, at best.

Before the ferry system opened, Hutch made a trip to the address listed on Hargreaves' driver's license to see if there were any clues that might help the team. The search turned up nothing. The home itself was impressive in many ways, yet it was largely contractor beige throughout with no real personalization of any kind. The only contents were a large shelf full of books and DVDs and a large bronze cross near the front door. There were no photos or personal items beyond clothing. Hutch made a note to track down the realtor involved with Hargreaves' purchase of this property to ask some questions. Thinking back to the mountain of paperwork required to buy his own home, Hutch wondered how someone bought a house like this with fake identification. *Could Hargreaves have simply paid cash for the place, eliminating the need for any backgrounding?*

On the way back to the docks to monitor the outflow of visitors, Hutch received a call from Eric. "Hutch, Hargreaves' prints came back from AFIS. Your victim's real name is Lonnie D. Palmer from Willow City, Texas. I don't have anything further at this point."

"Eric, I appreciate the quick response." Hutch notified the members of the law enforcement team about the identity of the victim, even though it added little in terms of the potential apprehension of his killer.

A long day became longer as the throngs of tourists arrived and departed undeterred by the heavy police presence. Amazingly, the idea that there might be a murderer loose on the island did not seem to deter anyone. After all, it was high season. The smell of horse shit and fudge was peaking.

In the days that followed, fewer police were in force on the docks to greet vacationers as they returned to the mainland. Video from the docks showed happy faces coming and going to the island with just about everyone carrying a suitcase. Whether it contained a gun was another matter. Without a clear description of who they were looking for, the effort seemed to have been a futile and useless gesture. By the end of the week, the case of Hargreaves/Palmer cooled as quickly as the night air on the island. The working assumption was the shooter had escaped.

CHAPTER 19

Anticipating the amount of time he would spend in the car that day, Nick Hayden decided to take full advantage of the early morning sun with a five-mile run. How long had it been since he'd had a run? Time at his parents' house had been kept by beers drunk and TV shows watched. But things were different here, and the run had given him time to consider the work ahead of him, as well as the twists that had appeared yesterday. So, Tina Matheson, until recently the head of the religious niche and seemingly responsible for the crisis at Weston, was Emil's daughter and Mallory's sister. *Half-sister*, he heard Mallory ringing in his head. *What the fuck is that all about?* Fortunately for Nick, he had only a few minutes before all thoughts of this latest news were replaced by his legs feeling like they were on fire, and the real possibility that last night's dinner might reappear. After building a considerable sweat, he congratulated himself on taking care of his body's needs. The story of Tina would be front and center soon enough.

By the time the BMW rolled to a stop at the front entrance of Weston Insurance, Nick had showered, shaved, and was working on his second cup of Starbucks. On cue, Mallory stepped out from under the awning shading the front doors and moved toward the curb when she recognized Nick's car. Wearing a knee-length floral dress and a light, white sweater, Nick surmised this might be the most conservative clothing she owned. Not sure how he would be received after the tension from yesterday, Nick was surprised to find her in a cheery mood.

"Is this my dark roast with cream?" she said, entering the vehicle.

Buckling up, Mallory offered a "thanks" as she sank into the leather seat and began to sip the coffee as the vehicle left the Weston compound. The two traveled in silence for several minutes until Hayden hit cruising speed on Highway 41 South for the ninety-minute drive from Neenah to the northern suburbs of Milwaukee.

Nick thought to himself that he had forgotten the two seasons in Wisconsin: football and construction. As far as the eye could see, striped orange construction barrels lined both sides of the southbound highway. From time to time, orange barrels also denoted the edge of the northbound half of the road as well. There were multiple signs indicating a work zone for the next stretch of miles, though there was no activity.

Fifteen minutes into the high-speed obstacle course, Nick broke the silence with a question focused on the business of the day. "Mallory, can you give me some background on the broker we're going to visit, as well as how the whole submission process works?"

"Sure. Let's start with the procedure first. Essentially, a broker represents the client, *not* the company, when putting together an insurance program. The broker is looking for the best overall deal for their client regarding terms and price, but most deals are inevitably driven by the negotiated premium. The broker earns a fee from the client for their work and expertise. Since many brokers specialize in some lines of coverage, they might approach many potential companies, particularly those that offer them incentives. Hungry insurance companies, like Weston, threw tons of upfront dollars at the brokers while also offering back-end compensation if the business is profitable."

Taking in his first lesson in insurance marketing, Nick let Mallory's overview sink in while working hard to keep up with signage in the changing work zones. "So, even though a broker's primary job is to represent the client, they might still earn money from both the person they represent and the company involved in a deal. How is that ethical?"

"Remember yesterday, I said you get the luxury of asking dumb questions? You hit the nail on the head," Mallory replied. "I agree, it's hard to see how one person can serve two masters. However, in Weston's case, we signed up for this by pushing brokers hard to throw some business our way at the absolute lowest price and with the most favorable conditions. In retrospect, no other self-respecting company would have met such terms. The smart money, meaning every other carrier, walked away from some of the deals we made while we went all in."

Continuing to absorb the details, Nick replied, "Why would any company do what Weston did?"

"We were driven by a growth strategy with aggressive targets. Early on, we did grow. Even with the losses we suffered, we still made a decent profit. Then, Emil and the board decided to push growth even harder. Weston literally doubled down looking for more religious institution business controlled by other brokers in the niche, based upon Tina's recommendation. It was the first time the company had ever used brokers as part of its distribution strategy, and it was like we had discovered a printing press for hundred-dollar bills. Everyone at the home office looked like a goddamned genius." Mallory paused.

"But?" asked Nick.

"But we were not as smart as the brokers. Some cut corners, withholding information about their clients or simply didn't provide it at all. Not necessarily enough to be lies, but at the same time, not always totally truthful either. This was some of what Robbie Mueller was alluding to. Since everything seemed to be going so well, our underwriting process got lax on top of not being sure what was critical to know about the type of insurance exposures we were signing up for in pursuit of revenue. Then . . ."

Nick finished Mallory's sentence, "Then . . . the losses started coming in."

"Exactly. Looking back now, it seems so simple. Even though we grew like crazy, we were losing money on every dollar of business we did. That was about the time when Emil and the board started having second thoughts about the whole mess and our supposed broker partners."

Looking at the endless cornfields on either side of the highway and thinking through their conversation, Nick had another question. "If the brokers claimed to be Weston's business partners, why didn't they take a longer-term view and act in good faith?"

"Bingo. You're pretty astute for a guy who doesn't know anything about insurance. The truth is Weston had previously only worked with contracted professional agents who represented the company. We had never worked with brokers before, and we forgot that distinction. Using the word 'partner' was feel-good bullshit, especially since everyone knew brokers represent their clients, not the company. My guess is the brokers were making so much money based upon what we threw at them, there was no incentive to move the business back to the companies they normally did business with . . . remember, the smart money. Another red flag we missed," said Mallory, feeling some confidence.

"How about one more dumb question?" asked Nick.

"Shoot."

"Why are we making the trip down to see this broker, what's-his-name?"

"Marco Ricci, from All-American Brokerage. My thinking is you should have some firsthand experience with a broker since the decisions around their selection and use probably will be a significant aspect of your final report to Emil and the board. All-American is our largest broker, and Ricci is their primary producer."

"What do you know about Ricci in particular, Mal?"

"Nothing. Frankly, while I've seen this guy's name before, I've never met him."

"Of course, the firm's name must be All-American?" asked Nick rhetorically. "Also, Mallory, this is *our* report, not mine," which drew a smile from her. "We are actually partners in sorting out this mess. So, where does Weston currently stand with Ricci?"

"For the moment, nowhere. In theory, Weston still has a tenuous business relationship with this firm but has slowed in accepting any new business from them given the direction of the program. It's a topic I'm sure will come up today. Even though Weston generated revenue of several million dollars in premiums, we paid a multiple of that in losses on the accounts All-American brought to us. Basically, Weston took a bath in this so-called partnership," said Mallory, using her fingers to make air quotes in reference to the word. "Combined with the other brokers, the current and future losses are potentially enough to put the company at risk of surviving. If you thought it was tough to look Robbie Mueller in the eye when he asked about his future and that of his team, imagine the other employees not associated with this niche who could lose their jobs too."

"How much money did All-American lose?"

"None. Weston was the risk-taker. We took the premiums and the losses. Yet we paid All-American big commissions, not to mention some profit-sharing checks based on our early good results. All-American made out like bandits on this deal."

"Given everything you said, Mal, this ought to be an interesting meeting to say the least," replied Nick.

The discussion ended as Mallory guided Nick off the expressway onto an exit ramp, through a detour, and into the parking lot of a nondescript office complex of identical cookie-cutter buildings. All-American Brokerage was housed in one of several low-rise, modern, brick structures surrounded by trees and manicured grass. After locating the signage on the property, Mallory and Nick eventually found the address. The sidewalk leading to All-American was lined with colorful flowers planted in red cedar mulch. Entering the lobby of the building, Nick and Mallory found another set of directions and guided themselves to the brokerage firm at the opposite end of the complex.

A glass door with the business's name opened into a sterile area where elevator music played quietly in the background. They passed a small sitting area and approached a counter guarded by a middle-aged woman with jet-black hair who wore too much makeup and smelled of drugstore perfume and unfiltered Camels.

"Can I help you?" asked the woman politely with a raspy voice.

Mallory jumped in. "Nick Hayden and Mallory Swenson from Weston Insurance to see Marco Ricci, please."

"I'll let him know you're here."

Both took a seat while the receptionist made a call to Ricci. Taking in their surroundings, Nick found nothing impressive about the space right down to the magazines on the coffee table that were uninteresting, even when they had been current six months earlier.

Ricci cut quite a swath as he made his way into the small greeting area. Wearing pinstripe pants that were no doubt paired with a jacket left in his office, Ricci also sported a pink shirt and monochrome tie of the same color. The ensemble was set off by matching suspenders in addition to highly polished Italian leather shoes. Ricci was well-tanned and had slicked back hair à la Michael Corleone. Nick began to feel underdressed for the meeting, wearing a jacket, a button-down shirt, and pressed black trousers. Ricci stood only five and a half feet tall, a fact that became even more apparent when Mallory and Nick stood to greet the broker, both towering over him.

"Good morning, and welcome to All-American Brokerage," said Ricci, offering his hand to Nick. Turning to Mallory, he paused briefly, looking her up and down in a slow manner that made both visitors somewhat uncomfortable before he extended his hand to her. Nick watched as Mallory's features froze in place. "Come on back to our conference room." Leading the way at a double-time pace through a series of narrow halls lined with empty cubes, Ricci chattered on in monologue about the history of the brokerage firm, a maintenance issue in the building, and the weather before they arrived at their destination.

The conference room amounted to little more than a broom closet containing a small, round, wooden table with a phone, four mismatched chairs, and a Keurig machine sitting on a dorm-sized fridge. Squeezing into the area, Nick chose a seat. As Mallory entered the room, Ricci brushed the length of her body with his as she made her way past, getting her attention as well as Nick's. However, neither said a word as Mallory took a seat as far away from the broker as possible. Unfortunately, her only option was directly across from Ricci at the small table.

"I've got a couple of new submissions for your religious niche that you can take back to the office," said Ricci. "For some reason, I can't seem to get a return call from your underwriters."

"Based upon what I've heard, I think we have enough business from All-American on our books," Nick replied. "I'm told Weston Insurance lost millions of dollars on the accounts you've provided."

"So, you're not here looking for more accounts like Tina used to?"

"No. Actually, we have been charged by Emil Swenson, the CEO, to determine why Weston is losing so much money in the religious niche. In fact, we're building an exit strategy so the company can leave the market." As Hayden concluded, he caught Ricci in a stare-down with Mallory's chest across the table. Ricci startled himself back to consciousness when Nick's voice stopped.

"Well, that's a shame. I liked Tina, but I think I could have done some serious business with Mallory here."

Nick rose to his feet. "Listen, scumbag, we made the trip down here to talk with you about what went wrong, but you've done nothing but disrespect my colleague with your juvenile conduct. If you are any kind of representation of the broker population for Weston's business, it's pretty evident to me that you and your buddies were a major part of the problem." Nick motioned with his head to Mallory for them to leave. But Ricci was not finished with the conversation.

"Listen, I don't know what you do, Hayden, but you have embarrassed me. I am a professional insurance broker with twenty years of experience. Nobody comes into my office and humiliates me the way you've done with your accusations," his voice raising.

Listening to Ricci but doing his best to keep his cool, Nick continued toward the door.

"Weston is a joke anyway. They had no clue how to treat us brokers and our clients," Ricci continued to chirp.

Nick stopped and turned as Ricci concluded, "I'm amazed Weston is in business in the first place." As the broker ended his sentence, Nick took a step forward, putting his right forearm under Ricci's chin, and pushed, raising him off his feet to eye level with the former PJ.

"Look. You can say what you want about Weston Insurance," growled Nick. "Based on what I've seen, their employees are top-notch and professional."

"Please let him go, Nick," pleaded Mallory. "He's just not worth it."

Upon hearing Mallory, his brain kicked in. Nick raised Ricci a couple of inches higher to inflict some additional pain, and then released his hold on the broker. "The company will send you a letter terminating our business relationship, asshole. In the meantime, you can consider it cancelled effective immediately."

Ricci coughed a few times, but quickly regrouped, responding with an aggressive move towards Nick but stopped short when the larger man squared to face him while holding his ground.

"Little man, you've already made a series of bad decisions relative to the business I represent. Go ahead and make it one more if you want." Nick paused without blinking. Ricci, doing the calculus involving the muscular man, finally chose to stand down. "Oh, and before we go, I believe you should apologize to Ms. Swenson for your poor behavior towards her."

Ricci's eyes got big for a moment, believing Nick was adding insult to injury. However, the broker, now cowed by the confrontation, uttered an almost inaudible, "I'm sorry."

Nick held the door for Mallory as they exited the office. Emerging into the parking lot, both took a deep breath of fresh air. "Wow, that went well," Nick offered, eliciting a nervous laugh from Mallory. "How about we hit a truck stop on the way home to take a shower to rinse the slime off of us, and then find some lunch?"

"Amen," retorted Mallory.

CHAPTER 20

Nick and Mallory were both quiet as they reflected on the meeting, each for different reasons. Nick thought through the exchange with Ricci given the losses Weston had incurred while quietly cursing himself for having lost control, while Mallory focused on her personal interaction with the broker. After they found their way back to the highway, Mallory looked over at Hayden. "Nick, thanks for standing up for me," she said in a small voice.

"You're welcome. Ricci was one sleazy son of a bitch. He was totally inappropriate with you. I'm not sure who at Weston signed up to do business with this guy, but they sure missed on reading the tea leaves. Even with what little I know about this business, all my alarms went off the second we met him."

"You know, when I bought and paid for these . . ." looking down at her chest, "I thought I would have more confidence in myself. If anything, I feel like every guy I work with just stares at them and has no respect for me. I seem to attract nothing but assholes. I just feel worthless sometimes."

"Listen, Mallory, you are who you are. You're smart, attractive, you know your business, and you should have confidence in yourself based on that. Don't let some asshole like Ricci ruin your day because of their behavior and make you feel like it's your fault."

"I just thought I would attract a better type of guy . . ."

"Who's to say you won't?" Nick decided to go for a laugh. "I mean, *I'm* off-limits because for the duration of this investigation, I'm the boss." Mallory gave him a stare, and then seeing the smile in his eyes, cracked up.

"So, no pining for you?" she asked.

"I don't see you as a piner," he replied.

She shook her head and reached for the dashboard, tuning in a local station.

A half hour later, they pulled over at a roadside diner in a small town just off the highway. The exterior of the restaurant looked like a vintage travel trailer constructed of highly polished chrome that gleamed in the sun. Inside, it was outfitted in 1950's décor, complete with signs from state fairs long past, plastic red and white tablecloths, and a large retro jukebox with push buttons to play the 45s inside. After being approached by a heavy-set waitress with a name tag that announced her as "Babs," Mallory ordered a salad and iced tea while Nick chose a cheeseburger, fries, and chocolate malt.

Once Babs left the table, Nick whispered. "Bad choice, Mal. This is not a salad kind of place."

"Tell me about it when you have your heart attack on the way home," she countered.

Babs returned, holding a large round tray with their drinks: Mallory's tea, Nick's malt, and a large metal mixing cup containing his extra malt and a long spoon. Mallory was already beginning to second-guess her menu choice.

"Should I start stretching to perform CPR on you?" asked Mallory as Nick ignored her diving into the malt.

"Screw you. I ran five miles today. I'm going to savor this."

"Nick, we started this conversation before, but never finished it. You said you were a PJ in the Air Force. What exactly is a PJ?"

"How long do we have?" asked Hayden, sucking hard on his straw to get the malt started.

"What kind of work did you do?"

"First of all, PJ is short for pararescueman. Essentially, it's the Air Force's version of Special Forces."

"Seriously. You mean like Navy SEALs?"

"Yes, except that when a SEAL gets wounded, we're the people they call to get them out of trouble. PJs are tasked to rescue, recover, and return any American, military or civilian, or member of Allied Forces wherever and whenever needed. That's what the official line from the website says anyway."

Babs returned with the main courses. Looking at her salad, Mallory immediately knew Nick had been right, and she began to stare at his cheeseburger.

"What does rescue and recover mean?"

"Just exactly that. The PJs' motto is 'That others may live.' Basically, we go into harm's way and do whatever is necessary to bring our people home . . . alive or dead. If a pilot is shot down behind enemy lines, we go. If there is a helicopter crash, we parachute in. If there is a ship taking on water and people are in danger of drowning, we're there. Most of the time, we're first responders providing medical treatment," said Nick.

"It sounds dangerous," she replied, picking at her salad.

"I guess. But, if we didn't do our jobs, a lot of good people would likely die."

"You said you provide medical treatment. Are you a doctor or nurse?"

"Neither. We're like paramedics on steroids trained to deal with battlefield trauma. PJs are given more leeway to administer drugs and perform emergency procedures than civilian paramedics since there are generally no hospitals in forward areas."

"You said you might have to drop in to help someone?"

"Yeah. It's all part of our long training course. PJs have a year-and-a-half training cycle that includes the medical piece, but also advanced weapons, free-fall parachuting, combat diving, mountaineering, operating boats, and rescue swimming, for starters. By the way, this is a damn tasty burger."

"Thanks for reminding me. The salad sucks," she said, putting her fork down. "How come I've never heard of the PJs?"

"Probably because our press agent isn't as good as the one representing the SEALs."

Taking a sip of her tea, Mallory followed up with another question. "How many rescues have you done?"

"I don't know. I really don't. If someone lives because I've done my job, that is how I keep score."

"Oh my God, I'm sitting with a real hero."

"Hardly, I just did my job. Every PJ does."

"Why did the Air Force choose you for this job?"

"They didn't. I signed up for it. In fact, it was a job I was born to do. I absolutely loved it. It gave me so many opportunities I wouldn't have otherwise had. I've traveled all over the world. Made lifelong friends . . . the kind of people that would be there for me and have my back anytime I ever need them."

She paused. "You know, when you were describing being a PJ, you used the present tense." Nick's eyebrows went up. "Are you really done with it? Or are you thinking about going back? Or is the exciting world of insurance the next chapter?"

Nick blew out a long breath. "Basically, after eight years, my body was shot. I just couldn't do the work to my personal level of satisfaction. My knees and shoulders aren't right. I've been shot a couple of times, stabbed, almost drowned. It was just my time to leave. I'd like to be able to play golf when I retire someday. Also, being a former PJ doesn't translate well to the real world. So, for now, insurance is where I'm at in life. But I don't think I'm in danger of becoming a lifer."

"I'm guessing Mr. Ricci did not intimidate you when he lunged at you then?" asked Mallory with a chuckle.

"Let's just say I wasn't too worried. Hey, can I ask you a question about Emil that's been bugging me?" said Nick, changing the subject.

"Of course," responded Mallory with some trepidation.

"When we met with him last week, Emil gave us the same story about the religious program that was essentially what we heard from everyone else. From my standpoint, it seems like Weston's poor results shouldn't have surprised anyone. However, when I went back over the notes from our conversation with Emil, he said something about getting 'justice.' Do you have a sense of what that means? How does a company expect or achieve justice?" he asked.

"Frankly, Nick, I'm not sure. I've heard Emil make the same reference when talking with senior staff members about ending this program. But, I'm not sure how anyone, let alone an insurance company, gets justice from the 'Christian fuckers,' as he likes to say. Maybe you should ask him to clarify this thought at our status meeting tomorrow."

"I'll take it under advisement for the time being," he said, finishing his malt with a Scotch whistle as he drained the cup with his straw.

"Nice," she said, responding to the sound. "On the way home, can we hit a McDonald's? I'm still hungry," looking down at the salad she had pushed around the plate, but not eaten. "I hate to say it, but you were right."

"That must have been hard for you to say. By the way, I told you so."

"Hanging out with you must be what it feels like to have a brother. You're such a dick."

CHAPTER 21

The following morning began bright and early as Nick met Mallory outside Emil's door. Anita greeted the pair with a smile. "He should be available shortly."

"Thank you, ma'am," responded Nick. With an awkward silence given the two visitors waiting, Nick decided to make more conversation. "Anita, how long have you worked for Weston?"

"Well, longer than I care to admit. I started out as Emil's secretary way back when he was managing sales here. As he got promoted, he asked me to keep working for him. I've been his admin since he became president . . . all told, we've worked together for more than thirty years," she said with a proud smile. "Oh, and I've known this lovely young woman for longer than either of us would care to admit," offered Anita to Nick as she looked at Mallory. "Pretty much watched her grow up," she said wistfully.

"Nick, Anita has kept Emil out of trouble during his time at Weston," commented Mallory. "That should be worth some kind of special award."

"Thanks, Mallory. I'll take it up with him. Good to chat with you both." Then, as if she were cosmically connected to Emil, Anita looked at Mallory and Nick and said, "He's ready for you."

A courtesy knock on the large wooden door was followed by the command from the other side to enter. Emil was bent over his leather-bound journal, writing. He did not look up as Mallory and Nick took their seats across from the CEO, who remained head down for another awkward sixty seconds as the visitors looked at each other. Then, the CEO shut the book. "It must be time for our update."

Gesturing them to the couches, Emil grabbed his coffee. "How are you two getting along?"

It was an interesting question. One that might be subject to great interpretation depending upon who took the bait. Did Emil really care about their relationship, or was it directed toward their investigation? Nick chose the latter. "Fine, sir. We have been making great progress interviewing many of the internal staff members. Also, we've gotten good cooperation from Legal who, on a preliminary basis, does not see a problem with Weston withdrawing from the religious program in the states where we do business. However, we still have several senior staffers to talk with before we start digging into some files."

Emil nodded as Nick spoke and then countered. "I got a complaint about you two yesterday from one Marco Ricci of All-American Brokerage. Nick, he says you told the brokerage that Weston was done working with their firm. Oh, and he also said you physically threatened him, then pushed him up against a wall. He's thinking about suing Weston."

Nick and Mallory sat up a little straighter at this news exchanging glances. Before Nick could reply, Emil continued, "Nick, I don't know what happened yesterday, but I've been around long enough to know there are two sides to every story. Frankly, I wish you would have punched that slippery little bastard. I remember meeting Ricci and wondering how this guy could represent the religious community period. Unfortunately, it took several years to get my answer. It was an expensive one at that. He cost us millions. I told that little son of a bitch he'd better get a good lawyer if he has the balls to sue us." Emil's look had transformed into a smile. "Keep up the great work, you two." And, just like that, they were dismissed.

As Mallory left the office, Nick lingered by the door. "Emil, I need a minute."

"Sure, Nick. What's on your mind?" said the CEO as the door closed.

"Emil, I've got a problem. When we discussed my assignment, you explained that you wanted me to help get Weston out of the religious niche and then determine the factors that led the company to what people have described as the brink of bankruptcy," said Nick, who paused. "You didn't tell me that Tina Matheson, the person who was instrumental to the program, was your daughter. I'm struggling with the idea that you were not forthright about this obvious problem." Nick took a breath after getting the words out, still feeling his blood pressure rising.

Emil remained seated on the couch as Nick sat back down opposite him. "I'm sorry about that, Nick. I truly am. Please don't consider it a breach of trust. When we first spoke about this job, one of your objections was that there were more qualified people to do this. Frankly, there are. I am approached by consultants all the time. And they do serve a purpose. But they essentially parrot back whatever findings the client already knows. They are also in constant selling mode, looking for their next paycheck as well. Finally, every one of the national consultants we could have hired know all about Weston and my daughters. Further, they know Tina in particular and constantly play up to her, thinking she'll be in a place at Weston to dole out more money to them, if they can protect her.

"When Tina first came to Weston, she and I had had a period of estrangement. It followed her mother's death. But of course, long-term Weston employees knew who she was. When asked, Tina told people she'd changed her name to honor her mother, and although I'm sure some found it odd, no one really challenged her on it. But her identity was well-known.

"Nick, as I told you, I need you to get to the root causes of failure here, taking *all* the personalities out of the equation. If Tina is culpable, both the board and I need to know. Your report needs to be above reproach. Frankly, you bring a perspective that I couldn't necessarily get from anyone else. Oh, and I apologize if you think I've deceived you in any way."

Emil's words echoed in Nick's head as he considered the explanation. While Nick still had issues with what Emil had done, the old man's response seemed almost reasonable given the circumstances. He considered a follow-up question about Mallory's story, but decided not to raise it with Emil, at least for now.

Nick rose. "Thank you, sir," he said, shaking Emil's hand.

"Nick, my door is always open to you on any issue," said Emil. Nick made a mental note of Emil's words for future reference.

When he returned to his office, Mallory was waiting for him in one of the side chairs across from his desk. "So, did you and Emil get things straightened out?"

"For now, I guess. He's an interesting guy and seems to be thinking way ahead as I continue to tread water in the corporate world. But I also have to give him credit for having my back on this Ricci thing." As they sat together, Nick noticed a change in Mallory's demeanor and appearance, seeming more confident. *What kind of daddy issues do you have?* he wondered. "What's next on our agenda, Mal?"

"On Monday, we start with Frank Raymond and then interview Tina Matheson. You have the weekend to prep. Do you want to compare notes on Sunday afternoon?"

"Perfect. Why don't you come over at three o'clock? We still have your second bottle of wine to get through, and I grill a great steak."

"I'm in." Before Mallory left the room, Nick received a call from the front desk. Putting it on speaker, Nick answered. "What's up, Cassie?"

"You have a visitor, Nick. I didn't see him listed on your schedule. This gentleman says he would like to come up to your office to talk with you."

"What's his name?" asked a puzzled Nick.

Hearing some inaudible discussion, Cassie replied, "The man's name is Dirk Diggler." Listening to the discussion, Mallory made a face like the name meant something, but couldn't place it.

"What does Mr. Diggler want, in particular?"

After more background chatter, Cassie responded, "He says he's a bill collector. He wants to talk to you about some gambling debts you owe his boss. Oh, and this gentleman says you also owe quite a bit in interest too."

Mallory looked aghast. But Nick shook his head with a smile that now confused Mallory even more. She moved on her chair, literally to the edge of her seat, as Nick continued. "Cassie, can you describe this guy?"

"Nick, it's hard for me to do since he's standing right in front of me and can hear me."

"Okay, Cassie. Let me ask you this. Is he short and stocky with a muscular build?"

"Why, yes. Definitely."

"Can you put this on speaker, so he can hear me?"

"If you want me to, sure." Nick heard a click.

Speaking a bit louder for the benefit of his unknown guest, "Cassie, does this guy have a bunch of low-life tattoos on his arms?"

Cassie hemmed and hawed before answering timidly, "Yes, he has some tattoos."

"Is he a swarthy-looking guy who looks like he doesn't have a pot to piss in?"

Nick could imagine Cassie blanching at hearing the description that was loud enough for the visitor to hear, whether she agreed with his assessment or not.

Not waiting for Cassie's response, Nick finished the call. "Tell Diggler I'm coming down."

Considering the previous day's confrontation with Ricci and after listening to the exchange, Mallory was concerned. "Nick, do you want me to call 911?"

"We won't need to call for an emergency vehicle. Come on along."

When they stepped into the lobby, they both saw a man standing in front of the reception desk, now charming a smiling Cassie. In his late twenties, he had short, brown hair cut with a bleached-blond mohawk. Tanned and muscular, the man had a sleeve of tattoos on each arm and wore a tie-dyed t-shirt, long-cut cargo shorts, and sandals. When he heard the elevator door open, the man turned toward Nick. But before the visitor could react, Nick quickly descended upon him, surprising Mallory and Cassie.

CHAPTER 22

"P-Man!" shouted Nick as he moved across the lobby and put the man in a bear hug, lifting him off the ground.

"Did I get you, Boss?"

"You had me at 'Diggler,'" said Nick. "Why didn't you let me know you were coming?"

The mood for both women lightened considerably given that it was clear the two men knew each other.

"I'm between assignments, and I hate timetables. I thought I'd surprise you when I got to this part of Wisconsin. Boss, it is so good to see you."

Stepping back for a moment, Nick looked at the ladies. "Let me introduce you both to a true warrior and national treasure, Philemon Ignacio Costello IV."

"Please, call me Phil," he said, giving Mallory an unexpected hug.

With a confused look, Cassie responded, "I thought you said your name was Dirk Diggler."

"Only in his dreams, Cassie," interjected Nick. "Dirk Diggler is the name of a character in the movie *Boogie Nights*. A well-endowed porn star. P-Man pulls this kind of crap all the time. I guess I haven't seen him much lately and was a little slow on the uptake."

Mallory jumped into the conversation. "How do you know Phil?"

"He's my best friend. We served in the military together. P-Man is an active PJ."

Mallory stuck out her hand. "Phil, it's an honor to meet you. Nick has told me a little about the PJs and their jobs. Thank you for your service."

Taking her hand, Phil replied very formally, "Ma'am, it is indeed an honor to serve you," which made Mallory blush for some reason.

"Phil, come on up to my office so we can catch up." After getting a badge from Cassie, Mallory, Nick, and Phil jumped on the elevator. "What are you doing in Wisconsin?"

"Boss, you know I'm a surfer. What better time to do this than in the summer?"

"Surfing? In Wisconsin?" asked Nick.

"Windsurfing. Supposed to be quite the rush."

"Wait," exclaimed Mallory. "Your normal job has you jumping out of planes, getting shot at, working in combat zones, and you're looking for a *rush* while on vacation?"

"Yeah. Want to come along?"

"No, thank you. But I think Cassie and her sometimes-boyfriend have all the equipment for windsurfing. You might talk with her later."

"Will do. Thanks."

"I'll leave you boys some time to talk but would love to hear some of your stories later," Mallory said, moving back to her cube.

Phil and Nick went into his office. "God, it is so good to see you, P-Man," Nick said again after closing his door.

Phil lowered his head. "Boss, I'm sorry I couldn't be there for you when your parents passed. You are my only brother. For you to lose your mom and dad was like me losing my parents. I was deployed and couldn't get leave."

"Thanks. You were there in spirit," Nick replied.

After a moment of silence, Phil asked, "What the hell are you doing working for an insurance company, man? Were all the prison guard jobs taken?"

Nick shot back. "What's the story on your hair? Did you lose a bet?" he said, laughing. "Actually, the president of the company was a friend of my parents and a fellow veteran. Suffice it to say he offered me a gig, some serious money, and put me up in a deluxe house. The guy wouldn't take no for an answer, and I wasn't smart enough to wiggle my way out of the offer. Even though you are barely housebroken, you are now an official guest at The Lakehouse until you leave. You'll be impressed."

Phil was half listening to Nick, looking out of the small window alongside the doorframe. "And, the surroundings here seem nice too," he said, peering through the glass at Mallory.

"According to the command structure, she works for me, making her off-limits in my book. But I know she'd like to find a quality guy. You know anyone?"

"Fuck you," Phil replied without missing a beat.

With a gentle knock on the door, Emil Swenson let himself in. "Hello. I understand we have a distinguished visitor here . . ." The words came out of his mouth before he saw Philemon in his beach apparel.

Jumping out from behind his desk, Nick took control. "Sir, I'd like to introduce you to Phil Costello. He's my best friend and an active duty Air Force Pararescueman. Phil, this is Emil Swenson."

Costello straightened up and turned on a huge smile, thrusting his hand toward Swenson. "It is a pleasure to meet you, sir. I understand from your bio that you were a distinguished Navy pilot back in the day."

Nick rolled his eyes. He had seen Phil go into his charmer act previously but was surprised he had done some research about Swenson, and likely the company, before his visit.

Having gotten past Costello's appearance, Emil responded enthusiastically, "Well, I was once. But it is such an honor to have a man of your caliber here at Weston Insurance."

Reaching into a pocket of his cargo shorts, Phil replied, "I have a gift for you, sir," handing it to Swenson. "Knowing your military background, I thought you might appreciate these mission patches. One with the official PJ emblem and motto . . ."

Swenson carefully unwrapped the patches from the tissue as though they were fine china.

"...and a second one says what we do."

Swenson held up a green and black stitched patch to see the likeness of Elvis Presley surrounded by the words, "If He's Out There, We'll Find Him."

Emil let out a belly laugh. "I haven't seen these in years, Phil. Looks like the quality of the mission patches has improved immensely since I was in the service. I understand their significance and can't thank you enough for them." Changing gears, Emil asked, "How long are you in town for, Phil?"

"I'm not sure. But I have a couple of weeks of leave left."

"Well, I would be honored if you would attend our company's summer picnic next week, if you're around. You can bunk in with Nick at The Lakehouse. There should be room for you."

"Thank you, sir. Nick was just telling me about the place you've put him up in. I just might take you up on your invite. When we were deployed in Afghanistan, Nick used to tell stories about how beautiful the Wisconsin summers were. Spending some quality time here is exactly what I need," said Phil with a surreptitious glance out the window.

"Then, by all means, please stay. Why don't you two get out of the office and enjoy the day. My guess is you've had a long week," he said, looking at Nick.

"You're a good guesser, Emil. Thanks."

Swenson disappeared as quickly as he had arrived.

"You still doing that mission patch deal?" asked Nick, turning to Phil.

"Boss, the civilians eat them up like candy. I always have a couple in my pocket, just in case."

"Let's take the CEO up on his offer and get some lunch before he changes his mind," said Nick, grabbing his jacket.

"Okay, but I've got a stop to make before we head out," said Phil.

Leaving Nick's office, Phil made a beeline for Mallory's cube. After getting her attention away from a computer screen, Phil made his move. "Ma'am, looks like I'll be staying here for a while. If I'm not being too forward, I'd like to give you a gift," pulling yet another set of patches from his pocket. "These are mission patches worn by the PJs in the field." He laid them on her desk. "They are a symbol of who we are and what we do. One is from my official unit, but the second made me think of you," he said with a twinkle in his eye.

"Why, thank you, Phil," said Mallory, looking puzzled, yet appreciative.

Nick grabbed Phil, announcing they were leaving for the day. "See you at three on Sunday afternoon. By the way, we'll have a third for drinks and dinner," nodding toward Costello.

After they left, Mallory opened the first tissue-covered package to find a camo-colored patch surrounding the image of an angel with the PJ creed, "That Others May Live," emblazoned beneath. Pulling back the tissue on the second patch, Mallory saw a red cross with a suggestive drawing of a beautiful young woman with the words, "The Louder You Scream, The Faster We Come." Although there was no one around her, Mallory's first reaction was to quickly close the tissue over the top of the patch and look over both shoulders to see if anyone was there. When she knew she was alone, she pulled out the patch a second time, smiled, and quietly exclaimed to herself, "Oh my."

Before Nick and Phil left, they stopped to see Cassie in the front lobby. "Rumor has it you are a windsurfer?" asked Nick.

"I'm a rookie to say the least, Nick. I had a boyfriend who was really into the sport. He's history, but I still have all the gear."

"Great. Any chance you could give Phil here a couple of lessons this weekend? He's a classic surfer dude from way back but has never used the sail before. He's staying with me at The Lakehouse."

The conversation brought a smile to the young woman's face. The prospect of hanging out with a good-looking guy sounded like a deal to her. "Sure. Give me your number, and we'll make it a date," she said, looking up at Phil.

Once the PJs left the building, Cassie dialed the number she had been previously instructed to call. Her call went immediately to voicemail.

After the prompt, Cassie left a message. "Sir, Mr. Hayden has left the office for the weekend and has a friend in town. Also, I'm not going to be making any reports to you. There is something wrong about this. If you want to fire me, go ahead."

CHAPTER 23

It had been an idyllic weekend in Wisconsin with sun. Perfect temperatures and enough air to make it exciting for the windsurfers. Mallory arrived at The Lakehouse on Sunday to prep with Nick for their interviews the following day. Dressed in a turquoise caftan with sandals and her hair pulled back into a ponytail, Mallory held her briefcase in one hand while juggling a bottle of red wine under her other arm. As Nick met her in the foyer, she presented him with the bottle. "Reinforcements," she said, moving past Nick into the great room. She found Phil and Cassie sunburned and unconscious on separate couches.

"Looks like I missed quite the party," said Mallory quietly, looking suspiciously at Phil as she passed through the room into the kitchen.

"Hardly," replied Nick. "They've been out on the lake for two solid days enjoying the weather. They came back to the house periodically for food and beer, but my guess is they are both worn out."

"Why is Cassie here?"

"You told me she had the windsurfing equipment, and I asked. P-Man wanted to give it a try. Cassie was more than happy to give him some lessons."

"I'll bet," responded Mallory with a sound of disgust, looking back into the other room.

"Is something wrong? What's going on?" asked Nick.

"Can we talk privately?"

Stepping out onto the deck, Nick closed the sliding glass door behind him. "What's up?" he asked.

"Nick, can I ask you about Philemon?" said Mallory.

"Sure."

"It's just . . . uh, what kind of man is Phil?"

"What do you mean?"

"Well, on Friday, before you left the office together, Phil came out to my cube, and we had a short conversation. He told me he was going to be in the area for some time, and I felt like . . . we made a connection of sorts. He sounds like an interesting guy; someone I'd like to find out more about. Then, two days later, I find him hanging out with another woman."

"Yeah, and now they're sleeping together," chimed in Nick.

"Shut up. I don't think that's funny at all," replied Mallory.

"Mal, lighten up. Like I told you, I was doing Phil a favor by setting him up to learn windsurfing from a local. There's nothing going on between them. Cassie is cute, but Phil is a stand-up guy. While he puts on quite the act, he's not into carving notches into a bedpost. In fact, with his job, my impression is he's not looking for any complications in his life right now either. But, not telling tales out of school, Phil did ask me about you and your situation."

"What did you tell him?" asked Mallory.

"I said you were a recovering lesbian."

"You did not," said Mallory loudly, her eyes widening in horror.

On cue, the sliding door opened to a shirtless Phil holding a cold beer. "Hey, Mallory. What's going on, Boss?" he said groggily.

"Just business talk," replied Nick. "We have some interesting interviews coming up this week with our little project, and we needed some time to prep. Where's Cassie?"

"She just left," said Phil. "I think she was as wiped out as I am." Then, looking at Mallory. "Thanks for making the suggestion about the sailboards. It sounds like Cassie just went through quite a breakup. She's a sweet kid. Spending some time on the water was good for both of us. Man, it was as much fun as anything I've done on the ocean."

Mallory responded with a convincing, "You're welcome."

"Well, I'll let you to get back to work. I need to take a shower. What time is dinner?"

"Work takes as much time as you allot for it," replied Nick, declaring that cocktails would begin in a half hour with dinner to follow whenever they got around to it. With that, Phil disappeared back into the house.

"I've read all the material you provided to me about Frank and Tina, and I think I'm ready. What are you anticipating?" asked Nick, looking at Mallory and half waiting for another unknown bomb to drop.

"As I said, Frank's an odd duck. A vocal person who wanted Weston to leave the religious niche. The only pushback you might get is when we ask to review some of the claim files. My advice is if he comes on too strong, find some potential malady you might exploit. He's a hypochondriac. He'll put distance between himself and any suspected microbes."

Nick made a mental note. "I'm glad you aren't interviewing me. Any insights about your weird family dynamic and/or Tina, beyond what the files and everyone says?"

"Frankly, Nick, I'm not sure what you're going to get from Tina aside from a lot of attitude. She is not worried about her job. In fact, I'd say she thinks she is on a track to become the next CEO at Weston Insurance once Emil steps down."

"After you left the meeting on Friday, Emil gave me his reasoning for holding back on telling me about his relationship with Tina. His reasoning made sense, saying he didn't want a consultant to be potentially influenced by Tina, who you've said is on the fast track to the corner office. But, since I don't know how the family tree intertwines with the religious institution mess, you need to fill in the blanks for me. Oh, and by the way, you promised a backstory before the interview with her."

Nick had her cornered, and he could see from her expression that telling the story would not be much fun. "Can I get you something to drink?"

"Oh, yeah," replied Mallory.

After returning with two beers, Nick sat on a chair opposite Mallory. After taking a long draw, Mallory took a deep breath. "As I understand it, Emil found his way to Weston after serving his country; he and Clara had been married before Emil joined the Navy. After he was discharged, they settled in the area and put down some roots. Emil was a top-notch salesperson, and it wasn't long before he and Clara became the 'it' couple in town. They hosted big dinner parties and became connected with several charitable organizations."

Mallory took another sip of her beer. "A couple of years later, they had their first child, Tina. Life was great for about six months until Clara was diagnosed with ovarian cancer. You can only imagine what it must have been like. A successful family being dealt such a blow. Anyway, Clara went through extensive treatments and was quite sick for months. None of the doctors were sure if Clara would live or die. During Clara's treatment, she and Emil became close to one of her primary doctors, a young resident. In fact, at the depths of Clara's chemotherapy, Emil became too close to the doctor and became involved with her."

Nick was transfixed by Mallory's story. "How close?" he managed to say.

"Let's just say close enough that the relationship resulted in the birth of a girl . . . me." Mallory finished her beer and got up to get another round. Nick noticed she stood at the refrigerator door for a full minute.

When she returned, Mallory continued without a missing a beat. "The doctor, who was my birth mother, had absolutely no interest in me. I'm not sure how much credit is due Emil, given the circumstances, but I understand he sent her a big check essentially to leave, surrendering any legal rights to me. Basically, go away and never come back . . . which she did. I have no idea who the woman was, whether she's alive or dead, and I don't care to know. Anyway, Clara recovered from her cancer. However, even though she survived, the treatment she received basically made it impossible for her to have any more children. Clara was left with the mess caused by Emil and in a quandary: split up the family or accept that Emil had another daughter. I don't know if the fact she was sterile entered the equation or not as she thought through her options. In the end, they agreed to keep me, raising both of us as their daughters."

"Wow, Emil must have been a helluva salesman," commented Nick.

"Right. I can't imagine putting myself in Clara's shoes. Going through a terrible battle with cancer and then finding out my husband had a child with the doctor who got me through the process? I'm not sure I would have been so forgiving. But she was smart. She knew that people would wonder about my existence when she was so sick, so she went away at the end of her treatments, and when she came back . . . there I was. I look enough like Emil so that no one doubts my paternity, and if anyone questioned my maternity, well, Clara accepted me and raised me as her own. No one who saw her with me ever doubted that. Including me. She was the only mother I ever had. Tina and I grew up as sisters never really knowing the full story. We were very close and did everything together since we're only about a year apart in age."

Mallory stood up from the chair and moved toward the railing of the deck, facing away from Nick as if foreshadowing the next chapter of the story. "Twenty years later, Clara was diagnosed with breast cancer, a very aggressive type. There was nothing anyone could do. She died within six months." Mallory's voice began to crack. "Our whole world crashed. During the grieving process, Emil had too much to drink one night. He told Tina and me the entire story about his affair with the doctor. Even though Tina and I were innocent bystanders, everything changed between us in an instant. Tina moved out of the house and legally changed her name to Matheson, Mom's maiden name. When she left, she told me she couldn't be around me anymore, since I would be a constant reminder of her father's infidelity."

Nick felt compelled to stand and comfort Mallory, who was now sobbing and shaking. Nick held Mallory for a full minute until she calmed down.

"Mal, I'm so sorry."

"Nick, it felt like I lost everything at that point. My mother and my sister. Tina left for college. I chose to stay home close to Emil and go to work at Weston. I skipped college. Never really did anything to pursue a career. Partied too hard with the local crowd for my own good. But Emil has always taken care of me, probably overpaid me, turned a blind eye toward my expenses, which are more than I make, and bought me the house next door. He is my father, and I love him. The weird thing is Tina eventually returned to Weston to work and reconciled with Emil. But our relationship has never been the same. My observation is Tina would do just about anything to gain his approval. I just don't get it."

"Thanks for the heads-up," replied Nick.

The sliding door opened. Phil emerged wearing a fresh t-shirt and clean shorts, holding a beer. "Were you able to get your business wrapped up?"

"Oh yes. And then some," Nick responded. "I need to do some food prep before firing up the grill. Just sit tight while I go to work," he said, stepping inside, leaving Mallory and Phil alone on the deck. Of course, he could still hear them.

They each took a chair, taking in the view in what ultimately became an awkward silence. After several minutes, Phil finally spoke up. "Are you alright, Mallory?"

"I'm fine. Just lost in thought about these meetings, I guess," she replied unconvincingly.

"Mallory, I just got a sense that something is wrong. I hope I haven't done anything to upset you." Then followed another thirty-second break in the conversation.

"Oh God, no, Phil, you haven't," said Mallory, turning towards him.

"It's just I don't meet a lot of interesting professional women like you. You make me a little nervous, to be honest."

"Nervous. Seriously. Nick told me about what you guys do for a living. It scared me just to hear about your work," said Mallory. "Why would I make you nervous?"

"Let me rephrase. I generally don't meet professional women who are confident, smart, and beautiful," replied Philemon. "Can I get you something to drink?"

"Sure, I'll have a beer with you," she replied.

"Great. I'm on it," said Phil, springing from his chair. As he walked behind her towards the door, his hand gently brushed her hair on the way. She sat back in her chair to bask in the sun with a broad smile on her face.

CHAPTER 24

Nick was the first arrival to the conference room early Monday morning. With a bagel in one hand and his Starbucks in the other, he was catching up on current events online when Mallory appeared in the doorway.

"Nick, something's happened that you should be aware of. The police chief on Mackinac Island released some details of a murder that recently occurred there involving a Barry Hargreaves."

"Okay. So why do I care?"

"This Chief Hutchins said Hargreaves was shot in the last week. There was a delay in announcing the murder since the victim was using an assumed name. Hargreaves was actually named Lonnie D. Palmer. That name popped up in my Google Alerts this morning. I set it up to see if any of the questionable people who were involved with the religious program ever showed up in any new ventures. Weston covered Palmer's ranch in Willow City, Texas. A wide spot in the road in the Hill Country near San Antonio. Palmer had a church camp for at-risk kids," explained Mallory.

"Sounds like a noble cause," replied Nick.

"Yeah, it was, until some of the campers were severely injured and arguably tortured at the ranch. Then, several kids died. We paid millions on behalf of Pastor Lonnie. Another risk courtesy of Marco Ricci."

"Our favorite asshole," replied Nick. "Why would Palmer leave Texas, adopt a new identity, and go to Mackinac Island unless he had a reason to hide from someone?"

"Good question. Who knows?" said Mallory.

"Maybe we can have Mr. Raymond comment during our meeting?"

At that point, the gruff voice of Frank Raymond, Vice President of Claims, boomed from around the corner and unseen to Nick. "Comment on what?" he said brusquely as he appeared at the conference room door.

"About a guy named Lonnie D. Palmer. By the way, I'm Nick Hayden."

"A Christian fucker . . . him, not you," retorted Raymond. "A pleasure to meet you. Call me Frank. Good morning, Mallory," he said, entering the room.

"Well, Frank, apparently someone didn't like him very much and ended up killing him on Mackinac Island. We don't know too much more than what Mal was able to find on Google, but he had changed his name to Barry Hargreaves."

"The world is now a better place," said Raymond coldly. The slightly built man was in his fifties. Standing just under six feet tall with dark hair parted to one side, he wore tortoise shell glasses. Raymond was dressed in a dark three-piece suit, albeit one that seemed at least a size too large for him, a black shirt, and contrasting tie. He sat in the chair opposite Mallory but was clearly focused on Nick. "Let me give you the story on Palmer," launching into a monologue.

"Lonnie D. Palmer was pretty much a vagabond preacher moving from town to town in Texas. A failed evangelical pastor who was determined to build a church and deliver the word of God to sinners in the wilderness. Physically, he looked like kind of a milquetoast. Average build, probably in his early forties. Really nothing special about the guy except when he spoke. Then he became larger than life with a booming voice and a big personality. He was incredibly well-read too. Turns out he was a no-nonsense fire and brimstone preacher with the unique ability to quote passages of the Bible with equal aplomb as the Second Amendment of the United States Constitution, which protects his gun rights. However, for whatever reason, Palmer never connected with the locals. His church opened and closed in record time. As he was about to leave Willow City, a long-lost uncle died, bequeathing Pastor Lonnie a huge ranch. One hundred and fifty acres, complete with a small home and several outbuildings. Pastor Lonnie said during the depositions it was a sure sign from above that he should change his mission in life. He founded Palmer Ranch to do the work of the Lord by helping those less fortunate."

"Depositions? Sounds like the story gets better?" commented Nick.

"Just wait," said Raymond. "Anyway, Pastor Lonnie didn't have any money to fix up the ranch, so he went on a fundraising tour of the local towns. After not getting the results he wanted, he decided to go after the bigger charity dollars in San Antonio and Houston. Palmer quickly figured out that people with serious money just lying around were more willing to part with it if the welfare of children was involved. So, Palmer decided his ranch would be to provide the word of God to inner-city, underprivileged youth.

"This guy was the consummate hustler. Pastor Lonnie preyed upon local contractors for free carpentry and plumbing to make the outbuildings into livable dormitories for his kids. Somehow, he found a local vendor to provide a never-ending supply of food for the campers. Whatever was needed to improve the quality of the ranch, Pastor Lonnie played upon the heartstrings of whoever had what the Lord required to make the ranch a success. Air conditioners for the dorms. All-terrain vehicles for use on the ranch. Buses to transport the kids. Even cattle were donated to add to the experience, under the guise of teaching the campers responsibility. You name it. Everything provided at no cost to Palmer Ranch.

"For several years, Palmer Ranch ran like a well-oiled machine and did some good things. The ranch was viewed as the model for helping at-risk urban youth. But, after a couple of years, there were rumors of mental and physical abuse of campers by the counselors, once 'problem children' themselves," said Raymond, using his fingers to make air quotes.

"At first, an ambulance would show up at Palmer Ranch intermittently, but soon began making regular visits. In one instance, a camper needed treatment for heat exhaustion because they had worked him too hard, according to the internal report. It was considered a simple mistake: the camper's work had not been monitored closely enough. Then a camper died of heatstroke resulting from a punishment. Shortly thereafter, an emergency vehicle took a third child to the hospital with multiple broken bones, including a skull fracture. And then the claims started to roll in big time."

As Raymond told the story, Nick and Mallory were now paying close attention to every word.

"The funny thing though is there were no investigations of any kind by any agency. No criminal complaints or charges brought by local law enforcement. Nothing. Whenever he was questioned by the powers that be, Pastor Lonnie was always highly cooperative, pointing out these rare incidents should not overshadow the good work being done at Palmer Ranch.

"At some point, a reporter from a local San Antonio television station took it upon herself to investigate Palmer Ranch after hearing about the injuries and deaths there. After she talked with the leaders from several area youth clubs and social service agencies, the journalist tracked down a number of former Palmer campers from the greater metro area. The stories were consistent. Essentially, a gang mentality raged inside the ranch with the leaders from competing local factions serving as both counselors for the camp and as recruiters for when the campers returned to the real world. Those who resisted were beaten, tortured, or raped. One of the principal means of control by the 'counselors' was the use of a hot box, constructed of wood and corrugated metal. Those who were deemed unruly were placed in what became known as 'the strongbox' and denied water until they repented for their sins.

"A full week-long exposé by the TV station highlighted the injuries and deaths of the campers. The series portrayed the deplorable conditions of the food prep areas, the lack of maintenance of the donated materials, and pointed out how the air conditioners in the barracks had failed long ago. Drug use was also rampant with low-level traffickers operating out of the ranch. The final evening of the series depicted Pastor Lonnie as a hands-off leader who was more interested in accepting monetary donations for his personal use. The funds, it was revealed, were channeled into a collection of luxury vehicles, updates of the ranch house, and a staff comprised of a security chief, a maid, and Palmer's personal chef.

"Public outrage followed with a swift demand for a criminal investigation into Palmer Ranch, Pastor Lonnie, and the deaths and injuries. The press vilified Palmer as a money-grubbing and uncaring clergyman. Pastor Lonnie remained steadfast, responding he had taken in tough and difficult kids off the streets with a laundry list of problems. He was doing the best he could to reform them, pointing out there were few, if any, similar ministries willing to do this kind of work. Pastor Lonnie was quoted as saying these kinds of kids could only be saved by 'tough love' and the Bible. Yet, he acknowledged his failure in this noble effort and his loss of control of the ranch where the inmates were now running the asylum. Pastor Lonnie's parting shot was that he was appalled by the level of violence perpetrated by a few campers and then revealed he himself was scared to death, afraid to leave the confines of his personal home. Pastor Lonnie tried to turn himself into a victim.

"The local prosecutors conducted their own probe, but after several months called it inconclusive. Yet, with an upcoming election, the district attorney chose to press charges against Palmer for the misuse of charitable funds and negligent homicide for his role in the deaths of two campers. The pastor retained a well-known defense attorney to represent him at trial. Given he'd stolen so many of the donations, he could afford a big-time attorney and all the justice money can buy. In the end, after months of legal wrangling, depositions, motions upon motions, and strong testimony, a jury of his peers could not convict Palmer beyond a reasonable doubt on any count. Pastor Lonnie was a free man.

"Seriously?" questioned Nick.

"But Palmer had lost in the court of public opinion. Then the real vultures were out. Several members of the local plaintiff's bar actively recruited former campers who might be able to lead the lawyers to Pastor Lonnie's money. Civil suits began to pile up, seeking extraordinary damage amounts. However, Pastor Lonnie had learned how to play the game too. He tendered defense of these claims to us, demanding that Weston protect him and pay for his four-hundred-dollar-an-hour attorney. We had some reports that Pastor Lonnie had moved significant amounts of cash to offshore accounts just in case he lost in court. Finally, the asshole filed for bankruptcy, declaring he had poured everything he owned into Palmer Ranch and was now destitute. He even petitioned the court that his homestead, Palmer Ranch, be excused from his list of assets.

"With no money beyond the insurance limits available for settlement, all the attorneys went to their clients, urging them to take whatever they could get from Weston, minus their share of course, before it dwindled to nothing. All told, Weston got stuck for $3 million in exchange for full releases. I can't even begin to tell you how much the defense costs were, but they approached roughly another million.

"After we settled all the claims, Palmer Ranch mysteriously burned to the ground. We wrote Pastor Lonnie another check for a million. Then, he dropped off the face of the earth. Gone . . . at least until today. Anyway, it's just another beautiful chapter in the religious book of business," he said disgustedly, wringing his hands and taking a deep breath. "Do the police have any suspects in the shooting?"

"Not that we know of, sir," replied Nick.

"Well, there is a long list of suspects they can run down. But enough with Palmer and claims war stories. He got what he deserved. What can I do for you today, Nick?"

"Sir, I've been charged by Emil Swenson to look into Weston's religious program and build an exit strategy for the company. I've got a pretty good perspective from the underwriting staff and Legal about how the company got into trouble with this program, but I'd like to add your perspective to our after-action report."

"Exit strategy? Well, it's about damn time. After-action report? Sounds like words from a military man. Did you serve, Hayden?"

"Fresh from my discharge from the Air Force," said Nick.

"Chair Force, huh?" said Raymond, chuckling. "I was a ground pounder in the Army before finding my way to Weston. What did you do?"

"I was a pararescueman."

"Damn, Special Forces. You must be one serious customer, son. Let me shake your hand for all the work you and the PJs did for our brothers and sisters over the years. It is truly a pleasure to meet you."

"Thank you for your service as well. Mr. Raymond . . ."

"Please call me Frank."

Nick smiled at Mallory, who returned the grin, recognizing that her strategy to insert his military service into the conversation had worked.

"Alright, Frank. Give me your perspective about the religious program."

"Well, Nick, I think I just told you. For me, it was hot garbage from the get-go. At first, we seemed to get the garden variety type of claims, old people slipping and falling at the church, wind claims on steeples, food poisoning from spoiled potato salad at church picnics . . . that type of thing. It wasn't long though before the claims seemed to get nastier, involving all sorts of deviants with kids, women . . . other men. Then we had some serious injuries from activities that were questionable as to whether they should have even been part of a church. We were covering zip line courses, ATVs . . . things we knew little about. We insured arsonists, gangbangers who were dealing drugs out of the back door, every type of scum like our buddy Palmer. Just unbelievable."

"Frank, how did this happen?"

"I'm sure we went into the market with the best of intentions, but we got greedy. The quick and dirty answer is we chose brokers who led us to slaughter, but we weren't smart enough to see it."

"How would you assess Christina Matheson's role in this program?"

Frank paused, shifting in his chair, choosing his words carefully.

"Listen, Tina is a smart young woman. A true leader in this organization. If anything, I would guess she must have been misled by some of the brokers. Perhaps she did not control her underwriters carefully enough."

Both Mallory and Nick could detect a notable softening in Frank's responses about the program when Tina's name surfaced.

"This was Tina's first big deal for Weston. I can't hold that against her. She's a good kid. At this point, I believe she would do almost anything to clean up this mess, especially for her father who's had quite the track record of success."

"Frank, I was led to believe you were very critical of this whole program. Is that correct?"

Frank thought carefully. "Any criticism was not in taking the risk with entering the program. It's not about personalities. I was most critical of leadership for not getting us out of this business sooner. I think I made that plain to Emil, if that's what you're getting at. We had some knock-down drag-out fights in his office about this mess. But I felt it was part of my job to speak up." Throughout his answers, Frank remained remarkably calm. For whatever reason, Nick had expected more in the way of fireworks when he pressed the Vice President of Claims.

"One final question, Frank. Do you have any problem with Mallory and me going through some of the claim files to see what we can learn?"

Frank paused ever so briefly before responding. "No. Help yourself. I believe Mallory knows how to access them through the system. I'll provide you both with the necessary passcodes. Have fun. When you get a firsthand look at what came across my desk, it will make your skin crawl."

"Thanks, Frank, we really appreciate it."

As he was leaving, Frank stopped and looked at Nick and Mallory. "Hey, if you are both free, I'm having a small cookout at my farm this week. Also, I understand you have a buddy staying with you . . . Titus?"

"Philemon," both Mallory and Nick chimed back in sync.

"At least I got the testament right. Bring him along. Dress casually."

"What do you think, Nick?" asked Mallory after Frank left the room.

"I think you nailed your assessment of the man. It fits with everything else we've heard over the last week or so. He seems like one pissed off customer. Maybe even not so much about the program, but at life in general. Question. How would Frank have known about Phil being in town?"

"I already told you, Nick. It's a small town," offered Mallory. "I noticed you chose not to tweak his hypochondria."

"Timing is everything, Mal. I'll keep that in my back pocket for the time being."

CHAPTER 25

The table was now set for Christina Matheson's interview. Nick was not sure what to expect. For the most part, Weston's employees were concerned, but cooperative in providing details about how the religious program had gone so wrong. Even Frank Raymond had been helpful in painting the larger picture. It was also clear to Nick that Mallory had put him into a position to succeed in this assignment. But even though he had prepared for these interviews, he still considered himself a fraud. *Him, taking on the cornerstone interview of his investigation with little insurance knowledge. Outgunned and feeling at a distinct disadvantage, despite Mallory's help. Shit.*

Nick felt no better when Tina glided confidently into the conference room. Wearing a cream-colored business suit jacket, matching skirt, and high heels, she was the epitome of professionalism. In her early thirties, Tina was also beautiful, with carved features, deep blue eyes, and the high cheekbones of a model. Her hair was a tussle of varying shades of sun-bleached blonde set off against her lightly tanned skin. Nick judged her to be roughly five feet, two inches tall, accounting for her heels, but her lithe, athletic body gave her the appearance of being taller. She made herself comfortable in the chair at the end of the table, crossed her legs, and smiled as Nick, who was somewhat flustered, tried to organize his materials. Tina gave an indistinct nod to Mallory while waiting for Nick to begin the conversation.

"Err . . . Christina Matheson, I'm Nick Hayden, and I'm here . . ."

Matheson's demeanor changed instantly, cutting him off. "I know who you are and why you're here. Everyone at Weston does. You're a muckraker asking questions about our religious institution program."

"Not exactly. Emil Swenson, your father . . ." Nick said for emphasis, ". . . has asked Mallory and me to complete a review of the program to determine what went wrong."

"Who said there is something wrong with the program?"

"Pretty much everyone, Christina. Apparently, the board recognizes the issues, senior management, including Emil, your general counsel, and even Mr. Raymond. The underwriting team is scared to death they are going to lose their jobs. As it's been explained to me, the results of this program potentially threaten the core financial base of Weston Insurance in its entirety."

Matheson sat still, staring at the wall for an extended time without responding. Nick and Mallory politely waited, giving Tina time to gather her thoughts. After the silence became uncomfortable, Nick spoke up.

"Christina?" asked Nick. "Christina, are you feeling alright?"

"I'm fine," she responded brusquely, coming out of her trance-like state. "You are trying to assign blame, laying these results at my feet in an attempt to destroy my career."

"No, that's not the case at all. In fact, the employees here have talked about the need for risk-taking and your level of professionalism. We are simply trying to understand what lessons could be learned from what took place so they aren't repeated by Weston in the future. However, as we understand it, you were responsible for conceiving and developing this program, were you not?"

"Yes."

"Based upon what you know now, what might have been done differently?" asked Nick.

Tina drifted off again, lost in an extended stare at the wall behind Nick. A dead gaze held long enough to make him turn around to see what had caught her attention. But there was only a beige wall behind him. After another long, awkward silence, Nick tried to get the woman's attention once more, using her less formal name to draw a reaction. "Tina?" After a short pause, Nick tried again with more volume. "Tina?"

"I'm sorry. You were saying?" she asked, rejoining the conversation.

"Tina, are you feeling alright?"

"Are you a doctor, Mr. Hayden?"

"No, I'm not, ma'am."

"Well, there you are. I've never felt better, but I've had enough of this witch hunt." Tina stood to leave the room before a stunned Nick could get out of his chair.

Then, gathering himself quickly, he let out a loud growl. "Sit the fuck down, Tina!"

Stunned by the demand, Tina actually retook her chair. Mallory remained in her chair, looking like a statue, unmoving while watching what was taking place.

"Listen, Tina, we're here to do a job on behalf of the board and the CEO," said Nick in a steady, but relentless tone. "We are looking for answers to legitimate questions about the religious program . . . your program. Now, I suspect most people at Weston are less than direct with you. But my take on this mess is that you've totally fucked this program up and are scared to death about what our findings will tell the board. You know, the people that will decide whether a manager like you stays or goes. My advice is to quit being some CEO demon princess wannabe and cooperate with the investigation if you want your opinion represented in our report."

When Nick ended his soliloquy, the conference room was dead silent. But Nick was in a stare-down with Tina, never having lost eye contact with her, until she blinked. Mallory had not dared to move during Nick's speech, melting into the wall. Then, Tina rose calmly from her chair.

"I'm sorry, Mr. Hayden. You're right . . . most be people here do not talk to me as directly as you have. May I have some time to rethink this before you write your final report?" she replied calmly.

"We've got some time before we conclude our findings. Can we get together again in the next week?"

"Sure. And thank you," said Tina as she left the room.

After closing the door, Nick looked at Mallory. "Any idea about what's going on with your sister?"

"Hell no . . ." she said.

"Is Tina a healthy person?"

"Tina can be aloof, a bitch, and look like she's bored or unengaged with a conversation. I'm not sure what was on her mind today. My impression is that she's fine health-wise, but remember, we don't talk."

"She just seemed lost during the conversation, like she had checked out for a minute or two at a time. When she went blank, something from my military training clicked, but I can't recall exactly what. Could the religious program and the poor results be causing her that much stress?"

"I have no idea, but something's not right. Oh, and by the way, Tina happens to be a master manipulator, so maybe she was just playing games today," said Mallory disgustedly. "Either way, that little session was a waste of our time. I was hoping for some insights from the person responsible for this problem."

"Keep Tina on your short list of people to reinterview." *At a minimum, I can stare into those blue eyes again,* thought Nick. "At any rate, we do have some solid themes emerging about the program. Let's take Frank up on getting our passcodes so we can dig into some of the claim files."

Although Frank provided Mallory and Nick with the appropriate log-ins to enter the claim system, it was not user-friendly or intuitive. Even Mallory, who was considered a wizard of Weston systems, was stymied. After several hours of frustration to access any information, Nick dialed Frank's extension to get some help.

"Nick, I apologize for the system problems. We work with an antiquated database, and we have absolutely zero confidence in the outputs. The staff here muddles through, but the fact of the matter is our technology is poor and unreliable. We are forced to keep a hard copy paper file for every claim so we can work on it when the system crashes . . . a weekly occurrence. I've bitched about this to Emil for years without success and been told we don't have the resources to get the system replaced."

"Frank, thanks for your honesty about the system problem. But Mal and I really need to go through the files to get a sense of what has taken place over the years. Is there anyone you could send over to our conference room to give us a tutorial?"

"Nick, we just don't have anyone we can spare. However, if you would mention this issue in your report to Emil and the board, I might be able to come up with a solution for you by tomorrow morning."

"Okay." As Nick put the receiver back on the phone box, he looked at Mallory. "Is it just convenient no one outside of the claims department can access or work in their system?"

"What do you mean, like they are trying to hide something? The claims processing system has been an issue for Weston for years."

"I don't know. I may be suspicious for no reason. Raymond said he hoped to have an answer for us by the morning. Looks like we're at an impasse. What exactly are you expecting when we go to Frank's house for dinner this week?"

"Who knows? I've never been invited before. But it should be interesting to say the least."

CHAPTER 26

Early the following morning, Nick walked through the darkened lobby, still contemplating the claim file issue, and spotted a dozen roses waiting for Cassie at her workstation, courtesy of Phil according to the large card. Nick arrived at their conference room hoping Raymond had come through with a solution to the problem. *Be careful of what you wish for.* Flipping on the lights, Nick found hundreds of thick paper files laying in deep piles around the room, stacked on the floor and the conference table. In the middle of the table, Nick saw an envelope on top of a shallow white box. Putting down his morning coffee, he opened the note. "Sorry for the mess, but here are all the religious program claim files and a dozen donuts. See you at the farm tonight." The note had been signed by Frank.

"Fucking A," said Nick to no one in particular. Opening the white box, he sat down in one of the leather chairs and began to eat a cream-filled Long John.

Seeing the light on, Mallory entered the room with a "Good morn…" before stopping in her tracks when she saw the stacks of files. "What the hell is this?"

"Frank's fix to our file review problem. I've seen cleaner rooms on *Hoarders*. Have a donut before the rats get them," replied Nick, gesturing towards the box. "At least they're tasty."

Searching through the mountain of files, Mallory could find no semblance of order in how they were arranged. "I'm not sure how we do any data mining with what we have. At least there are names on the file jackets, along with the claim and policy numbers."

"Well, considering I'm not sure what we're looking for anyway, I continue to get more suspicious of Frank the more 'helpful' he becomes. He's delivered all the files we've asked for. But without a way to sift through them all and make any sense of the details, we might be here for years."

"Not to mention death by a thousand paper cuts."

"It's almost as if he's intentionally overloaded us with information to obscure what might be relevant. Mallory, when you talked about reviewing the files, did you have an approach in mind?"

Moving a stack of files from a chair, Mallory took a donut and sat down. Deep in thought for several minutes, she finally replied, "I don't think we ever intended to look at every file. We could see the bigger picture with some statistics that are readily available. Thinking about it, you should call your newest, bestest, football buddy—Mr. Woods. He provides a list of complex files and those with high projected payouts to the board each quarter. That would be my starting point. Can you see if he will meet us for lunch today?"

"That's genius, Mallory. At least for now."

****

Jonathan Woods was thrilled to get a call from Nick inviting him to lunch. In fact, he cleared his calendar of meetings for several hours after noon, just in case lunch ran long. They agreed to meet at a sports bar called The Office, not far from Weston's building. The Office was nothing more than a large pole building with a stylish circular metal bar sitting underneath a bank of flatscreen televisions, allowing patrons to watch whatever game was on at the time. Decorated primarily in Wisconsin Badger red and white, the room contained framed jerseys and signed sports memorabilia, along with football helmets representing all the local high schools. Beyond the bar were rows of high-boy tables and booths all strategically placed near more television screens.

Jon arrived early, chose a booth, and had been served an iced tea by a cute dark-haired girl wearing cut-off shorts, a baseball cap, and a referee's jersey. Nick and Mallory stepped from the light into the darkened pub, letting their eyes adjust until they spotted Woods.

"Hi, Jon. Thanks for making time for us today," said Nick.

Although he wasn't sure what Mallory was doing in tow, Jon was nonetheless pleased to see Nick. "Hey, Nick. Hello, Mallory," he said as a polite afterthought. Jon was dressed impeccably, sporting a maize and blue tie, apparently in honor of Nick's alma mater.

"This is quite the place. I'll have to put it on my short list for football season," observed Nick.

"You're right. Even though you might not believe it, I come here to watch Badger games with some old Madison buddies from time to time. They have about a hundred beers on tap and some great burgers and wings," recommended Jon.

Mallory studied Jon carefully. Based on everything she knew about the man, he didn't look like a wings kind of guy to her. Their waitress took drink orders from Mallory and Nick and disappeared.

"What can I help you with?" asked Jon.

"First of all, we both want to thank you and your team for the prompt legal opinions that chart the course for Weston to leave the religious market. I can only imagine how many strings you had to pull to get us that material so quickly."

"No problem," responded Jon, taking a sip of his tea.

"At our meeting, you recommended we look through some of the claims files to get a better sense of what had taken place with the program. Well, we got hard copy files today . . . enough to stack up to the ceiling in this place," he said, looking up. "Rather than plow through every file, Mallory suggested you might be able to provide us with a list of large loss closed and pending files you share with the board."

Jon reached in his pocket and took out his phone, tapping in a number. "Marcy, can you email a copy of the large loss list from the religious institution program to Nick Hayden and Mallory Swenson ASAP for me? Thanks, Marce.

"You're all set. My admin should have it on your laptop by the time you get back to the office. It's in an Excel format, so you can manipulate the data any way you need to."

"Impressive. We really appreciate it, Jon."

The ref returned to take their food orders. "Don't you dare order the salad here," Nick joked, looking at Mallory. When the server left, Jon looked at Nick. "Can I ask you a question?"

"Sure," replied Nick.

"What's it like to run down the tunnel at the beginning of a Big 10 football game with one hundred thousand fans screaming at the top of their lungs?"

"Jon, you can't even imagine," replied Nick. He went onto describe the feeling for Woods and answer another hour's worth of football questions as Mallory sat silently eating her wings. While he spoke, Nick wondered if she was really a wings kind of girl.

CHAPTER 27

Mallory arrived at The Lakehouse promptly at five o'clock to pick up Nick and Phil. "Gentlemen," she greeted them as they jumped in the Jeep. "I think I know where I'm going, but if not, you're my navigator tonight, Nick."

Phil immediately noticed Mallory was smartly dressed, wearing a white and blue striped sundress and sandals. "Hey, Boss, do I look good enough for this corporate gig tonight?" asked Phil.

"What, is that a clean pair of cargo shorts? You've been wearing the same outfit since you got here," said Nick.

"Bullshit. These are camo shorts, in case you didn't notice. I've been wearing the beige ones all week. Plus, I'm on vacation."

"Well, the button-down peach shirt is a nice change. Do they make those for men, too?"

"The shirt is salmon-colored, dickhead. Are you representing some People's Republic in your plain blue shirt, or was your blue blazer at the cleaners?"

Listening to the back and forth, Mallory entered the conversation. "Girls, you both look very nice."

"Why, thank you, Mallory," answered Phil, ending the tête-à-tête until she located Frank's property. "This doesn't look like a farm to me. I don't see any cows," said Phil as they drove up the long gravel-covered road to the house.

"I think Frank just calls it a farm since he has forty acres of land," replied Mallory. "He's never been married. My guess is his home will be impressive."

"I take it you and Frank don't get together for drinks regularly?" asked Nick.

"Not on a bet," she said as the vehicle came to a stop in a makeshift parking lot near the front entrance.

Phil saw a variety of late-model Mercedes, Porsches, and BMWs already parked. "Last time I was at a party like this, I was the one parking the cars."

"The night's not over, P-Man," replied Nick, getting out of the Jeep.

After ringing the doorbell in the large stone entranceway, Frank greeted them wearing a casual long-sleeve button-down shirt and a pair of jeans while holding a drink. "Mallory, Nick, Malachi."

"Philemon, sir," Phil corrected his host while sticking out his hand in introduction. "Thank you for the invitation."

"Damn, I'm sorry. I'll get your name right eventually. Nice tangerine shirt, Philemon," he said as he turned to lead them through the house to the kitchen where all the activity was.

"I noticed he didn't confuse your name with any saints," Nick whispered to Phil.

As they followed Frank through the house, it turned out Mallory was right again. It was a cross between *Architectural Digest* with a heavy dose of *Field & Stream*. The great room was immaculate, distinguished by a collection of large exotic wall-mounted animals from almost every continent on the planet. "How long have you been a big game hunter, Frank?" Nick asked.

"Everyone needs a hobby, Nick. These mounts are outputs from another one of mine. You'll see after dinner tonight," replied Frank, piquing Nick's curiosity. "The bar is set up in a room off the kitchen, and there are appetizers throughout this portion of the house. Please, help yourselves, and be comfortable," he said, looking at the three of them.

As they rounded the corner, they heard a familiar voice. "Nick, Philemon."

The source turned out to be Cassie, who was serving as the bartender that evening. "Hello, Mallory. What can I get you to drink?" Mallory settled for white wine while Nick asked for a rum and coke. Phil took a moment to survey the back bar.

"Cassie, I'll have a Monkey 47 and tonic. By the way, you look cute in your bartender's tuxedo."

"Thanks, Phil." Cassie rewarded him with a smile. "I'm just helping out Mr. Raymond tonight. I can use the extra money. By the way, I love your coral shirt. Oh, and thanks for the roses. They are beautiful."

That portion of the conversation caught Mallory's ear as she lingered with her drink to listen discreetly.

"Cassie, thanks for the great weekend. I enjoyed spending time with you. Next time I'm in town, how about I teach you to skydive?"

"I'm in," she said excitedly, handing him his drink. "Don't be shy about coming back for more," she said coyly.

Not sure exactly what they were getting into, the group of three strategized to remain together as they found their way to Frank's large deck. Several familiar faces were seated at the various round tables, including Jon Woods and Emil. They were flanked by up-and-coming junior executives that Nick and Phil had not yet met. Notably, all were wearing blue blazers, prompting a silent head nod from Phil. Standing off by the railing alone, staring into the distance, was Tina Matheson looking beautiful in a floral wrap dress, but she appeared detached and out of place. Nick watched the boys in blazers each take their turn to talk with Tina. Based upon Nick's assessment, it was an obligatory conversation to make sure each had face time with one of the company's less well-liked movers and shakers. With Frank temporarily out of pocket, Emil jumped in as impromptu host, taking care of introductions. The young executives were courteous, but far more interested in making points with the leaders than wasting their time on these unknowns.

Emil called Nick and Phil over for a sidebar chat. "This might be old hat for you guys tonight, but we're all in for an annual treat."

"Excuse me, sir?" asked Nick, looking confused.

"You'll see later."

Nick and Phil exchanged glances, not sure what to make of Emil's comment. Both motioned for Mallory to join them, rescuing her from a pedantic young attorney from Jon's staff who was interested in more than a conversation with her.

"Mal, any idea what's going on tonight?" asked Nick.

"Not a clue. Remember, Frank likes Tina, not me necessarily."

Nick joined a conversation, taking a seat near Emil, while Mallory went off to find something to eat. Phil worked his way back to the bar on a personal quest of drinking his host out of the expensive gin. With Nick now working the crowd, Mallory and Phil found their way to an empty table to sit and talk.

Taking a bite of her bacon-wrapped scallop, Mallory took advantage of the time alone. "Phil, why do you refer to Nick as Boss?"

"I guess . . . because he is."

"You mean, he outranked you in the Air Force?"

"No, we were peers from that standpoint. Nick's just a natural leader. We met in the first phase of PJ training called Indoc, a process to sift the wannabes from the real thing. We started with about a couple hundred guys in our class. Several weeks later, it was just him and me. Had Nick not taken time to help me improve my running, the graduating class would have been just one. I wouldn't be here now without him. I owe the guy so much."

Taking a sip of his drink, he continued, "After our initial assignments, we were stationed together in Afghanistan and became working partners. In every situation, no matter how bad it was, Nick always seemed to keep his cool. Even when we were taking fire."

"Taking fire?" questioned Mallory.

"You know, the enemy shooting at us when we were on a rescue."

"Oh my God," she exclaimed.

"Nick is a true professional. More than once, he calmed an injured soldier while we worked on him, telling him everything would be okay . . . and it generally was. He just inspires confidence in people. When we met, I could swim circles around him. However, after I gave him a few lessons, Nick now leaves me in the dust . . . if that's possible in the water. Personally, I don't think there's anything he can't do . . . even insurance."

Mallory smiled.

"Mallory, can I ask you something?"

"Sure."

"I don't have too much leave left. Are we going to get this romance started or what?"

Before she could answer, Frank took center stage. "Tonight, we're going to do some shooting with guns from my private collection." Following Frank like baby ducklings, there was an excited buzz from the small group. Around a large hedge, the partygoers found a rack of expensive weaponry, including AK-47s, Heckler & Koch, and Mausers and M40s, among others.

"Wow, alcohol, tobacco, and firearms together! Only in America . . . and some third world countries," yelled an excited Phil, earning strange looks from others in the group.

Frank announced a tournament with each guest being given three rounds for shooting targets at two hundred yards. Cassie moved through the crowd with each person choosing a numbered slip from a box, signifying the shooting order. Of the sixteen participants, Nick ended up with number eight, while Phil drew fifteen. Mallory passed but was interested in watching the show.

Before the competition started, Frank made a final proclamation. "We're shooting to win the traveling trophy won last year by . . . me," he said, holding up a cheesy homemade plaque with two green plastic shotgun shells glued to a wooden base to faux oohs and aahs coming from the group. "Remember, we're playing for honor here. You can assume any shooting position you wish and take any weapon available. Who's up?"

As it turned out, one of the junior attorneys had drawn the first shot, followed by several other members of the blue blazer club. With minimal experience with weapons of this type, all chose an AK-47 because they had seen them in movies. However, none even came close to hitting the metal target. Shooting at number seven, Emil chose an intimidating Sig Sauer Tactical 2 sniper rifle. It was clear Emil had done this once before, ringing the metal target twice. Nick followed, asking to use Emil's weapon since it was warm. Before dropping into the prone position, Nick gestured to Phil. "Any final advice, P-Man?"

"Just don't embarrass us, Boss."

"Thanks. No promises though, since I haven't shot a weapon like this in quite a while."

Taking his time, Nick lay on a mat, trying to remember his advanced firearms training. Taking a deep breath, he focused on his target. In quick succession, Nick rang the bell three times followed by a round of applause from the group.

"Who's next?" he said, standing up confidently.

"I am," came a woman's voice from the back of the group. Tina Matheson stepped around the attorneys, taking the Sig from Nick. Kicking off her wedge heels and putting on a pair of shooting goggles, she then carefully assumed the prone position in her wrap dress. Taking her time, Tina rang the bell twice to wild applause.

Looking downrange, Phil uttered a "Damn, nice shooting, ma'am," eliciting what appeared to be a rare smile from her.

Nick reached down to Tina with a hand up, unsure if she would accept it. But she did. "Congratulations," Nick offered, acknowledged by a broad smile in return. Tina stood next to Nick, even taking his arm for a time as the show continued.

By the time Phil's turn came, no one else in the group, besides Nick, had a perfect score. With twilight now becoming a factor, and even after several drinks, Phil and his chosen Mauser rang the bell three times to the delight of the small crowd. Everyone knew the final competitor was their host. Frank was intent on keeping his own trophy, but his guests could feel the pressure building. After several years of hosting this exclusive event for Weston brass and wannabes, no one had even come close to challenging his skill level.

Frank picked up a Remington MSR from the gun rack. Slowly approaching the shooting mat, he assumed the prone position before squeezing off three perfect shots, earning polite applause.

With the contest apparently over, the group began to migrate back to the deck when Emil stepped forward. "Frank, I think there should be one more round with only those with perfect scores competing in a shoot-off," he said, baiting Frank, who was content to have tied the PJs.

"Emil, we're losing the light, but I'm up for the challenge if Nick and Philemon are. However, we'll also shoot from three hundred yards out," pointing in the general direction of another metal target.

"Who's up first?" asked Phil, who had nothing to lose.

Making up the rules as they went, Frank said they would keep the same order. The group became totally silent as Nick settled with the Sig Sauer. He looked over at Mallory, who smiled back at him with an encouraging look. Siting in the target, Nick relaxed and pulled the trigger. There was a general gasp of disappointment from the crowd as they realized the bullet had missed its target.

"Looks like it's up to you. Make sure you summon all your redneck powers," said Nick, handing the weapon to Phil.

Nick moved off to the side between Mallory and Frank while awaiting Phil's shot.

"Nice shooting, Nick," said Frank, quietly offered his gratuitous condolences.

"Thanks, sir, you make it look easy. Hey, when you shot, I noticed you had a raised patch of irregular skin on the back of your neck. It's probably nothing, but I thought I should mention it to you."

Frank began to feel around on the back of his neck with both hands searching for the area. "Seriously? I didn't know about it. You have a medical background, don't you?"

"Yes, but I'm not a doctor. It might be something you want to have checked out though."

Mallory stifled a huge smile, biting her lower lip upon hearing the conversation. Unable to contain herself, she turned, stepping away from Frank and Nick.

"I've never seen anything like that before. Better safe than sorry though, sir," said Nick with his voice raising at the end of the sentence like he was not being entirely truthful about his diagnosis.

In the meantime, Phil had taken aim and, after a short pause, fired to be rewarded with the corresponding clang of the target echoing downrange. The small crowd erupted with a loud ovation.

Frank slowly moved toward the mat. While most didn't notice, one of Frank's hands was busy feeling the back of his neck, searching for what now must surely have morphed into a cancerous patch of skin.

"You play dirty," said Mallory, quietly tittering as she slid back over to Nick.

Finally settling into his shooting position, the crowd held its collective breath while the executive took aim for what seemed like an eternity. More than once, his left arm reached to touch his neck as Frank drew a bead on the metal target. Squeezing the trigger, the shot left the rifle. However, the group heard nothing but the sound of crickets coming from the field as they paused to contemplate the proper protocol. Within thirty seconds, there was a smattering of courteous applause from the partygoers.

"Man, I won!" Phil exploded with a scream. Jumping up and down, he began to receive congratulatory high fives from the blue blazers, while Frank, still in the prone position, was scratching at his neck. Inspired by the turn of events, Cassie ran toward Phil, jumping into his arms before planting a huge kiss squarely on his lips.

Taking in the sight, Nick nudged Mallory. "I didn't do this for me. I did it for Frank. He needed a case of humility. By the way, Phil is the worst winner I've ever seen. He is going to grind old Frank's ass for as long as we stay here."

"Where's my plaque? Where's my plaque?" Phil began yelling. Emil responded, awarding the hideous prize to Phil. "Frank, will you be putting my name on the trophy? Man, I'm going to have to come back and defend my title next year. I owe it all to my new lucky apricot-colored shirt," howled Phil. "I need a drink," as the newly crowned champion led his followers back to the bar.

Nick helped Frank off the ground. "You shot well, sir. Thank you for the invitation tonight." Frank said nothing, still scratching his neck trying to understand what had just happened. "Let's grab Phil and get the hell out of here," said Nick to Mallory. When she disappeared into the group, Tina approached Nick. "Nice shooting," she said before giving him a hug and another smile. Then the three of them made a quick exit from the shooting range, leaving Frank behind as the light of the day came to an end.

By the time they got back to The Lakehouse, Phil had calmed down but was still caressing his new hardware and a now empty souvenir highball glass that once belonged to Frank. Mallory pulled up to the front door to let the men out of the Jeep. After Nick got out of the vehicle, Mallory asked him if she could have a moment alone with Phil. Once Nick was in the house, Mallory looked at Phil, who was now standing outside the passenger door.

"Do you remember what you asked me at the party?" But before Phil could respond, Mallory continued. "Tomorrow. Six o'clock for dinner. I'll pick you up here. Leave your damned plaque behind."

Before he could say a word, Mallory drove away. Both ended the evening returning to their respective homes with huge smiles on their faces.

CHAPTER 28

The following morning, the early sun and the lake called to Nick to take a long swim. The cool water felt like home to him as he practiced a variety of strokes back and forth between the dock and a raft floating offshore. After thirty minutes of solitude, Nick heard a splash. Stopping mid-stroke and treading water, he saw Mallory had jumped into the lake from her dock and was making her way towards him.

"Morning, Nick. Where's your swim buddy? I thought you were a professional?"

"I am, or I was anyway. You're right, probably not good form, but where's your swim buddy?"

"I'm looking at him. You've been working out for a while based on what I could see from my house, and the water's cold. Interested in some coffee?"

"Sure," responded Nick, realizing this was breaking new ground in their relationship.

Mallory had brought two towels to her dock, obviously denoting some level of premeditation with her plan. Emerging from the water, Nick noted Mallory was wearing a one-piece red racing suit before she pulled on her terry cloth bathrobe. After walking up the path to her house, Mallory brought coffee, cream, and fruit to a weathered teak table on the patio. The heavy wooden chairs were outfitted with bright blue and red cushions, and the table was shaded by a large matching umbrella standing in the center. However, at that time of day, several maple trees provided enough morning cover from the sun.

"What's up?" asked Nick after wrapping himself in a towel. Picking up a cup of the steaming brew, he waited for an answer.

"What do you mean?" replied Mallory.

"This is a first for us. Morning coffee? Good stuff, by the way."

"Papua New Guinea. I guess I wanted you to know something. After I dropped you off last night, I asked Phil on a date." She sounded as though she was seeking approval from Nick.

Nick thought about Mallory's statement. It was neither a question nor a declaration requiring a response, even though it was clear she wanted one. "That's great, Mal. I told you Phil is a great guy. You've seen him at his best and his worst during the past week . . . particularly last night when he was pimping Raymond."

"I just couldn't sleep last night thinking about him. Any ideas about where we should go tonight? You know, things he might like to do?"

The devious side of Nick thought he could plant the seed with Mallory about taking Philemon to places he absolutely hated, like the ballet. But, given Mallory's level of excitement, he resisted the urge. "Phil's one step removed from being a caveman. Buy him a steak and a drink, and he'll love you forever. He's low maintenance."

"Thanks, I want to make a good first impression."

"I think you already have," replied Nick.

"Oh, and FYI, I need to leave work early today to get ready."

****

Ninety minutes later, they were roughly in the same position, only holding paper coffee cups and dressed for work around their conference room table amidst the avalanche of paper. Each was now studying a copy of the large loss list provided by Jon, trying to develop a strategy for digging into the hard copy documents. For whatever reason, Jon had sorted the list by occurrence date. After thirty minutes of silence, Nick said, "I'm not really seeing anything here but incredibly large dollar amounts. The dates of the claims really don't tell me anything."

Mallory nodded in agreement but remained silent.

"Mal, what do you see?"

"I guess the same thing. However, if anything, remember what Frank said. It seems to corroborate our interview. Weston had a normal pattern of losses early in the program, but then picked up momentum with some serious claims after that."

"Jon said we could sort the data any way we want to with the Excel attachment," said Mallory after another long thirty minutes passed. "Should we try a different search criteria?"

"I don't think we have much to lose," responded Nick, still staring at the original document. "What do you suggest?"

"How about a sort based upon the type of loss?"

"Go for it. Is that something you can do?"

"Piece of cake," she replied, already focused on her laptop and tapping away at the keyboard. In less than a minute, both were now staring at another record.

After another frustrating hour, Nick looked up. "I'm still getting nothing out of the data. A lot of large losses, but the fires are separate from the heavy liability claims, which are cordoned off from the sexual misconduct files."

Mallory nodded. "Okay. How about if we simply sort based on the size of the loss or the reserve amount of the pending claim, from largest to smallest?"

"Let's go in that direction and see what we find. Maybe something will jump out from the data that makes sense?"

Sixty seconds later, each was now focused on reading the output of their third attempt. Five minutes had passed when Nick uttered, "Holy shit." He continued reading the overview of the losses captured. "I can't believe the size of the claims Weston has paid or will pay. I guess I knew that intuitively from all the interviews with the staff and our broker friend, but these dollar amounts are eye-popping."

"I've been working at Weston for quite a while but have never seen a series of individual claim totals like this in one market segment," replied

Mallory. "Looking at the data in this way, it's not hard to understand why the board made the decision to leave the religious institution niche. It doesn't take a genius to see how the company might be on the fast track to going out of business. It's so bad, it's almost like someone was putting on poor accounts intentionally."

"Agreed. While we might be moving in the right direction with this sort, we still have a mountain of files in this room. Does it make sense to somehow focus on smaller chunks of information? What if we started by studying the details of the ten worst claims in terms of dollars to see if we can come to any conclusions?"

"That seems like a reasonable approach," replied Mallory. On her copy of the list, she took a highlighter and drew a line between file numbers ten and eleven. Although the strategy did seem sound, they were now faced with the practical problem of locating those ten files from the mountainous stacks, separating them from the others. That task took the better part of the afternoon, made more complex by the realization that several of the thick files had multiple companion folders. Whoever had delivered the material to the conference room either hadn't taken that into account or deliberately separated the case files to make any search more tedious.

Promptly at four o'clock, Mallory looked at Nick and said, "Gotta go," making a beeline for the elevator, almost taking out one of the young mail delivery interns in the process.

Nick smiled to himself as he continued the arduous process of locating the complete records so they could start their review the following morning. After completing the task, he realized he had a night to himself since Philemon was out on the town with Mallory. Poised to get a head start on the analysis, Nick segregated the materials for the first file on the list, placing it in his briefcase. Labeled *Minnesota diocese (Donovan)*, it was by far the largest file. In fact, it had so many additional folders it required a second full briefcase that he scrounged from his office. "Some light reading with takeout tonight sounds perfect," he said to himself, clicking off the lights with both hands full of insurance documents. He headed for home with a side trip to a tired strip mall housing a dingy Chinese restaurant for an order of General Tso's chicken and a side of crab rangoon.

After arriving at The Lakehouse, Nick dropped both briefcases on the floor while setting the food and his keys on the table in the foyer. "Honey, I'm home!" he yelled.

Phil came around the corner wearing a pair of jeans, sandals, and a floral Tommy Bahama shirt. "Hey, Boss. Damn, that smells good. What do we have?" he said, pawing through the plastic bag containing Nick's dinner and pilfering a crab rangoon.

"I thought you were heading out with Mallory tonight?"

"Five minutes," said Phil, speaking with his mouth full and holding up five fingers when they heard the roar of Mallory's Jeep. "Looks like my ride's here. Don't wait up, Boss," he said with a wink. Smiling, Phil grabbed another rangoon and disappeared out the front door. Nick heard Mallory hit the gas, and the silence he loved so much returned. *No planes, no armor, no shooting. Solitude.*

Nick changed into shorts and a t-shirt before grabbing a Stella, both briefcases, and what was left of his dinner as he settled on the deck. Pulling out the first file, he took a long draw of beer and began to read. Although he wasn't expecting compelling reading from an insurance file, he breezed through the pages like a best-selling novel, learning the sordid details about the molestation of a series of young boys, including those with special needs, over an extended time by a Father Edward Donovan. A series of depositions from all the players, including Donovan, were included, as were photos of the kids involved, medical records, attorney opinions, attorney opinions about attorneys' opinions, and official assessments regarding the impact of the trauma on the children. Recognizing this was real life and not fiction raised the hair on the back of Nick's neck at what this supposed holy man had done to destroy the lives of so many children, so many families.

He noted the entry of a Minneapolis-based attorney who had raised the stakes of the sexual molestation claims with a stepped-up social media strategy, drawing even more attention to the transgressions of Weston's insured. Ultimately, after all the denials and obfuscations from the diocese, the file reflected a settlement with Weston paying $20 million. The story ended with internal file notes indicating the settlement had been sealed by the courts with the diocese kicking in even more money. Donovan was compelled to undergo counseling as his penance, but, amazingly, there would be no prison term. Then, the pages ended. Unlike a great novel, there was no final resolution. Nick searched the briefcases for some more pages but found none. The maddening tale ended abruptly. There was no conclusion. There was no afterword.

After reading the Donovan story for almost four hours, his beer was hours dry, the takeout was cold and untouched beyond what Phil had filched, and the sun had disappeared. Nick's entire body was quaking and he began to gasp for breath, his mind racing about how such a travesty could have gone on for so long. Although he was happy the children had been compensated for their pain, he was also incensed that so much money was paid on the backs of Weston employees now at risk of losing their jobs. The diocese and their priest just walked away, as did the broker who had made a healthy commission on the deal. Nick could now understand Emil's point of view and his frustration. *Christian fuckers!*

Nick decided to grab another beer, trying to make sense of it all while contemplating the stars, sitting on the deck in an Adirondack chair. Within fifteen minutes, the beer was gone. Mentally and physically exhausted, he fell asleep and did not move from his chair until morning light.

CHAPTER 29

Nick was awakened by two loud splashes in the lake below, as well as muffled talking and laughter from people doing their best to be quiet but failing miserably. It didn't take long for him to figure out who the offenders were: Mallory and Philemon. He stood from the wooden chair, taking several minutes to straighten up before walking to the deck rail for a better look. It was apparent neither remembered their swimsuits on the way to the lake.

"Hey, you with the hairy ass, good morning!" yelled Nick from above.

The sound of splashing stopped immediately, replaced with silence aside from the sound of Phil. "Hey, Mallory, I think he just insulted you." Taking an elbow in the ribs for his comment, Phil yelled back. "Did we wake you, Boss?" the sound echoing off the trees along the shoreline.

Nick moved closer and could see two heads peeking up from the opposite side of the swim raft. "No. I'm used to seeing naked people cavorting in my backyard," which brought more giggles and laughing from the water. "Stand fast, I'm coming down to the shore."

"Nick, please stay where you are," Mallory yelled back.

However, it was too late. Nick moved quickly down the path to the water. Now standing only one hundred feet from Phil and Mallory, who had repositioned themselves on the opposite side of the raft, Nick yelled, "Mallory, I read the diocese of Minneapolis file last night. Have you ever run across the name Father Edward Donovan?"

"Yes. I think most people have heard that name," she said, her head popping up over the swim platform to make eye contact. "He molested a bunch of kids in Minnesota."

"Right, and Weston paid a fortune to settle the cases," said Nick.

"Can't this wait? The water's freezing."

"That's not my problem," replied Nick. "One more question, and I'll leave. After the settlement, did Weston ever find out what happened to Donovan? I'd like to talk with the priest to learn more."

"Good luck with that. A couple of months ago, I got a Google Alert about Donovan. He was shot and killed in Appleton while he was supposedly being rehabilitated from his pedophilia. The murder is unsolved, even though everyone seemed to know why."

"Appleton? You mean just down the road?"

"Yeah."

"I'd like to talk with the police about the killing and find out if they have any leads. I'd say you've put in a full day and probably the night too. See you in the office tomorrow morning. I'll let you know what I find out."

"Thanks," both Mallory and Phil responded in unison.

"Oh, and I'm thinking about readjusting my telescope," said Nick as he turned to walk back to The Lakehouse to the sound of more cackling.

****

By ten o'clock, Nick had made several calls to the Appleton Police Department without success. On this third attempt, he was able to get out of the phone tree and connected with a live person. After explaining who he was and his interest in the Donovan case to several employees after each transfer, he was finally directed to Detective Chuck Nowitzke. However, Nowitzke's phone went directly to voicemail, announcing he was out of the office and could not be reached. The message directed those requiring immediate assistance to contact Officer Anissa Taylor. After getting Taylor's extension, he heard a similar notice that she was out of the office. Frustrated, Nick made his final call to Nowitzke, leaving a message outlining specifics and requesting a call back at the officer's earliest convenience.

CHAPTER 30

Chuck Nowitzke's head felt like it might explode. In fact, he concluded it might be the most humane thing that could happen to him, aside from being charged with the hotel's cleaning fee for the resulting splatter. Gathering his thoughts into what was now a mid-morning game plan, he broke down the key elements, including rising from the bed, becoming upright, finding his way to the bathroom, and urinating. However, as he lay in his bed, he had serious doubts as to whether he could get the order correct. The bright sun filling the room was no help. Apparently, a maid had left the drapes open a crack the prior day. To his dismay, the sliver of light that found its way into the room seemed to follow his head on the pillow, and he was powerless to stop it. He realized he had spent the night in his clothes, yet somehow had managed to kick off his shoes and one sock. Then, he recalled he was at The Tropicana Hotel in Las Vegas for a homicide investigators conference that began that morning. Working backward in his mind, he remembered attending a pre-conference cocktail party at Caesars' the night before. Yet, after finding the open bar, and with little food to soak up the alcohol, he was hard-pressed to recall the people he had met or how and when he had gotten back to his room down The Strip.

Continuing to ponder the events of the prior evening, his phone rang. With a gargantuan effort, he compelled his body to roll over, getting to the call before it went to voicemail.

The cheery voice of Anissa Taylor greeted him. "Good morning,

Chuck. Where are you? I've been looking all over the conference room for you but can't seem to track you down."

"Good morning," Nowitzke responded with a croaky voice. Straightening up on his bed, he continued, "I'm running a little behind schedule. My pants and jacket did not come back from the cleaners as promised. Save me a seat, and I should be there within the hour," before clicking off his phone. *If Taylor can't figure out my lie when I get there, I'll have some serious doubts about her future as a detective.*

The National Society of Homicide Investigators meets annually at revolving sites around the country. These civil servants experience the best that money can buy at a new destination each July. Typically, that means hotels peddling off-season rates looking for booking days. The rotation traditionally included sites such as Miami, Phoenix, and Dallas.

After a cold shower, Nowitzke pulled some new clothing from his suitcase. He felt each degree of the searing heat as he stepped out of his Uber in front of Caesars' at the main entrance. Although he had made it to the hotel, the next order of business was finding his meeting room, which was no small task in the sprawling resort. Walking through the casino, the loud ringing of the slot machines reverberated inside his skull between his temples. Nowitzke found a coffee kiosk and ordered a large with a double shot of expresso. Although the air-conditioning was running overtime in the hotel, he was still sweating thirty minutes later as he located the conference area, finding his name badge, one of two still unclaimed, at an unattended table outside of the large double doors. Drinking the warm coffee, Nowitzke strategized he would wait for a scheduled break and then blend in with the crowd upon their return to the meeting, hoping beyond hope Taylor had indeed saved him a place. Scavenging his own seat at this point in the morning surely would have him sitting ringside. Great for a Vegas title fight, but problematic for one going to a business meeting in his current condition. Waiting patiently on a red velvet couch, Nowitzke sat quietly, studying the garish casino. As he finished the coffee, the meeting doors opened, and those trapped inside spilled out in two columns headed for their respective restrooms.

Hundreds of people of all shapes and sizes exited the auditorium. Although some were dressed in uniform, the majority wore jackets and business attire.

Wearing a long, sleeveless, black dress and matching blazer, Officer Taylor found Nowitzke slumped on the couch outside the room. Assessing Nowitzke's appearance, she cheerfully commented, "Classy. Were there any survivors?"

"I didn't think my bullshit dry cleaning story would hold up. Congratulations, detective, you have honed your investigative chops to a new level," Nowitzke growled.

"Let's put it this way. I saw a more lucid homeless guy sitting on the sidewalk this morning who looked better than you do now. It doesn't take much of a detective to figure out how you spent your evening."

Chuck smiled to himself. Months earlier, Taylor would never have stood her ground with him, much less needle him about his appearance. She had come a long way since they had met on that snowy March morning to investigate her first murder. Even though murders were hardly routine in northeastern Wisconsin, the pair had been called in by police agencies in sister cities in the area to assist with other homicides that had occurred during the year. Taylor's growing confidence was a significant addition to a package that already included collegiate good looks, blonde hair, height, and intellect.

"What happened to you last night?" Taylor asked.

"I ran into my dream girl . . . a tall, blonde bartender with a heavy pour," replied Nowitzke.

Not really listening to his response, Taylor launched into a recap of the morning. "You missed quite the opening speaker. A gold shield detective from New York City talked about investigating a series of mob murders, finding body parts of the victims around the city. Fascinating."

"Taylor, I haven't had breakfast yet. By the way, you need to get out more often. Are you up for some blackjack tonight?"

"I'm not sure. After you ditched me last night, I played some of the slot machines and drank the complimentary watered-down vodka."

"No, I'm talking about real cards and real vodka. Trust me, you can lose your money twice as fast as on any machine."

A silent time clock went off in the collective heads of those attending the conference as the herd reformed, moving back into the room.

"Who's the next speaker?" asked Nowitzke.

"Not sure," said Taylor. "The agenda said he is a small-town police chief who is doing a case study on an open homicide. I think he's from Michigan. Oh, and you're welcome, I saved you a seat. Just promise you won't puke on my new dress."

"I'm not in a position to make any promises to you. I trust we are sitting toward the back of the room, so I can get a nap in before lunch."

One of the conference organizers, who doubled as the primary emcee, gave the traditional introduction of the speaker, outlining every credential earned by the man. A tall and lean law enforcement officer stepped from behind one of the long burgundy curtains on the side of the stage and made his way to the podium wearing a sharply pressed blue uniform. It was obvious from the various ribbons on the uniform that this was an impressive individual.

"From the great state of Michigan," the presenter completed his intro, ". . . please welcome Chief Keith Hutchins of the Mackinac Island Police Department" to polite applause from the crowd.

Hutchins had attached a battery-powered lavalier microphone to his collar to enable him to roam around the stage. Introducing himself as "Hutch," the chief outlined his purpose for the case study.

"Ladies and gentlemen, I'm looking for your help and insights. Earlier this year, a murder took place on Mackinac Island, a vacation spot with roughly five hundred full-time inhabitants, but a million visitors annually. As you might guess, we don't have many murders on our island. In fact, the last one took place in the '60s. This is an open case, and I have incorporated the details into a PowerPoint presentation."

Nowitzke slumped, whispering to Taylor, "Jesus, a PowerPoint." He wedged his arms under his chin to maintain a proper look of attention even though he felt like nodding off.

Hutch continued. "I want this to be a dialogue. If you have questions or observations about what was done or not done during the investigation, please speak up. We have several microphones circulating in the audience so everyone can hear. If you have a theory or see something we missed, I want to hear it. I don't care about my ego . . . I care about solving this crime."

Moving to the other side of the stage to keep his entire audience engaged, Hutch continued, "There are several interesting aspects to this case. The male victim was a new resident on the island and was largely a loner. One evening, after stargazing, he was shot with a large caliber rifle. During the initial phase of our inquiry, we found that the victim, Barry Hargreaves, was living under an alias. Once we learned the man's name, Lonnie D. Palmer, we determined he was a former preacher who operated a Texas-based ranch for underprivileged kids. He had also been a source of controversy, having been investigated for child abuse and murder. Our initial thinking was the killer was not a resident of the community. Thus, someone tracked the pastor down and planned to murder him before escaping off the island. Pretty ballsy stuff."

Nowitzke opened his eyes, his head now raised, looking at the stage. Was this possible? Another religious figure killed by an unknown assailant with a long-range rifle. Nowitzke and Taylor exchanged looks, noting the striking similarities to their Donovan case, even though they knew the odds of the killer being the same person were seemingly small. Fighting off his hangover, Nowitzke was now totally absorbed in Hutch's presentation, wishing he had not killed and maimed so many brain cells the prior evening. Taylor began taking notes and making observations of similarities and differences between the cases.

Hutch reviewed his findings, outlining them item by item. He projected the police photos of the body, discussed the statements of important witnesses, and talked about the combined efforts of the local authorities on the island and adjacent ports to identify the shooter before eluding capture.

After fifty minutes, Hutch paused. "I have two final pieces of evidence to share. The first is a grainy video taken from a local business's CCTV system showing the final moments of the victim. Notice how a slightly built individual with a suitcase approaches Palmer. At first, we thought this might be a concerned person trying to provide medical help." He ran the snippet of video back and forth for the audience. "Notice how he reaches down and appears to check Palmer for a heartbeat. Then, for some reason, our Good Samaritan pulled out a collapsible baton, breaking both the victim's legs." As the video rolled, Hutch noted several in the audience whose heads snapped in time with each of Palmer's legs.

"Our conclusion was that this was the shooter. Also, while we surmised that the likely perpetrator was not checking Palmer for a heartbeat but shoving a piece of paper into one of the victim's jacket pockets." Hutch continued to run the video back and forth for the audience, who was mesmerized by the presentation.

"When we opened the document, we found a letter containing a single line of text."

Again, Taylor and Nowitzke looked at each other. This could not be a coincidence.

Hutch clicked to the slide, flashing a photo of the wording on the large screen. In very large print, the words appeared. '*197. If he break another man's bone, his bone shall be broken.*'

Nowitzke blurted out a question even before raising his hand. "Chief Hutchins, what does the sentence mean?"

From the stage, Hutch spotted Nowitzke. "Frankly, we're not sure. It's clear it meant something to the shooter and the connection to the victim. We know Palmer was accused of injuring and killing several kids. But, beyond that, the words are somewhat obscure, and the real answer is . . . well, we don't know."

Taylor's hand went up. "Hutch, the verbiage looks like ancient text. Is this a Bible verse?"

"Good question. That was our first assumption, but after running the sentence past a couple of local pastors, they agreed it was not from the Bible. After that, I decided to put the words into Google. Turns out it's a passage from the Code of Hammurabi."

"The code of what?" Taylor followed up.

"Hammurabi," said Hutch, repeating the finding. "I did some serious research on that myself. This code was one of the earliest sets of laws ever committed to writing. It was created in 1780 BC by Hammurabi, the king of Babylon. A thousand years before Moses came down off Mount Sinai. Essentially, it's a collection of legal principles listing crimes and punishments, and settlements for disputes. It addressed everything from theft, murder, and property damage to marriage rights, children's rights, women's rights, and slave rights. The laws were carved into obelisks for all the citizens to see. Two hundred eighty-two rules of conduct that set the norms for behavior that were absolute and binding upon everyone, including the king. In fact, since the laws were committed to the obelisks, they could not be changed, giving rise to the phrase still used today when we say something is 'written in stone.'"

Another question emerged from another officer near the front of the room. "How come I've never heard of these laws before?"

Hutch paused and smiled. "Another big finding for me. My guess is most everyone in the room has heard at least one or two of these laws. 'An eye for an eye, a tooth for a tooth,'" he offered.

Heads across the room began nodding in acknowledgement.

"Needless to say, these laws were fairly Draconian and old-school," concluded Hutch, looking at the emcee who was pointing to his wristwatch, telling Hutch his presentation was over. "I've run out of time today. If you have any information that might be of assistance, please contact me." He flipped to his final slide, showing his name, phone number, and address. Even though the group was intrigued with Hutch's presentation, most did not see his particulars since they had already turned to leave the session in favor of lunch smelling of rubber chicken wafting from the adjacent room.

Hutch was shutting down his laptop while Nowitzke and Taylor fought their way to the front of the room, moving upstream against traffic. Climbing onto the stage, Nowitzke introduced Taylor and himself. "Chief Hutchins, we really enjoyed your presentation. In fact, there are elements of your case that are incredibly similar to an unsolved case that we investigated this past winter."

"How so?" said Hutch, looking puzzled.

"Well, there are several interesting parallels. Both involved the murder of a religious figure by an assailant at long range with a sniper rifle. That alone seems to be reasonably coincidental, but there are a couple of other details that are more compelling. Both victims had some serious issues. Your former pastor was suspected of injuring and killing kids while ours was a convicted pedophile priest. However, the clincher is a letter we found in the priest's room that also had a single line of text. It wasn't the same as the one you presented, but pretty damn similar and written in the same style. Based upon your presentation, my guess is it's another law from the Code of Hammurabi. During our investigation, we asked a priest whether the text was a verse from the Bible, but got a no. It never occurred to me to type the phrase into Google. There was a number in front, just like your example, but the wording seemed so obscure."

Hutch listened intently as Nowitzke provided the details of the Donovan murder. "It's interesting to say the least. While there are some differences between the sets of facts, I agree the presence of the two documents might link the cases . . ." said Hutch, ". . . although, I think we've all been wrong before. Even so, I think we owe it to the victims to at least see if there is a connection. Is there any way we can exchange information, including the ballistics reports, photos, autopsies, and the like? You've seen most of what I have."

"Hutch, I need to clear this with my chief. I can't believe there would be a problem, but I just need to cover myself."

Hutch, Nowitzke, and Taylor exchanged business cards and set a provisional timetable for a more in-depth phone discussion once they all returned to their respective jurisdictions.

Buoyed by what he'd heard and the new direction of a cold case,

Nowitzke talked Taylor into lunch at one of the local bistros in the complex, forgoing the group meal. "Anissa, I think we just paid for the trip. Let me talk with Chief Clark about getting cleared to send our data to Hutch. My advice to you as a senior investigator is that we blow off the rest of the day's presentations and change our flights to head home tomorrow. You can get your pool time in this afternoon and I'll piss away some money at the tables and we can meet for dinner later."

Although it was her first professional conference and she wanted to learn more, the prospect of a poolside lounge chair with an umbrella drink in the Nevada sun was much too powerful to pass up. Taylor took Nowitzke's suggestion. "See you tonight."

****

With Taylor nursing her sunburn and Nowitzke licking his financial wounds, morning came before the sun rose. They boarded a shuttle to McCarren International Airport to catch the first plane back to Wisconsin. After checking a long list of voicemails, Nowitzke looked at Taylor. "You're not going to believe this. I got a message in the last day from some local insurance guy that wants to talk to us about Fast Eddie's murder. Not sure what he wants, but what a small world. I'll call him back when I get into the office tomorrow."

Taylor gave an unenthusiastic nod, looking for a place to put her head down to sleep for the short ride to the airport.

CHAPTER 31

The Weston Insurance annual summer picnic was one of the most hated and loved corporate events of the year for the employees and their families. Hated, because it was a full July Saturday carved out of a short summer calendar that most employees felt could be better used elsewhere doing almost anything other than rubbing shoulders with the organization's leaders. At the same time, the outing was loved given the overwhelming affection and respect everyone felt for the day's host, Emil Swenson. Typically, he worked the crowd like a politician in an election year, glad-handing employees and their families, kissing babies, and making everyone feel welcome. Emil viewed the picnic as an opportunity to thank his extended family for their hard work, putting his money where his mouth was to prove it.

Traditionally, the event was hosted at a private club that Emil rented each year. The facility was set on a mass of land consisting of approximately one hundred acres of broad meadows surrounded by large maple and evergreen trees. A sprawling single-floor brick structure was the centerpiece of the property. Guests were greeted by Emil in the front entranceway fashioned by several massive roughhewn wooden beams and aged metal creating a dramatic architectural triangle rising roughly two stories. Once through the double entry doors, the partygoers had the run of the building, which boasted bamboo flooring, high ceilings, and impeccable furnishings. Two rows of white-clad servers lined the route, holding trays with flutes of champagne and mimosas on a path to the rear patio that opened onto a sand beach fronting a lake. The frontage included a boathouse with a dock and boat launch. Off the shore, two floating rafts bobbed in the water. The first raft, closest to shore, had a slide and a large sun deck. The second was located roughly another one hundred yards beyond and was intended as a resting place and a reward for the heartiest of swimmers.

A massive white tent was erected off the patio, offering seating for all 400-plus guests. Tables set for eight were covered with white linen and centerpieces decorated with wildflowers. Two portable bars flanked each end of the expansive multicolored brick patio boasting numerous tables sheltered from the sun by brightly colored umbrellas. Additional servers worked the crowd, passing hors d'oeuvres and taking drink orders for those trapped in a conversation. Ironically, even though the level of service was that of a high-end resort, Emil insisted the luncheon include only Wisconsin fare, meaning grilled bratwurst, burgers, chicken, and several types of potato salad with raw vegetables.

With a near-perfect cloudless day and a light breeze across the water, Emil's luck for exceptional weather had held for another year.

Nick arrived at the picnic stag, dressed comfortably in a golf shirt, shorts, and sandals. He was somewhat surprised that the picnic offered valet service. *Nice touch*, thought Nick as he tossed the keys of his Beamer to an earnest young woman who was wearing Weston's corporate colors before going to greet his host.

"Good morning, Emil."

"Glad you could make it, Nick," said the CEO, extending his hand. "How goes the investigation? Where is your friend Philemon and Mallory?"

Before Nick could answer, Phil and Mallory pulled up in her Jeep. Phil was wearing a white Packer t-shirt he had found in one of Nick's drawers, covered by a Tommy Bahama floral shirt, camel cargo shorts, and flip-flops. Mallory sported a black bikini under a wrap dress, black sunglasses, and a wide-brimmed hat.

"Good morning, sir," said Phil. "I appreciate your invitation today. You have been very generous to me during my time here."

"When is your leave over, Philemon?" asked Emil.

"In the next couple of days," he said looking at Mallory, who frowned.

"Hello, Mal," said Emil. "You're looking very festive."

"Thanks Emil. Good to see you outside the office," she replied, kissing him on the cheek. "We're heading in to find a patio table. We'll save you a seat, Nick." Mallory and Phil joined hands and walked through the house followed by the gaze of both Emil and Nick.

As they watched, Emil commented to Nick, "I don't think I've seen Mallory this happy in years. I know she likes working with you."

Nick took the compliment in stride. "Well, Emil, any bounce in her step isn't from me. Those two have become quite an item in a short period of time. It's also been a good thing for P-Man, er, Philemon too."

After a short pause, Emil turned his attention back to Nick. "Will you be in the office on Monday to give me a briefing about how you're doing?"

"No problem, sir. Things are interesting to say the least."

"I also have a personal matter I need to discuss with you. Why don't you catch up with Mal and your friend?"

"Thanks, Emil," said Nick, pondering Emil's words.

As he turned into the house, Nick noticed Tina Matheson emerge alone from a metallic white Audi convertible near the temporary valet stand, flipping her keys to one of the young men. Glancing back, Nick thought she made quite the statement in her casual print dress and her blonde hair pulled back, wearing oversized white sunglasses adorned with sparkling jewels that caught the light. *Once you get past the bitch part, I never realized that Tina was so beautiful.* Carrying a wicker beach bag, she strode confidently up to the front door to meet her father. However, Nick never saw her greeting to Emil as he was commandeered by Phil, who was looking for a bar and a private conversation. A Stella and a gin and tonic later, Phil led Nick to a quiet spot at a patio table away from the crowd.

Nick started the conversation. "So, where have you been keeping yourself lately?"

"I'm sorry, Boss. I know I dropped off the radar. It's just Mallory and I hit it off so well, and we've been spending a lot of time together. Part of the issue is I need all the extra sleep I can get since we can't keep our hands off each other."

"P-Man, I'm happy for you. I haven't known Mallory much longer than you, but what I do know is I can see the attraction. We're brothers. What's good for you is good for me. You owe me no apologies."

Phil's face showed a huge sense of relief. "I just didn't want you to feel abandoned because I found a new, um, interest.

"I need some advice, Boss. My leave is up in the next couple of days, and this is the first time I'm not excited about going back to work after some time off," said Phil.

"What are you going to do?"

"I owe the Air Force another year. After that, I have no idea. If I did stay in the military, I'm not sure I could do my job based upon how my body feels. Eight-plus years has worn me down. You know what I'm talking about. For the time being, I'm rotating back to Lackland to train prospective PJs. That helps me with the physical toll, but yelling at a pool full of rookies is only fun for so long. Beyond pararescue, there are no other jobs in the Air Force that interest me." Nick thought back to his original visit to his recruiter and how he came to the same conclusion years ago. Phil continued, "I'm not sure what I can do outside the military. And honestly, I feel like Mallory is going to factor into this."

"It sounds like you've begun the conversation every PJ needs to have with themselves at some point. Coming into this job, you knew the demands of the work. The plain truth is that PJs have a short shelf life."

"I get that. However, you've made the transition from the Air Force. How are you handling things, Boss?"

"I'm doing my best. The so-called real world is a different place. Now don't get me wrong. I like most of the people I work with at Weston, and there is a huge level of respect for the military. But P-Man, we've lived by a creed using words like 'honor' and 'valor.' The people I work with know those words, yet, I'm not sure they have the same meaning, at least in the business world. Most of the civilians take their lives and their freedoms for granted. The biggest hardship they face is spending too much time in the Starbucks line each morning. When you're chasing dollars, the goals just don't seem as worthy."

Phil sat back, studying his old friend. "So, Nick, that's what your work's all about. I mean, how are *you* doing?"

Nick paused, staring off into space briefly. Then, very quietly, he responded. "P-Man, the truth is I'm struggling. Jesus, I've had what feels like a couple of panic attacks. They come from time to time . . . I mean, even when there's nothing threatening me. But then all of a sudden, I just lose it. For no reason I can figure out. Thank God I haven't embarrassed myself with an attack around someone else." He slumped in his chair a little further. "I've felt like I lose my cool too easy too. Pushed some idiot broker up against a wall the other day. He was being a dick, but I was just unprofessional. And on top of losing my parents, and the job I loved, I think I'm drinking too much." He bent at the waist, rubbing his face with one of his hands without making eye contact.

Philemon took in everything Nick said. "What are you going to do? I mean, there's help available to veterans."

"I know . . . but I haven't looked into it yet. I'm still hoping just to work through it all."

"Does that mean you're not going to be a career guy at the insurance company, Boss?" asked Philemon, trying to lighten the mood of the conversation.

"From what I already know, there are only a handful of people I've met at Weston that set out to join the insurance industry. I have no idea where I'm going, but I can tell you the words 'insurance' and 'career' will never be in the same sentence for me once this gig is over. As you're thinking about retiring from pararescue, if you find a job you like, get two of them, one for you and one for me. By the way, thanks for listening. You came to me for advice, and I didn't mean to dump this on you."

"No problem, Boss. You're a work in progress. If you *ever* need to talk, you call me. Can I ask you about Mallory?"

"Sure. What would you like to know?" said Nick warily.

"Just tell me about her. Mallory has changed my thinking going forward. Beyond making a living as a civilian, I'm tired of being alone. When we were saving the world, a lot of prime life passed us by. I think I might be in love with her. But I don't know. Signing up for another hitch and being gone on a tour a year at a time wouldn't seem to help matters though."

"Right now, you and Mallory are in lust. From my patio, it sounds like a pair of howler monkeys in the spring. If you have to wait a year, so be it. You'll find out if it was meant to be during that time. San Antonio is an easy flight from Wisconsin. If I had to guess, Mal would like this to work out too. The fact of the matter is that I really don't know her too well. We just started working together. I will tell you she has some issues though. For starters, there is one fucked up family dynamic going on with her father, Emil, and her sister, Tina. Everything seems intertwined with the company, and I haven't figured that out yet. Like why one sister is a vice president and Mallory seems to fade into the woodwork sometimes. I have no doubt she's smart and knows her business. Oh, and we've had our disagreements. I just think you need to go into any relationship with her with your eyes wide open."

Philemon took in Nick's assessment but said nothing in response. "Don't read anything extra into what I'm telling you. She's an attractive young woman. I'm giving you insider knowledge. You take it for whatever it's worth. In the meantime, what were you thinking about doing for your next career?" said Nick, changing subjects. "Aren't you descended from a line of pastors?"

Philemon looked at him seriously. "Are you fucking kidding me, Boss? Me . . . a pastor? I think the Jesus gene skipped a generation with me. Anyway, you know I like my Sundays off."

"I wasn't sure you could have pulled it off either," laughed Nick. "Maybe you can study to be a dental assistant on your Saturdays or find work as a rock and roll singer."

Phil laughed. "I hear it pays well," aping Bon Scott and the AC/DC song.

"P-Man, the one thing the world doesn't seem to have enough of is government contractors. Worst case, if you leave the Air Force, you can probably find a gig that pays twice what you make now with a helluva lot less strain on your body. Give it time to work things out."

"Well, Boss, you should take your own advice. Stuff will work out for you too."

"Thanks, man. In the meantime, the most pressing issue is your drink is gone. Get in line and get yourself a double."

Philemon gave Nick a hug, heading back toward Mallory who was amongst a group of employees. On his way, Mal turned and smiled at him briefly before continuing her conversation with an employee from the administrative staff.

As he sat back down, Nick pondered where his life was going. The conversation with Philemon continued to bounce around in his head. He and Philemon were in essentially the same place. Both knew they could no longer do the job they loved so much with the PJs. Both were unsure about how their skills fit in the civilian world. Although the insurance business was getting more interesting by the day, the thought of another thirty years in that line of work made him want to throw up. *Maybe I should think about becoming a dental assistant?* Equally concerning to Nick was that he had no one in his life. While each of them might struggle transitioning to the real world, at least Phil had Mallory, for the time being. For Nick, finding a woman was too much to fathom at the moment. Rising from his chair to get a refill from the bar, someone walked up behind him.

"Can I buy you another drink?" said the woman's voice. It was Tina Matheson.

"I never turn down a beautiful woman willing to buy me a drink," said Nick, trying to hide his shock.

Tina smiled absently. Walking over to the bar, the people parted for her like the waves did for Moses. After grabbing another Stella and a Sauvignon Blanc, they found their way back to the table. Tina took a sip of wine from the plastic cup when Nick broke the silence.

"Seriously, no one could scare up a Reidel for your wine?"

"Looks like we spared no expense, except on the barware. I think we have one too many Loss Control people on staff worried about broken glass on the sand beach." After a short pause, Tina said, "Nick, I owe you an apology. I made some strong accusations about you that were unfounded. I know you were just doing the job Emil and the board hired you for. I know the religious program is falling apart and that you're responsible for finding out what went wrong. And I'm sorry I was a bitch that day."

"Tina, trust me, I'm not trying to move up the corporate ladder. Apology accepted."

"Thanks. I just wanted to clear the air. I look forward to meeting with you and Mallory again so I can add what I know so you can do your jobs." Tina stood, turned, and got lost in the crowd.

After she had left, Mallory approached Nick. "What was that all about?" she said derisively.

"She apologized for her behavior at the interview the other day."

"Wow. Looks like all that money Emil spent sending Tina to charm school is finally paying off. C'mon with me and join our table. You're not going to believe who is part of the group." She wrapped his arm around hers and they made their way through the crowd.

Nick and Mal found Phil, Cassie, C. Jonathan Woods, and his wife, Courtney, together around the table. Woods was dressed in black slacks, an open-collared button-down shirt, a blazer, and new loafers, apparently not understanding the word "picnic." Courtney, a tall and appealing woman with a tight bun of brown hair, had, no doubt, been coached by her husband into wearing a corporate-approved outfit comprised of a conservative sundress and sandals. Nick judged that Woods was likely in his early forties, but Courtney was probably a couple of years younger. Unfortunately, she traded additional years of age for her staid appearance.

Prior to Mallory grabbing Nick, she had made the polite invitation to the Woods to join their little group, never assuming they would.

However, the nuance of her graciousness was apparently lost on the attorney, who readily accepted. Based upon their brief meeting at Frank Raymond's home a few nights earlier, Philemon had quickly sized up Jonathan as a corporate type. Certainly, a type diametrically opposite to Philemon, particularly considering the blond mohawk. Seeing his opening, he purposely wedged himself in the seat between the general counsel and his wife in Mallory's absence. When she returned to the table with Nick, the color drained from her face seeing Phil in the middle of a Woods' sandwich. Yet, she managed to compose herself quickly, especially after seeing a purposeful wink from Philemon. Phil's final Weston corporate outing for the year was going to be epic.

The rest of the group milled around the table, sizing up their seating options. The look on Jon's face beckoned Nick to save him and to sit in the open chair to his immediate right. But Nick had decided to play along with Phil. Jon's comfort zone would be totally obliterated that afternoon.

"Cassie, looks like you're my date today?" said Nick.

"Sweet," cackled Cassie with delight.

Nick maneuvered the leggy redhead, wearing a pink bikini top and short shorts, into the chair next to the attorney. Jon was unsure of what to make of all this. It did not take a mind reader to see from Mrs. Woods' face she was not overjoyed that her husband was now seated next to the scantily clad receptionist. Certainly, nothing like this had ever happened at prior corporate events when she was surrounded by her husband's minions, all wearing their blue blazers. Nick and Mallory took the open spots as Mallory made the introductions around the table since it was clear these were not the type of employees who worked in the same circles in the Weston extended family.

Philemon started the conversation. "Woodsy, it's nice to see you're a man of the people sitting with us today. I would not have figured that," he said with a smile before draining his drink.

Both Mal and Nick stifled a laugh at the attorney's new name, assuming it would not stick beyond today. Then, after a pregnant pause at the table juxtaposed against the din of the party surrounding them, Courtney looked directly at her husband. "Oh my God, Jonathan. No one has called you Woodsy since college," she said loudly.

Considering his wife's remark for a moment, Woods took a sip of his Chardonnay and nodded. "You're right, Courtney. You know what, I miss those days."

The ice officially broken. Phil disappeared from the table only to return minutes later holding a tray with six large shot glasses filled with a pinkish orange mixture.

Mal looked at Phil warily. "What do you have there?"

Looking at the entire group, Phil said a little too loudly, "It's time for 'sex on the beach.'" Passing the glasses around the table, he was sure Jon or Courtney would balk. However, neither did. Phil told the group that on the count of three, they would each down their shot together. And, they did.

"Wow. That was refreshing," said Courtney, putting her glass on the table. "May I have another?"

Cassie squeezed out of the table, making the run before reappearing with another six shots. She also made the third run. Courtney made the fourth. In short order, the table with the general counsel and his wife was setting a new precedent as one of the loudest groups at the picnic. Jon's jacket came off, folded on the chair behind him with his shirtsleeves rolled up. Courtney had pulled out her bun to reveal shoulder-length hair, softening her appearance. An outsider would have thought this was a group of old friends that had gotten back together based upon the raucous laughter coming from what was now the "fun" table.

The typical employee was interested by the mix, while the attorneys, with their spouses or significant others, were confused on several counts. First, that their leader was sitting between a muscular man sporting a mohawk with two arms full of tattoos and the redheaded receptionist. Second, that C. Jonathan was not holding his typical court discussing new legal precedents. From the standpoint of those subjected to the picnic because of their attachment to a house attorney, it was a welcome

change, especially when they found their way to the bar to find out what
their new friends were drinking. Upon hearing the name of the beverage,
the women giggled while the men howled and more shots were poured.

Even Emil, who wondered about the atypical din coming from
the Woods' table, swooped in for a closer look. "Is everyone having a
good time?" he quizzed, leaning into the group between Phil and Jon.
Courtney answered, "Emil, this is the best time I've ever had at the
employee picnic. In fact, I've already had 'sex on the beach' four times
today."

Emil went a shade pale, unsure of how to respond to Courtney.
As he paused wondering what to say, eyes from those around the table
flitted nervously back and forth in abject silence before the dam burst.
Deafening laughter erupted from around the table, saving Emil, who
seemed to join in with the fun but quickly moved on to greet more of
his guests.

Following lunch, the group of six found that they were the center of
attention. A second and third layer of chairs clustered around them with
others hoping to join in the fun. The individuals found many layers of
common ground, and the conversation devolved into several sidebar
exchanges. Woodsy picked Nick's brain about the upcoming football
season. Cassie confided to Courtney she wanted to go back to college to
become a nurse. Courtney told Cassie that ironically, she had graduated
from nursing school, but decided to become a full-time Mrs. marrying
an up-and-coming corporate attorney. Mallory and Philemon simply
held each other's hand, quietly soaking in the moment knowing the
clock on his leave was ticking.

Several employees began to migrate to the sand volleyball court set
up on the beach while others headed for the cool lake water to swim. A
former high school volleyball player, Cassie began recruiting for a team
at the table, enlisting Philemon, Nick, and a less than thrilled Mallory.
Although Woodsy and Courtney seemed game, they had not come
dressed to roll around in the sand, promising to be better prepared the
following year.

When Nick rose from the table to head to the volleyball court, he noticed Frank Raymond off at a small side table having an animated, yet quiet, conversation with Emil and Tina. She had changed from her sundress into a black-and-purple-striped racing swimsuit with a towel draped around her waist. As he passed Tina, who was on her way to the lake, she turned and smiled while Nick responded with an approving glance. Nick kicked off his sandals, took the phone out of his pocket, and stripped off his shirt to prepare for his volleyball game. In the process, he caught Tina looking back at him in a double take.

Expecting a friendly game with his fellow employees, Nick was shocked when the first volleyball came rocketing into the sand at his feet, courtesy of Robbie Mueller.

"P-Man, looks like they take their volleyball seriously here."

"Great, my goal today is to not get hurt," said Philemon.

The game quickly devolved into something only resembling volleyball despite the net, a white ball, and the occasional spike. Even so, while the players knew they weren't qualifying for the Olympic team, it didn't stop them from diving for loose balls, arguments over the score, or trash-talking. An hour later, the sand-covered combatants agreed to a fifteen-minute beer break. Several members from each team ran to an old-fashioned metal horse trough filled with ice and bottles, retrieving armfuls for all the players.

"Looks like I need to start doing more running," huffed Nick, dropping to a knee next to Mallory and Philemon.

Phil was lying with his head resting on one of Mallory's legs in the shade holding two bottles, one for rehydration and the second which he ran back and forth across his forehead like a cold compress. "I'm going to be hurting tomorrow, Boss. Emil throws a helluva party."

"This happens every year," said Mallory. "Even by Monday, half the employees will still be limping around the office."

As the break extended to twenty minutes, an urgent scream went up from the direction of the water. "Help! Help!"

CHAPTER 32

Nick was quickly on his feet on a dead run for the beach. Philemon was close behind with Mallory trailing. Then, they heard a second scream. "Please, she's drowning! Hurry!" Then, there were more shouts coming from the swimmers standing on the raft closest to the beach pointing in the direction of the second floating platform.

When Nick got to the water, he spotted Cassie standing on the shore. "Nick, someone was swimming between the first and second raft when they began to struggle in the water," said Cassie, pointing in the general direction of the original shriek.

"Call 911!" Nick yelled to Cassie as he hit the water, swimming hard in the direction of the furthest platform. Nick was in his element again. Even though he was tired from the volleyball game, he didn't allow himself to feel any exhaustion, now focused on what he had been trained to do. He felt the adrenaline coursing through his body, but quickly stabilized his stroke pace, feeling no panic. If there was a drowning in progress, Nick knew time was a definite factor, wondering if he had enough speed to cover the distance. Then, once he did, would he be able to find the victim in time?

As he made it to the first raft, several swimmers there pointed to an area about fifty yards further away where they had seen the woman struggling before going under. Getting a sense of his target zone, Nick turned briefly to see Philemon coming up from behind. Nick powered out a final sprint to the area. Then, Nick sucked in all the air he could and dove deeply into the clear water. He felt the layers of cool water under the surface as he searched, but he could not locate the victim. Forced to surface, he took another deep breath, diving deeper. Then, he spotted her. She was motionless, floating in ten feet of water in a contorted position. It was then he had a realization. *Oh my God, it's Tina.* Nick swam back to the surface again, yelled to Philemon, and dove deep, focused on Tina's location.

Nick was able to get a hold on Tina's body and, placing his mouth to hers, tried pushing air into her lungs but got no response. Tina's eyes were open and staring straight ahead. Her fingers were curled into gnarled balls, and her body was spasming violently. Nick put his left arm around Tina's neck and began pulling hard for the surface. After what seemed like an eternity, he emerged from the water, trying to keep Tina's head above the surface. Finding his position relative to the raft, Nick turned, pulling Tina as they moved toward the platform. Philemon saw Nick and swam directly toward the raft knowing he would have to help get Tina out of the water. As Philemon hoisted Tina's body onto the platform, Nick popped out of the water. Tina was not breathing and had no pulse. Nick began mouth-to-mouth while Philemon started with chest compressions. As he worked, Nick noticed Tina's body had now relaxed from its previous twisted appearance. However, he didn't know if that was good or not. The PJs feverishly continued working on Tina. In the distance, they heard sirens from emergency vehicles moving in the direction of Emil's home. Closer though, they also heard a boat motor getting louder as if headed straight for them.

After a minute, Nick again checked Tina. She had a faint pulse but was still not breathing. More mouth-to-mouth and chest compressions followed. Nick yelled, "C'mon, Tina. You're tougher than that. Come back to us!" Philemon and Nick continued their work. Then, Tina let out a loud gasp, vomited violently, and began breathing, albeit shallowly. By then, the boat they could hear was almost upon the raft. Both men saw Mallory piloting the skiff, her face showing no emotion. Nick and Phil gently placed Tina into the small craft. Finding an emergency kit, Nick pulled out a thick wool blanket, wrapping Tina in it to keep her warm for the trip back to the dock. Mallory turned the boat and moved toward the sirens and the flashing bubble lights of the ambulance, fire trucks, and police cruisers.

Still weak, Tina looked up to Nick. "Thank you," she croaked.

"Hey, you just scared the shit out of me," said Nick, smiling down at her while taking her hand to comfort her.

****

A small army of first responders were clustered on the shore surrounded by a hushed crowd as the small craft finally made it to land. Two local EMTs were first to greet Mallory's skiff and tried to assume control of the situation. But Nick was having none of it, shouting them down.

"Gentlemen, I'm a former Air Force Pararescueman and have been trained in water rescues. One of you needs to back the ambulance up to the dock." There was a hesitation on the part of the one who looked like he had formerly been in charge. "*Now*," ordered Nick. Not sure what was happening, the EMT turned to retrieve the ambulance. Looking at the second EMT, Nick ordered, "Once that ambulance gets here, bring out your oxygen tank and all the warm blankets you have. Now let's set up a saline drip." The second EMT also looked confused for a moment, not used to taking orders from a civilian at an emergency scene. Nick got in the man's face and invoked his command presence. "*Did you understand what I said?*" Finally, the EMT seemed to engage, nodding affirmatively while also making eye contact with a local deputy sheriff that was watching the proceedings. "I assume you have a radio hooked up to a local hospital?" asked Nick.

The EMT's head bobbed up and down. The radio was tethered between the EMT's belt and white shirt. Nick grabbed the microphone, turning and pulling the EMT in his direction. Making contact with the doctor on call, Nick gave a succinct report of what had taken place along with the condition of the victim, whom he described as stable.

"Billy . . . is that you?" the doctor asked questioningly.

"Negative, Doc, but this is Billy's microphone. I'm Nick Hayden."

"And, just who are you?"

Nick left out the particulars but proceeded to tell the doctor the course of treatment he was engaging in for Tina.

"Sir, I'm Dr. Lassiter. Please let the EMTs do their job," replied the physician.

Listening to the one-way diatribe from Nick, the deputy stepped forward. "Sir, I need you to stand down," said the officer to Nick. "Trust me, these guys know their jobs."

"Yeah, but I know their jobs better . . . trust me," replied Nick, drawing a glare from the deputy.

"Sir, if you don't stop interfering with the EMTs, I'm going to arrest you for disorderly conduct."

As the ambulance was preparing to roll to The Hobart Thompson Hospital, Nick moved toward the back to attend Tina. However, the lead EMT told Nick that he was not making the trip and glanced at the deputy. Ignoring the EMT, Nick was halfway into the emergency vehicle when he felt a hand on his back. "Okay, buddy, you've been warned," barked the deputy. In a single movement, Nick wheeled, landing a fist and knocking the deputy down. A melee ensued as the two men rolled around on the ground. Philemon pulled Nick from the pile and both went back to the bottom as several of the first responders jumped on the PJs. Before he could get to his feet, Nick found he had been handcuffed.

Nick heard the fading ambulance siren from the back of a police cruiser along with Philemon. "At least you got a punch in, Boss. What the hell was that all about?"

"Jesus, Phil. That's what I was talking about before. I know my old job better than either of those two bozos. I wanted to complete the rescue . . . like the old days."

"Boss, the hard truth of it is that your old days are over," said Philemon, the words hanging hard in Nick's head. "You're a civilian now. You can't just jump into any rescue situation and take over. It pisses people off."

Then, the cruiser door opened. "It's your lucky day, assholes. Mr. Swenson called my boss and asked him to release you both. Said you're fucking heroes for saving his daughter," said the burly cop. "But I think you hit like a woman," he said, looking at Nick.

"You look like you know how hard a woman hits, asswipe," replied Nick.

****

Philemon dropped Nick off at the hospital. An hour later, he was cleared to visit Tina. Gently opening the heavy door, the room was dark with subdued lighting. Aside from the beeping coming from the series of monitors attached to her body, the room was still. Tina had been sleeping, but the sliver of light from the hallway woke her.

Once her eyes adjusted to the light, she saw Nick. Then, she started crying. "I'm so embarrassed about everything today. I'm so sorry for any trouble I've caused anyone."

"Tina, I'm sure you didn't set out today to have a near-death experience. Stuff happens. You're safe."

She took Nick's reassurance in stride.

"I do have three questions for you though. How long have you been an epileptic?"

Tina blanched, managing to croak, "How did you know?"

"A couple of things. The other day in our meeting, you zoned out several times with a blank stare. That got me thinking. When I found you underwater today, your body was twisted and contorted. Over the years, I've had some medical training and put things together on the ride over here. I assume you were swimming and had a major seizure?"

"I did. It was so scary." Tina paused. "One moment I was enjoying the day. Then I just lost control of my body and blanked out in the water."

"Are you getting treatment for it?"

"I haven't been. In fact, I was trying to keep this a secret and didn't want anyone to know for fear I wouldn't be considered for my next job at Weston."

"Tina, I'm only a glorified EMT, but you need to talk with your physician about this. You saw what happened today. It could have been worse. Imagine if you'd had a seizure while driving a car and injured someone else. There is no stigma with epilepsy. It's treatable. No one has to know beyond your doc."

"I will, Nick. I promise I will," said Tina as the day began to take effect on her.

"In the meantime, Tina, your secret is safe with me." Nick rose to leave. "Get a good night's sleep."

"Nick, I can't thank you enough for saving my life."

"It's what I used to do. Make sure you thank Philemon and Mallory too. They were both part of the effort."

"I will. Also, when I get back to the office, can we reschedule my interview to answer your questions about the religious program?"

"Absolutely. In the meantime, get well."

"You said you had three questions?"

"Yes, I did. When you feel up to it, will you have dinner with me?"

Whether it was the stress of the day or the meds in her body, Tina had faded off to sleep. Unsure whether she'd even heard the final question, Nick left the hospital.

****

It was long after dark when Nick returned to The Lakehouse. He was surprised to find his car parked in the front driveway along with Mal's Jeep and another vehicle he didn't recognize. Having taken an Uber home from the hospital, he was greeted by muted lighting and voices coming from the deck.

"Get yourself a beer and join us out here for a nightcap!" yelled Phil.

Mallory, Cassie, and Phil were sitting comfortably around a small gas flame built into a table, talking through the events of the day. They waited for Nick to sit down before pouncing with the obvious question.

"Is Tina going to be alright?" asked Mallory.

Nick took a long draw on his Stella. "Yeah, she's going to be fine, thanks to you all. You each reacted perfectly in a difficult situation, but you saved Tina's life."

There was a collective sigh of relief with Nick's news. The night ended with the friends in silence enjoying the fire and a sky full of stars.

CHAPTER 33

At seven thirty Monday morning, Nick arrived outside the large wooden doors of Emil's office for the requested briefing. Anita was on the phone but acknowledged him with a smile as she waved him past. For whatever reason, Mallory had not been invited to this session, but Nick was now feeling comfortable in his role. After a light knock, Nick entered the room to find Emil writing in his journal. Without saying a word, Emil pointed towards the coffeepot, motioning Nick to take a seat on the couch. Nick sat, sipped his coffee, and waited.

A few moments later, Emil closed his book and stood, walking slowly to the couch and taking a seat opposite Nick. Gathering himself, Emil began, "Nick, I've been doing a lot of reflecting on my life lately. Tina's near drowning was the capper for me. I know I have not always been the best father. I've been preoccupied with business, sometimes missed important moments. You know, the things that make a difference in someone else's life. I can't say how grateful I am to you for saving Tina's life. I can't even comprehend what life would be like without one of my girls." The old man's voice cracked.

"I've sent a case of Monkey 47 gin over to The Lakehouse for Philemon," Emil continued. "I noticed he was partial to it at Frank Raymond's house the other night. What can I do to thank you?"

Nick paused, taking a drink of his coffee. "Emil, I'd like you to let me out of my contract. I'm in over my head. I don't know your business. I'm taking a lot of your money, but not bringing you any value."

"Bullshit," said Emil, forcefully shaking his head. "You're doing a fine job. The people you're working with speak highly of you. Also, I appreciate your ethics. We have people at Weston that aren't necessarily earning their keep as much as you are yours. I simply can't grant your request . . . it's the one thing I can't do. Please finish the job. This may be the most important report the board and I will ever receive. I need you to stay."

"Emil, I appreciate your kind words, but there's more to it than the work. Working with Mallory—"

"What's wrong with working with Mallory?" replied Emil. "I thought you two were getting along?"

"We are, but Emil . . ." Nick struggled to find the right words. "We've previously talked about Tina and that she is your daughter. And, without jumping to any final conclusions, Tina is pretty much the primary issue . . . the person responsible for all the pain here at Weston. It's no big secret since everybody here, including you, seems to know it. But then you also assigned me Mallory. A very capable person, and we are getting along, but you never told me that she was your daughter too. Again, something everyone around here seems to know, but me. You've asked me to investigate the religious niche on an ethical basis, but there are so many fucked up Swenson family dynamics complicating the process and intertwined with Weston, I'm starting to wonder if that is even possible," he concluded with a frustrated tone. "What else haven't you told me about that I should know? Why should I stay? I need a reason."

As he spoke, Nick watched Emil turn away and walk towards his desk. He took a moment before he faced Nick again, and Nick braced himself for anger, even rage, that his personal life was the topic of conversation. Instead, Emil looked tired. And for the first time, Emil also looked his age, and then some. He eyes met Nick's, and his expression seemed to fidget, his mouth twisting with some unsaid words. Instead of sitting, he moved to the coffeepot and slowly poured himself a cup.

Nick sat motionless as Emil stood near the coffeepot. With his back to Nick, Emil continued. "Nick, I have prostate cancer. In fact, I've had it for quite a while, but have been too busy to do anything about it. My famous last words. After a recent exam, the doctors concluded that I missed my treatment window and gave me months to live, at best."

Nick was stunned. "I'm so sorry, Emil. What . . . what can I do?"

"Nick, just keep at your work. Please don't walk away now. I know I should have told you more about my girls and my relationships. I should have told you about Tina and Mallory upfront, but it's been such a crazy time for the company and for me . . . personally. Work has always been everything to me, and so I've just kept working through it all. They're going to have to take me out of here with my boots on," he vowed. "Please keep this to yourself for now. Neither Tina nor Mallory know. When the time is right, I'll talk to each of them." Emil began to stare at some of the memorabilia on his shelf. "If something does happen to me, you'll report to Jonathan Woods until you complete your investigation. In the meantime, we need to keep working to make this right. I want to work to make this right too. Say you'll stay. Please. I need you to finish this mission."

Mission. Yes, Nick recognized the technique. His father had showed him how important it was to use the right words when selling an idea to a customer. Nick knew he didn't owe shit to Weston, but his sense of mission, the importance of completing a job once you start it, that he understood. If it was just the words, he could have walked out of Emil's office and headed to the parking lot. But then where? Back to his parents' house in Door County, where he had no friends and no function? An unfamiliar house in an unfamiliar place where he could spend his time with neighbors his parents' age? Listening to them tell him how proud they were of him. And hoping to God it was actually true.

He saw Emil watching him, and any doubts Nick had about the man's illness melted away. It wasn't a line. He could tell from Emil's overall appearance that despite his best efforts, he was sick.

Finish this mission.

Nick stood up, and looking Emil straight in the face, simply nodded and walked out. He would stay.

Leaving Emil's office, Nick played back the meeting in his head, thinking through the old man's words "We need to make this right." Although it seemed to fit Emil's earlier theme of seeking justice, he could not make sense of it. Still lost in thought, he wandered back to his office when he heard the phone ringing and managed to pick up the receiver just before it went to voicemail.

"Mr. Hayden, this is Detective Chuck Nowitzke with Appleton PD returning your call from last week."

"Officer, I was calling about the Donovan case. I work for the insurance company that covered the diocese, and we paid out a small fortune in losses to many victims because of this guy. I understand Donovan was shot and killed in the spring. What can you tell me about where the case stands?"

"Nothing, Mr. Hayden. This is an active file still under investigation. I can confirm what you've probably read online. Donovan was shot and killed from long range by an unknown assailant with a high-powered rifle. Donovan died at the scene. We have a laundry list of suspects, but the case is not closed at this point. We do continue to get new leads on this case on a regular basis. I'm sorry I can't help you."

Not one to give up easily, Nick continued. "I've been asked to close out the company's religious program and just want to be thorough. Is there anything I can say to make you change your mind?" No sooner had he finished his sentence than the line clicked and went to a dial tone.

Gathering his thoughts about next steps, Nick concluded he had done all he could with the local police. In fact, he reasoned that if the roles had been reversed, he probably would have given the same answer as the detective. Nick turned on his laptop and was in the process of getting online when he heard a knock at the door. Tina Matheson had poked her head into the office. With her blonde hair pulled back, she was wearing a trendy black-and-white plaid dress and black jacket. She looked rejuvenated and was smiling.

"How are you feeling?" asked Nick, looking up from his desk.

"Never better. I had a great night of sleep on Saturday and a relaxing

Sunday at home. I've already followed up with my doctor about being evaluated for that other little matter."

"Great."

"I brought you something . . . just a small token of thanks," she said, handing him a bottle of Caymus, an expensive red wine, with a shiny red bow attached. "I also put a bottle on Mallory's desk. Would you see she gets it?"

"Of course."

"I also sent a bottle of Monkey 47 gin to your friend Philemon at The Lakehouse."

"P-Man will love it, but he'll likely need a liver transplant before he ships back to Texas."

"As to your last question, the answer is 'yes.' Pick a night this week, and I'll buy."

She had heard him after all. "We can debate who's paying later, but I'm looking forward to it."

Tina disappeared, moving down the hall back in the direction of the executive wing.

"What's up with Tina?" asked Mallory, who had arrived at her cube just after watching her sister leave Nick's office. "She actually said good morning to me," looking at the bottle of wine on his desk. "Giving up on coffee for something stronger?"

"You tell me. She left a bottle on your desk to thank you too. Maybe we can drink our lunch together?"

"What did the hospital put into her IV? Heroin? How's your morning going?"

"I'm batting about five hundred." He explained about the level of cooperation from the Appleton detective and his pending date with Tina.

At the latter news, Mallory stepped into Nick's office, closing the door. "Are you serious? Tina?" she said with her arms folded.

"Mal, first, this was a courtesy heads-up to you. Second, it's just dinner."

"I just assumed any boss of mine would have better taste. Nick, I like you. But Tina's got one of those large brass hotel carriers full of emotional baggage tethered to her all the time. I know because I've got matching luggage. I just don't want to see you get hurt."

"Aside from the occasional sucking chest wound, PJs don't get hurt. Getting back to business, I think our focus needs to be on the top ten files we carved out the other day. I've read about Donovan and am doing some follow-up research after talking with the police. Each of those files end with a huge payment to someone, but we don't necessarily get the rest of the story. It might not make a difference, but finding any unusual patterns buried in the documents might lead us to some conclusions. At least we can say we went the extra mile from an investigative standpoint if anyone asks."

"That makes sense," agreed Mallory.

"Why don't you take half, and I'll keep the rest. We can then compare notes about anything interesting. You take the Palmer file since you're familiar with it."

Retiring to the conference room, they began plowing through the mountain of records. Nick found several articles about the life and death of Donovan from the Minneapolis area press. As he completed a surface review of his internet search, the facts of the priest's death were just as the detective said. Donovan was shot by a high-powered rifle, dying in a blizzard this past spring. Mal completed reading the Lonnie Palmer file and was concluding her backgrounding of their former insured. He might have died on Mackinac Island as Barry Hargreaves, but as Lonnie Palmer from Texas, he fit the profile of a Christian fucker.

The effects of the volleyball game combined with three hours hunched over a laptop caused Nick's back to cramp. Looking at Mallory, he said, "Up for getting out of here for lunch?"

As they got into the elevator, Nick asked, "What did you find out about Palmer?"

Mallory recapped the facts as they reached the first floor, walked through the lobby, and got into Nick's car. "We insured the ranch in good faith," she concluded. "The mission of the organization was solid. Our people had no way of knowing Palmer would abuse kids. In hindsight, though, we should have asked more questions of the broker."

"Let me guess . . ." said Nick. "Marco Ricci?"

"Give the man a cigar."

"It's pretty clear that Palmer changed his name to leave his past life behind him," concluded Nick. "Were you able to get any specifics about how he died?"

"Based upon what I read in *The Mackinac Island News*, he was shot from long range by a high-powered rifle. There aren't too many other details in the article, but I'll keep working."

Nick looked confused. "Mal, I'm not talking about the Donovan file. I'm asking you about Palmer."

Now Mallory was confused. "Nick, that's who I was talking about."

"So, both Donovan and Palmer were killed in the same way. That seems like one helluva coincidence, doesn't it?"

"Yes, I guess. It's not like all of our scumbag insureds get shot after we close our file."

Nick mulled over the set of facts as they arrived at their restaurant. "I wonder if the Appleton Police detective would care about this. I'll give him a call after lunch to see if this changes anything in terms of his level of cooperation."

CHAPTER 34

While Mallory began to read the next file on her stack, Nick decided to make a final plea to the detective he'd spoken to earlier that morning.

"Nowitzke," Nick heard, connecting on the first try.

"Detective, this is Nick Hayden from Weston Insurance calling. I talked with you . . ."

Nowitzke interrupted. "Mr. Hayden, I remember you. Nothing has changed since this morning. The Donovan case is active, and I can't release any details about it to you."

"Well, Detective, something *has* changed. My partner and I are doing a review of Weston's claim files. We found a remarkable similarity between the Donovan death and another former insured, a man named Palmer. At least, he was Palmer when we insured him. For whatever reason, he changed his name to Hargreaves after we paid a ton of money on his behalf for abusing kids at his ranch in Texas. According to what we have been able to piece together, both men were shot from long range with a powerful rifle."

Nowitzke was stunned. After the conference in Las Vegas, here was another connection between Donovan and Palmer. "Mr. Hayden, where did you say Palmer was murdered?"

"I didn't. But the shooting took place on Mackinac Island."

Nowitzke's head was spinning. First, the story by Hutch. Now, some insurance guy is calling with the same report. It was a lead that could not be passed up.

While Nowitzke remained silent, Nick kept pushing. "We have some pretty extensive files on both losses and the circumstances around them. Maybe there is a connection between the two shootings, maybe not. But, if Weston has some information in its files that could establish a link or a motive, wouldn't that be important to you? Worst case, you're only out the meeting time."

There was another long pause from Nowitzke. "Mr. Hayden, thanks for calling."

Nick waited for the line to go dead again as it had that morning. However, something he said must have clicked with the officer.

Nowitzke continued. "On the condition you bring your files along, do you have time to meet later this week?"

****

By five o'clock, Mallory had finished reading several volumes of a file entitled "Mount Zion Baptist Church of Birmingham," quickly pronouncing the exercise a colossal waste of time. The historic Alabama church had burned to the ground the prior spring caused by a lightning strike that was witnessed by several observers. Numerous fire departments responded promptly, but the structure's old wood was like kindling, and the building was quickly engulfed in flames. The state fire inspector confirmed what everyone already knew. There was no controversy. No hint of arson. Mother Nature was just being a bitch that day. Weston promptly paid the policy limits of $14 million. Once the matter concluded, the leadership of the church wrote a letter to the company thanking it for the excellent service and offering to endorse Weston as a carrier of choice. At least, until the cancellation notice arrived.

As Mallory slogged her way through the fire loss, Nick was buried in the details of a major claim at Bethany Lutheran Church of Munising, Michigan. In fact, the loss with the potential to be the largest claim ever handled by Weston.

****

Mason McMillan answered his first call out of seminary, arriving at the church in northern Michigan with his new wife, Jennifer. In short order, the vibrant and ambitious couple breathed new life into the dying church. Then, it happened.

McMillan had organized a day-long snowmobile ride as part of a youth event. The plan was to take advantage of the fresh powder, riding west through the wooded backcountry. They would find a place for lunch off the trail and return, completing the 100-mile trip before sunset. Twelve riders, youth and chaperones, all on their own snowmobiles, appeared at the church at eight o'clock on a frigid morning in late December. In fact, one of the attendees brought a separate snow machine for the young pastor to use. Never having ridden before, McMillan received a brief lesson about the operation of a snowmobile, including the throttle and braking, right down to how to operate the heated handgrips. One of the riders even provided McMillan with a helmet.

The trip began on a cold and crisp Friday morning with the sun shimmering on the new fallen snow. After leaving Munising, it was not long before the group made its way onto the trails in the backwoods. Moving up and down over the hilly terrain, there were vistas of Lake Superior that were hard, if not impossible, to reach during the summer. Cutting through the woods, the trail narrowed to a single file, and then, it broadened into wide roads before dumping out onto frozen lakes.

Reaching a wide portion of the trail, Billy Gagnon, a member of the youth group, challenged the pastor to a race. After much goading, McMillan accepted, believing it would help cement his bond with the kids. The race would be a sprint on a long straightaway, which ended before the trail continued in a sweeping turn back into the woods.

Gagnon, an experienced rider, and McMillan pulled up, side by side. With two hours of experience under his belt, the pastor felt confident in his ability to handle the sled. Aside from the wind blowing the light snow across the trail, there was no sound in the hinterlands until one of the chaperones yelled, "Go!" Both Gagnon and McMillan remained even for the first quarter mile when the pastor looked down and saw that his machine was now doing sixty-five miles per hour. Backing off slightly, Gagnon pulled ahead and was the easy winner at the makeshift finish line. Trailing, but still moving at high speed, McMillan whizzed past Gagnon, who had stopped. Whether the throttle stuck or the inexperienced McMillan confused the gas for the brake, he continued on reaching the woods until squarely hitting a sturdy oak tree with a grinding crash. The impact demolished the sled, catapulting McMillan headfirst over the handlebars into the tree with a sickening thud.

Although the helmet had saved McMillan's life, he was severely injured. Amidst a group of teenagers alternately crying and praying, one of the chaperones called for help. A Flight for Life helicopter arrived, taking McMillan to Marquette General Hospital where he was rushed into emergency surgery. Nine hours later, the neurosurgeon found the young pastor's wife in the waiting room and informed her that while her husband had survived, he would be a quadriplegic for the rest of his life.

The file reflected a coverage opinion from outside counsel to C. Jonathan Woods that under Michigan law, McMillan was, in fact, injured while on the job. He was entitled to wages, medical benefits, and rehabilitation services. Since McMillan was only twenty-seven, Woods' math on the pastor's average weekly wage through the balance of his natural life was, as he termed it, "significant." However, that portion of the claim would be overshadowed by the ongoing medical cost and rehab.

****

Nick told the story to Mallory and Philemon over beer and nachos at The Office, their new favorite watering hole.

"I can't even imagine," said Mallory. "I feel so bad for the couple."

Both PJs were silent. Although the facts and the country were different, both had experience with this. More than once, they helped save the life of a soldier with a severe injury. But their involvement ended when the soldier was flown out by helicopter. They never heard the rest of the story when the wounded warrior returned home to his young wife and family who were left to pick up the pieces.

"Sorry to have been a downer tonight," apologized Nick.

"What happened to Pastor McMillan?" asked Mallory.

"Based on what I was able to find, he must be one tough son of a bitch. The McMillans are together, still living in northern Michigan, and have opened an outreach ministry to help other para- and quadriplegics. Think about that for a moment. I saw their website. There was a nice photo of the two of them smiling in front of what looked like a log home. Him in a wheelchair and his wife standing behind him."

"Man, I don't think I'd have the strength to go on if that happened to me," said Philemon, staring at his drink.

They sat in silence briefly amid loud shouts by other people around them watching a Cubs game.

After a few moments, Nick started the conversation again. "P-Man, it's your last night in Wisconsin, and we told you we would take you wherever you wanted to go for dinner, and you picked this place."

"I've got everything I need with you two," he said, smiling at Mallory. "That, and a selection of one hundred beers on tap."

"When do you ship out?" asked Nick.

"Tomorrow at oh-dark-thirty. I should be in San Antonio by noon and bitching about the heat and humidity five minutes after that."

"Look, I'll pick up the tab for the damage we've done so far and get out of your hair," said Nick. "It's your last night together. You don't need me hanging around. By the way, what do you want me to do with all that Monkey 47 gin?"

"Save it for my triumphant return to Wisconsin."

"I thought it would have been gone by now," Nick said kiddingly.

The two PJs hugged goodbye. Philemon looked at Nick. "Boss, a man's got to know his limitations."

"Thanks, Dirty Harry. You travel safe, and we'll see you when we see you."

Philemon looked solemnly at Nick. "Remember, Boss, if you ever need me, just tell me when and where and I'll be there."

"I assume you're on airport duty?" questioned Nick, looking at Mallory.

Mallory nodded yes.

"Remember, we meet with Appleton PD tomorrow morning," said Nick.

Phil and Mallory watched Nick walk out the door just as another thunderous shout erupted from the Cubs fans.

When Nick got back in his car, he took a breath. He had spent the day with Mallory and not said a word about Emil's cancer. Compartmentalizing information, decisions about what to share and what to hold inside had been part of the deal as a PJ. He thought back to the McMillan case and how "he'd never been there, after." After. Was there going to be an after? Would he have to be there for Mallory, who'd become a friend, when she learned her father was sick? What would Tina expect from him, if anything? Or would he be long gone when the news broke? He had promised to keep Emil's secret, and he would honor that promise. But for the first time in a long time, he would have to deal with the consequences. As he sat alone in his car thinking, he felt beads of sweat forming on his forehead and his body stiffen. Then, it felt like something was sitting on his chest as he gasped for air. Yet, having had several prior attacks, he managed to calm himself. After several minutes, he wiped his brow and headed home.

CHAPTER 35

The Appleton Police Department was located on Walnut Street, not more than twenty-five minutes from The Lakehouse. Nick and Mallory arrived at the same time but had come from different directions with her detour to the airport. Each was carrying a large briefcase, with Nick hauling the Donovan file and Mallory bringing the Palmer material.

"Did P-Man's flight leave on time?" asked Nick.

Mallory nodded yes as she tried to look upbeat. But, based on the condition of her makeup, it was clear she had cried at least once.

"How do I look?" asked Mallory.

"Not to sound insensitive, Mal, but you look like you just came from an Alice Cooper concert."

"You are such a dick. Give me a minute so I can fix my face in the car, okay?"

Minutes later, they entered the building and presented their identification to a stern-looking woman behind glass off the lobby. Upon receiving visitor badges, they were buzzed into a narrow hallway. As the heavy metal door closed behind them, they entered a hallway painted light blue with beige industrial carpeting. Proceeding down the hall, the walls were lined with a series of color photographs featuring the Appleton Police making a difference in the greater metro area. Nick and Mallory were unsure of where to go until a tall and attractive blonde woman in uniform poked her head out of the doorway of a conference room. Officer Anissa Taylor introduced herself, inviting them into the room. The sterile hallway theme continued in the windowless room containing a large wooden table, several office chairs, a laptop, a star-shaped phone for conference calls, and an open box of donuts with three lonely orphans. In a chair at the far end of the table sat a disheveled and puffy-looking man in a wrinkled blue sports jacket with brown hair, a thick mustache, and three days growth of beard, staring down at the contents of several large files. Upon seeing his visitors, he stood, mindlessly introducing himself as "Nowitzke" and pointing the visitors toward chairs across the table from Taylor.

There was an awkward tension in the room until Nick jumped in. "Thank you for your time today. Detective Nowitzke, Ms. Swenson and I have been charged by Weston Insurance Company's CEO and board of directors to do a deep dive into their religious program with the intent of closing it down."

"Why is your company leaving that line of business?" asked Nowitzke.

"Great question," responded Mallory. "Frankly, the company lost its shirt over it. For whatever reason, we ended up doing business with the wrong accounts that brought us an outrageous number of large losses. We just can't make a profit insuring churches."

Taylor had been taking notes of the conversation on a yellow legal pad. Looking up, she asked, "So, I understand your company had the distinction of insuring Edward Donovan?"

"Well, kind of," said Nick. "We covered the diocese he worked for and ended up paying the claims for his victims."

"Would you mind telling us how much Weston paid?" asked Nowitzke.

"We insured the diocese for two years with a limit of $10 million for each term. Because the molestations continued over both, we ended up paying $20 million in losses plus whatever we incurred in expenses."

Both Nowitzke and Taylor let out a simultaneous gasp at the numbers.

"However . . ." Nick continued, ". . . the entire settlement was much larger and involved several other carriers along with the diocese contributing additional funds."

"That's a shitload of money," commented Nowitzke.

"Tell me about it," replied Nick.

"Can you tell us the names of Donovan's victims?" probed Nowitzke.

"No, since the claims involved minors, the records and the identities of those who received settlements were sealed by the judge."

Taylor and Nowitzke exchanged looks. "We were told the same thing," said Taylor.

"Changing gears, why does the insurance company care about what happened to Donovan?" asked Nowitzke.

"I'm not sure it necessarily does. Originally, we were just being thorough and trying to follow the assignment we'd been given from the CEO to tie up all the loose ends before giving the board our report. Part of our process was to do a review of the biggest losses. We knew Donovan had been murdered, but something clicked when we ran across the Palmer claim and his subsequent shooting. Taking your advice from the other day, we looked over all the reports on the web and found some interesting similarities between the deaths of both men. We had no way of knowing if law enforcement has a database for murders or whether you were working them. Worst case, we thought it was worth reporting this coincidence to the police."

Sitting back in his chair, Nowitzke replied, "First of all, there is no national database for unsolved murders. That being said, I'm not sure how much I can add to the Donovan case for you. He was staying at a local rehabilitation center here in Appleton, getting treatment for being the scumbag child molester he was, when he got shot back in March by what amounts to a sniper. 'Fast Eddie,' as he was known in Minneapolis, took two bullets to the chest. We found a shell casing in the snow on the roof of an adjacent building, but not much other physical evidence. I even tracked an individual through the snow in hopes I might find the killer, but I came up empty. Taylor and I followed the trail back to Minneapolis but ran into a brick wall. In fact, several of them. As I said on the phone, we have no suspects, and this case remains open."

Nick thought about Nowitzke's response. "What do you know about the Palmer case, if anything?"

Taylor responded, "Actually, not much on a firsthand basis. Chuck and I were at a detectives' conference last week in Las Vegas when you left your message. Interestingly, the police chief of Mackinac Island presented a case study of the Palmer killing, looking for thoughts and opinions about the open case. Chief Hutchins indicated no suspects have been identified, and while there is a minimum of physical evidence, he has some video of a person he believes to be the killer. The upshot of the matter is someone gunned down the former pastor, known to the locals as Barry Hargreaves, with a high-powered rifle. After some digging, it turned out Hargreaves' identification was fraudulent, and a check of fingerprints indicated the victim was actually Lonnie D. Palmer."

"Do you know why he changed his name?" asked Mallory.

"We don't. However, Chief Hutchins said Palmer had lived as Hargreaves since moving to the island last year. The police don't know if he was running from something or someone or simply wanted to start a new life," replied Taylor.

"You said you had the misfortune to insure Palmer, too?" asked Nowitzke. After getting a nod from both Mallory and Nick, he continued, "What was the story on his claim?"

Nick recounted the tale as related by Frank Raymond, complete with details about the beatings and murder that Palmer was responsible for.

"How much did Weston have to pay because of Palmer?" asked Nowitzke.

"$3 million to the victims and their lawyers, defense costs, plus another million as a parting gift after Palmer likely torched his house," replied Nick.

"Another scumbag," commented Nowitzke.

"Don't get us started," replied Nick. "These are just two in a stack of claims we're plowing through right now. Every one of them has a big payout." Looking at Nowitzke, Nick continued. "Detective Nowitzke, aside from the coincidences surrounding the shooting of Palmer and Donovan, is there anything else you can tell us about how these murders might be connected?"

Until now, the entrance to the conference room had been open. Nowitzke looked at Taylor, whereupon she rose and closed the door.

Nowitzke righted his chair and leaned into the table as if he was about to divulge a secret. "Frankly, we don't know too much about the Palmer killing, having just learned of the case last week. We've only spoken with Chief Hutchins briefly at the conference. At this point, we're jumping through a couple of procedural hoops so we can all lay our cards on the table to see if the murders are in any way connected." Nowitzke paused. "Assuming this doesn't leave the room, I can tell you about one additional interesting detail. When Donovan was killed, we searched his room as part of our investigation and found this." The detective pulled a sealed plastic bag containing a piece of paper from one of the large files, sliding it across the table to Mallory and Nick.

Nick picked up the document and held it so they could both read it together. "What does it mean?" asked Nick.

"We don't know exactly," replied the detective. "However, we do know the sentence is pulled from the Code of Hammurabi."

"The code of what?" replied Mallory.

"Hey, we're just learning about this stuff too. But, basically, this code was a series of laws that were written by a king, Hammurabi, long before Moses came down off the mount," replied Nowitzke.

"Okay?" questioned Mallory.

Taylor picked up the story. "During the presentation by Hutchins, he showed a screenshot of another similar letter pulled from Palmer's pocket after he was killed. It was different from this one, but in the same style. Hutch said it was a verse from Hammurabi."

"Well, I'm no detective, but that certainly sounds like a correlation considering both victims were bad people, along with time, space, distance, and the fact most people couldn't tell you about the Code of Hammurabi," said Nick.

"We agree, but for now, we're at a bit of a standstill waiting to take the next steps with our investigation," said Nowitzke.

"How can we help?" asked Nick.

"I'm not sure you can. I'm sure part of the issue will be the cost of the trip to Mackinac Island."

"Detective, I'd like to meet Chief Hutchins and listen to the discussion. If Weston took care of the expense of chartering a plane to Mackinac, would you and Officer Taylor be interested in tagging along?"

CHAPTER 36

When Mallory and Nick arrived back at Weston's home office, Cassie was on the phone. When she saw them enter the lobby, she began waving furiously at them to get their attention. When Cassie finished her call, she stepped out from behind her desk, coming out into the lobby.

"Guys, I just wanted to let you know Frank Raymond is looking all over for you, and he's in a bad mood. He's been walking through the building and calling me every half hour to see if you've returned."

"What does he want?" asked Nick. Mallory looked puzzled as well.

"He didn't tell me. But he said when you came into the office that I should give him a call. He seems pissed off about something, but God knows."

"Thanks for the heads-up, Cassie. Give him a call to let him know we're back just like he asked you to do. In the meantime, we're going to get some coffee and take the long way back to our conference room and let him stew some more," said Nick.

Cassie smiled and went back to her desk.

Nick looked at Mallory. "What's this all about?"

Ten minutes later, they were back in the conference room pawing through the files when Raymond entered. He was bright red with a large vein in his forehead that looked like it might burst.

Nonchalantly, Nick looked up from his file. "What's up, Frank?"

Doing his best to keep himself under control, but largely failing, he launched into his answer. "When I gave you access to the claim files, you were not supposed to take them from the building. I understand you discussed them with the local police. In particular, the Donovan and Palmer files."

Mallory looked pale given the tirade from the senior officer of the company, but Nick was nonplussed. "Where did you get your information, Frank?"

"Well, well . . . that's confidential. But I know you did it."

"Frank, first, you never told me we couldn't take the files from the building. In fact, I've done it twice. I suppose I could get permission from Jon, if necessary. Do you think he's going to have a problem with that?" C. Jonathan Woods' admiration for Nick was well-known at this point. Nick let that sink in before continuing. "The first time I took the files was to read the Donovan case at home. The second time was today when we met with Detective Nowitzke at the Appleton Police Department."

"Why were you meeting with the police?"

"Frankly, Frank, that's none of your business. These are corporate files and part of the assignment given to us by Emil. I made the decision to take the files for our meeting with the police. Mallory had nothing to do with that. If you want to blame someone, I'm responsible. However, we report to Emil and him alone. We know they are valuable company property and have safeguarded them. Oh, and just to let you know, we might have to take some files out of the office in the future. If you've still got a beef with me, take it up with Emil or Jon or whoever the fuck you want to."

Raymond stood at the doorway of the conference room fuming and breathing hard, trying to compose himself before slamming the door when he left.

Once he was gone, Mallory looked at Nick. "Frankly, Frank?"

They both started to laugh. "It just slipped out, and it was all I could do to keep it together after I said it," said Nick.

"What the hell was that all about?" asked Mallory.

"I have no idea. Maybe that growth on the back of Frank's neck is acting up again? You said it yourself. He has a passive-aggressive personality. Maybe he's concerned that we're sharing details of his work. Who knows?"

They were both silent for a moment and then burst into laughter again, as quietly as possible.

****

By the end of the day, Nick hadn't learned too much from reading about the destruction of Shepherd of the Sea Evangelical Church in Fort Lauderdale, Florida. According to the photos of the original structure, the building had been beautiful. But, located one hundred feet off the beach, it was no match for Ava, a Category 3 hurricane on the Saffir-Simpson scale. The sustained winds and storm surge produced an Old Testament-like result, literally wiping the church off the face of the earth. The account was the product of his old buddy, Marco Ricci, who earned a fat commission while the total loss cost Weston $8 million.

"I'm no genius, but what company insures a building like that thinking a major storm won't be a problem?" mused Nick out loud. "Fucking Ricci drove another bad deal with an inexperienced underwriter."

His comment stirred Mallory from her file about the flood loss sustained by the New Hope Church in Red River, Minnesota. According to background data, the Red River overflows every spring like clockwork with the run-off from snow. A winter of exceptional snowfall engorges the river, bringing it to a flood stage that places the entire town at risk. Even though the church had been around for more than seventy-five years before Weston agreed to insure it, no one at Weston bothered to ask why New Hope had a new structure. From what Mallory could tell from the file, it was because the church had been rebuilt on the same plot of land adjacent to the river after having been destroyed by flood ten years before. For whatever reason, the Weston underwriter agreed to provide flood coverage even though that was not typical for the industry. Mallory noted that Weston paid just under $4 million to settle the claim.

Stretching in her chair, she looked at Nick. "Reading these files is getting depressing. It's no wonder Weston lost money doing all the stupid things we did."

"You know, maybe we're looking at this all wrong," said Nick. "The property files reflect what we already know. Weston made poor underwriting decisions, in many cases driven by unscrupulous brokers. Of course, on the theory that God hates trailer parks, and apparently churches, Weston also had some terrible luck."

"What are you saying?" asked Mallory.

"The property claims are pretty cut-and-dried. Nasty losses with big payouts, but once the file is closed, Weston owes nothing more. The liability files seem worse. Higher payouts where Weston has been or could be on the hook for years to come. Of the remaining files, let's focus on the liability claims."

"That makes sense," said Mallory. "It will also save time and an enormous amount of emotional energy."

"Someone here was asleep at the switch," concluded Nick.

After a pause, Mallory replied, "Speaking of that someone, is tonight your big date with Tina?"

"Yes," replied Nick.

"Where are you going?"

"If you must know, the Packerland Steakhouse."

"At least you should enjoy the food and the setting. I've haven't been there in some time, but the place is full of autographed football memorabilia. You might even see a player come through. Also, if the conversation gets dull, you can watch the big-screen TVs in the bar."

"Thanks for the tip, Mal," Nick replied, just as his cell rang.

Nick listened to the first minute of the call, then responded. "Sure, the day after tomorrow works for us . . . Yes, we'll have our files along . . . Let me see if I can pull the arrangements together tomorrow and get back to you to confirm." The call ended with, "Thanks, Chuck."

Clicking off the cell, Nick explained to Mallory that it was Detective Nowitzke, and they had a tentative meeting with Chief Hutchins on Mackinac Island.

As Nick stood to leave to head to his dinner with Tina, Mallory grabbed her phone and began to search for charter planes. "Have a nice time. I'll make myself useful and see if I can find us a plane."

CHAPTER 37

Nick was running late. He had stopped at home to change his shirt, splash some water on his face, and grab a sport coat. When he got out of his car in front of the Packerland Steakhouse, the aroma of grilled meat told him he was in the right place. Entering the restaurant, he saw Tina sitting near the end of a long brass bar facing away from him, nursing a martini and watching one of the televisions Mallory had described. Nick judged she had definitely not just come from the office. Dressed in a tight black dress that was off one shoulder and halfway up her thigh along with black stiletto heels, he was happy he opted to wear a jacket. As he approached, she turned and flashed a smile at him.

"Wow, you look beautiful tonight," he exclaimed.

"You clean up pretty well yourself. Would you like something to drink before dinner?"

The bartender had seen Nick approach and overheard the conversation. Nick ordered a Stella and sat down next to Tina on one of the raised stools.

"This is quite the place," said Nick, looking around.

"I know you played college football and thought this might be fun," replied Tina. "I'm a Packer fan myself and enjoy the entire season, college and pro. Before we get our table, we should look around at all the stuff. They've got framed photos and autographed footballs all over the place. Also, in the main dining room, there's a replica of the Lombardi Trophy. Oh, and the steaks here are incredible."

After Nick's beer arrived, he looked at Tina. "What should we toast to?"

Her eyes glistened for a moment and then she replied, "How about to life?"

"Damn straight," Nick responded as they touched glasses. *Emil's life. Stop, don't go there. Just enjoy the company of a beautiful woman.*

"How are you feeling, Tina?"

"I'm great. I've seen the doc, and she has me on some meds that should control my symptoms. Sitting in that hospital bed overnight gave me a chance to think. I've begun to look at things differently and feel like my outlook is more positive now." Tina took a sip of her drink. "You know, Nick, I went back to that dock at Emil's and saw just how far out on the water I was when I had my seizure. I can't believe the ground you covered to rescue me. People have told me that I was lucky you were there."

"You sure scared the hell out of me. Candidly, I wasn't sure I could get to you in time."

She grabbed his hand. "I know I've told you before, but thank you. I'm sorry we got off to a bad start. It was my fault."

As they were finishing their drinks, they meandered through the bar and took in the mementos. The bar was decorated in heavy wood, and the floor was covered in large, old-style, black-and-white checkered tiles that had some wear to them, giving them a more authentic look. Framed photos and signed everything from former coaches and players were displayed. A large dining room showcased oaken bookshelves and tables covered in white linen tablecloths. The staff wore uniforms with white jackets embroidered with the name "Packerland Steakhouse" above the lapel pocket. The ambient lighting surrounding them created a relaxing atmosphere.

A lissome hostess, who knew she was attractive, seated Tina and Nick at a large window table.

"This is pretty impressive," said Nick.

"Just wait until they bring out the steaks for you to see."

A waiter placed a wine list on the table and asked if either had been to the restaurant before. While Tina said she had, she wanted Nick to see the presentation. The waiter returned, carrying a large silver tray displaying an impressive sample of several cuts of red meat before launching into his spiel about their quality.

Tina and Nick each chose a large tenderloin filet and a wedge salad to go along with a high-value cabernet that jumped off the wine list.

As they waited, Nick asked, "Can we have one ground rule tonight?"

Tina looked at him and smiled. "I guess I'd like to hear what you're proposing before I agree."

"Fair enough. How about no discussion about actual work tonight?"

Tina raised the remains of her martini, nodding in agreement. As the wine and salads arrived, they had each survived a flurry of small talk before Nick broke some new ground.

"Tina, can I ask why you chose to work for an insurance company? After talking with so many people at Weston, I haven't found too many that set out with that goal in mind."

"Let's not talk about work, but why do I work in insurance?" Tina laughed, and waved off Nick's attempt to explain. "No, it's okay, I think I see the difference. I don't know too many people that made it their goal to join the industry either. After I graduated from college, insurance kind of found me. At the time, people weren't beating down the doors to hire new graduates. Since eating seemed important at the time, I was offered a job to become a broker at a firm in Minneapolis after going to an on-campus career fair. Of course, my father worked in the industry, but that was just a coincidence. When I started in insurance, I made a promise to myself it would not be a career."

"Will you keep your promise?"

"Who knows. I like my job and would like to move up at Weston, but there are some days I think I'd rather be running a coffee shop. You accepted Emil's offer, even though you have no experience. Why?"

"My military career was over." Nick paused, took a breath. "My parents were dead. I didn't know what I was going to do. When your father invited me to Weston, I thought he wanted to make a connection because my parents had died. They were old friends, and my father actually worked at the company."

"I know," replied Tina. "He was a bit of a legend, like Emil. I'm sorry about your parents."

After a short silence, Nick continued his story. "Anyway, Emil offered me a job, and I wasn't smart enough to be able to talk my way out of it. But I can tell you it will not be a career for me. Don't get me wrong, your father's a wonderful guy, and I appreciate his help. However, I have no idea what my next job will be. Although running a coffee shop might be fun . . . if it had a wine bar in the evening."

"Now you've got something," Tina agreed.

The waiter cleared the salad plates and brought out two massive knives in preparation for the slabs of beef that followed.

"Can I ask you why you returned to Weston after your stint as a broker?"

"Has Mallory, or even Emil, told you about my mother, about what happened at the time of her illness?"

Nick nodded. "I don't know too much aside from the fact that you and Mallory do not share a biological mother." Nick tried to sound clinical, with no judgment and no opinion on the matter.

"After Emil told us about his affair, I flipped out. I was young, made some strong statements, and just left. After several years of stewing about what happened, I decided I wasn't necessarily happy in Minneapolis and wanted to have a chat with Emil. You should understand that even before I left, he wasn't necessarily father-of-the-year material. He had thrown everything into his work. He was 'old' when we were born and was always more engaged in work than either of us. When both Mallory and I began working for him, he insisted that we call him 'Emil,' instead of 'Dad,' to keep things 'professional.' Neither one of us has ever gone back to 'Dad.' I can't speak for Mallory, but part of the way I cope with his past, his affair, is by seeing him more as a father figure, like so many other Weston employees do. But, he's a better father figure than a father, I suppose. Actually, I ended up looking to Frank Raymond in Emil's absence."

"Seriously? Frank doesn't come across as a warm and fuzzy type that would have time for a young woman."

"I get that. He's got some issues. But for whatever reason, he took an interest in me and has been a mentor for many years, even after I came home."

"How did your conversation with Emil go after you returned?"

"Even after all I had said and done, he said he loved me and was proud of what I had accomplished. He invited me back to Weston and found a place for me. Over the years, we've made our peace. I have come to respect him. In fact, I would do anything to please him. He is my father after all. I'm not sure that's much of an answer, but it's all I can give you.

"I would do anything to please him." *Like trying to create an enormous niche market, while ignoring all the signs that it's a huge mistake?* Nick was on the verge of asking when he remembered his own ground rule for the night. He switched gears.

"I get it. So, if you've reconciled with Emil, why do you and Mallory seem not to get along?"

Tina finished chewing her food, took the napkin off her lap, and wiped her mouth. "Nick, I know you said only one ground rule, but I'd like to add one more about Mallory."

"Alright. I wasn't trying to pry, but I was."

"It's fine. I'm not ready to discuss it with you. Maybe we can talk about Mallory at some point in the future."

"Well, good for me."

Tina looked confused. "Why?"

"It implies we have a future of some sort. Perhaps a second date."

"Don't go overboard," replied Tina. "We'll see how this one finishes first," she said with a knowing glint in her eye.

After carving another edge off his steak, Nick looked at Tina and made his move. "You know, you're reaching dream girl status for me?"

Tina put down her knife and smiled. "Oh really. How so?"

"Let's see. A beautiful woman with a brain who likes steak, wine, and football. I think that pretty much checks everything on my list."

"Who was on the list before me?"

"No one. You're the first to hit all my criteria. I've never really had time for anyone in college or with my work in the Air Force. Being on constant deployments, I didn't think it would be fair to anyone. If I wasn't on a deployment, I was only looking for R&R and to get healthy."

"You mean with your friend Philemon?"

"Yes, but even though he likes football and steak, he doesn't fill out a dress like you do. It's just not quite the same."

Tina laughed. "I'm kind of in the same boat. Most of my adult life has been focused on work. In some respects, I'm like Emil. Although I've had some opportunities, there was nothing ever serious for me."

"So, we're two kindred souls lost in the world."

"At least until now," Tina replied.

CHAPTER 38

When Nick arrived at the conference room the following morning, Mallory was there waiting for him. Before he could take off his jacket, she started.

"So . . . spill it," she said.

"Spill what?"

"You know, tell me about your date with Tina."

"Oh that," he said coyly. "We had some drinks, a nice conversation, and an outstanding dinner. The collection of Packer stuff at the restaurant was amazing."

"Sounds more like a business dinner than a date."

"Oh yeah, and then we did it in the back of her Audi in the parking lot."

"Screw you. You barely fit in the front of an Audi."

"Well, I thought that's what you wanted to hear. Hey, did I push you for details of your time with Philemon?"

"No," came a sheepish reply.

"You know why?"

"Because you're an officer and a gentleman?"

"That, and because P-Man gave me all the details anyway." Before Mallory could find anything to throw at him, Nick finished. "Just cut me a little slack on this, please."

"Okay," replied Mallory. "Well, since my night was not anywhere near as exciting as yours, I made arrangements for us to fly out of the Appleton International Airport tomorrow morning at eight o'clock.

We can fly directly onto Mackinac Island. I couldn't believe they had their own airport designation symbol. It's MCD, if you're ever playing airport trivia. I also talked with Nowitzke and Taylor to coordinate with them. We'll meet them at the airport. Chief Hutchins will pick us up in Mackinac."

"How long is the flight?"

"According to the NetJets website, forty-eight minutes, one way."

"Piece of cake. We should be home in time for dinner. Thank you for making the arrangements."

After ordering roses to send to Tina, Nick spent the rest of the day prepping with Mallory to discuss any links between the deaths of Donovan and Palmer with law enforcement.

****

The sleek, white and black Embraer Phenom 300 looked like an oversized bullet glistening in the sun as it sat on the tarmac of the executive wing of the Appleton airport. Mallory and Nick arrived at the airport together about the same time as Nowitzke and Taylor. Following a quick greeting, the group found their way to the NetJets office where they met their pilots, Bryan Mitchell and Heidi Dileo. Dressed in matching white shirts and blue pants, they introduced themselves and confirmed the destination. Mitchell, a tall and energetic man in his early forties, appeared to be the senior member of the team. Nowitzke, a nervous flier, was happy to see some grey hair on Mitchell's temples after studying Dileo. The short and trim woman had her black hair pulled into a bun and was the epitome of professionalism. However, Nowitzke observed a little too loudly that she looked like last year's junior prom queen. Taylor rolled her eyes. "Chuck," she said in a voice that matched Nowitzke's. "Your comment could be carbon-dated."

Mitchell responded, "Sir, don't let looks deceive you. Dileo is your pilot today. I'm her copilot. She graduated at the top of her class from the United States Naval Academy and flew fighters. Two tours in the

Persian Gulf." Mitchell held up a couple of fingers. "She's a trained killer," he said for effect, leaving the detective unsure if he was joking about his last comment or not.

As the group moved toward the plane, Taylor balked. "Don't we have to go through screening and TSA?"

Dileo smiled. "No, that's the beauty of a private flight, no lines. Climb aboard and watch your heads. There's only about five feet of clearance on board. Make yourselves at home."

Climbing the stairs, each passenger quickly found a large leather seat and buckled in. Since the plane was equipped to handle seven people, they could each spread out. Appointed in wood and gold trim, the cabin was more than comfortable.

"Hey, I can't go fly coach after this. I'm officially ruined," said Taylor.

As the engines spun up, Mitchell poked his head through the door from the cockpit. "Has everyone here flown before?"

The pilot saw all four heads nod.

"Does everyone here know how to operate a seat belt?" The question was directed specifically at Nowitzke. The group chuckled at the detective's expense. "Just to manage expectations, there will be no bags of peanuts today, and you have to help yourself if you want coffee from the galley once we're airborne. It's a quick flight, and we're number one for takeoff. See you in Mackinac." Mitchell shut the cockpit door.

When the jet touched down, Nick could see several single-engine planes clustered around a modern-looking white building that looked more like a house than a terminal. Literally cut out of the woods, the airport had no control tower, meaning that planes arriving or departing were responsible for avoiding collisions, not that there was much air traffic on Mackinac.

Stepping from the plane onto the tarmac, each member of the party stretched to the full extent of their height after emerging from the somewhat cramped interior that Nowitzke labeled a flying culvert. "But it still beats flying commercial," said the detective as they walked toward the house.

"Nick, do you have any timetable on your meeting today?" asked Dileo.

"Ma'am, we're not sure how long this will take," shaking his head no.

Dileo pulled a business card from her front shirt pocket. "Here's my cell number. Give me a call about thirty minutes before you want to leave so we can file a flight plan and get you home."

Once Dileo turned back towards the terminal, Mallory pulled up alongside Nick. "Your new girlfriend isn't going to like you getting phone numbers from hot young pilots."

"Good point," said Nick. "You're now in charge of making the call so we can leave this afternoon," he said, handing the card to Mallory.

"Shit," replied Mallory, jamming Dileo's card into her purse.

"Curbside service" took on new meaning as a horse-drawn carriage stood in wait outside the terminal along with Chief Hutchins, Chad Acosta, and the driver. Nowitzke and Taylor greeted Hutchins before making introductions all around.

"First time on Mackinac Island?" Hutchins threw out a general question.

The visitors' heads all shook yes aside from Nick, who explained that his parents had been frequent visitors over the years, bringing him to the Grand since he was a teenager. "It's always a treat to come to the island," said Nick.

After the easy glide from the plane ride in, the sway of the burgundy-colored wagon and the clip-clop of the horse's hooves on the pavement offered quite the contrast. "It's a quick one-mile trip to the hotel," said Acosta. "We reserved a conference room there for our discussion, but we have to make a quick side trip." The two large black horses seemed to know the way through the woods and down Annex Road. Though they became confused trying to turn left automatically into the hotel property before the driver intervened, demanding they continue onto Cadotte Avenue before coming to a stop outside the Little Stone Church.

A steady flow of tourists moved up and down the street, enjoying their vacations without giving a second thought to the group stepping out of the coach. Once they had assembled, the first instinct of the visitors was to turn around and look back up the hill, taking in the majestic old hotel. However, Chief Hutchins quickly got their attention when he announced this as the sight of the Palmer murder. In short order, Hutch pointed out where the body was found, where they believed the shooter was positioned, and how the scenario played out, up to and including the grisly discovery by the honeymooners. For Nowitzke and Taylor, it was a clinical afterword to Hutch's presentation in Las Vegas. Each asked a few clarification questions, but for them, the picture was crystal clear. For the civilians, there were different reactions. Although Nick had seen combat, hearing the details and graphic narrative of the cold facts took him back downrange. He suddenly became pallid and started to sweat profusely as the reality of what had transpired set in. Then, his knees locked as Hutch talked about the direction of the shot as confirmed by the pattern provided by the arterial spray from Palmer's wound. He took several deep breaths trying to calm himself. *Another attack. Fucking PTSD. I need to fight through this without anyone seeing me.* Then, he felt someone seize his arm.

Mallory took charge, walking him a few steps away from the immediate area to a place where a prevailing cool breeze moved over the grass. "Are you alright, Nick? Take a few deep breaths and close your eyes," said Mallory. "Let me know when you want to step back into the conversation."

The law enforcement officers and Acosta were so engrossed in talking through the finer points of Palmer's murder that they didn't realize the two Weston employees had stepped away. Several minutes later, his color returned, and they rejoined the others at the coach before climbing aboard for the short ride back up the hill to the main entrance of the hotel. Nick gave Mallory a long, grateful look.

Acosta whisked them through the lobby to a space denoted as the Gerald R. Ford Conference Room. For the first-timers on the island, the elegance of the lobby left quite an impression on each of them. Within the small blue conference room, several tables had been pushed together and covered with a red cloth into one unit, surrounded by nine padded leather chairs. A large-screen television sat in one corner of the room while a coffee station had been placed in the opposite corner.

Once everyone had taken their places and the door was closed, Hutch picked up from where he had left off on the street. As he concluded his review, Hutch produced a plastic evidence bag containing the actual letter with the line from Hammurabi, passing it around the room. "Note the phrase about the broken bones," said Hutch before playing the grainy video of Palmer's murder. For those seeing it for the first time, Hutch noted again the collective head snap in sync with each of Palmer's legs.

When Hutch finished, Nowitzke stood, offering the comparative details about Edward Donovan's death. Not to be outdone, he also produced an evidence bag containing the letter with the single line from Hammurabi. A full hour later, including a give-and-take of questions from Hutch and Acosta, Nowitzke explained how he and Taylor had followed the trail to Minneapolis where it dead-ended.

The discussion then moved on to the physical evidence gathered at the respective scenes. Nowitzke offered photos of the degraded boot prints he had tracked through the snow. Hutch countered with the bloody boot prints of Palmer's killer. The only points of agreement were that the prints were roughly the same size and appeared to have been left by tactical boots. However, this led to another sidebar conversation. "Chuck, while the prints you found appear to be close in size to those left by the killer on Mackinac, everyone who lives in the upper Midwest knows a footprint in the snow can increase in size depending upon the local conditions. That's assuming, too, the photo of the print you took was from the killer. The plain fact is that Target sells boots with similar tread patterns by the boatload. It might just be a coincidence." Nowitzke grudgingly agreed with Hutch's conclusion.

Nowitzke then produced the shell casing he had found at the sniper's perch while Hutch offered an evidence bag containing the slug that had fallen from Palmer's body onto the street. "I have one additional piece of data," said Hutch forebodingly. "The preliminary forensics report from our people arrived this morning. They concluded the weapons used on Palmer and Donovan were different. Even though the slug and the casing certainly came from sniper rifles, that's the only similarity."

Nowitzke nodded in agreement. "I got our report early this morning and read it on the flight here. Our people came to the same conclusion. Different weapons were used in each murder," his voice falling off to silence. "I can't argue with the science, but I continue to wrestle with the similarities between the death letters. That cannot be a coincidence, but it's the only connection between the two murders."

Mallory chimed in. "I'm no expert, but the paper quality is essentially the same, like it came from a standard printer. The font and the ink look identical between the letters."

"Oh, and there is at least one more coincidence," said Nick, getting the group's attention. "Weston insured both entities. But beyond that, we couldn't find any connection between Palmer and Donovan aside from being responsible for the massive payouts we made."

Hutch looked at Nick and Mallory. "Okay, let's talk this through. How many other religious accounts did Weston have?"

Nick deferred to Mallory, who was more familiar with those details. "A little over a thousand," she said.

Chuck followed up. "Does Weston exchange data with other carriers who offer coverage for religious institutions?"

Mallory said, "No. But even if we did, I'm not sure any other insurers would even know about any murders. These incidents only came to our attention because we listed the names of some of our bad actors on Google Alerts. Had we not, I'm not sure we'd even know about the fate of Donovan and Palmer."

"So, the only other coincidence is Weston's bad luck?" said Hutch to no one in particular. Focusing on Nowitzke and Taylor. "While there are similarities between the Donovan killing and that of Palmer, my conclusion is we don't have enough evidence to call this a serial killing."

"I agree," nodded Nowitzke. "The letters suggest a link, but I wouldn't go advertising this broadly. The fact of the matter is, aside from the killers, only the people in this room know about the Hammurabi connection. If there are any copycat killers, they wouldn't know about this specific detail. Aside from that, I don't have any suggestions regarding next steps to take or even who should be taking them."

Nick looked at Hutch and Nowitzke. "Since you've looked at these murders from your own individual perspectives, can you climb into each killer's head and tell me what you think? I'm just curious."

Hutch stood up from his chair. "Boy, Nick, that's tough to say. Looking only at the Palmer killing, I'm not sure I could answer your question. I guess my inclination would be to focus on the victims. As I understand it, Palmer was investigated for child abuse and murder, but not convicted, not even arrested. The campers were underprivileged and had few resources. They don't fit the profile of a sniper tracking down Palmer, who was living under an alias, and then shooting him. Palmer also ripped off donors, but I don't see anyone from that group being out for blood. Sorry, it's not much of an answer," he concluded.

Waiting for Hutch to finish, Nowitzke responded. "I'm not sure I could answer your question either, Nick. In the Donovan case, you have a pedophile priest who molested kids for years. Like Hutch, I'd also start with the victims to provide a clue about the perpetrator. But you have any number of different possible directions," he said, pausing. "Maybe someone who was abused by a priest, meaning any priest, when they were younger grew up and is now looking for retribution? Perhaps it's a loner looking to become famous when they are eventually caught? Perhaps some religious zealot who ascribes to all the portions of the Bible, except the 'Thou shall not kill' part? We don't know who Donovan's victims are, but my instincts tell me it wasn't one of them anyway. Even if there was a vendetta by a family member, someone would also have had to find Donovan and then be willing to go to prison for shooting him. A real question is who had the resources to track Fast Eddie down along with the motivation to kill him? God knows?"

Taylor spoke quietly, "You know, it occurs to me that both men committed horrific crimes, but neither was convicted nor did any jail time. Essentially, neither paid any real price for their crimes."

"That's a good point," said Hutch. "Nobody likes to see a criminal get away with it. But, seeing someone doing it and being motivated to mete out justice on their own are two different things. Even for a victim, it's a lot to take on, the planning, and the execution, just to make it right."

For both Nick and Mallory, the phrase, heard so often spoken by Emil, jolted them both. The conversation ended on that note. The group had talked through all the details again, coming to no conclusions. But as the group packed up, Nick and Mallory looked at each other, both wondering the same thing: Was someone at Weston involved? Who?

Unknown to Nick or Mallory, both detectives were wondering the same thing. As the others excused themselves to use the bathroom before lunch, Nowitzke and Hutchins quietly shared a thought.

"Chuck, do you think someone from Weston could be involved in these cases?" asked Hutch.

Nowitzke shrugged. "Possible, I guess. But what's the motivation for someone there to do this? Even if it is, I doubt it's one of these two. Why would they volunteer the information? There's no way either one of us would have connected those dots."

"Fair enough. But if it is someone at Weston . . ." Hutch continued, ". . . Nick and Mal better be watching their backs."

Nowitzke just nodded.

Acosta had catered a deli lunch into the room. However, the conversation had waned as much as the collective appetite of the group. After picking at their food for an hour, the security chief walked them through the lobby, serving as a docent talking about the history of the Grand. One wall along their path spoke volumes of the prestige enjoyed by the hotel over the years with a series of photographs of past United States Presidents, politicians, and movie stars who had stayed there while on the island. The short hotel tour ended with another coach ride back to the airport.

"This looks like my kind of place," said Nowitzke.

"Get your platinum card, and let's make an afternoon of it, Chuck," said Nick.

Nick gave the high sign to Mallory to call Dileo to get the plane ready for the return trip home. Hutch and Acosta thanked the detectives and the Weston staff for making the trip to the island. The primary takeaway was it was not a wasted trip, but the result was unsatisfying. Yet, Nowitzke and Hutchins both knew it was only a matter of time before one or the other would get a break in their case.

CHAPTER 39

On the short plane ride back to Appleton, Nick tried to sleep. But his brain would not let him as it churned, replaying the entire meeting in a never-ending loop. When the Embraer landed, he and Mallory took a rain check on happy hour with the police officers. Nick was convinced that all the pieces to the puzzle were right in front of him, but he just couldn't put them together. *Was this now part of the mission?* On the drive home, still deep in thought, Mallory roused him with a question she repeated for a third time.

"What's on your mind?"

"I'm sorry. Were you talking to me?" asked Nick.

"I was trying to, but your head was somewhere else."

"I just keep thinking about the meeting today, and something bothers me."

"Like?" Mallory questioned.

"A couple of things. Hear me out and tell me what you think. During the discussion, Hutch and Nowitzke talked about the killer and the crime in terms of the victims. Who are the victims here?"

"What do you mean? As in the abused kids, those injured and killed?"

"Mal, think about this. Who else was a victim of these crimes?"

After thinking it through, she said, "I suppose Weston Insurance was the victim."

"Absolutely. However, no one ever thinks of a company, let alone an insurer, as a victim."

"Anyone else?"

"Well, I guess, going with your logic, Weston's employees."

The BMW came to rest in front of The Lakehouse.

"Got time for a drink?" asked Nick.

"Based on the discussion, I'm guessing yes."

After they had each grabbed a Stella and moved to the deck, Nick continued his stream of consciousness.

"Do you remember when Chuck made the point that the only coincidence between the killings was the death letters quoting Hammurabi?"

"Yes, and you said the other was that Weston insured both entities who were associated with Donovan and Palmer."

"Yes, so Weston is a common thread," concluded Nick. "Remember Hutch commenting it was really bad luck to have insured both." He took a pull on his beer before continuing. "Then, there was a discussion that neither Palmer nor Donovan were in plain sight. Both needed to be found. Donovan at his rehab stint and Palmer living a new identity on Mackinac."

"Right. And someone said that would require resources . . ."

". . . and motivation," chimed in Nick, "but I'll get back to that shortly. Who would have the resources to be able to track down these guys?"

"Someone with a lot of money and time . . . and inclination."

"Like an insurance company?" asked Nick.

Mallory was silent.

"The next thing that jumps out to me is that someone said neither Palmer nor Donovan were convicted or did any jail time," said Nick.

"That was Anissa."

"Correct. What would you call that?"

"Call what?"

"The fact neither of the perpetrators were convicted nor served time."

"I suppose . . ." said Mallory, pausing, ". . . an injustice."

"Do you know anyone that has talked about getting justice lately?"

After a thirty-second pause, Mallory exclaimed, "Wait, Nick. Are you really saying Emil might be the shooter?"

"It might be a wild theory, but doesn't it all fit in a weird sort of way? He had the opportunity."

"How so?"

"Mal, he has access to all the data from the files. He watched the program flourish until the crushing losses started to come in. Then, he has said on several occasions that the religious institution losses have put the entire company at risk . . . his company. He has the budget of a CEO and his schedule is his own. Oh yeah, and he's a combat veteran who has been trained to use a rifle."

"But he's an older man," protested Mallory.

"A motivated older man who's pretty damn spry for his age. Each of these murders was done from long distance. He wasn't planning on hand-to-hand combat with either of the victims."

Nick thought for a moment and continued. "At my last meeting with Emil, I had asked him if he would let me out of my contract. He said he wouldn't because I needed to complete the investigation of the religious institution business. But he also said we—both he and I— needed to work to 'make this right,'" Nick said, using air quotes. "He was definitely referring to an exit strategy. It's his company, and this whole program is the single blot on his record at Weston. The man who wrings his hands when he talks about the Christian fuckers? Mal, you have to admit, it's a valid theory."

Mallory sat staring straight ahead, her face ashen, showing no emotion. Nick had made a compelling case.

Tears began to stream down Mallory's face. "Can we stop talking for a moment?" she said, pulling her legs up to her chest and wrapping her arms around them. Remaining silent, Mallory began to gently rock back and forth, her brain shifting into overdrive as she picked through the specifics of Nick's argument.

Nothing but the sound of loons on the lake filled the air. Nick drained his beer. "Mallory, I am so sorry for saying any of this."

"I know. I get it. But I just can't believe it. Emil, a killer? Weston might be more at risk then ever, but what would push him over the edge to plan and kill these guys?"

Knowing that his life is going to be over very soon; wanting to "make it right" before he goes, thought Nick.

Nick was at a loss for words. However, in his mind, he now had put everything together. "Mal, can I get you a blanket?"

"Thanks. I'd like that. And can you get me something stronger than a beer?" She hesitated for a moment. "Nick, are you going to tell Nowitzke about this?"

"I don't think I'm ready to quite yet. I think we need to do some more digging, if possible, with some internal records to fill in more of the blanks before offering what could be a wild theory to the police. I think I owe that much to Emil."

Nick went into the house before reappearing with a pair of heavy highball glasses and a bottle of Jack Daniels. He poured two glasses, handing one to Mallory.

"Nick, can I ask you something?"

"Sure."

"What happened on Mackinac Island today? You almost seemed to seize up, and I was worried about you."

Nick took a long pull of his Jack and stared off toward the lake. "Mal, I had a flashback of some sort today. Frankly, I've been struggling with PTSD since I returned from my last tour. Panic attacks mostly. Unprovoked ones. They come and go at random . . . some fucking combat veteran for chrissakes. I am so embarrassed."

Mallory let a moment pass before responding. Then, she sat forward in her chair towards Nick. "It's no big deal. I can't even fathom what you must have seen and experienced. My God, you've done your service to the country. My impression is PTSD is pretty common for returning vets."

"Not for me it isn't. I just am not myself. That little file throwing incident with you . . . I would never have done that in my prior life. I seem to just fly off the handle from time to time in anger and rage. Little things, and some bigger ones, like our buddy Marco Ricci, set me off. Oh, and I've been drinking way more than I should to compensate." He filled his glass again.

"Have you seen anyone to get help?" asked Mallory.

"Yeah, about the PTSD, anyway. Supposedly the temporary kind. I'd been getting some counseling before my parents . . . I will beat this," he said resolutely. "But the process of working through this just sucks, Mal."

Mallory leaned over and filled her own glass again. "Your secret is safe with me. Since the night is going in a tailspin with my supposed murderer father and your anger issues, can I ask you another personal question?"

"Sure, why not?"

"When you were talking with Jon Woods, he asked you about your football career. Now, I don't know anything about football, but I Googled you. Based what I read, I gather you were a pretty good player. He asked you a question that was debated quite a bit in some old articles. It was about you choosing to go to Michigan over Wisconsin. Everyone around here seemed shocked by your decision. Maybe it's nothing, but I never saw your answer, and it made me wonder."

Feeling the effects of the alcohol, Nick stood, steadied himself, and walked to the edge of the deck. "Well, it's a long story."

"I'm not going anywhere, Nick."

"The bottom line is I fucked up big-time back in high school. And when you eff things up to the extent I did, there's a ripple effect that led me in other directions." He drained his glass and set it on the railing. "By the time I became a senior, I had worked my whole life to be an athlete. My father and mother sent me to camps, which helped, but it was my deal. My ticket." He paused. "But I knocked up my girlfriend. A little speed bump to my plan, and that of my father. Man, I can still see the look of disappointment on my parents' faces when I told them the news. It was the first time I'd ever felt anything like that from them before. And then I lost control of the situation.

"A couple of days later, my father told me he was in the process of 'fixing' things. He bought off the girl, Hannah, and her family just to keep everything quiet. It wasn't that long ago, and having a baby in school wasn't great, but not the scandal it had been in earlier generations. Anyway, he pulled out his checkbook and the whole thing was done. I never saw Hannah again. I never heard if she had a boy or a girl." Gazing at the lake, he continued, "I often wonder where that baby is. A teenager by now. I think to myself whether I've run into her or him in passing without ever knowing.

"Well, Dad may have taken care of the girl, but my father's money still wasn't able to bottle up the secret for the locals. I felt ashamed . . . like a black cloud was following me. Before everything took place, I was set to go to Wisconsin. It was one of his dreams for me. Like I owed him for bailing me out. So, I said screw it. Michigan came calling, and I took their scholarship. I just needed to get out of town and get a fresh start, Mal. My darkest secret. But then I compounded things."

"How so?"

"When I graduated from college, the prevailing wisdom was that I would get a shot at the pros. My father was really pushing me hard to get an agent. He actually told me to quit school after my senior football season and spend all my time working out to beef up. But, when I looked in his face, I could still see a trace of disdain for what I'd done. It was still there four years later."

"But you were a success," said Mallory.

"By most people's standards, I suppose. I wanted to earn his respect. I could see that playing football at the next level wasn't going to help me earn that back. So, I said fuck it and joined the Air Force, just to spite him. And I found the most dangerous job I could, Pararescue. I was going to earn his respect or die trying. My penance as it were.

"I wanted to show him what I was really made of. Not a fuck-up. When I decided to leave the military, I wanted to see the look on his face with me in my uniform. But that never happened. I know he loved me, but the son of a bitch died before we get to make our peace," he said, tearing up. "He died feeling like I was a disappointment."

Mallory listened while nursing her drink. "Nick, I know what it feels like to be a disappointment," she said, standing up and moving towards the rail near him. "In fact, I have that feeling every day when I go to work. I hear people talk. 'Why isn't Mallory on the fast track? What's wrong with Mallory?'"

Nick looked at Mallory. "You know you shouldn't listen to what people say. You've got skills that most wish they had."

"So do you.

"Mal, I've never told anyone the whole story before, not even to Phil. I hope you will keep my secret?"

"You can trust me."

CHAPTER 40

Early the following morning, Nick's head was throbbing. As he settled into his conference room with a cup of coffee, he had three unexpected visitors. One that was a pleasure, one that was not, and the third best described as bizarre.

"Good morning, stranger," Tina said, entering the room with a big smile before dropping into a chair across from Nick. "How was your trip to Mackinac Island?"

"It made for a long day," said Nick, wondering how Tina knew about it. *This is a small place.* Evidently, Mallory booking the plane and using Weston money to pay for it made the grapevine plenty fast. Unwilling to discuss too many details or offer his theory about her father that still needed vetting, he tried to shut down that portion of the conversation. "Actually, I'm not sure how much progress we made, if any."

"What were you looking for? I mean, why did you and Mallory need to go?"

"Tina, suffice it to say, there was a murder on the island involving a former customer."

"Oh my God, a murder? Somehow connected to a client of Weston? Who was it?"

"I'm really not at liberty to talk about it, Tina. What I can say though is that the police are working the case hard."

"Do they have any suspects?"

"Yes. There's a videotape of the murder. However, at this point, they haven't identified the shooter." After a pause in their conversation,

Nick shifted the discussion. "I really enjoyed our dinner together the other night."

"Thanks for the flowers. They're beautiful."

"I've been thinking about another date, assuming I survived round one," said Nick.

"While the Russian judge gave you low marks, you pulled through by the skin of your teeth," Tina replied with an even bigger smile.

"How about a road trip?"

"That's a pretty big step. I'm not sure I'm ready for that," replied Tina. "What are you thinking?"

"My parents left me a home in Sister Bay. It's the height of the vacation season up there right now. How about a long weekend there, leaving on a Friday around noon? Oh, and it's a big step for me too."

"I've never been there. What would we do?"

"Golfing, exploring, biking, dinners, drinking wine by the fireplace, hot tubbing, that type of thing."

"That doesn't sound like much fun at all. What about the sleeping arrangements?" she asked.

"You'd have your own room and bath. I'd be in the master suite and lock myself in at night in case you're tempted to get to me."

Tina laughed. "Can I think about it?"

"Another good sign for me. Also, Mallory and I would like to talk about the religious institution program again when you have time."

"Sure, Nick. Let me check my calendar, and I'll get back to you," said Tina as she rose and headed for the door.

As she exited, Tina was met by Emil. Yet she offered no greeting to her father, refusing even to make eye contact with Emil as he entered. "Next," he said, closing the door. "Nick, I've been thinking about when I would tell my daughters about my health issue. As I'm sure you know, Weston is a small place sometimes," never lighting on a chair.

"Tell me about it," Nick agreed.

"I wanted to give you a heads-up that I will ask both Tina and Mallory to a meeting at the end of the day. I'm just going to rip the bandage off and tell them about my cancer and the prognosis. The last thing I want is for them to get this news from someone other than me."

Nick winced. "I can certainly appreciate that. How are you feeling, sir?"

"Remarkably well for someone that will die soon," said Emil. "How's your work coming along?"

"Fine. I think the best way to describe it is we're making slow but steady progress."

"Keep at it, Nick. Jobs depend upon getting this right," said Emil as he departed.

How could this man be a killer? Like everyone else, Emil had his flaws, but accusing him of murder took things to a new level. Nonetheless, even after sleeping on it with his brain grinding through the night, Nick woke up even more convinced Emil must be the shooter. His mind wandered to how Tina would react to Emil's announcement, pondering the amount of emotion she might have. What about Mallory? Her father had been her focus, healthy or not, her entire life. She'd never been away to school, never worked for anyone else. As Nick settled back into his chair to read one of the remaining files, he took a sip of his morning coffee when he saw Frank Raymond standing at his door.

"Good morning, Frank," said Nick.

Raymond just stared at Nick in an odd way and extended his right hand, giving him the finger. Then, as quickly as he appeared, Raymond turned and left without saying a word.

Nick sat stunned for a moment. Then, he burst into laughter. "What the fuck was that all about?" he exclaimed to himself.

Approaching from the opposite direction as Raymond, Mallory heard the commotion coming from the conference room. "What's going on?"

Elaborating only about his final visitor, Nick told Mallory about what had taken place.

"Are you serious? What do you think he meant by that?" asked Mallory.

"I have no idea. I couldn't tell if he was pissed off at me or if that's his sense of humor and he was trying to be funny about something. It was just so weird. That's breaking new ground for me. But you've said all along he's a bit of an odd duck."

"Maybe he's upset you're dating his mentee?" she said, referring to Tina.

Nick let Mallory's comment pass. "I'm not going to worry about it." He stood and closed the door, drawing a serious look from her.

"You want to know what I think about your theory, in the cold light of day? You want me to comment on my father being a potential killer?"

Nick nodded.

"I'm having a tough time accepting your theory about Emil being the killer and want to try and prove you wrong. I'm going to dig into his travel records, expense accounts, and other unusual cash outlays and compare them to the dates Donovan and Palmer were killed for starters. However, recognizing that where Donovan was shot is just down the road, I'm pretty sure Emil wouldn't be looking for any mileage reimbursement there. Beyond that, I'm not sure what the next steps would be. Best case, we find Emil was not involved."

"Sounds like a plan. For the record, Mal, I'm not holding out to be right. I hope you're able to exonerate Emil. Are you able to check those kinds of records without rousing any suspicion internally?"

"I think so," said Mallory, pausing as if dreading her next comment. "Nick, if I can't clear Emil through travel records, do we have to contact Detective Nowitzke about this?"

"Mal, let's get some more specifics first. If my theory is off base, the last thing I want is for Emil to get thrown under the bus publicly for something he didn't do," replied Nick.

"One last question. Although the jury is still out, based on what we've learned from our file review so far, the murderer would appear to be targeting people that were individually responsible for large losses at Weston. If your hypothesis is correct, should we be warning Mason McMillan? After all, his work comp claim will likely be the biggest loss in Weston history."

"I thought about that last night too. I see a difference between his claim and those associated with Donovan and Palmer, though. While Weston will pay big bucks over the remainder of McMillan's life, everything I've read about the guy suggests he is a righteous man who had a terrible accident. His punishment is being in that wheelchair. Contrarily, Donovan molested kids, and Palmer beat and murdered them. And they got to go on with their lives. The worst thing that happened to Donovan was rehab. Palmer was living in luxury. Do you see the difference?"

"Essentially, you're contending that Donovan and Palmer were Christian fuckers, while McMillan is not."

"Well said. That's the way I would look at it, even though I'm trying to play junior psychiatrist on a potential serial killer and could be wrong," said Nick, pausing. "Even if I am wrong about this and the killer is only focused on large-dollar losses, what exactly would we tell McMillan if we did contact him?"

"I guess you're right," Mallory conceded.

"Do you have a Google Alert on McMillan, just in case?"

"I will today."

They agreed the rest of the day would be spent with Mallory making internal inquiries into Emil's travel habits. Nick would focus on one of the remaining files, Hopkins Ministries.

****

It was roughly three that afternoon when Emil's admin, Anita, came to the conference room looking for Mallory. Although Nick made an earnest attempt to read the file, his concern for Mallory and Tina and their pending meeting would not allow him to concentrate. "I'm not sure where she is, Anita." Upon hearing Cassie's voice paging Mallory through the overhead intercom, Nick knew the time had come. Suddenly, Mallory appeared in the doorway.

"Did you learn anything from that file?"

"No," came the flat answer. "Have you been able to track down any details on Emil's comings and goings relative to the murders?"

"Not yet, but I've got some sources willing to quietly give me a hand in Accounting," she replied, still sounding confident in her direction as she drifted reluctantly out of the room.

"Mal, call me if you need anything."

"What could I need? It's not like I'm spending my time trying to figure out if my father is a serial killer, or anything like that." She smiled ruefully and walked away.

"Nothing like that," Nick said to the empty office.

CHAPTER 41

Shortly after Nick returned to The Lakehouse for the evening, the heavens opened, pelting the area with rain. With a chill in the air, he flipped the switch of the propane fireplace and was immediately rewarded with a flame and some heat. He found himself standing in front of the refrigerator searching for something to eat. Although it was well-stocked, nothing really appealed to him. He wasn't even sure if he was even hungry. Frustrated by the depressing direction of Emil's health announcement and his pending theory labelling a man he liked as a killer, he decided to catch up on the local news. However, the heavy rain scrambled the satellite signal, leaving him with an error message that filled the impressive ninety-inch screen. Now, officially bored, he resolved to grab some rain gear and brave the night in search of nothing in particular. Picking up the car keys, he opened the door and was startled to find Tina standing in the rain totally soaked.

"Do you mind if I come in? I had nowhere else to go," she said without any expression.

"Please do," said Nick. "I know that feeling tonight. Let me get you some towels." Nick went into the guest bath, finding several oversized towels before raiding his own closet for a comfortable hoodie and a pair of sweatpants. "Here you go. The clothing will be too big for you, but they always keep me warm."

"Thanks," said Tina, heading for the guest room to change.

"Can I get you something to drink?"

"What do you have in the way of brown liquor?"

"I have no idea," said Nick.

"Then surprise me," she said in a somewhat detached way as she stepped into the other room.

Nick heard the shower and bathroom fan kick in. Taking another Stella from the refrigerator, he sat on the leather couch opposite the fireplace and waited. The call for a brown liquor signaled the worst in his mind, even though he already knew what was coming.

Fifteen minutes later, Tina appeared, looking remarkably refreshed with her hair dry and in place but like she had shrunk in the rain wearing Nick's oversized sweat clothes. "While they are a couple of sizes too big, you were right about them being warm," she said, locating her drink and sitting on the opposite end of the couch.

"Why were you out on a night like this?" asked Nick.

"It's a long story," she said taking a sip of her drink, leaving her momentarily breathless from the alcohol. "Anyway, Emil called me in for a meeting late in the day. When I arrived, Mallory was already there. Since we generally don't meet with our father together, I knew immediately something was up. In his own style, he got down to business and told us both he had late-stage prostate cancer, that he'd waited too long to seek treatment, and the prognosis was he would die in the coming months. Just like that. No emotion. No nothing. It was about the same as if he was telling us he was buying a new car."

"Tina, I'm so sorry," said Nick.

"Mallory cried at the news. I was stunned. Emil has always been so healthy and full of life. I took a more clinical approach, peppering him with questions. Had he gotten a second opinion? Was he absolutely sure no treatment would work at this point? Was he certain about the prognosis? Yes, yes, and yes, he replied. Mallory became even more emotional, and the more she cried, the angrier I got. Then, I just left the room, leaving the two of them behind in Emil's office. By the time I got to the parking lot, it began to rain, but I didn't care. I drove around for a while but didn't want to go home. I needed to talk with someone and ended up here. I stood outside for ten minutes unsure if I should even be here and then wondering if I should be telling you all this. As I thought things through at your front door, I got drenched. Then you opened your door before I could knock." Taking another sip of her drink, Tina got more comfortable, drawing up her feet under her and cradling her glass with both hands. "I'm sorry for intruding, Nick."

"I'm glad you're here," he said reassuringly, but decided he would do more listening than talking, at least for the time being.

"You know, I think back to all those years I wasted by intentionally not being part of his life. I'm so glad I reconciled with him and got the chance to work with him at Weston. I learned so much from Emil."

"He's not dead yet. Hopefully you can build some more good memories with him in the coming months," said Nick.

"I agree. But right now, I'm just so pissed off."

Nick said nothing. He heard the rain beating on the windows as Tina took a breath.

"I'm angry about the stupid disease. I'm angry with Emil because he didn't take care of himself. I'm angry at myself," Tina said emphatically.

"Why are you mad at yourself?"

"Because when Emil told me he was going to die, I couldn't cry. Here's Mallory blubbering away, and I'm just a stoic sitting there without any emotion. Why couldn't I cry, Nick? I just don't get it. On the way here tonight, I started thinking about a lot of things. Like why I'm still pissed at Mallory after all these years. My God, she's Emil's daughter . . . my sister. We were so close when we were young. It wasn't her fault we didn't have the same mother. It was Emil's, but I punished her. Then, this whole religious institution program mess. It was my chance to make Emil proud. But I failed. I went for the quick money and hoped to catch the attention of the board so I could move up in the organization. Yet, it seemed like everything I did . . . every choice I made along the way . . . was wrong. Then to compound matters, I did what every failed executive does. I bailed and tried to distance myself from the program and let others take the fall."

Tina paused and took a long sip of her drink. Nick could hear the rain pelting the sliding door. "Nick, I've never told anyone this, but . . . I've actually met Mallory's mother."

"Seriously? How did that happen?"

"Several years ago, when I was a working at the brokerage, our firm hosted an industry function. I was at a cocktail party in the middle of a conversation when I saw a woman that I thought was an older version of Mallory. Her spitting image really. I worked my way across the room and introduced myself. The woman said she was Dr. Natalie Hickman. We actually hit it off and hung out together for much of the evening. The more we talked, the more mannerisms she had that looked exactly like Mallory. A beautiful woman. We sat together at lunch the following day. During some of our small talk, I poked around with some more personal questions. Profession? Oncology. Married? No. Any children? She hesitated, but said no. We exchanged business cards at the end of the conference. Since we were both living in greater Minneapolis, we agreed to get together for drinks after work one night about a week later. After my second martini, I finally worked up the guts to ask her the question that was stuck in my brain.

"When I got the question out, Natalie blanched and said nothing. When I launched into Swenson family folklore, the woman looked like she was about to have a panic attack. Then, into our third round of drinks, she looked at me. "Who are you? Do you work for Emil? What the fuck is going on? Are you a setup for something?"

"When I told Natalie who I was, she seemed to relax. No, I was not trying to track her down. Our meeting was by pure happenstance. I had no agenda. When we talked, she filled in some of the blanks from her end about Emil and what took place years before. She said she had struggled with the idea of her having an affair with the husband of someone she was treating. But she also said she couldn't help it. You know, Nick, she never even asked me the name of her baby?"

Nick was riveted to the story. "What happened to her, Tina?"

"Interestingly, she took a job in the local area here within the last year. We still get together for drinks or dinner from time to time. Please, Nick, you can't breathe a word of this to Mallory."

"Jesus," replied Nick. "Don't worry, Tina. I wouldn't know how to even broach the subject with Mal."

Nick thought that for someone who hadn't been able to cry at the story of her father's pending death, she had certainly dropped an emotional bomb on him. Everything from family history and more details than he cared to learn, the estrangement of the sisters to a serious, but healthy, admission about what had happened to Tina's religious program. As he was processing everything Tina had said, he needed another beer and refreshed her tumbler with another Jack Daniels and ice before she continued.

"You know, I would do anything to resolve the religious niche mess," said Tina. "I want to make it up to Emil and the employees I've put at risk. I want to prove to Emil that I'm not a failure and show him I can be a great leader. I also want to give Emil the justice he deserves." Tina began to cry inconsolably. Unsure whether her catharsis was primed by the pressure of her job, the news about her father, the alcohol, or the entire lot, Nick's only reaction was to slide down the couch alongside Tina and take her hand while the rain continued to buffet The Lakehouse.

Tina was still resting against Nick an hour later after she had cried herself to sleep. He was also comfortable. With the fire still blazing, he finished Tina's drink, rescuing it from her other hand. The storm had passed. Looking out onto the lake at the full moon, he was in no hurry to move. When Tina roused herself, she was confused by her surroundings before looking up at Nick.

"I've got to get to bed," she said tiredly, pulling herself off the couch.

Nick stood up, taking her glass and his empty bottle to the kitchen when he noticed Tina was not moving toward the door. Instead, he saw his sweatshirt laying on the floor next to his pants in a trail moving in the direction of the master bedroom. Poking her head around the corner of the doorframe, Tina looked at him. "Aren't you coming?"

CHAPTER 42

The morning sun found its way through the master suite's east window, streaming onto the bed and Nick's face, waking him. He felt a gentle touch on his shoulder. Turning his head, two blue eyes were looking back at him.

"Did I wake you?" asked Tina.

"No, I think it was the sun," he yawned.

"Can you tell me about your tattoo and the scars around it?" asked Tina, looking at the circular design of an angel under a parachute with the words "That Others May Live" across the bottom.

"I earned it in San Antonio during a night of drinking and debauchery. Philemon talked me into getting a tattoo and, like a dumb shit, I agreed. Basically, I asked the artist if he could recreate a mission patch for me. Since Phil used them to pick up women, he had a full supply along, and I took the tamest one. It's the motto of the PJs."

"Can you tell me about what the PJs do?"

"It's pretty simple really. We're part of what's called the Guardian Angel Weapon System. Essentially, if someone is injured or needs help, our job is to go . . . no matter what."

"Like you did for me?" asked Tina.

"Yes."

"What about Philemon? Did he get a tattoo as well?"

"Oh yeah, he got one too. While the tattoo guy was working on me, Philemon passed out. I asked the artist if there were any rules about where you could put a tat. Turns out there aren't any. P-Man woke up the following afternoon with both a splitting headache from the liquor and a burning sensation on the left cheek of his ass. Since you can only sense pain in one part of your body at a time, he didn't know why his ass hurt until he sobered up the next day. Once he figured it out, he found a beautiful drawing of a helicopter surrounded by the words, "If You Go Down, We Come."

"Are you serious?" replied Tina, not believing the story.

"Next time he's here, ask him about it. He'll probably give you a peek. The funny thing is I didn't even have to pay for Phil's tat. The artist thought the once-in-a-lifetime story was so cool that he considered it a donation in honor of Phil's service."

"So, what about the scars on your arm?" Tina asked, still fingering the several raised miscolored areas on his shoulder and upper arm.

"That's a longer story," said Nick.

"I'm not going anywhere," replied Tina.

Nick smiled. "The scars are from a rescue in southeastern Afghanistan a couple of years ago. A helicopter crashed in hostile territory, and our team was called to respond. A couple of pilots were ferrying several Army Rangers on a mission when their Chinook helicopter started taking fire from ISIS. On route, we were told all the Rangers were killed when the helo crashed, along with one of the pilots. By the time we got to the site, the locals had found it and were waiting for us. Early in the war, the insurgents figured out a rescue team would always come, and it was their opportunity to kill more Americans. Anyway, when we arrived, I was the first to get on the ground, using a rescue hoist. As soon as I touched the earth, all hell broke loose. Bullets were flying in all directions when I heard the pilot yelling to me from the wreckage. Once I took cover, the locals started shooting at the Pave Hawk helicopter I just left. A bullet hit the helo's engine. When it started smoking, the pilot made the decision to get back to base or risk having more people stuck on the ground."

"Wait, they just left you and the other pilot all by yourselves with all the bad guys?"

"Yeah, but they had no choice. I checked over the downed pilot and, miraculously, he had only minor injuries. Luckily, we had other friends looking out for us."

"What other friends?" asked Tina.

"When we head out on a mission, the PJs are just a part of a Combat Search and Rescue team. A team includes fighter jets, reconnaissance aircraft, and special refuelers. That day, our best buddy was an Apache."

"An Apache?"

"An attack helicopter. It's incredibly nimble, and the weapons system is connected to the helmet of the pilot. Wherever the pilot looks, the weapons follow. This type of helicopter is totally decked out with anti-tank missiles and a thirty-millimeter chain gun. When they made their presence known to the ground fighters, I relaxed. The Apache kept the insurgents busy for several hours before more help came. Once it did, the injured pilot and I got on a cable dropped from another Pave Hawk helicopter, and we made it safely on board."

"So, where did the scars come from?" asked Tina.

"A now-deceased ISIS ground fighter who thought it would be fun to shoot at us on our ride up the hoist. I took several rounds to the upper arm. My pilot was unharmed. The Apache driver got in the last word."

"These are bullet scars?"

"From an AK-47."

"My God, you're a hero," exclaimed Tina.

"Hardly, and I hate that term. The morning network news programs throw that word around pretty loosely . . . like every time someone rescues a cat from a tree. I've met some real heroes that no one ever talks about, least of all the media. I was just doing my job, Tina. Just like all the other PJs still deployed. By the way, what time is it?"

"Nine thirty."

"Shit. I need to get into the shower and get to work."

"So do I. Meet you in the shower," said Tina as she jumped out of bed and stood naked in front of him.

"Tina, I'm already really late."

"You know you get a standard fifteen-minute break at Weston?" asked Tina.

Nick looked puzzled. "Yes, but I never take them."

"You've got some comp time coming."

"Damn, I guess that's why you're in senior management."

CHAPTER 43

By the time Nick arrived at the conference room, it was late morning. His clothes were uncharacteristically disheveled, he did not have his signature Starbucks in hand, and his hair was still wet from the shower. Mallory, seated at the far end of the table, never looked up even though she heard him arrive. Her head down, she was engrossed in studying the initial batch of internal accounting records documenting Emil's travels.

"Good morning, Mal," said Nick, eliciting a guttural response from across the table.

"Mal?" he continued in a softer tone, this time earning no response.

"Mal, how are you doing?" his volume increasing. "Please. I really want to know."

Looking up from her work, Nick saw her face was red and blotchy. Taking a moment to compose herself, she finally replied in a hoarse voice, "Emil is dying of prostate cancer, but I think you already know that, don't you?"

Nick found himself wondering why Emil had told her about Nick's knowing. He was about to try to explain, but Mallory started speaking again.

"When I left for that meeting with Emil yesterday, I thought the worst thing I could go through was thinking my father was a serial killer. Then I learn that Emil is sick, dying actually. Philemon is in San Antonio, and I think I'm in love with him, but now he's halfway across the country. He can't be here for me, for this. The capper was last night when I just decided to work, all night, get lost in my work. I watched the sun rise from Weston and came home to shower and get ready for a new day and saw *her* car parked in front of your house. I knew it wasn't because Tina had made an early morning coffee and donut run before stopping by."

"Mal, Tina came to me last night struggling with Emil's announcement too. One thing led to another, and she ended up staying the night. It certainly wasn't to spite you."

"And once *she* told you the news, did you think that maybe I needed a little attention, a little support? Or is all that less important than the work we've been doing together? You introduced me to Philemon, and once he entered the picture, things changed. I'm so happy to have found him, but I hate that he's not here, especially with everything else going on with work and Emil. But I thought you were my friend. You are the first person at Weston who ever really cared about me for me, not just the boss's daughter. And now you are involved with Tina, and that means I can't rely on your friendship." Mallory's eyes started to tear up, and Nick approached her, giving her an extended hug until she calmed down.

"Mal, I don't have so many true friends that I could discount anyone. With everything that's happened in the last couple of days, maybe you should take some time off." Nick was not ready to talk about the progress of his relationship with anyone, certainly not Mallory.

"I can't take any time off, Nick. You know that. I am more anxious than anyone here to disprove your theory about Emil. Now more than ever," said Mallory.

"Okay, but you've already put in a full day and night working on this and have moved the ball along. Why don't you at least take the rest of the day off? Do you have any sense of when you'll get all the records on Emil's travel?"

"We should get everything by tomorrow morning," replied Mallory. With that, she picked up her briefcase and headed slowly for the elevator. At least Emil had not betrayed his trust. Nick didn't want to think about what Mallory would say if she knew that he had known the whole time what Emil was going to tell them.

****

Nick pulled the Hopkins Ministries file from his briefcase, determined to finally read the document after a previous false start. This file was different than the others with the internal work housed under a jacket with a red cover. Looking over the rest of the stack, he noticed immediately that none of the other files had such a designation. Leaning back in his chair, he put his feet on the table. He had barely completed page one when Tina came into the room and closed the door. "Damn, you always make quite the entrance," said Nick, marveling at how put together she was in her tailored black business suit and heels. "What's up?" he asked, moving back to a sitting position.

"Nothing. I just missed you."

"What's it been? Three hours?" he said.

"Almost. Nick, thanks for last night. After hearing Emil talk about his cancer, I just lost it. I really didn't have anywhere to go, but I didn't want to be alone either. You're a great listener. By the way, the sex was incredible. I think you've now met all *my* criteria. Anyway, driving to the office this morning, I decided I needed some time away to deal with this Emil stuff. Is your offer to go to Sister Bay still on the table?"

"Absolutely. When would you like to go?"

"Could we leave at noon tomorrow? I'm sure we both have things to take care of in the morning before we head out."

"Noon it is. By the way, Tina, you have also crossed off all my relationship requirements last night . . . several times, in fact. And that was even before we played submarine in the shower," replied Nick. "I'll meet you in the lobby tomorrow at twelve o'clock."

As Tina turned to leave, Nick got her attention. "Hey, one last rookie question before you go. Why does this claim file have a red cover when none of the others do?"

"It means it's still active."

"Active? Meaning what?"

"We've had some claims, but for whatever reason, the file is still a working document. Weston must still be handling some additional open losses for the insured. Based on the pile sitting on the table, this looks like the only one still open. What file is that?"

"Hopkins Ministries," Nick said as he held it for her to see.

Tina blinked a few times, then her face shifted to a knowing look. "Yes, Hopkins Ministries. That will make for some interesting reading." Her expression had gone almost completely neutral, and Nick started to fear another epileptic moment, but in a few seconds, everything in her face shifted.

"See you tomorrow," she said with a wink.

Excited at the prospect of spending a weekend with Tina, Nick sat back again, getting comfortable, when the conference room phone buzzed. Anita, Emil's admin, was on the other end.

"Nick, Emil is wondering if you have time to give him an update on your progress."

Moments later, Nick approached Emil's office for the impromptu afternoon session. Traditionally, they met in the morning, but this timing worked well for Nick with his pending trip home the following day. Anita was on the phone at her post, standing guard duty, when Nick arrived. "Good afternoon, Nick," she said with her characteristic smile as she waved him through. Despite the unusual timing, Emil sat at his large desk, writing in his journal. Nick took his traditional place on the couch, crossing his legs while waiting politely for the old man to finish his daily ritual.

As Emil rose from his desk, Nick beat him to the punch with a question. "I thought you typically wrote your journals in the morning, sir?"

"You are correct. However, I had some thoughts this afternoon I just needed to commit to paper. My time is growing short, Nick, and my head has been filled with feelings, opinions, and judgments I had to capture. If nothing else, I feel like I have a new level of clarity about things I never had before. As quickly as I put them in my journal, something else pops into my brain. Keeping a journal is something you should consider, Nick. In the coming years, when you go back through them, you might see how your thinking has changed over time." After his monologue, Emil stared off into space briefly.

"Nick, can you give me any insights about how Mallory and Tina took my news yesterday?"

"Well, Emil, I'd say the reaction of each was what you might expect. Mallory was totally broken up by your announcement. She's compensated by diving deeper into her work. She'll be fine over time, but you caught her off guard," said Nick. "Tina was angry. Not at you, but at the circumstances. As much as she is into her job, my impression is she's having trouble concentrating." Nick also made the decision to leave out the details of his night with Tina.

"Fair enough," said Emil. "I just wanted to get your opinion." The CEO stood and moved over to his large trophy case. Taking out a football in a Lucite case, he returned to the couch. "Nick, I appreciate all the work you have done and continue to do on behalf of Weston. I want you to have this little memento from my collection."

"Emil, I can't accept this," said Nick, looking down at an autograph on the ball.

"And why?" queried Emil.

"First of all, it's one of your personal possessions. Second, you know I played at Michigan, and this ball has been signed by a Badger," laughed Nick. "In fact, it's signed by the asshole who broke my nose."

Emil started laughing. "Yeah, I know. I was there. After seeing you get up after that goal line hit, I was happy to see you weren't seriously injured. As I recall, the Badgers gave you a fight, but the Wolverines prevailed. Anyway, I just wanted to give you something that would always remind you of me."

"That will definitely not be a problem, Emil. Thanks . . . I think," said Nick gratefully, putting the ball and case under his arm.

Before he left the office, Emil approached Nick, giving him a long hug.

"Are you okay, sir?"

"Never better, Nick."

As the doors closed behind him, Nick realized he hadn't given the CEO any update on the investigation. In some respects, he was relieved since his theory about Emil being a killer was still possible. The fewer details he had to provide to someone that might be involved in this bizarre scenario, the better. At the same time, while everything pointed to Emil as the prime suspect, his act of kindness did not fit with Nick's hypothesis. The football felt like a parting gift, and knowing how little time Emil had left, the phrase took on more meaning.

Making the decision to take his briefcase and work home, Nick stopped dead in his tracks after passing Frank Raymond's office. Raymond's door was closed, but Nick could see the executive pouring through a mound of papers spread across his desk. Nick knocked on the door and wedged his body halfway inside the office. When Raymond looked up, he saw Nick standing in the doorway with a football under one arm.

"What can I do for you, Hayden?" asked Frank.

With an expressionless face, Nick slowly raised his left arm. Without a word, he flashed his middle finger at the executive for several seconds before pivoting and turning back toward his conference room. Frank's delayed reaction came moments later, his booming laughter reverberating off the walls of the executive wing.

CHAPTER 44

Nick had made his way back to The Lakehouse and was on his third attempt to begin reading about Hopkins Ministries when he heard Mallory's Jeep scream to a stop in his driveway followed by excited pounding on the front door.

Nick had barely made it to the foyer by the time Mallory barged into the house. Almost hyperventilating, she could scarcely get her words out quick enough. "I think your Emil theory may be right. After I left work, I got a call from my friend in Accounting. Things are lining up, just like you thought."

"Mal, slow down," said Nick calmly. "Take me through what you've found. Can I get you something to drink?"

"Do you have any brown liquor?" asked Mallory.

"Yes, in fact I've had quite a run on the stuff lately," said Nick, making a joke that was lost on Mallory.

Moving out to the deck, Mallory did her best to contain herself, launching into her findings before Nick could even take a seat. "Nick, do you remember Chuck Nowitzke talking about whoever killed Donovan needing resources to locate him in the first place?"

"Yes," replied Nick.

"As part of Weston's internal financial process, the company still uses an outmoded control practice of having two executives sign off on any individual expense over $10,000. I asked Accounting to look at all the expenses needed to resolve the Donovan claim. As you can imagine, this was a pretty costly loss. We paid expert fees and made huge payments to outside counsel, not even counting the payouts to the victims. As part of that review, we ran across an invoice from a company known as Miller Investigative Services. Miller's billing was charged to the Donovan file, but *after* the claim had been settled. One of the executives that signed off on the invoice was Emil."

"Interesting, but hardly conclusive," said Nick. "Maybe someone just needed a signature. In my short time at Weston, I've seen Anita looking for an officer to sign something to process a bill. Has anyone talked with Miller Investigative Services or seen a report?"

"No one seems to have a copy of that report in the building, so I called Miller on the pretext of making sure their bill had been paid correctly. After playing along, I explained I was Emil's admin and that there was some confusion about the original report. I told them it had been misplaced and asked for a second copy to be sent to me. The document arrived this afternoon via email. The narrative is extensive, but the critical part, as far as I'm concerned, includes a reference to a memo noting Donovan undergoing counseling at a church-owned treatment center in Wisconsin. Since there aren't that many types of facilities in the state, the investigators had little trouble discovering Donovan's whereabouts."

"Alright," said Nick. "Would Weston have any reason to locate Donovan after the file was closed?"

"I can't think of one," replied Mallory.

Nick sat back in his chair. "I'm certainly not sold yet. Finding Donovan and shooting him are two different things."

"Agreed," said Mallory.

"Do you have anything that ties Emil to the killing?"

"Well, not exactly. Only circumstantial evidence at best. Remember how Chuck talked about the storm here on the day Donovan was shot?"

"Yes."

"I remember the day now, but never made the connection. The storm was so bad that Weston delayed the opening of the business day until noon. My source can confirm Emil was in town that day based on a mid-morning stop at a local service station for gas for his company car based on a receipt he turned in."

"Mal, that's not much in the way of evidence. The fact he was in town during a snowstorm makes him a suspect along with the other couple hundred thousand people who live in the area."

"My point is that for a guy who travels significantly for work, the receipt verifies Emil was in town that day."

"I assume there's more," said Nick.

"Nick, Weston's expense records place Emil on Mackinac Island on the date of Palmer's death."

"Really?"

"It appears Emil attended an industry conference for CEOs and up-and-coming executives on the island. In fact, he gave the keynote address to the group."

"Do you have any evidence tying Emil to the shooting?"

"Of course not. Chief Hutchins laid out everything for us in detail, and he's stymied as well. Again, my point is Emil had the opportunity to shoot Palmer with his presence on Mackinac."

"Keep going," said Nick.

"That's it," said Mallory. "Look, Nick, I'm trying to move past all the emotion of Emil being involved and just resolve the matter one way or the other." She hesitated for a moment. "Can I ask you a hypothetical question?"

"Sure."

"What if we concluded Emil killed these people? Essentially, he's provided justice against a pedophile and an abuser where the system failed. You could make the case he's ensured that neither of these monsters will ever hurt anyone else. If that's the case, hasn't he done society a favor? Can we let this just run its course?"

"What, and write it off as a sort of Christian fucker karma?"

"I'm asking the larger question, I guess. Doesn't it infuriate you when the news reports about a child molester, or a wife beater, or someone on their fifth drunk driving offense getting off with a little more than a slap on the wrist?" She took a breath. "Or a teenager texting instead of watching the road?"

Nick stared at her, feeling the red of emotion that he worked hard to control.

"Of course it does, Mal. The system is far from perfect. But, if you think that through, where would it stop? Who's to say when vigilante justice is ever over? If Emil is the prime suspect, when does he decide enough is enough? To some extent, what you're saying makes sense in a weird way, considering the nature of the crimes. But what if Emil starts killing people because they're involved in a car accident that causes a large loss to the company? Not because of the reason for the accident, an actual accident, but because of the losses?"

"Obviously, that would be wrong, and there are limits. Nick, I'm not advocating anything. I'm simply asking whether the world is a better place because of Emil's alleged killings."

"Probably. But we live in a country where the rule of law needs to be enforced. I don't even see this as a grey area. If Emil's committed these crimes, he's no better than the people he's killed."

"In my head, I know that. I guess I'm just sick these priests and pastors could get away with their crimes, and now I feel like I'm on a path to ensure my father doesn't get away with his." She paused for a moment. "Now I feel embarrassed for even having raised the thought with you."

"No problem, Mal. I'm writing this off as a philosophical question followed by a reasonable debate. In the meantime, please stay the course with your internal investigation. By the way, I thought you took the afternoon off?"

"I did."

"Mal, you need to develop some hobbies."

Mallory gave him a tired grin, and she left for the rest of the day. Nick sat for a few minutes, not trying to think about how differently things would have turned out if he'd allowed Mallory to provoke him with her "texting teenager" example. What if he'd lost control? *You didn't.* He shifted back to work, telling himself the sooner he wrapped up here, the sooner he could plan for his time with Tina in Door County. He felt motivated.

CHAPTER 45

"I said a weekend, right?" Nick asked Tina jokingly as he hefted her large suitcase into the trunk of his BMW, leaving barely enough room for his overnight bag.

"I wasn't sure exactly what I needed, so I may have overpacked a little."

"At least the trunk lid shuts," said Nick as they got into the car, pulling out of the parking lot precisely at noon.

It was a beautiful late summer day with blue skies and brilliant sun as they made their way north on the four-lane highway, leaving Neenah and Weston Insurance in their wake. The several-hours-long journey took them through Green Bay before they entered Door County, the peninsula of Wisconsin that juts out into Lake Michigan. Billed as the "Cape Cod of the Midwest," Tina confessed to Nick that she had never visited that part of the state but was excited about what she had seen on various websites. But she was also interested in spending quality time with Nick on his home turf.

As the highway winnowed down to two lanes north of Sturgeon Bay, the pace of the journey slowed as they made their way through a series of small, but quaint tourist towns that sprang up along the road. They took their time making several stops at roadside markets that sold fresh fruit, produce, antiques, and cherry-flavored everything, from jams to pies. Nick pulled off the main highway, and they meandered through the backcountry of farmland, large orchards, broad meadows, and deep woods. After several years of duty around the world, Nick was still able to find his way to one of the many well-preserved working lighthouses that dotted the Lake Michigan shoreline.

It was late afternoon when Nick pulled into Sister Bay. Despite the heavy tourist traffic, he still managed to find a parking space just off the road below the top of the hill where he remembered a bar with outdoor seating. Finding a table, he and Tina had a view of the entire town that was buzzing with life. Sister Bay had been cut out of the woods and rested on the shore of Green Bay. Nick took a deep breath. The air was clean and clear with a slight chill coming in off the water. However, both Tina and Nick, who were wearing t-shirts, shorts, and sandals, were comfortable in the late afternoon sun. As they ordered drinks, Tina could not believe the level of activity in the small town, with its population of around eight hundred now bursting with thousands of tourists. People were everywhere, milling about comfortably in the restaurants and on the streets. While Nick and Tina waited for their drinks, they watched a small traffic jam on the main drag caused by tourists who decided to exercise their right of way, as granted by the state of Wisconsin, in crossing the busy two-lane road.

"I forgot about how many vacationers come here at this time of year. A traffic bottleneck happens every five minutes during the season," said Nick. Looking at Tina, he asked, "What do you think?"

"This is such a beautiful place," she exclaimed after taking a sip of her Chardonnay. "I've always heard people talk about Door County, but I just never made the trip. There is so much energy here, but at the same time, I feel so relaxed." She reached over and took Nick's hand. "Thank you for bringing me to such a special place."

"I haven't been able to enjoy this place much lately. When my parents retired here, they invited me back hoping I would put down some roots in the area. With all my travels, I wanted to do just that. But after the accident, I ended up with their dream home, which was obviously not the plan. For now, though, I'll enjoy it until I figure out my next steps. Who knows, I might just become a full-time resident."

"What are the winters like here?" asked Tina.

"Not a whole lot different from those in Neenah. Wisconsin winters are Wisconsin winters. Snow, ice, freezing temperatures, high wind. But there are fewer people here and fewer places open for business. Many of the residents leave for a while for a warmer place. Snowbirds. There are definitely no traffic issues in Sister Bay in the dead of winter. Frankly, a little solitude might be good for me . . . except for this weekend."

Tina smiled. "What are we doing for dinner? Are we going to need a reservation?"

"Not tonight. I'm cooking at home."

"How are you going to make that work? We didn't bring anything besides some snacks and the cherry pie we bought at the market," said Tina.

"Tina, if there is one thing I learned in the military, besides attention to detail, is to always have a P-A-L-N, plan."

She laughed at the irony.

"Actually, my parents . . . no, I have a neighbor who's been watching the house since I went to work at Weston. He's the neighborhood watch guy, retired, like most of the folks in my area. He's helped out by making sure the lawn gets mowed, and other neighborly stuff. I called him after we made our plans and asked if he would do some shopping for me. I think his wife probably did it, but either way, the fridge is stocked. Steaks and salads are on the menu, and I might even be able to whip up an appetizer."

"Well, I'm taking care of dessert," she said suggestively.

"Good, that was the other part of my P-A-L-N."

"So, Mr. Man-with-the-Plan, what's next?"

"I'd like to have another drink and enjoy the scenery," he said, looking at her.

****

As evening approached, the Beamer's headlamps guided their way off the county highway and down the long, gravel-covered private drive cutting through a meadow filled with wildflowers. From the car, Tina and Nick saw lights from the log-hewn home that sprang up out of the field. Nick turned left between two lighted limestone knee walls, which revealed a recently cut lawn and a variety of trees planted about the expansive yard. Rolling to a stop in front of the refurbished cabin, both Tina and Nick got out of the car and heard nothing but the sound of the breeze moving over the meadow.

"Man, I never get tired of that," said Nick.

"Tired of what?" asked Tina.

"Listen."

"I don't hear anything."

"Exactly. When was the last time you could say that?" asked Nick.

"I don't remember."

"Mom and Dad rebuilt an old cabin that has been here for generations. But they also did some remodeling and upgrades to suit their needs," said Nick as he wrestled the bags from the trunk. "About the only thing you'll hear is a random vehicle going past on the main road, an occasional pack of coyotes at night, and the bells tolling from several local churches in the evening or on Sunday morning. Aside from that, it's just total peace here."

Nick dropped the suitcases in the foyer and walked into a cozy room covered with old barn wood. In the corner stood a floor-to-ceiling stone fireplace. "Most of the furnishings came from the local area," commented Nick. "I guess I would describe the place as comfortable. We can take the rest of the tour later. I'm starving," he said, steering Tina toward the updated kitchen.

"What can I do to help you with dinner?"

"How about if you pick a wine from the cabinet, pour a couple of glasses, and relax. I'll fire up the grill?"

Following dinner, Nick chose another bottle of red, and they found their way to several comfortable chairs sitting near the pool and hot tub on the patio. The scent of wildflowers wafted through the courtyard carried by a gentle, warm breeze, and aside from the glow from the pool, the only light came from the sky.

"Nick, I can't remember the last time I saw so many stars," Tina exclaimed.

"We're far enough north that you can see stars here that aren't visible in the city, even a small one the size of Neenah. It's another thing about this place that never gets old."

They sat in silence together, sipping their wine and holding hands while marveling at the heavens.

Finally, Nick broke the quiet. "Can I ask you about Frank Raymond?"

"Oh, Nick, do we have to talk about work stuff?"

"No, it's not about work. I'd just like to know more about the guy. My impression is you're close to him. I'm just trying to understand."

Tina took a sip of wine and a deep breath. "Perhaps the kindest way to describe him is as an 'oddball.' Many people have used worse to describe Frank. He's never been married. He's got few friends, if any, aside from my father. Yet, in some ways, he and I are close. He became my mentor at work when I returned to Weston."

"How did that happen? I would have thought you would have left most people at Weston behind with your technical knowledge after several years at the brokerage firm," said Nick.

"You're pretty good. I felt like I was in decent shape technically, but I needed someone to guide me through the politics at work. Frank filled that bill. Even though he's a hypochondriac and somewhat off-putting to many, he's very smart. Actually, our professional connection was an extension of our relationship before I left for college."

"How so?" asked Nick.

"Well, as much as I love Emil and would do anything for him, he was wrapped up in his business when I was young . . . an absentee father. I understand how that might happen now. Anyway, I'm not sure how things developed, but Frank ended up filling some of that role for me. Kind of the weird uncle, I guess, even though I didn't think so at the time. When I was a kid, he took an interest in me. Taught me how to bait a hook and fish. When I got older, he taught me how to shoot a gun, which evolved into learning to hunt. Frank's a great teacher and was patient with me. I knew he wasn't my father, but he took a genuine interest in me. When you're a kid without that feeling from a dad, you go where you can to get it. The best part was I didn't have to share him with Mallory. Frank came to my school concerts and volleyball games. There was always a distance, but I'll be forever grateful for what he did for me. Even now. We don't agree on everything, but he tells me what he thinks. The further I've gone in my career, I've found that hearing a true opinion from someone is pretty rare."

Nick sat quietly, taking in Tina's story. "That's kind of sad. I'm sorry."

"Don't be sorry, Nick. For the most part, I wouldn't take a do-over on my life." She paused. "Can I ask you a question?"

"Shoot," replied Nick.

"Is that hot tub up to temperature?" she asked, carefully putting her wine glass down on the patio before stripping off her clothing. "Let me check," she said, walking toward the spa.

"It must be time for dessert," replied Nick.

Tina glided slowly down the steps into the tiled tub, turning on the jets on her way. As she sat down, she looked at Nick. "Can you bring me my wine glass?" she asked, bobbing in the water.

"Sure." He knelt to hand her the glass after giving her a long kiss. Then, in one motion, Tina stood up in the tub and, knowing he was somewhat off balance, pulled him into the water fully clothed.

When he came back to the surface, Nick said, "Nice move." Now stripping off his sodden clothing, he said, "No one ever did that to me at Indoc."

"What, kissed you while you were handing one of your boys his wine?"

"Smart-ass. Remember, I was a PJ and can tread water for quite some time."

"Is that all the Air Force taught you about doing in the water?" Tina asked playfully.

"Pretty much. But I learned some other stuff along the way," he said, moving toward her.

CHAPTER 46

Nick's mother used to quote an old saying, that "Nothing good happens after midnight." The saying floated through his head when his phone began to vibrate at three in the morning. Switching on a headboard light, he saw that Tina was still asleep. When Nick heard Mallory on the other end, he could tell she had been crying.

"Nick, I'm so sorry to call you at this hour, but Emil's in the hospital. The ambulance just brought him there. Apparently, he had hired a nurse to live at his house to help care for him. Anyway, she found him unresponsive about an hour ago when she went to check on him. It's not good. The nurse guessed that Emil has just hours to live."

"We can be there in a couple of hours, at best," replied Nick.

"Where are you?"

"In Sister Bay."

"I assume you're with Tina. She must have turned off her phone, because every call I made to her went directly to voicemail. Please tell her she needs to come to the hospital *now*."

"We're on our way."

Nick felt a moment of dread before waking Tina and having to deliver the news that her father was on his deathbed. As Nick spoke, Tina sprang out of bed, fueled by adrenaline. There were no tears or emotions, only a sense of urgency. Within thirty minutes, both had showered and dressed. Since they had been in Nick's home for less than ten hours and had little time to spread out, repacking went quickly. Guided largely by the full moon, they sped through the little towns in darkness, working their way back to the highway. The lack of traffic, when compared to what they had seen the prior day, made it feel like the rapture had occurred overnight, leaving them as the only two people left on the planet. After they made it to the highway, Nick's BMW and truckers hauling their loads were the only vehicles on the road. Both Tina and Nick were quiet, but for different reasons. Tina appeared to be lost in thoughts about her father. Nick was focused on the task at hand, simply trying to beat the clock. The GPS indicated the journey time was just under two hours, and Nick was determined to beat that estimate.

Arriving back in Neenah, they drove through the quiet streets just as the sun was starting to rise. The only traffic consisted of early morning joggers. Tina navigated for Nick until they saw a large blue neon hospital sign letting them know they had arrived at their destination. Nick quickly pulled into the covered entranceway to let Tina out of the car. She dashed from the vehicle, meeting a night security man who had completed his shift. He opened the hospital door and got out of the way as Tina ran towards the information desk. After parking the car, Nick followed a similar trail, finding his way to Emil's room. As he approached the room down the darkened hallway, he heard whimpering coming from the room. By the time he made it to the doorway, the whimpering had turned into full-blown sobbing. He was too late. Emil passed away after leaving "do not resuscitate" orders. As such, the doctor and nurse were in the process of leaving the family to grieve on their own. Mallory was on a couch curled into a ball with tears streaming down her face as she stared out of a picture window. For Tina, the dam burst after hours of contemplation as she stood at the end of the bed, holding onto a handrail and sobbing uncontrollably. As Nick entered the room, the sisters saw him and simultaneously began to move toward him. In what was one of the most awkward moments of his life, Nick had Mallory with a death grip hug on one side, while Tina was squeezing the life out of him from the other. He was the buffer providing the emotional space for each woman as they cried out, mourning their loss. After several uncomfortable minutes, Nick broke their clench and was prepared to send them to their separate corners when Mallory and Tina eyed each other momentarily. Seeing what was taking place, Nick began searching for an imaginary whistle to referee when the young women, unexpectedly, began to hug each other. With each of the sisters now telling the other they were sorry for all their transgressions over the years amidst renewed wailing, Nick headed for the door saying he needed some coffee, but also simply to get out of the room. Despite all of their history, their friction, they had each other. He had no one. Somehow, for some reason, he hurt more now than he had since coming back to Wisconsin. And he needed to have that hurt all alone.

CHAPTER 47

Although they knew it would take some time to completely heal all their wounds, Mallory and Tina agreed that partnering to carry out their father's last wishes would be a good first step. However, Emil was already ahead of them, having completed a detailed plan for family, friends, and employees to celebrate his life. Nonetheless, even with Emil's connections and reach, Mallory and Tina still needed to make sure the day their father had counted on went without any problems.

To no one's surprise, Emil did not want a religious funeral. The man who spent the last few years referring to "Christian fuckers" had no interest in saying goodbye from a church. His body had been cremated, and Tina and Mallory had been presented with an urn and an American flag.

The employees of Weston Insurance were granted the day off work with the closure of operations in memory of their CEO and were invited to an exclusive dinner at Emil's country club. Following the lavish cocktail reception and plated prime rib and lobster dinner, several flat-screen televisions were positioned around the room. Immediately, before the dessert course, the lights in the room dimmed and Emil's face lit up the screens.

"Thank you all for coming today," said Emil from the other side. "My hope is that you have enjoyed this gala commemorating my life. I don't know how many funerals I've attended over the years that did not do justice to the life of the dearly departed. The last meal I wanted served in my memory was watered-down punch and ham sandwiches.

I trust you enjoyed your meal and wine today. Before you get to the dessert course, I wanted to offer a couple of parting thoughts. And yes, for those of my critics in the room, and there are some for sure, Emil will get the final word." His attempt at humor got the desired response from his employees.

"Thank you all for your hard work. I loved Weston Insurance and all my employees, present and past. It was truly an honor to work with you and enjoy the kind of success we had over the years. I know I'm far from perfect, but I've had a wonderful life. I feel love in my heart for my beautiful daughters, Christina and Mallory, and hope they can find a way to mend whatever differences they have so they can go back to being the close sisters they were when they were young.

"Finally, after much personal reflection, I want to leave you all with this thought. Although I've made some great decisions over the years, I also feel remorse for the bad ones too. In fact, I'm drawn to something called The Code of Hammurabi, one of the first sets of laws written by a king for his followers more than 3,000 years ago." At the mention of Hammurabi, Nick almost choked on the water he was sipping and began frantically searching the room, hoping to make eye contact with Mallory. "The forty-eighth law from the great king states, 'If any one owe a debt for a loan, and a storm prostrates the grain, or the harvest fail, or the grain does not grow for lack of water, in that year he need not give his creditor any grain, he washes his debt-tablet in water and pays no rent for this year.' This wise man was talking about debt forgiveness. It's something I have not always believed in but have come to realize how important a concept this should be in our world and for Weston Insurance."

While Emil largely had the crowd in the palms of his hands from the grave, the employees seemed lost and confused to some extent by their fallen CEO's reference to a long-dead king, with Nick and Mallory being the exceptions. Hearing the tape, Nick was now more convinced than ever that his theory about Emil must be correct. He couldn't find Mallory, but he wondered what she was going through, knowing what the quote seemed to confirm.

Emil then took control of the room for the last time. On cue, a group of servers entered the large dining room with trays of champagne. Tina briefly paused the video until each employee had a glass. Then, hitting the play button, Emil continued raising a similar glass on-screen. "Let me make a final toast to Weston Insurance and its wonderful employee base. Here, here!" Emil concluded his pre-prepared speech. "Enjoy the rest of your day off, and best wishes."

A round of applause set off spontaneously, continuing until C. Jonathan Woods rose, standing in the center of the room. "Ladies and gentlemen, on behalf of the officers of Weston Insurance, thank you for coming today. After dessert, it was Emil's desire to keep the bar open for a final after-dinner drink."

Nick wondered if "Sex on the Beach" was on the drink menu as he tried to find Mallory in the crowd. However, Mallory was already moving like a salmon upstream against a throng of employees, working her way toward him. When they finally met, they moved off to a quiet corner of the room. "I'm assuming you had not seen Emil's final address to the troops before today?" Nick asked quietly.

"God no, Nick." Mallory looked genuinely shaken. First with her father's death, and now this obscure reference that probably meant nothing to anyone in the room except to her and Nick. "Had I known about the details of Emil's speech, I would have said something to you before the dinner. I was totally shocked Emil would make a reference to Hammurabi. What does it mean, Nick? Were you right about Emil?"

"I'm not sure. I keep hoping I'm wrong, but this is one helluva coincidence. Who was Emil talking to? I don't think it was either of us since we've never made any reference to Hammurabi in our meetings with him. Was Emil's message meant for someone else in the room? I don't know what his intent was."

"It would be quite the fluke that Emil would mention Hammurabi by accident," Mallory conceded. "It's not like Emil went around quoting the guy on a regular basis."

"Mal, unless Emil was in the know, him making a Hammurabi

reference would have roughly the same odds as being struck by lightning while winning the lottery. Obviously, we need to tie up all the open issues you've been working on before coming to any final conclusions regarding Emil and talking with Chuck," said Nick. "Any idea when that might be done?"

"I should know something in the next day according to my contacts."

"Alright. I'm taking Emil up on his offer and heading home. Can you talk to your sister and discreetly get a copy of Emil's remarks? I'd like to see it again and talk this through in the morning. Hopefully, we'll have all the pieces of information we need by then."

"I will, Nick. Enjoy your afternoon off. I'm heading back to the office to clear up some other details."

As Nick moved towards the door, he saw Tina and Frank Raymond in an adjacent room opposite the large dining room. Although he was unable to hear the conversation, it was clear to him they were arguing. In fact, it was a very heated argument. Changing his direction to intercede on Tina's behalf if needed, both she and Raymond saw him approaching.

"Is everything okay?" said Nick, looking at Tina.

"Yes, Nick. We're fine. We were having a disagreement over an aspect of the religious institution program."

"Since I'm responsible for its dissolution, is there anything I need to know?" asked Nick.

"No, nothing," growled Raymond. "It's old business, and I think we have it resolved."

Looking at Tina for confirmation, she nodded her head. "I'll talk to you later, Nick," she said, essentially telling him to leave.

****

When Nick turned into the drive at The Lakehouse, he saw an unfamiliar small car parked there. Pulling alongside the silver Toyota Prius, he could see Cassie behind the wheel, waiting for him. Seeing the BMW come to a stop, she got out of her car at the same time as Nick.

Still wearing a short black dress from the funeral, it was clear to Nick the redhead had been crying.

"Cassie, are you okay?"

"Yes, Nick. I just needed to talk with you and didn't want to do it at work. Do you have a minute?"

"Sure. C'mon in," he said, holding the heavy front door for her. "Can I get you something?"

"Do you have any bottled water?" she asked.

Nick pulled two bottles from the refrigerator, including one for himself. Handing Cassie her water, he took a seat in a large chair opposite of her on the couch. "What's going on, Cassie?"

At his question, she began crying again. "I'm so sorry, Nick."

"I know. I'll miss Emil too."

"Well, I'll miss Emil, but that's not the reason I'm here." As her eyes moistened, she continued. "Nick, I need to confess something to you. I've been spying on you." Before he could form a reply, Cassie resumed. "Please don't hate me. I like you. But, please don't hate me."

"Cassie, I don't think I could hate you if I tried. Exactly how have you been spying on me?" he asked calmly.

"I was told to report your comings and goings from work, who you were meeting with, what was said if I could find out, your travel schedule, and anything else about the work you were doing," she said.

"Why were you doing that?" asked Nick, who was puzzled.

"Someone thought you were going to hurt Weston Insurance Company with your investigation. They thought you might go too far, beyond what you were supposed to, and create real trouble for the company."

"Why would I do something like that, Cassie?" asked Nick. "Weston is a fine company."

"I was told it's because you haven't been an employee that long and that you aren't one of us."

"I'm not sure what that means," said Nick, pausing. "Who asked you to spy on me?"

Cassie was shaking as she took a long drink of her water, mustering up her courage to speak. "It was Frank Raymond. He wanted to know everything about you. In fact, he told me if I didn't do it, he would see to it that I would be fired. God, I hate that man. But I couldn't lose my job, Nick. I have bills to pay, and I love what I do at Weston. Frank swore that if I said anything, he would personally make my life a living hell. So, I agreed. Then, after I saw how nice a person you were and how you were working with Mallory, I didn't think you were trying to hurt the company. If anything, you made things more fun around here. I tried to stand up to him several times, but he kept bullying me with threats. Please don't hate me," she implored.

Nick shook his head. "Cassie, I'm sorry for what you've had to do. But I'll be honest with you. I'm not sure how much information you could have given Raymond about me." Nick's response seemed to reassure her. "Cassie, I do need to talk with Mallory about this though. Do you understand? Your secret will be safe with us."

"Okay, Nick. I trust Mallory. But no one else, please?"

"Absolutely, no one else." From her reaction, it looked like the weight of the world had come off Cassie's shoulders as they rose from the couch together.

"Thanks for listening, Nick. I feel so much better for having told you." She moved toward him, gave him a hug and a kiss on the cheek, and quickly made her way toward the front door.

Nick waved as she pulled out of the driveway. He took a sip of his water. "Fucking paranoid Frank."

CHAPTER 48

The following morning, Mallory's car trailed Nick's from The Lakehouse into the parking lot of Weston's building. Getting out of their cars, they looked at each other, mouthing simultaneously, "We need to talk." They walked together in silence through the lobby and on the ride up the elevator before making it to the sanctuary of their conference room.

Nick closed the door. "What did you find?"

"I got several calls yesterday afternoon, including one from my internal source," said Mallory. "As I was about to leave work for home last night, I got a call from Miller Investigations. They still think I'm Emil's admin and, apparently, hadn't gotten the word that he died. Anyway, they were trying to track down an unpaid invoice for payment on the Palmer case. For whatever reason, it never dawned on me to follow-up with them beyond the Donovan file. I told them I'd see that it would be paid if they'd email me a copy of their billing and the report. I got both almost immediately. After looking over the report, I didn't find anything we didn't already know. But then I wondered where the originals were and, more importantly, the executives who signed off on the expense. My Accounting source is an early riser, so I called her around seven this morning. She tracked things down and found that the approved invoice had somehow gotten attached to another billing and was overlooked. It turns out Emil was one of the signees. Care to guess who the other was?" asked Mallory.

"Frank Raymond?" replied Nick.

"You're right."

"Well, it's certainly not much of a stretch. The larger open question is why anyone at Weston tracked down anyone connected with a closed claim file," said Nick.

"Agreed. Maybe we should ask Frank?"

Nick considered the suggestion. "Perhaps, when the time is right. Did you find out anything else?"

"Yes, and this is a biggie. Remember I told you Emil was at the Grand Hotel during the week Palmer was shot? After hearing Emil's Hammurabi reference yesterday, I did some digging, starting with his private nurse. She told me Emil was limiting his travel because of his illness but confirmed he made the trip to Mackinac Island for the meeting. Apparently, he chose to attend because he was delivering the keynote address on the opening night. She said it took everything in Emil's power simply to get up and get dressed for work every day. Evidently, he kept quite the game face because I never noticed any real change in him."

"He must have been one tough guy," concurred Nick, thinking back to their final meeting. "But, if he was that ill, how did he manage to shoot Palmer? You remember the video showing the presumed killer running off into the night?"

"Nick, I had the same questions. So, I called my Accounting source. Turns out Emil *was* on the island. But he left after the first night. His hotel bill confirms it. I just assumed he was on Mackinac for the entire conference. Palmer was murdered after Emil returned home. My father was not the murderer," Mallory concluded triumphantly.

"So, basically, there was no way Emil was the shooter . . . at least for the Palmer killing."

"Right. Also, since Emil knew he wouldn't stay for the full meeting, he invited several other staff members to represent the company, including Jonathan Woods, Frank Raymond, and a couple of other senior managers."

"Wait, Frank Raymond was on Mackinac Island when the Reverend Lonnie was offed? That's interesting considering what happened to me after the funeral. When I got home, Cassie was in her car waiting for me. She had been crying. She told me she had been spying on me."

"Spying on you?" asked Mallory.

"Those were her words. She had been asked to report about my schedule, who I talked to, anything she could learn about what was said during our investigation. That type of thing. Any guesses on who might have asked her to do that?"

"Frank Raymond?"

"Bingo," said Nick. "The way she explained it, Frank threatened to fire her unless she did what he said."

"He doesn't have the authority to do that," replied Mallory.

"I would have assumed as much, but she probably didn't know that. Frank was just being a bully. Why would she lie? Anyway, she finally worked up the nerve to tell me. She was very upset about the whole thing," he said, pausing. "Based on what you've been able to find, Emil was not Palmer's killer. But, Mallory, do you think he could have been the shooter for Donovan?"

"No, Nick, no I don't. But remember you're talking about my father. I'm hardly unbiased, but no. If the only thing tying these killings together is the relationship to Weston, that would suggest that more than one person was involved. I have a hard time with that. I can't imagine Emil being a killer at all."

"I agree. Even though the early facts seemed to point to him, I can't see him killing someone in cold blood. Given what we know, and you hit it on the head, the shooter must be associated with Weston in some way. Remember what Chuck said. You need to be able to prove motive, means, and opportunity. Mal, can you come up with anyone else here who had the motive?"

"Frank Raymond comes to mind first. He had to deal with all the injuries and emotion caused by these men of God. He made it no secret he was pissed that Weston cut major checks to the victims or to the actual source of the problems and then watched as the perpetrators walked without any punishment. Frank was Emil's good friend and may have been looking to give him the justice he had called out for. For a guy like Frank, killing off the Christian fuckers makes sense."

"Okay. What about the opportunity?" asked Nick.

"Like Emil, Frank has pretty much all the resources of Weston Insurance at his disposal. He signed off with Miller Investigative on tracking down those that got lost after the claims closed. He could disguise his travel to the areas where the killings took place by attending insurance industry functions and meetings, pretty much wherever he chose to go."

"Can you have your source verify Raymond's expense records to see if he was on Mackinac Island when Palmer was shot?" asked Nick.

"Piece of cake. But, what do we do about the Donovan killing? It's the same problem we had when we thought Emil was involved."

"There is no perfect solution for that aside from determining if Raymond was in town at the time. That was your first instinct with Emil, and I can't think of anything better at this point. Maybe something else will crop up as you go through the details." said Nick. "Mal, what about the means to be the killer?"

"Even though we thought of Emil first, Raymond may actually be the better suspect of the two. You were there for his big shooting event and saw only a portion of his gun collection."

"Absolutely. I was shocked at the size of his arsenal."

"FYI, he also has a huge number of handguns. You know, as I think about it, that might also explain why the ballistics are a problem. Frank has the luxury of swapping out the rifles for each killing, making him almost impossible to track down."

"That makes total sense. A gun nut with all the tools, the resources, and a vendetta. Let me ask you the one thing I didn't when I rolled out my Emil theory. Can you see a guy like Raymond being able and willing to kill multiple people like this?"

"I think you hit it before. Frank Raymond is a bully and a nut job. He seems to delight in using his power. I can picture him shooting any one of these people and not thinking twice about it. He would also enjoy the idea he could do this and get away with it. I'll follow up on Raymond's travel expenses and see whatever else I might come across that places him at the scenes of the crimes." As she was about to leave the room, Mallory stopped before opening the door. "Nick, should we be talking to Nowitzke and Taylor about what we know?"

"Mal, I'm not sure what we know just yet. If we accused Frank and, for some reason, were wrong about this, we would damage Weston Insurance and Emil's legacy unjustly. Remember how close we were to thinking that Emil was the shooter at one point. Once we nail the documentation on Raymond, we go to Chuck and Anissa. Fair enough?"

"Yes," replied Mallory.

"I also don't think this discussion should go beyond this room. Agreed?"

"Does that include pillow talk with your girlfriend?" asked Mallory.

"Yes, Mal, it does."

"Alright, then. By the way, I should have a copy of the disc with Emil's funeral speech by this afternoon. What are you working on?"

"I'm still trying to get into the final file on Hopkins Ministries. It's the last of the top ten. Who knows if that will be another colossal time-waster or not?"

CHAPTER 49

The thick red file jacket, designated at Hopkins Ministries, contained more than a single document. It was a collection of dubious events that Weston Insurance was financially responsible to resolve on behalf of the account. Nick read how Hopkins Ministries found its way to the unsuspecting Weston Insurance, courtesy of their broker, Marco Ricci. Following a tumultuous first six months with the account generating multiple eye-opening losses, the underwriting file was internally flagged for cancellation at the end of the policy term. However, through a comedy of errors, fate interceded. When the cancellation should have taken place, the underwriter responsible for the account was stricken with a lengthy illness. With no manual intervention in place, Weston's processing systems renewed the policy for a second term with no price increase. Nick cringed as he read the results. From a claim standpoint, Hopkins had become one of Weston's best customers. At the heart of the files, the one common thread of all the turmoil was Brother Turner Hopkins.

Raised in the streets of Chicago, Hopkins was the product of a black father and a white mother, neither of whom had much time or use for their child. Early on, Hopkins realized he needed to figure out the ways of the street to survive. And he did so, excelling at learning new and different ways to steal. In a more traditional setting, Hopkins would likely have been a success as well. Gifted with a near genius-level IQ, he grew into a handsome young man who looked more like a frat boy than a street hustler. Combining his intelligence with street smarts, Hopkins built a burgeoning local criminal empire. He also recognized he didn't need to get his hands dirty in the process since he could always find willing young men to provide the required muscle when needed.

A natural leader, many were drawn to his charismatic personality, though Hopkins' ability to provide his people with drugs and guns, as well as food and shelter, made many dependent upon him. By age twenty, Hopkins was generating a cash income for himself of more than $100,000 a year. He also developed enemies in the process. Even though Hopkins managed to avoid scrutiny by the police, his operations drew the attention of several long-established street gangs who felt their territorial rights were being violated. One of the faction's leaders, named Luther, was very interested in what Hopkins had been doing, hoping to tap into the money flow. More charmer than gangster, Hopkins resorted to diplomacy in meeting with Luther and the other rival gang leaders, trying to work out a partnership. But rather than working together, Luther and his counterparts demanded more than half of whatever Hopkins was earning. Hopkins was also warned by Luther that if certain monthly minimums were not met, he and his followers would be killed.

Rather than taking a chance on antagonizing the street gangs, Hopkins decided to reinvent himself. However, despite a generous skill set, he was unsure of his course of action until meeting a local street preacher, Jarvis Wallace. Known on the street as "Scratch," Wallace was a reformed heroin addict who had developed an uncontrollable junkie itch. After Wallace collapsed in the street and was unresponsive, the local police intervened, taking the kindly old addict to a sympathetic priest who recognized the problem and proceeded to cure him with the Bible and cold-turkey rehab. During his recovery, Scratch learned just enough about the good book to paraphrase it to the less knowledgeable. Now, five years later, Scratch's ministry was a local street corner where he yelled for others to repent while seeking donations in an old black bowler hat placed at his feet.

As Hopkins watched Scratch, it occurred to him that the preacher had invested minimal resources in his business, had a large potential audience, and operated with impunity from criminals and gangs who didn't see his moneymaking as a threat, consequently leaving him alone. Although Hopkins was not formally educated, he took Scratch's business model and transformed it into a larger, more sophisticated operation with broader reach.

Hopkins' first order of business was to steal a Gideon Bible. After reading it from cover to cover twice, his level of recall allowed him to retain large passages. Still, while Hopkins could quote Scripture flawlessly, he did not care about the underlying theology. His only interest was how the words might be used to generate cash flow.

Beginning modestly, Hopkins staked out his space in a busy corner of the Loop in Chicago preaching to businessmen and women rushing to meetings and trains. A week into his first venture as a street preacher, Hopkins realized the pocket change he generated was not the income he hoped for. He began to watch Sunday morning television as a guide to success for what he judged were more polished individuals in rival franchises. Hopkins concluded that he needed to make several changes to his approach. First, he decided to move his operations from the urban area of unbelievers to, what he deemed, the more gullible folks in the Bible Belt. He also concluded that he needed to upgrade his appearance to create the look of a successful pastor. For Hopkins, that meant wearing three-piece suits and getting expensive haircuts. Finally, while he intended to deliver powerful sermons, Hopkins theorized the *real money* in preaching was in performing miracles.

To make that type of transition required making some fronting cash before leaving Chicago. Carefully choosing his associates, Hopkins hatched a plan to target several known drug dealers protected by Luther. Over a long weekend, Hopkins and his crew worked at lightning speed to rob the pushers of cash and whatever product they had before skipping town. The gutsy venture netted Hopkins roughly $25,000, which he viewed as a respectable parting gift from Luther.

Over the next several weeks, Hopkins and his refugee crew traveled through middle America before settling in Springfield, Missouri, as the home for his new church. As part of his exit strategy from Chicago, Hopkins recruited young men who could offer a respectable look, but also had brains and the willingness to adapt. Anointing them with the biblical reference, The Sentinels, they were tasked to support Hopkins' new ministry in a variety of ways, not the least of which was protection. Hopkins believed it was only a matter of time before Luther and his associates would come calling, looking for the stolen money and drugs. He hoped The Sentinels would discourage any such conflict. Ever-present around Hopkins, The Sentinels always carried small arms, including machine pistols, concealed under their suits, providing the preacher with an entourage of good-looking young men, earning a level of respectability for potential members of his church.

To save money, Hopkins contracted to have a large tent erected as the host site of his church and generated interest through social media. While he drew small crowds initially, his powerful voice and stage presence, supplemented by his ability to quote Scripture, became a powerful combination. In short order, his lengthy and sweaty sermons, where he often stripped off his jacket and vest to work the crowd, became his trademark. Working five nights a week, Hopkins began to expand his reach, pulling in larger crowds each evening. With his church now established, he attempted to lure even more followers with the promise of performing miracles.

Learning how to conduct 'miracles' through online research, Hopkins determined The Sentinels were an essential part of an elaborate plan to gather information about the church attendees before each service. Each Sentinel was tasked to mill around with those seeking a miracle, learning names, stories, and maladies. Anyone with serious issues was steered away from the stage to a section where they could only catch a glimpse of the preacher. Those who fit Hopkins' profile were moved to the aisles near the front of the house. Once the service began, The Sentinels communicated with Hopkins via a concealed earpiece, guiding him to the seats of the targeted parishioners. With The Sentinels feeding Hopkins background information on each person seeking a cure, the preacher generated immediate credibility, calling out those individuals by name and identifying their specific problem or ailment.

Hopkins added to the theatre by using his commanding voice to call out the demons inside of the person. Among those targeted were individuals who would bravely tell the audience they were legally blind, after admitting privately before the service they had some minimal level of sight. Upon curing the blind, Hopkins asked each of those who were cured to shout out the color of his brightly colored tie to the crowd as proof of a miracle. Hopkins also routinely healed the deaf. Before each such miracle, Hopkins would stand back-to-back with his parishioner, loudly asking questions and demonstrating to the crowd the person could not hear him. Then, moving back in front of the subject, Hopkins would implore the devil to leave the person's body. Of course, only lip-readers were chosen by The Sentinels. Those cured would appear to be able to hear Hopkins' commands, validating his power.

Learning from local carnies, Hopkins added a parlor trick to his repertoire, lengthening legs to cure crooked backs. The Sentinels routinely selected individuals in the audience seated next to people with canes. Walking down the aisle of his church, Hopkins would stop and direct someone to stand and pick up the cane. Hopkins would theatrically invoke the power of the Lord, take the cane from the person, throw it away, and tell them to run up and down the aisles. Every night, the audience was mesmerized at the sight, never realizing the cane belonged to another who actually needed it. Following each miracle, Hopkins blessed those healed by placing a hand on their heads and pushing them backward into the waiting arms of The Sentinels. Although Hopkins took credit for hundreds of miracles, no actual healing took place. Yet, for some reason, none of his subjects said otherwise. Perhaps the reason was a mild threat from The Sentinels about people who undid their moment of holy glory, meeting with even worse demons than they had experienced before Brother Hopkins. The illusion was complete, and the crowds attending his services became standing room only.

Then, Brother Hopkins benefited from a true miracle himself when a college film crew documented one of his services for a local cable channel. Hopkins' good looks and charisma were an immediate hit. The exposure earned him a regular weekly Sunday morning time slot, which quickly became syndicated regionally. His miracle business exploded with so many requests that Hopkins could not fill them all in person. Not to be deterred from making a dollar, the preacher directed those needing his power to send a prayer card with their request, along with a $100 donation. It was a small price to pay to provide help to a person in need. Consequently, Hopkins' income soared from thousands of dollars to just over a hundred thousand dollars weekly.

While the additional television exposure paid dividends, Hopkins was concerned it also gave the location of his ministry to his enemies. As such, he decided to upgrade The Sentinels, replacing his original crew with former military types. Each new member of the team met Hopkins' physical profile, even though most had been dishonorably discharged from the service for a variety of reasons. Now feeling invulnerable, Hopkins went about performing the Lord's work surrounded by these supposed professionals.

In just over 18 months, Hopkins took ownership of a large gated estate outside of Springfield. He also bought a lavish vacation home on the coast in Miami. His lifestyle required a collection of vehicles, a designer wardrobe, luxury watches, and leasing a jet to travel between his homes and from place to place as his ministry demanded. In fact, Hopkins declared to the world that he would take his power on the road to small towns throughout the Heartland so the people could benefit from his miraculous talent. Hopkins Ministries was working as planned. At least until Ernest Mayberry wandered into a tent revival one hot August night.

Mayberry, a Florida native, had suffered a serious spinal injury as the result of a car accident on Interstate 75 several years prior. Following numerous surgeries on his C4 vertebrae, Mayberry was in constant pain, unable to hold a full-time job, and desperate for a miracle. The fact that Mayberry didn't consider himself a Christian was not an issue for him. Settling into a chair about an hour before Hopkins would take center stage, Mayberry was approached by one of The Sentinels. Upon providing his story and the type of cure he needed, Mayberry was shuffled by Hopkins' staff to the back rows of the tent and encouraged to complete a prayer card. The Sentinel who interviewed Mayberry knew immediately that he was exactly the wrong person for the Hopkins show. Not to be deterred, Mayberry moved back towards the stage, taking an aisle seat as the crowd streamed into the tent. Unnoticed by anyone from Hopkins Ministries, Mayberry waited patiently for his chance for healing.

On an evening when Hopkins declared miracles surely would come true, his earpiece was not working properly due to the humidity in the tent. Without the coaching from The Sentinels, Hopkins naturally assumed the frail, bent, and unkempt old man standing in front of him had been cleared by his team. Mayberry told Hopkins and the audience he had constant back pain because of a car accident. Brother Hopkins knew immediately that this malady was off-script. However, implored by the crowd, he called out for a miracle nonetheless. Hopkins blessed Mayberry, calling on Satan to leave his body. Then, Hopkins put a strong hand to Mayberry's forehead, causing him to fall into the arms of The Sentinels. Unfortunately, the preacher's blow severed the man's already deteriorated spinal cord, resulting in instantaneous paralysis in his arms and legs. Mayberry collapsed to the floor on cue but had lost control of both his bladder and bowels in the process. With stench adding to the already thick air, Hopkins realized that Mayberry was in distress. Yet, rather than calling for immediate medical attention, he beckoned The Sentinels to remove the man from the stage for his own "safety" before moving onto his next subject. The sixty-year-old Mayberry never regained consciousness and died in the back of the house before the end of the service.

Weston settled the case out of court with Mayberry' unsophisticated and estranged daughter for $2.7 million. Claiming her grief would be salved with all the happiness that money could buy, she promptly moved out of her trailer park to a more suitable home. The Mayberry incident became the first chink in the Hopkins Ministries' armor. Shortly thereafter, Weston was placed on notice about a series of sexual misconduct claims by several female members of the ministry, alleging Brother Hopkins had repeatedly taken liberties with them. In some cases, there were additional accusations of gang rape by The Sentinels. Those claims were evaluated to be worth several additional millions of dollars.

Following a flow of new complaints on the heels of the Mayberry case, Hopkins received much greater scrutiny from the local Springfield media. Then, a YouTube video surfaced showing a tipsy Hopkins at a high-priced gentlemen's club surrounded by his Sentinels and several strippers. Hopkins responded to any criticism saying he needed to go where the sinners were if he was to save them. Rumors also persisted that many of his Sentinels were trafficking in drugs. Eventually, Hopkins wrote off such chatter as wild speculation, invoking Berra's Second Law indicating "anyone who is popular is bound to be despised." Despite growing pressure on his ministry, Hopkins remained largely above scrutiny, and the money continued to roll in.

CHAPTER 50

Just after noon, Nick felt the conference room walls closing in on him after reading the Hopkins Ministries file. He shook his head in disgust. Weston had found its way to yet another Christian fucker. When Mallory came into the room, she could see by the look on his face that something was on his mind.

"Is something wrong?" she asked.

"Mal, every time I think I've seen it all, I read one of these files and get pissed off all over again. Weston has insured some serious assholes, but this Hopkins guy is at the top of the list."

"How so?"

"He preys upon the weakest of the weak . . . people with serious illnesses who really need a cure. He takes their money and provides them with false hope. He's a very slick charlatan. There's no documentation any of his miracles worked, but people keep lining up for more. Hopkins is laughing all the way to the bank. He lives a lavish lifestyle protected by a small army of misfits. Oh, and the file also says he's been assaulting female members of his staff. Weston will be making payments on this guy's behalf for the foreseeable future. This is a new low," said Nick, throwing the file against the wall.

"How does he get away with it?" asked Mallory.

"He seems to be toeing a very fine line, and I'm not sure he's even breaking any laws. Mal, you've seen the type on Sunday morning television. As far as I know, he hasn't asked anyone to put their hand on the TV screen to transmit a miracle yet, but I'm sure he would if he could figure out a way to make money at it. He continues to draw full houses, and now he's taking his show on the road." Nick had worked himself into a frenzy. "I need to get some air."

"How about a late lunch?" asked Mallory. "I've got some interesting updates for you about our buddy, Frank."

Within fifteen minutes, they were at The Office. Although Nick seriously debated about choosing the Long Island Iced Tea, he had since calmed down, opting for the sweet variety instead. Taking a sip of her lemonade before their sandwiches arrived, Mallory started the conversation.

"Frank was on Mackinac when Palmer was shot. Weston's records confirm it."

"Were you able to find out where Frank was when Donovan was killed?"

Mallory and Nick paused for a moment as the young lady in her referee shirt served their food.

"We've talked about this, Nick. The only thing I can confirm is he was in town. Apparently, Frank had a staff meeting in his office on the afternoon of the day Donovan was shot."

"So, we've clearly got him at one site and potentially a second."

"Should we call Nowitzke?" asked Mallory.

"Let's wait. After thinking about this, I could see Frank being incensed enough to want to take a pot shot at Brother Hopkins. I wonder if we could proactively monitor Frank's upcoming travel schedule through your contact in Accounting. With all corporate travel funneled through that department, maybe we could get some advanced warning if he plans to hit the road."

"That's true. But how would we know if he was going somewhere to shoot someone?"

"Well, Mal, we don't. However, after reading the Hopkins file, he fits the same profile as Donovan and Palmer. If Frank is the shooter, he will be drawn to Brother Hopkins. If, and when, Frank books a trip to somewhere that coincides with the preacher's schedule, it would likely be more than a coincidence."

"If that's the case, how will we be able to keep tabs on Hopkins?"

Nick took a breath and then a sip of his drink. "The file said Hopkins promotes his ministry through social media. I haven't looked at Facebook lately, but I wonder if he has an active account."

"I do Facebook," said Mallory, pulling out her phone and bringing up Turner Hopkins. "Wow, he is incredibly active, posting photos of his miracles daily and asking for donations. He has also posted the locations of his traveling circus for the next two months. Hopkins has a quarter-million followers."

"Why don't you make it two hundred fifty thousand and one, Mal? That way, you'd be dialed into what Hopkins is up to. If we get an inkling he and Frank are going to cross paths, we can react."

"What are we going to do if that happens?"

"I have no clue at this moment. On the other hand, you spending time following a sleazy spiritual leader can't hurt. Had you known, maybe you could have saved all the money you paid your plastic surgeon and got your boobs for free with your very own miracle?"

"Thanks, but no, Nick. I've had enough offers of the laying on of hands." replied Mallory. "By the way, I watched Emil's celebration video again and got nothing new out of it."

"I don't get it. How would Emil ever come up with a Hammurabi reference without some knowledge of what's going on?"

"I don't know," said Mallory. "Maybe Emil figured out Frank was involved and was trying to call him off? There is no good explanation, and we can't ask Emil. I've put the video in your office. Be my guest and come up with something I missed."

****

When they returned to the office, Cassie was on the phone but waved forcefully to get Nick's attention.

"Nick, Tina was looking for you. She asked me to catch you since she figured out you were out of the building. She said it was very important you see her this afternoon. She's in her office right now."

Approaching Tina's office, Nick had a sense something was not right. Several cardboard boxes were sitting on the floor by her desk next to a locked green plastic container whose contents were destined for shredding. Ironically, many of Tina's personal items decorating the shelves behind her remained in place. Tina was seated solemnly at her desk and smiled weakly as Nick entered.

"Thanks for tracking me down, Nick. I wanted to give you a heads-up before any official word comes down from management to the employees and policyholders. I spoke with Mr. Woods today. He's been slated by the Board of Directors to take on the leadership role at Weston with Emil's death. Woods told me that given what we all seem to know about the religious program and my hand in it, both he and the board thought I should take some time off."

"Tina, did they fire you?"

"No, they asked me to take a 60-day leave of absence. I've been struggling with my father's death, and I agreed that taking time off would be a good idea. They'll keep me on the payroll, and I'll recharge. I've been on a burn-out track anyway. When I come back, Woods said he would find a suitable role for me . . . at least that's what he told me," Tina said unconvincingly.

"How could the board draw any conclusions about the religious program until we've completed the investigation?" asked Nick.

"Nick, you have two different assignments. First, everyone knows how bad the results were and that I was the program manager. Those are facts and certainly not a secret. Nothing you would tell the board would change that. After thinking it through, I accept responsibility for the whole mess. The board is more interested in hearing about what could have prevented the problems in the first place so they aren't repeated."

"Okay. So, what will you do?"

"Kick back and do a lot of thinking, for starters. I've booked a flight to an all-inclusive in Mexico. Nothing but sun and daiquiris for me for the next couple of weeks after I take care of business here." She hesitated.

"Nick, would you like to spend some time together? Maybe after your assignment is complete here?"

"That would be nice, Tina, but I'm not sure when things will wrap up."

"As long as it's not more than two months, I'll wait. You won't see me for at least a couple of weeks. Can we spend tonight together before I leave tomorrow? Nothing special. Just sex, wine, and sex."

Nick smiled. "I guess I better start stretching."

****

When Nick returned to his office, he found the DVD of Emil's final message on his desk and popped it into his laptop. After the third time of pausing, rewinding, and playing the short speech, he agreed with Mallory's conclusion. There was nothing new to be learned. Yet, Nick sensed they were on the right track and that a resolution would come together sooner than later.

CHAPTER 51

At six o'clock the following morning, Nick woke to the buzzing of his cell phone.

"Morning, Nick. It's Mallory."

"Jesus, Mal. Don't you ever sleep?" Nick asked, swinging his legs over the edge of the bed.

"When can you get to the office? There have been a couple of developments. There's some serious activity taking place on Facebook with Brother Hopkins and with Frank Raymond's travel plans. I think something big is going to happen in the next couple of days."

"Alright. I need to take a shower and will be in shortly. You said developments, plural. What else is going on?"

"Nick, I got something here that I don't know how to handle, and I'm scared to death. When can you get to the office?" asked Mallory.

"I'm on my way," replied Nick. As he clicked off his phone, Tina, who had been sleeping next to him, stirred. "What's going on with Mallory?" she said, pulling the blankets up around her for warmth.

"Work stuff . . . an insurance emergency."

"Is there such a thing? Anything I can help with?"

"No, remember, you're on sabbatical."

"Wow, that sounds so much better than being pushed into a leave of absence."

Tina then pushed the blankets away, revealing her naked body. "Are you sure there's nothing I can help you with?"

"Not after last night, unless you've got a bottle of Gatorade next to you. Will you be alright?"

"Absolutely. Promise me you'll stay in touch so we can get together soon."

"Let's just say I'm highly motivated," Nick said, looking at her body. Reaching down to her, Nick gave Tina a deep kiss before hurrying off to the shower.

****

Mallory was on her third cup of coffee when Nick arrived. Her caffeine-charged report began before Nick could take off his jacket and sit down. Keeping a business-like focus, she launched into her findings.

"Nick, you were right about Hopkins on Facebook. He is very active and seems to be up early with responses to his followers every morning. However, he didn't reply to this one." Handing her phone to Nick, he read the incoming message to Hopkins:

"2. If a man charge a man with sorcery, and cannot prove it, he who is charged with sorcery shall go to the river; into the river he shall throw himself, and if the river overcome him, his accuser shall take to himself his house . . ."

"I looked it up. It's definitely from Hammurabi," she said excitedly. "It's the same style as the other letters we've seen, only in an electronic format."

"Mal, I'm not familiar with Facebook. Is there any way to tell who sent it?"

"It's from an account using a fake account name. *BLZebub.*"

"Beelzebub? Is that a reference to the devil?"

"Very good, Nick. I had to look that up too. Beelzebub was a fallen angel in Milton's book, *Paradise Lost.* Supposedly, Satan's second-in-command."

"Looks like my liberal arts degree is worth something after all. Is there any way to track this down to an actual person?"

"No. But this was only the first communication sent in the last week. Here is the second from Mr. Zebub to Hopkins overnight."

"196. If a man put out the eye of another man, his eye shall be put out."
"200. If a man knock out the teeth of his equal, his teeth shall be knocked out."
"Friday!"

"This is the Hammurabi reference most everyone knows, 'An eye for an eye, a tooth for a tooth.' Any guess on the Friday reference?" asked Nick.

"I would think it's the day of reckoning. I checked Hopkins' website and confirmed his traveling show will be at the Highland Theatre in Kansas City this Friday evening. It's a large outdoor amphitheater that can host up to ten thousand people," she added.

"What time *did* you get up today?"

Ignoring Nick, Mallory continued. "I thought the Friday reference could be about any Friday. But after doing some checking, guess who booked some travel to Kansas City for this week in the last day?"

"Frank Raymond?"

"Effing A . . . what should we do now?"

"For starters, talk to your NetJets people so we can get down to Kansas City ASAP. See if you can pull up any information about the Highland Theatre, along with the timing of the Hopkins show this Friday evening. In the meantime, I need to make some calls."

"Are you going to talk with Nowitzke and Taylor?"

"I think we need to. I don't know what their jurisdictional issues will be, and we have no solid evidence that anything is going to happen. I'll lay out the details for them in the context of everything else we know and let them make the call about what they want to do."

"I agree, Nick. But what if they decide it's not worth the trip? How do we stop Raymond?"

"We'll figure it out. This is what has you scared to death, Mal?"

"No," she said quietly. "I found this in my mail from yesterday. I only opened it this morning," she said, handing him a folded piece of paper. "Needless to say, no return address. Only a local postage cancellation on the envelope."

Nick opened the single sheet of paper.

"3. If any one bring an accusation of any crime before the elders, and does not prove what he has charged, he shall, if it be a capital offense charged, be put to death."

Nick looked from the letter to Mallory, who was shaking and staring off into space. "It's a death letter, Nick. Definitely Hammurabi. I checked that one too," she said, trying to maintain her composure. "I don't understand the passage's meaning, but it was clearly addressed to me. Why did I get this? And based on what's happened to others who've received similar letters, for some reason, I think I'm now a target."

"Okay, Mal. We're calling Nowitzke *now*," said Nick.

"Jesus. I can't believe Frank Raymond sent this to me," concluded Mallory. Unsaid was why Nick didn't get one too. "What are we going to do?"

****

It had taken several months to piece together. Luther eventually determined that several of his dealers were robbed by Turner Hopkins and his crew. Nevertheless, even after putting out the word he had some serious business with Hopkins, no one on the street had any information as to his whereabouts. Hopkins had dropped off the face of the earth. A year later, none of the locals had heard from or seen Hopkins anywhere until fate intervened.

Luther was making his regular monthly visit to see his elderly grandmother, whom he called Mama, on a Sunday morning. They talked about the summer heat, the Cubs, and her health in her stuffy and drab first-floor apartment. As always, Mama had her television on for background noise, tuned to a local religious channel. After an hour,

Luther rose to leave when he heard a familiar voice coming from the screen. Turning up the volume, he got a full look at the TV preacher. It was Hopkins. Even though he was much more respectable-looking than he had been while living in Chicago, there was no doubt it was him. Luther also took careful note of several serious-looking men in suits surrounding Hopkins as he delivered his message from the pulpit. Luther sat back down as he and Mama now paid rapt attention to the program. Luther was particularly interested when Hopkins Ministries flashed the list of upcoming events, including an old-fashioned revival meeting at the Highland Theatre the following Friday.

"Luther, can you get my purse?" asked Mama. "I need to send that nice young man some money."

"Mama, I don't think he's going to be around much longer to use it."

Moving into another room, Luther picked up his cell, calling his second-in-command. "Hey, man, it's me. Get a car along with some of the boys, cash, and weapons. We're taking a road trip to Kansas City, leaving this afternoon."

"Luther, I'm so happy you enjoyed learning more about the Lord this morning. Are you going to watch the rest of the program with me?" asked his grandmother.

He reached over and kissed her on the top of her head. "Sorry, Mama. I've got some old business to take care of."

CHAPTER 52

The Highland Theatre in Kansas City, Missouri, is considered a true masterpiece of the "Show Me" state, the adopted home of Turner Hopkins. Constructed in the early sixties, the original architect created a natural marvel, designing the theatre to take advantage of the rolling hills on the plains. The theatre had been lovingly refurbished over the years by a local arts community to maintain its state-of-the-art functionality. The most recent changes had increased the size of the stage with a large overhead canopy to protect the performers from the elements. An upgraded sound system and functional lighting were also added, along with meeting rooms, making the theatre a year-round income generator. The bowl was expanded and divided into sections, flanked by large pergolas to the east and west, providing patrons with access to multiple restaurants, bars, and supporting facilities. Opposite the stage at the back of the house sat two large towers that provided symmetry to the primary design of the main stage, along with additional lighting and technical features.

On a Friday evening in August, the Highland would host Hopkins Ministries.

****

When Nick contacted Nowitzke, outlining his theory about Raymond, the detective agreed it was primarily conjecture. However, he pronounced it "damn good speculation" nonetheless, especially given the ongoing connection to Weston Insurance. Nowitzke was also aghast that Mallory had received a Hammurabi letter, knowing how other recipients had fared. He was also curious about the timing of the letter. If Raymond was in fact the sender, why send a letter to Mallory before taking care of his supposed business with Hopkins? After arm-wrestling with Chief Clark, the decision was made to send Nowitzke to observe and coordinate with the local Kansas City authorities. On their private flight, Nowitzke, Mallory, and Nick talked through what they thought was about to take place, arriving two full days in advance of the Hopkins Ministries event. Mallory brought along a print-out of Raymond's itinerary, right down to the room number at the Marriott where he was staying. She and Nick had debated whether it would have made more sense for her to stay behind in Neenah, keeping distance between her and the primary suspect. However, Mallory would have none of it, insisting on making the trip.

After the plane touched down, Mallory and Nick picked up a rental car, dropping Nowitzke off at Kansas City PD before continuing onto the Highland. Posing as tourists, they took one of the scheduled tours of the complex, snapping numerous photos of the facility. They also took a couple of maps of the campus. Moving through the sprawling outdoor theatre, Nick tried to visualize where Raymond might position himself to take a shot at Hopkins. Despite his efforts, the breadth of the grounds offered any number of options that could serve as a potential sniper perch. Nick conceded that narrowing down the possibilities was purely guesswork.

Following their tour, they stopped at an electronics store to buy headsets with microphones so they could communicate with each other privately on the night of the event. Returning to the KCPD building, they found that Nowitzke had connected with his counterpart, Detective Thelma Waldron. Waldron was a twenty-year veteran of the force, starting her career as a female patrol officer. She was short with a stocky build and had close-cropped black hair spiked with product. Despite her stature, though, she had a commanding presence that was respected by her people and Nowitzke.

Waldron was skeptical of Nick's theory that Raymond would come to town to kill Brother Turner. But, while she remained unconvinced, the last thing she wanted was the murder of a popular television preacher taking place on her watch, whether the man was a fraud or not. Waldron also had strong opinions that Nick and Mallory should have no part of any police activity on the evening of the event. However, Nowitzke stood up for the two, reminding the Kansas City team that they were the ones who had brought this potential threat to the attention of the local police.

Eventually, Waldron caved on that point but required a limited role as observers for Mallory and Nick. Working together, with the available information provided by the Weston employees, the small group hatched a plan. With limited resources available, Waldron agreed that two plainclothes officers would follow Raymond from his hotel to the event on Friday evening. Once in the theatre, two different undercover officers would pick up Raymond's trail and monitor his activity. If he moved to a shooter's perch and had a weapon, he would be arrested on sight. Mallory and Nick were allowed in the venue but had to promise to remain away from the front stage and remain inconspicuous so as not to alert Raymond. Even though Mallory wanted to be involved, she was relieved to learn her position would be in a closed portion of the grounds, far out of any line of fire. Nick was also slated to be an observer but would be stationed in a different portion of the Highland where he could watch the events and comment accordingly. Without any jurisdiction, Nowitzke would be placed near the front of the house, posing as one of the stagehands. Short of an all-out emergency, Waldron had sworn him to take no action. Official communication would take place between the parties with small handheld devices provided by KCPD.

****

On the eight-hour journey from Chicago, Luther and three of his boys strategized about their plan. Piled into a black Escalade, Luther told them there was to be no booze or drugs on the ride to Kansas

City. He wanted them thinking clearly when it came time to deal with Hopkins. Any party favors brought along would be saved for the trip home. Luther also told the gang members that they would look for an opening to kill Hopkins prior to the show. However, if that was not an option, Luther explained that he would take the first shot at Hopkins. Knowing he would need help with Hopkins' bodyguard, he asked his crew to focus on the intimidating men in suits behind the preacher. He guessed the bodyguards would be armed. However, Luther and his gang would be ready, each carrying a Mac 10 machine pistol slung around their necks and concealed under hoodies. Luther surmised he would have one chance to kill Hopkins in what amounted to a public execution, if it came to that. And, for whatever reason, he believed he would be able to do so and escape back to Chicago.

****

Plainclothes officers picked up Frank Raymond as he stepped off the plane at Kansas City International. Then, they tailed Raymond's rental car to the Marriott where he checked in and went directly to his room. Promptly at six o'clock, Raymond went to the lobby bar and enjoyed two martinis before going into the steakhouse on-site. Aside from the insider information known to the two officers, Raymond was just another anonymous businessman in Kansas City. In the final report to Waldron that evening, Raymond was noted to have returned to his room at 10:06 p.m.

****

At eleven o'clock, a black Dodge Ram pickup truck arrived at the Jayhawk Inn near the Highland Theatre. After checking in, the lone occupant parked the vehicle under one of the lights in the lot and took two brown bags through the lobby up to the room. Ten minutes later, the lights in the room went out, although no one noticed.

CHAPTER 53

Over the course of his time as a miracle worker, Brother Turner Hopkins had played more elegant locations than the Highland Theatre. He had ministered to bigger crowds in larger cities. In theory, nothing should have been amiss. Yet, as he prepared for his performance that evening, Hopkins felt a disconcerting level of tension he had never experienced before. Sure, he had received previous death threats. In fact, he had trouble keeping track of all of them. That was why he hired The Sentinels in the first place, to provide security and to watch the crowd. As his makeup artist applied the final touches to his face, he took a stiff belt of tequila to calm his nerves followed by a rinse of mouthwash. The taste combination was horrible, but Hopkins wanted no one to detect alcohol on his breath during the service. Once he had completed his pre-show ritual, he blew off whatever anxiety he had been feeling and walked towards the stage.

Moving behind the curtains to one side of the platform, Hopkins peeked out to see another standing-room-only crowd. More miracles to perform. But more importantly, this would be a big money night for Hopkins Ministries. Over the last several months, Hopkins had quietly contemplated retiring altogether. For a street kid from Chicago, he now had more money than he had ever dreamed of and could not even fathom spending it all. He stashed millions of dollars in banks in the Caymans and in Switzerland, along with more cash in safety deposit boxes in at least five banks across the United States. Beginning to think like a businessman, he had become painfully aware his entourage was a crushing expense. Between The Sentinels, his support team, the marketing group, and his logistics staff, Hopkins was supporting roughly twenty full-timers whose salaries were cutting into his personal profits.

Hopkins mused to himself about simply picking up and quietly leaving the country, allowing for a compelling future backstory, if needed some day. He thought of selling his homes and moving to an obscure Caribbean Island, and concocting a story that, during his self-imposed exile, he had walked the path of Christ throughout the Middle East, reflecting on life. He judged his new island lifestyle would be doable with a single bodyguard and one personal assistant. With no wife, he would immediately become the most eligible bachelor in town, wherever he landed. If and when he decided to return to the United States, any missteps made in his previous world would have been long forgotten. Hopkins would be reborn with his absence, primed to become a spiritual leader on the national stage. He also would not have to deal with what he privately called the "dregs of the world" clamoring to be near him. He would also publicize his availability to participate on the high-paying boards of directors of religious schools and foundations, earning more money and doing far less.

With the start of the service nearing, Hopkins cleared his mind of this fantasy, promising himself to act in the coming weeks. For now, he needed to concentrate on this evening's performance.

****

The black Dodge Ram truck parked in a lot to the west of the stage about two hours before the show was to begin. The driver emerged wearing sunglasses and a brown baseball cap while carrying a black guitar gig bag. Having scouted the area, the supposed musician blended in with others as they all walked through security together. Aside from the three-hundred-fifty-pound rent-a-cop who was more interested in crowd control, there was no other security for the church service. The security guard never left his metal bar chair positioned by the gate and waved the musicians into the theatre. Mentally recalling the map of the campus, the guitarist walked to the elevator at the back of the open-air theatre, opposite the now-lighted stage. Taking the lift to the top floor of the technical services building, the individual found the metal service ladder and climbed to the roof. Sheltered in the perch well above the crowds and with no one at that level, the gig bag was opened. Thirty seconds later, the two pieces of a Ruger 10/22 assault rifle were assembled as the stock and action and the barrel came together with a simple twist. The semi-automatic weapon was completed with the addition of a Nikon P Series Rimfire scope. From the nest, the gunman now had a spectacular view of the entire facility, especially the stage.

****

Before leaving with KCPD for the Highland, Nick pulled Mallory aside. "Mal, why don't you sit this out? You don't need to go to the theatre. You'd be safe here surrounded by police while Raymond's drama plays out."

"Shut up, Nick," replied Mallory. "If it's so safe, why don't you stay here?"

"Mal, I didn't get a death threat. You did. That's the difference. I don't know what's going to happen." He paused. "I just don't want you to get hurt."

"I'll be fine, she said boldly. "Don't worry."

Having heard their conversation, Nowitzke approached the pair. "Mallory, I agree with Nick. Please stay here at KCPD. I mean, why take the chance?"

Nowitzke's plea was met with a stony look, her silence clearly communicating her intent. "Okay, then. Listen, even though we'll have a good handle on where Raymond will be, you need to wear this," said Nowitzke, handing her a tactical vest. "It's not fashionable and definitely not built for the sticky weather down here, but it should keep you safe . . . just in case," offered the detective. "Oh, and it's not up for debate, young lady," his tone eliminating any possible resistance.

"Thanks Detective . . . I guess." Grudgingly, Mallory accepted the idea, strapping on the black vest emblazoned with the word "POLICE" over her shirt, pulling the Velcro closures tight.

****

Under the watchful eye of the Kansas City police, the detectives were surprised when Frank emerged from the hotel earlier than expected. From across the street, the officers thought the thin man with the large glasses looked especially dapper that late afternoon, wearing pressed, khaki-colored, cuffed pants, a brilliant white shirt, and a black blazer. After taking the keys from the valet, he tossed his bag into the back seat of the vehicle and pulled into traffic.

"Our boy is on the move," said one of the detectives into his radio.

Knowing his destination made their work easy. The officers tailing Frank watched him arrive at the Highland grounds and walk into the theatre. The second set of officers picked up Frank at the entrance and observed him meandering through the complex. Frank walked right past Nowitzke, who assumed his position near the stage after hearing that the insurance executive had left the hotel. Frank lingered around the stage as if enjoying the sight. Five minutes later, he was approached by a man with brush-cut brown hair wearing a tailored suit. Following a short conversation, the Sentinel escorted Frank to the first row, removed a velvet rope, and placed him in an aisle seat.

Watching from the back of the house, Nick spoke into his handheld radio. "What's he doing?"

Speaking discreetly into his wrist, Nowitzke responded, "Nothing. He strolled in here like he didn't have a care in the world. He didn't bring anything from the car. The two officers trailing him said Raymond was never out of their sight. Frank talked to one of Hopkins' handlers and gave him a primo seat in the first row."

"No shit. Think he's looking for a miracle?" asked Nick.

"Or to get close to Hopkins," replied Nowitzke. "He's just sitting there with his legs crossed, like he's sitting in a park."

"Chuck, I'm assuming he doesn't have a sniper rifle with him?"

"You're pretty smart for a guy who's not a cop. He would need a miracle to hide a rifle where he's at, Nick. Damn, I'd love to get seats like that for a Packer game. Why do all the alleged serial killers always get the best seats?" said Nowitzke with a laugh.

"Okay, Chuck, you're the old hand at this. What do we do now?"

Waldron, who was also observing the proceedings from the East Pergola, chimed in. "We wait. Nick, stay in your position and watch from there. Mallory is safely in her position near the back of the house. If Frank decides to get up and move, we'll be all over him."

Nick looked across the expanse at a restaurant that had been closed for the evening. From his position at the mirror image restaurant on the opposite side of the theatre, he gave Mallory a quick wave. She acknowledged him with a smile before sitting down. Both had a sweeping view of the stage and the seats in the bowl below them.

As time dragged waiting for the show to begin, Nick began to have doubts about the theory, especially given the amount of police resources in play. "Mal, did I mess this up?" speaking to her through their private microphones. "I thought Raymond shot his victims from long range. What's going on? Has he changed his strategy?"

"Nick, just relax," replied Mallory. "I believe in your theory. Why else would Raymond be here? Your argument was compelling enough to convince detectives in two police departments to take serious action. Let's let things play out. We're going to know something soon enough."

"Are you doing okay?"

"Yes, I'm good," she said in her most convincing voice. "I just want this to be over."

"Remember to stay out of the line of fire."

"Duh," she replied through her private mic.

Over the course of the next hour, the Highland Theatre filled to more than capacity. Luther and his crew entered the complex individually and found single seats scattered in the front sections near the stage. Just before eight o'clock, the crowd noise began to grow in anticipation of the seeing Brother Hopkins.

CHAPTER 54

As the hour neared, loud Christian rock music was piped through the massive state-of-the-art sound system. Numerous sets of revolving, colored lights above the stage kicked in, further assaulting the senses of those assembled. As the tempo and volume of the music increased, flames from behind the stage shot upward into the night sky accompanied by laser lights piercing through the man-made fog that now wafted onto the stage. The combination of the sensory overload had the desired effect, working the crowd to a frenzied pitch. Then, more like a rock star than a religious leader, Hopkins, wearing a white-on-white suit, rose slowly on a mechanical platform from below the stage to a large ovation, bringing the crowd to its feet.

Above the din, Nick asked Nowitzke through the handheld. "Can you see Frank? With all the fog on the stage, I can't see him from here."

"Nick, he hasn't moved. We've got eyes on him all around the facility. Don't worry."

The house lights dimmed. Hopkins quieted the crowd, launching into an hour-long sermon about giving back. In his classic fashion, he moved like a caged lion around the stage, peppering his rhetoric with supporting Bible passages. He began sweating profusely and removed his coat and vest, stripping down to his shirt and tie. Hopkins hammered home the idea he would be the messenger if the crowd was willing to accept him. Now it was their turn to give back by providing him with their offerings. On cue, The Sentinels descended on the crowd with collection baskets. By the time they returned to the stage, the metallic chrome altar was overflowing with cash.

As the house lights came back up, Hopkins implored the crowd. "Are you ready for a miracle?"

"*Yes*," his flock screamed back in unison, almost as if they had somehow been coached.

"Showtime," said Nowitzke into his microphone as he watched the spectacle. With the masses heaving and shouting, the Kansas City officers reported that Frank remained calmly in his chair, to the consternation and puzzlement of the Wisconsin contingent.

As Hopkins moved towards the edge of the stage, The Sentinels began to line up those chosen to receive miracles. Near the front of the line was Frank Raymond, and he was moving toward the stage. From his position, Nowitzke spoke into his handheld microphone, telling his team to stand down for the moment. But Nick saw things differently. "Mal, something here just isn't right." He hurriedly walked towards the stage.

In front of Frank, the miracle line's pace was slowed considerably by an obese woman in a wheelchair. To direct the flow of traffic, one of The Sentinels took a position next to Frank, holding his hand up to slow the procession while his colleagues struggled to move the lady up a ramp towards Hopkins. With most of the attention by The Sentinels now focused on the woman, Luther saw his opportunity. Moving quickly out of his seat, he stepped into the line immediately behind Frank, camouflaging himself behind the well-dressed man so Hopkins would not see him until the last second. However, as Luther cut into the line, he inadvertently brushed Frank's back. Frank turned briefly, glancing backward to see who had touched him before refocusing on the stage.

Looking through the scoped rifle from the roof of the technical services facility, the gunman saw the glint of silver flash momentarily from under the coat of Frank Raymond. Then, he spoke calmly into his headset. "Gun, on stage. Frank's carrying a pistol in a holster under his jacket. You need to hoof it, Boss."

"Got it, P-Man. Now, get your ass out of here," replied Nick, transitioning from a fast walk into a dead run down the aisle towards the stage to stop Frank.

Confused by the private exchange being fed into her ear, Mallory could only respond into her microphone, "Philemon? Are you here?"

"It's me, baby. I'm on overwatch for the Boss but I'm packing up and moving. Keep your head and that sweet ass down."

"Gun, gun, gun!" Nick yelled into his handheld to the balance of the police team as he charged toward the stage. "Frank's carrying a pistol. He's going to shoot Hopkins point-blank in front of everyone."

Before the police could respond, Hopkins had completed his miracle for the large woman, taking time to make her walk the length of the stage. He then turned towards the short, well-dressed man who was next in line. Then Hopkins caught a glimpse of his old friend Luther smiling at him over the man's shoulder. As Raymond placed his right hand into his jacket, Hopkins yelled to The Sentinels, "Gun, gun, gun!"

In the next moments of confusion, there were several shrieks from the crowd as it surged towards the exits, disrupting chairs and knocking down many of the congregants. Frank was momentarily baffled, wondering how his weapon had been discovered, though he could not see Luther behind him pulling the machine pistol from under his sweatshirt. Several of The Sentinels reacted at the exact same speed as the others on stage, pulling weapons and firing, unsure of the target. Luther's initial burst caught Frank in the back, killing him just as he got a hand on the revolver. Yet, before he hit the ground, the nerves in Frank's hand clenched in a death grip, and the snub-nosed revolver discharged, sending the shot through his jacket into Luther's foot, dropping him to the ground. Recognizing he was late to the stage, Nick made it to Nowitzke's position, pushing the unarmed officer to the ground and protecting him with his body as the battle raged.

"Nick, I've got a muzzle flash to my left. Multiple flashes."

"What? Phil, get the fuck out of here, *now*."

In his private microphone, Nick could hear Mallory screaming, accompanied by the sound of gunshots raining down on her.

"Mal, are you alright?" yelled Nick. "Mallory, are you there? Please come in."

With bullets flying in all directions, The Sentinels were now focused on Luther, who continued to fire from the floor, taking out six of the bodyguards. However, the lack of discipline that had gotten them discharged from the military flared as several of The Sentinels fired their weapons haphazardly. One of those random bullets entered the back of Brother Hopkins' head, exiting with a blast tearing off his face as he dropped lifelessly to the stage. Once the police had pulled their weapons and advanced, the shooting on stage ceased with the entire gun battle lasting for less than thirty seconds. During the skirmish, Luther took several more rounds to the abdomen, bleeding out before he could get medical attention, abandoned by his crew who had been too afraid to jump into the fray.

Once the frenzy was over, Nick jumped to his feet and ran to the opposite corner of the theatre where he had last seen Mallory. He could see her lying under a picnic table curled up in a ball. "Mal . . . Mal!" he yelled. When he arrived, Mallory's emotions kicked in and she began to cry and shake beyond her control. Nick gently pulled her from under the table. "Were you hit, Mal?"

"Jesus, Nick . . ." gulping for air through her tears, ". . . I think so. I felt a big thud to my chest as bullets started hitting all around me. I wasn't sure where they were coming from so I managed to crawl under the table. I was scared for my life."

Nick did a cursory search of Mallory's vest, finding a mangled bullet lodged in the material. "God, it feels like my ribs are broken," she groaned.

"I don't think any slugs made it through the vest, but I need to check." Nick gently pulled open the Velcro closures of the vest, giving her a quick once-over checking for bullet holes or blood. Seeing none, he exhaled deeply, slumping down on the cement next to her. "Mal, I think you're fine. But you're going to have one helluva bruise."

"Hey, next time we go to a shoot-out, why don't you try harder to convince me to stay with the police," she grumbled and winced, trying to laugh through the pain.

****

A local journalist reported that there truly had been a miracle at the Hopkins Ministries tent revival that Friday evening. Despite all the bullets that had flown, only a single member of the congregation, an insurance executive from Wisconsin, was killed. Beyond that, no one else in the assembly, including the police, received anything more than scratches and bruises. In what was characterized as an assault on religion, Brother Hopkins had been needlessly gunned down, along with members of his protective group, by a notorious Chicago-based gangbanger, who had also perished. His motive was undetermined.

Although Waldron was not ecstatic with the result, she had been provided enough of the backstory about Hopkins to realize that some measure of justice had prevailed. The follow-up investigation added to Waldron's comfort level when the connection between the preacher and Luther revealed they were cut from the same cloth.

The local hospital had confirmed Nick's preliminary diagnosis of Mallory. The vest had done its job. No life-threatening wounds. However, Mallory had suffered two broken ribs, which made every breathe a new adventure in pain. She was also sporting a large purple bruise on her side that seemed to grow by the day. KCPD speculated that the bullets that hit Mallory must have come from one of the machine pistols fired from the stage.

Nowitzke was so thankful for Nick shielding him from the spray of bullets, he bought the beer for his new friends before they returned home. Upon returning to Wisconsin, Nowitzke promptly obtained a search warrant of Raymond's home, confiscating his arsenal for testing. In short order, the state crime lab confirmed the collection included the weapons that were responsible for the deaths of Donovan and Palmer. The only remaining controversy was a finding by the local medical examiner in Hopkins' final autopsy. Though the official report confirmed Hopkins had been killed by numerous bullets of the same caliber, there was also a large, unexplained pass-through wound in his chest. While he could not prove otherwise, the medical examiner surmised the wound might have come from a high-powered rifle. For Nowitzke, that aspect of the report was simply noise tied to an unwarranted conspiracy theory. He would have none of it since the evidence was clear Raymond was culpable for the various murders. Nowitzke made a call to Michigan, and investigative files in Appleton and Mackinac Island were officially closed.

Philemon continued to maintain that he had seen a muzzle flash coming from his left that evening, but there was no proof. Returning to Wisconsin in his new black Ram truck, he was simply happy for several days off and to be spending time with his best friend and Mallory on the deck of The Lakehouse over a Monkey 47 gin and tonic.

"Boss, I told you I would be there for you, whenever or wherever you needed me," said Philemon.

Nick smiled. "P-Man, there was never a doubt in my mind." However, he could not quell other growing questions about the entire episode.

CHAPTER 55

When Nick and Mallory returned from Kansas City, it was to a hero's welcome, of sorts. The entire Weston community was shocked about the death of Frank Reynolds and that he was implicated in the murders of men responsible for the outrageous claim costs incurred by the company. More stunning for those at Weston were the accounts of the firefight in Kansas City. While Nick and Mallory spent their time completing their report for the board, each received comments and spontaneous visits from colleagues curious to hear a firsthand account of the story or those simply offering support. Robbie Mueller offered Mallory a gentle hug as they passed in the hallway. Several of the claim handlers pushed Nick for details of the actual shootout. Even the typically stoic executive assistant, Anita Lathom, stopped at the conference room occupied by Mallory.

"Mallory, how are you doing?" asked Anita.

"I'm fine. Really. A couple of broken ribs and a hellacious bruise." She pulled up her shirt so Anita could see the large, now mottling green and yellowish area on her back. "Glad things have drawn to a close."

"Oh my, Mallory. I just . . . feel so bad for you," the image of the contusion burned into Anita's mind.

"It looks much worse than it is."

"Well, I just wanted to say how proud . . . how proud Emil would have been of your work," she concluded, fighting her emotions before quickly stepping from the room.

As far as the official report, C. Jonathan Woods could not have been more pleased. Nick had gone above and beyond in completing his assignment, detailing all the issues everyone already seemed to know. He also gave a very direct report to the board about the effect of unattainable goals and unrelenting pressure from management which drove the exceptionally bad results in the religious niche. Nick acknowledged that Tina Matheson was the key figure in the failure of the program. But he also deftly made the board itself culpable for not asking more questions of management as the results tanked over time. He completed his thirty-minute presentation by heaping praise on his partner, Mallory Swenson, who he said was instrumental in developing the findings and bringing the matter to a conclusion. In fact, Nick recommended the board reward her with a promotion and compensate her accordingly.

Following the meeting, Woods asked Nick to come to his new office to wrap up the details of his contract. As Nick sat in one of the familiar couches in Emil's former space, he looked over at the large desk, half expecting to see the former CEO laboring over his journals. It had only been a couple of weeks since Emil's death, but the office didn't quite feel the same.

"Nick, the board and I want to thank you for everything you did. Weston Insurance still has some work to do to clean up the mess caused by Frank Raymond, but you were fantastic," said Woods. "Is there anything I can do to convince you to stay at Weston?"

"Jon, I sincerely appreciate the offer. But, as I told Emil on several occasions, I'm not sure what I want to be when I grow up. I'm searching for something, but I'm not sure what it is. Weston Insurance, Emil, you, and the entire staff has been very accommodating, but I need to move on."

"Please let me know if you ever change your mind. I can always find a place for a smart young man like you to work here. Two final things. Emil bequeathed you that large cardboard box sitting on the table."

"What's in it?"

"It looks like a letter along with Emil's journals. He was very specific that you, and only you, should have them. Oh, and he told me he wanted you to read them."

"Seriously. Well, thanks . . . I guess."

Woods then slid an envelope across the desk. "Secondly, please take this as a token of our gratitude."

When Nick peered inside the envelope, he found a check. "Jesus, Jon, fifty thousand dollars?"

"Consider it a well-deserved bonus."

"Well, thank you, Jon. Can I ask, did you give Mallory anything?"

"We offered her a promotion with a significant bump in salary."

"Did she accept?"

"She's still thinking about it," offered Woods.

"By the way, before I leave, I have something for you too," said Nick. Woods looked surprised and pleased as Nick handed him a large shopping bag. The new CEO removed a football contained in a lucite case autographed by Wisconsin's All-American running back, Montee Ball.

"Damn, Nick. I can't thank you enough."

Nick hefted Emil's cardboard box and moved for the door. "Jon, I don't want to haul these journals home. Would you mind if I stayed at The Lakehouse and read them through the balance of the week?"

"No problem, Nick. It's the least we could do," staring at the ball. "Hey, Nick, isn't Ball the guy who broke your nose?" heard Nick as the door shut behind him.

Before moving back toward his office, Nick saw Anita dutifully sitting in her executive cube. She had been gone when he entered the new CEO's office, but now he could not avoid her. "How are you doing, Anita?" asked Nick as he put down the box of journals. It was a polite question, but the answer was clear on Anita's face.

"Not so good. Emil was more than a boss and a mentor. I also viewed him as a friend," she said with red eyes. "I'm not sure how things will change here with our new leadership. I don't know if I'll be keeping my position. I'm just scared, Nick."

Nick could offer Anita little more than a hug and comforting language. "Everything will be alright, Anita," even though he had no idea if it would be or not.

CHAPTER 56

Nick returned to The Lakehouse, hefting the box containing Emil's diaries from the trunk of his BMW. He juggled the heavy container while fiddling with the keys to the front door before entering and dropping "the gift" from Woods on the kitchen island with an audible thump. Then, after cracking a beer, he moved out to the deck. Nick could feel the change of seasons in the air. After serving at billets around the globe, it had been years since he had enjoyed autumn. Comfortable days. Cool nights. Happy memories of high school football games and trick-or-treating as a kid.

Wearing a light jacket and jeans, he sat on the deck of The Lakehouse taking in the fading orange sun. Aside from the call of loons on the lake, the only other sound was the breeze whistling through the pines. Closing his eyes, he pondered his time with Weston Insurance. What had taken place? He had taken a job he didn't want and stumbled into a murder investigation.

Nick always wanted to leave a place better than he had found it. Nonetheless, he wasn't sure that was the case here. Even though everyone agreed the matter was officially resolved, he felt uneasy. Despite the spectacular view, his mind was elsewhere thinking through the most recent series of events focused on the shooting of Hopkins and the death of Raymond. His beer sat untouched, sweating on the arm of his chair, when he heard the front door open.

"Just me!" yelled Mallory as she moved through the house. "You need a beer?" she yelled.

"No, I've got one," he responded.

"Another beautiful day in Wisconsin," said Mallory as she sat with her Stella in the companion chair. "So, the rumor has you leaving Weston and moving on."

"Well, for once, the grapevine at Weston has failed," replied Nick. "I'm on a track to leave, but I've got this feeling that there are a few loose ends to close on this whole shit show."

"You too, huh?" asked Mallory as she kicked off her shoes and curled her feet underneath her.

"Maybe I'm just overthinking this. According to Nowitzke, the police have closed their files, hanging the murders on Raymond. It's easy to understand why. Frank was an unlikeable asshole with a huge personal arsenal and a well-advertised beef against the Christian fuckers. But he deviated from his pattern, pulling a handgun on the stage in Kansas City and got killed in the crossfire. Why did he change tactics? He used long guns in all the rest of the murders. No one had a clue that he was even a suspect until we made a connection. Why go out in a blaze of glory with a handgun knowing full well that you might get shot . . . or worse, survive and end up becoming a prison bitch?" he asked rhetorically.

"Oh, and the Hammurabi letters. Now, and please don't take offense, Mal, but Frank seemed focused on killing Hopkins without a plausible plan to kill you."

"Sorry to disappoint you, Nick."

"You know what I mean. There's no way he could have shot Hopkins with his bodyguards in place and then have the time to come find you and murder you."

"But I did take a bullet."

"I know, and thank God for Kevlar. The slug was mangled, but there's no way Frank got off a shot at you. He only fired one based on the gun's magazine. You either took a random bullet from the firefight . . . or it came from somewhere else."

"I was afraid to even say that. But it fits with the one thing that's been bothering me. The medical examiner who did Frank's autopsy said there were numerous bullet holes in the body of a caliber like the guns used by The Sentinels and the gangsters. But there was also a large wound in Hopkins' chest that couldn't be explained. The ME contends that a rifle of some sort might have been responsible . . ."

". . . which fits with Philemon's assertion that he saw muzzle flashes that night," added Nick.

The remark hung in the air as both Nick and Mallory fell silent.

"What do you want to do, Nick?"

"That's just it, Mal. Law enforcement has closed the cases. If we go to Nowitzke with a *feeling* that there is the killer still on the loose, he'll look at us like we're nuts, especially since it was our theory about Frank. At least I would if I were in his shoes. The fact is I don't know that there is another murderer. We've got no real evidence that anyone else did anything. Who else would be a likely suspect? We went from Emil to Frank convinced that each was the killer. All the physical evidence points to Frank. Ballistics confirmed the weapons used were his," he said, pausing. "I've got nothing," he said, staring at the lake below them.

Mal took his hand. "Nick, look at me. You did exactly what you were asked to do by Emil . . . and more. You earned your money here and can walk away."

"You're right, Mal. Fuck it. Frankly, I want my life back."

"Are you done with Weston?"

"Not yet. Woods gave me Emil's journals with personal instructions from your father requesting me to read them. I'm not bringing them home, so I asked Woods for permission to stay here for a few more nights. Barring any brainstorm from you to the contrary with a mystery suspect we've totally missed on, my goal is to read his goddamned tome, clearing out the liquor cabinet in the process."

Mallory stood. "Everyone needs a goal, Nick. I can't blame you for wanting to go home," she said as both entered the house through the patio doors. "By the way, thanks for doing a solid for me with the board and my promotion."

"You earned it. If you need anything, you know where to find me, at least for the time being."

"Hey . . . there is one thing," she said hesitantly. "Lately, I feel like I'm being followed."

"Okay? Can you tell me anything specific?"

"Of course not," replied Mallory. "You know . . . just a stupid kind of sense that someone's watching me."

"What do you want to do?" asked Nick in a serious tone. "Is there anything I can help you with?"

"No. It's probably nothing," she concluded. "Having told you has already made me feel a little better."

"Like I said, if you need me, you know where I live."

Mallory gave Nick a hug and opened the front door to let herself out when she found Tina on the other side getting ready to knock. "You're back, Tina. Wow, you're looking nice and tan."

"Thanks, Mallory. I heard you're moving up in the world at Weston. Congratulations," she said as a vague afterthought, peering over her sister's shoulder into the house.

"Nick's in the great room," said Mallory, excusing herself as Tina moved past.

Tina found Nick in a leather chair in front of the propane fireplace. "Hello, stranger," she said, sliding over the arm of the chair into his lap and turning on a big smile. "I've missed you," she said before kissing him full on the lips before he could react.

"That's a helluva entrance," smiled Nick. "Welcome back. Where have you been?"

"Just clearing out my head at a luxury resort for the most part. I'm feeling ready to go back to work."

"Not to be a downer, but I'm sure you must have heard about Frank Raymond, right?" asked Nick.

Tina's expression was unchanged as she responded. "I saw it on the network news. I can't believe what they said about Frank on the television. That wasn't the man I thought I knew."

"By the way, Mallory was injured in Kansas City too. She took a bullet."

"Seriously? I just saw Mal!"

"She's fine, Tina. Mallory was wearing a vest. It saved her life. We were in Kansas City trailing Frank with law enforcement. The police in several jurisdictions believe Frank shot several Weston clients, like Edward Donovan and Lonnie Palmer."

"Oh my God," exclaimed Tina, putting her hand to her mouth. "Why? Why did Frank do it?"

"As best as we can determine, Frank was pissed off about the losses and the effect on Weston," concluded Nick. "I would read it as getting even . . . or giving justice to some."

"He was the only suspect?" asked Tina.

"Yeah, they got him dead to rights. The police confirmed he owned the weapons used. Mallory and I tracked Frank's travel patterns and confirmed most of the other details."

There was a long pause in their conversation. "I don't want to sound insensitive, Nick, but I've been thinking about you for several weeks. Oh, and I'm incredibly horny. Interested?"

Nick decided Emil's journals could wait another day before taking Tina's hand and moving to the bedroom.

CHAPTER 57

Despite spending the night with Tina, Nick's mind could not shut off his conversation with Mallory. In fact, he felt that sex with Tina had become passionless, almost like she was merely going through the motions. Leaving Tina sleep, he stepped quietly into the kitchen and made a pot of coffee. As it brewed, he flipped on the switch to the fireplace and grabbed the box containing Emil's journals, setting them on the coffee table. With the knife on his money clip, Nick sliced through the tape on the brown cardboard box. In the carton, he found a card on a stack of the well-worn journals. Tearing open the envelope, Nick found a handwritten note from Emil.

"Nick, after our many conversations, I have found writing a journal to be therapeutic in nature. As I've instructed Mr. Woods to talk with you, I have one last request. Please read all the journals I have enclosed. I trust you will do this one last favor for an old man. Best wishes, Emil."

It was all Nick could do but smile and shake his head at the request. But, for whatever reason, he felt compelled to oblige. He filled a coffee cup before dropping into his favorite leather chair and began to read. True to Emil's meticulous nature, each of the leather-bound books was numbered in sequential order. For whatever reason, Nick quickly realized the journal he started with was volume fifty-seven with the final edition noted as sixty-four. A quick scan of the first volume gave Nick the impression it covered the time period surrounding the inception of the religious institution program at Weston. He assumed the remaining records chronicled the remainder of Emil's life.

Plowing through the first of the books, Nick read about Emil's excitement for the religious program, believing it to be a game changer for his company by providing a new revenue stream through the brokers. He was also excited his daughter, Tina, had been selected to develop and manage the ambitious new program. True to Emil, the books followed no specific pattern and did not read like a novel. Scattered throughout the volumes were the former CEO's observations about the current events of the time, insights about personnel at the company, and reflections about his relationships with both Tina and Mallory. Continuing to be puzzled about why Emil had given the diaries to him, Nick read on, refilling his cup several times. By midmorning, Nick checked on Tina, who was still sleeping. He meandered toward the bathroom to take a shower, brewing another pot of coffee before taking the next volume and finding a chair in the shade on the deck, letting the marathon continue.

Just before lunch, he reached volume sixty, which detailed Emil's early misgivings about the religious program. Emil commented about the strong performance of other programs in contrast to the developing issues from, what he noted were from, Tina's baby. From what Nick could tell, the first of the early and ugly claims started to plague the company. On one day, Emil recounted a particularly harsh discussion with Frank Raymond about the claim problems and how his vice president was pushing him to get out of the business, predicting it would ruin Weston.

Tina found Nick sunning himself on the deck, taking a break between tomes. Wearing only an open bathrobe, she tried, but failed, to coax him back into the house. "Sorry, Tina. I'm on a bit of a mission and want to get this done. Your father gave me his journals to read."

"His journals?" she questioned. "Why? What's in them?"

"Your guess is as good as mine. Basically, it seems to be a recap of his life."

"Which part?" asked Tina.

"His final years, I guess. He talks about all sorts of things, including the development of the religious niche."

"Oh," she replied. "Is there anything I can do to distract you?" opening her robe.

"Distract has such a negative connotation. But no, I need to get this done."

"No problem, Nick. I have a late lunch scheduled today with Natalie Hickman. Tomorrow I plan on stopping by Weston to see where I stand with management." She reached down and kissed him on the forehead. "I'm going to jump into the shower and let myself out," said Tina, playfully flashing him on the way.

It took all of Nick's energy to refocus his attention to Emil's journals. Volume sixty-one yielded the first official use of the term "Christian fuckers," who were noted to be sucking the life out of the program. Grouped in and amongst the actual perpetrators, Emil included Marco Ricci, whom he characterized as an "oily little bastard." By the end of that chapter, Nick could tell Emil had seen the handwriting on the wall for the religious program. That volume also made the first note of Emil's prostate cancer and his ongoing notations to follow up with his doctor regarding treatment options. Emil documented Nick's arrival on the scene at Weston, whom the CEO labeled "a young man with management potential." To some extent, Nick felt the irony of reading a story he had already lived out as he became part of the narrative. By five o'clock, Nick put the journals aside, found a glass, and filled it with Jack Daniels. Watching the setting sun, he pondered the car wreck that was the religious program at Weston.

He was a total outsider from the insurance world, but it seemed to be common knowledge in general that churches had numerous high-profile losses. He'd seen so many of the stories on the television news. Trusting kids abused. He considered Tina to be as well-read and intelligent as anyone he had met in his limited time in the insurance field. *Why couldn't Tina see this coming?* Contrarily, the investigation into the religious program was like a choir hymnal, with everyone singing the same tune. Poor management. Too much latitude given to brokers. Not enough intelligent questions by underwriters. Pricing that was well below what the market commanded. *What caused Tina to miss the storm clouds on the program that were so evident to everyone else? Was it now Monday morning quarterbacking on the part of the Weston staff having seen the net results?*

By the time he filled his third snifter, he made the commitment to drinking his dinner, vowing to read the final three volumes the following morning. But the open questions churned in his brain as he fell asleep in the chair.

CHAPTER 58

Rising early the following morning, Nick completed reading book sixty-two over a pot of coffee. It ended with Emil editorializing about the murder of Father Donovan and how the justice system in America had failed. *Down to two more volumes*. Nick found his way to the shower. The journals added nothing new to what he already knew, but he was troubled, like he was missing something. *Enough with the journals for now.* Needing to get out of The Lakehouse, he resolved to clear out his office at work. It was a minor detail, but one that needed to be done before he could officially put Weston in his rearview mirror.

Stepping into the lobby in a t-shirt and jeans, he earned a smile from Cassie, who was at her post. In fact, she rose and walked around the desk to give him a hug. "I thought you had left Weston, Nick," said Cassie.

"Almost. I need to clean out my space, and that should be pretty much it. Do I turn my badge into you when I'm through?"

"Sure," said Cassie with a smile. "I'll get it back to Human Resources for you."

"I won't be long," said Nick as he stepped onto the elevator. When he arrived at his office, he found a small brown box centered on his desk with his things neatly placed inside.

"You didn't have much here, Nick," said a voice coming from behind him. It was Anita.

"Thanks," he said. "How are you getting along with your new boss?"

"I think I'm going to be fine. New challenges, but Mr. Woods seems to like my work. Can I walk you downstairs?" she asked, steering him toward the elevator. As they stepped into the lift, Nick continued the conversation.

"Anita, you're a long-timer here. Can I ask you something about the whole Mallory, Tina, Emil thing . . . do you know what really happened?"

"Yes, I know the details. What are you looking for specifically?" said Anita as she blanched.

However, before Nick could follow up with his question, they both heard shouting coming through the elevator doors before they opened on the ground floor. Tina was standing in front of Cassie, screaming. "Why isn't my badge working, Cassie?" yelled Tina, shaking the identification in the receptionist's face.

"I don't know, Ms. Matheson. I don't make those decisions," she said, holding her own. "You need to take that up with Mr. Woods."

"You know who I am, Cassie. Now, let me into the building, you bitch," replied Tina, her eyes wide with rage. "Is fucking Woods in the building?"

"Yes, Mr. Woods is. But you are not on his calendar," responded Cassie, her voice rising in response.

"Fuck you. I'm going into the building if I have to break the door down," replied Tina, moving toward the entrance. However, Cassie, who was taller with a more athletic build, stepped in front of Tina to block her attempt.

As Nick watched the surreal conversation, Anita had heard enough and stepped forward, yelling in a stern voice, "Enough! Tina, you know the rules as much as anyone," which stopped the shouting match.

Tina turned to see Anita and Nick both observing the exchange. When Tina saw Nick, she had a look of horror on her face, like she had been caught doing something. Then, before Tina could reply, a squad car with its light bar on pulled up to the front door of the Weston Insurance entrance in response to a panic alarm triggered by a button under Cassie's desk. By the time the officer entered the building, Tina's demeanor had changed like she had flipped a switch.

"I'm sorry, Cassie. I lost my temper and apologize," said Tina in the presence of the burly officer.

Although looking unsure, Cassie acknowledged Tina's act of contrition.

"What's the problem?" asked the officer.

"Just a misunderstanding on my part," offered Tina in a polite tone. "I'm sorry for causing any disturbance here."

"Is anyone pressing charges or have anything else to say?" asked the officer to the people in the lobby.

Anita stepped forward. "Thank you for coming today, officer. I think we can classify this as a verbal squabble that has been resolved. We're sorry to have caused a problem for you, sir." Both Tina and Cassie nodded in agreement in the presence of the cop, who was satisfied. He left Weston, followed closely by Tina, who made no acknowledgment of Nick.

As the air cleared, Anita asked Nick to step into a conference room adjacent to the lobby. Anita closed the door behind Nick after he entered. "Nick, it's none of my business, but I understand you have a personal relationship with Tina."

"Yes," said Nick. "You could say that."

"It's a small town, and I don't know otherwise, but you just saw the real Tina . . . maybe for the first time. You seem like a good guy, and I'm not trying to pry. But I wouldn't want to see you get hurt."

"Thanks, Anita. Looks like I'm getting my money's worth today. Now, about my question concerning Emil and his secret."

"Nick, it might be the worst-kept secret in Neenah. I can't share all the details of the story, but the basic details are fairly straightforward. Emil had an affair while his wife Clara was undergoing treatment for ovarian cancer. The child born from Emil's little dalliance was Mallory. The mother signed an agreement giving up her rights to Mallory and took a large check in exchange for her silence."

"Okay," said Nick. "That's pretty much what I've heard. Can I run a name past you?"

"What name?" asked Anita.

"Mallory's mother's name?"

"Nick, I've been sworn to secrecy about this. I worked for Emil at the time and was involved with finalizing the details. But I don't know if I'm at liberty to answer that question," replied Anita.

"Natalie Hickman," blurted out Nick. "The oncologist who was caring for Clara."

Without saying a word in response, Anita's look of puzzlement gave Nick the answer he had been looking for. "Who? I don't know that name. Who gave it to you?"

Nick's nonverbal response gave Anita her reply.

"Tina, huh?" asked Anita.

Nick nodded yes.

"Listen, Nick. I have no idea where she conjured up that name, but I can tell you without a doubt that I've never heard of anyone named Hickman. Remember how we started this conversation. I've known Tina pretty much her whole life. She's a manipulator and pretty much a psycho bitch."

Anita's words seared into Nick's brain as he left Weston. On his way home, he decided to contact Nowitzke. "Chuck, Nick Hayden calling. You're the only one I can call, and I need a favor. I need you to run an arrest record for someone."

"Sure, Nick. Why don't you come down to my office now?"

CHAPTER 59

Nowitzke was more than happy to see Nick, the first time since the shoot-out in Kansas City. "What can I do for you, Nick?"

"Can you run an arrest record for a Christina Matheson?"

"Sure. Anything for you. Who's this Matheson person?"

"A coworker at Weston," said Nick, leaving out any further details.

Nowitzke sat back in his chair for a moment like the conversation triggered something. "You know, that name rings a bell. One of our officers yesterday told me about a strange call at a local Appleton restaurant about a reported disturbing-the-peace issue. Seems like one of the patrons, a woman, sat in a booth for most of the afternoon, babbling on for several hours. Apparently, this lady starts talking loudly, disturbing others in the place, including the waitress. When the officer arrived, he approached the woman and questioned her. The woman just snapped, shouting that she was enjoying lunch with her friend and that she wanted to be left alone. The officer spoke to the waitress, who said that no one else had ever been in the booth. However, this lady insisted her friend, a Natalie Hickman, was with her the whole time."

Nick's eyebrows raised when Nowitzke said Hickman.

"So, the cop goes and checks the restaurant's video camera and damn, there was no one else at the table," said Nowitzke. "When asked for her identification, the woman gave the officer her driver's license . . . one Christina Matheson."

Nick blinked hard at hearing the conclusion of Nowitzke's story. *Jesus Christ!*

"The officer said the restaurant wasn't pressing any charges. They just want the woman to leave the place," said Nowitzke. "Our uniform said this woman was a fucking loon, Nick."

Stunned, Nick didn't remember leaving Appleton PD or finishing his conversation with Nowitzke. His first instinct was to go home. When he turned into the driveway at The Lakehouse, he saw Mallory pulling into the yard as well.

"Mal, what's going on?" asked Nick.

"Nick, I've got that feeling again . . . someone stalking me today. It scared the shit out of me, and I didn't know where else to go."

"Mal, get in the house now. We've got a problem," replied Nick.

"What?"

"Just get in the house and I'll explain," said Nick, scanning the area. Once inside, Nick locked the door behind them. "We need to read Emil's journals, just the final two volumes."

"Why?"

"I'll explain after we're through," he said, moving the final two chapters to the kitchen island, where they stood side by side and read the pages silently. They completed the first volume in thirty minutes without any revelations.

"Nick, this is stupid. Why are we doing this? I don't get it?"

However, Nick insisted, and the two dove into the final journal. Neither said a word until they had turned the final page. And then, they both stared into space, trying to articulate what they had read.

"Oh my God, Nick. Emil says without a doubt that Tina intentionally tried to bankrupt Weston with the religious program. It all makes sense now."

"You said it yourself at one point during our investigation. Words and music to her deliberately making poor decisions. Worse, she tried to frame Emil for the Donovan and Palmer murders if the police ever figured it out. But no one did until we started our investigation," responded Nick.

"But, why?" asked Mallory.

"I'll tell you why," said Tina, entering the kitchen with a handgun leveled at them. "Because Emil couldn't keep his dick in his pants when he fucked my friend Natalie while my mother was undergoing cancer treatment, that's why. I wanted to punish him. You know, everyone loved him but his family."

Both Nick and Mallory remained focused on Tina as she spoke. "Mallory, come over here now," barked Tina, tossing the extra house keys onto the island. "Nick, another set of keys to get into the house. Now, you stay where you are." Mallory timidly moved toward her sister, who placed a gun to her back.

"So, I take it you were the one who killed Palmer and Donovan?" asked Nick.

"Of course I did. An eye for an eye, right? Didn't you think Hammurabi was a nice touch? Frank Raymond taught me how to shoot a rifle years ago, and I got pretty good at it. Maybe not as good as a former PJ, but enough to kill those Christian fuckers. As our friend Frank said more than once after they died, the world is a better place. And he was right. Besides, if the killings were hung on a Weston employee, so much for the better for the downfall of the company . . . Emil's most prized possession."

"So, Frank wasn't the shooter?" asked Nick.

"No, he had nothing to do with this, Nick. At least until Brother Hopkins was killed," replied Tina. "I was in Kansas City and pulled the trigger. Even got off several rounds targeting Mallory, my little bastard sister."

Mallory almost fainted at the revelation.

"Why did Frank go to Kansas City?" asked Nick incredulously.

"He was my mentor. Smart in some ways, dumb in others. When he figured out I was killing off former Weston offenders, he confronted me. I told him I wouldn't stop until I killed off the worst of the worst or Weston was bankrupt. I used his weapons all along without his knowledge during scheduled work trips. When Hopkins' turn came up, I manipulated Frank to pull the trigger and save me from prison. Turns out the son of a bitch loved me." Tina paused for a moment. "Same as you, Nick. A different tactic with you though. Sex goes a long way to influence someone or keep in touch with an ongoing investigation. By the way, thanks for the orgasms."

"Mallory, did Nick here tell you I found your mother? He wasn't supposed to spill the beans. She looks just like you by the way," said Tina.

"Tina, you know you've got some mental issues," said Nick. "First of all, I have it on good authority that Natalie Hickman is not Mallory's mother. Further, there is no oncologist named Natalie Hickman in the state or surrounding area. You made it up. You even spent hours talking to your imaginary friend in a restaurant yesterday," said Nick. Suddenly, Nick could feel his blood pressure rising while becoming short of breath. He couldn't move. He looked at Mallory, and he realized he was not going to be able to save her. She was going to die right in front of him, and all he could do was stand and watch.

"Where exactly did you get your information, Nick?"

"From me," said Anita, who entered the kitchen from the deck with a rifle trained on Tina's head. "Now get away from my daughter," she commanded. All eyes went to Anita. "I was the mystery woman years ago. Emil suffered for Clara when she was sick. I was there for him in every way . . . and we got involved. When Mallory was born, I gave her up for adoption on the condition Clara and Emil would raise her. Emil came up with the story about the oncologist, telling it to protect me after Clara died. Even in little Neenah, we were able to keep our secret. So many years lost. Having to watch your daughter grow up without you is the hardest thing I've ever done. My cross to bear. But I won't let anyone threaten her, you psycho bitch," said Anita, raising her weapon. "Now put down the pistol or I will pull the trigger."

Mallory was dazed, blinking hard at the news. Tina did as well, trying to make sense of the lies she had heard for so long. As she computed what Anita had revealed, Tina relaxed a bit, lowering the pistol.

Nick found something deep within himself. His voice. He could speak. He could talk to Tina. "Tina, you need help. Please let Mallory go and drop the weapon."

The sound of Nick's voice woke Tina from her stupor. "I'm not going to any prison or mental hospital. The fact of the matter is Mallory here is still Emil's mistake." As she raised the gun to Mallory's head, there was a deafening blast. Tina's head exploded before she fell to the tile floor.

EPILOGUE

Nick's final act at The Lakehouse was to place the trophy won by Philemon squarely on the mantel of the great room fireplace. "Kitschy," Nick murmured to himself, stepping back to admire the tacky award. He headed outside, closing the front door behind himself just as a familiar Jeep pulled up.

"Just wanted to say goodbye and thank you, Nick," said Mallory.

"Thanks for what?"

"Giving me a mother again, for starters."

"I've heard through Nowitzke that his file re-opened and immediately closed again. Most importantly, no charges against Anita."

"Thank God. Visiting my new mom in prison on Christmas would have sucked," said Mallory.

"How are you two getting along?" asked Nick.

"Well, I'd say we're a work in progress. We have a lot to catch up on. A lot of questions mostly. We'll just need some time to figure out another fucked up Weston relationship," said Mallory. "How are you doing with the whole Tina thing?"

"The short answer is okay . . . I guess. Mal, I had no idea about Tina. It bothers me that I never had a clue," he said, pausing. "Nowitzke told me off the record that when the police went to her apartment to wrap up the case, there was no doubt she'd had mental issues for some time. You know him. Said Tina was a 'fucking loon.' He wouldn't give me any specifics, but . . . Jesus."

"Nick, Tina had a side none of us could see. Or maybe we just didn't want to . . . not even her sister."

"I'm sorry for your loss, Mal."

Both were lost in thought until Mallory changed the subject. "I've given my notice to Weston. I'm moving."

"Let me guess . . . San Antonio?" replied Nick with a wide grin.

"As I said early on, for a guy that doesn't know much, you're pretty smart. I want to see if Phil and I can be a couple. Also, I'm going back to school with Emil's inheritance to get a degree. Where we end up after that is anyone's guess. What about you? What's next?"

"I think I've turned a corner. More therapy. Less drinking. Maybe I'll buy a business. Who knows? A coffee shop with a wine bar was discussed at one point," he concluded with a vague smile on his face as he moved toward the driver's door of his car.

"Wait a minute, Nick. Come here," said Mallory, closing the distance between them.

Nick looked at Mallory with a questioning look on his face.

"Just trying to give you a proper goodbye." Mallory stepped toward Nick, gently took his head with her hands, and kissed him passionately until she was through. "God, I'm glad I got that off my chest. Oh, and don't be flattered. That was for me, not you."

"Whatever you say, Mal," replied Nick with a big smile. "When you get some time, come on up to Door County and find me."

She stood on the driveway and watched as the BMW pulled away.

ACKNOWLEDGEMENTS

Men of God is my first mystery fiction novel. The original idea was floated to my wife, Nancy, after dinner while I was still working full-time. Over many discussions (and bottles of wine), we talked about the story in generalities. Nancy encouraged me to get a whiteboard to keep track of the flow of new ideas, plot twists, thoughts, and options. While I have used that whiteboard in writing subsequent novels, I thought *Men of God* would flow from my brain through my fingers onto my laptop keys. That was until I retired from the insurance industry and began to write the first draft. It was then I realized I needed more than an outline of a good idea. I needed characters and places and scenes. At some point, I dove into writing the prologue. My wife was shocked that I was able to write fiction at all. But I was on my way.

I spent hours researching how to write a novel while also seeking to contact an interested Air Force Pararescueman. With the help of the PJ Association and Michael Jones, I found my way to Scott Gearen, a decorated veteran, who patiently answered my questions about life as a PJ. Scott was the first of many technical experts who helped me along the way.

With *Men of God* being a crime drama, I had the help of several other experts in law enforcement. Bill Larson, a retired detective, became my go-to person, providing ideas and answering technical questions. Arleigh Porter, an active police chief, also provided me with assistance, not the least of which included putting me in touch with other experts in the field. My brother, David Jordan, a retired officer, answered various procedural questions and provided details about K-9 units. Finally, my initial research on this project began with his captain, Matthew Barnes.

My golf partner, Brian Arndorfer, offered an insurance claims and legal perspective on several scenes in the book.

I thank each of them for their time and expertise. I also now understand what many other authors have communicated in their acknowledgements, i.e. that any mistakes or errors in presenting technical material is strictly on me.

Once I had an early draft, several members of my family contributed to *Men of God*. My daughter, Jamie Jeska, provided me with feedback and helped extensively with editing. Leah McDuffie, my other daughter and an active service member, added insights from a military perspective and served as a beta reader. My mother, Karen, provided me with encouragement along the way.

Other family members who offered critiques along the way include my sister, Lisa Lombard, and my cousin, Sue Menhennick, both voracious readers.

Several former coworkers and friends added perspective and feedback about the story, including Mary Witteborg, Walter Kilgus, Sara Sohns, Todd Hoyt, Kevin and Mikki Fronek, and Cathy Voelkel.

Further, the characters and storyline in the final draft evolved significantly due to the efforts of my editor, Margaret Dwyer. While it was difficult to adjust a work that I had spent years on, I respected her direction while trying to remain open to alternate ideas. *Men of God* is a much better book because of the editing process.

Finally, a big thanks goes to Shannon Ishizaki, owner of TEN16 Press, for taking a chance on a first-time writer. I appreciated the efforts of her team, including Kaeley Dunteman and Lauren Blue, to get me across the finish line.

If I've missed anyone who helped me, I apologize. *Men of God* was years in the making and has been influenced by so many. Thank you!

CPSIA information can be obtained
at www.ICGtesting.com
Printed in the USA
LVHW012320070920
665258LV00018B/2366